Ghost House
AND
Ghost House
Revenge

Clare McNally

Ghost House
AND
Ghost House Revenge

NELSON DOUBLEDAY, INC.
Garden City, New York

Ghost House

———◆———

For Michael, for believing

ACKNOWLEDGMENTS

Thanks to Mike and John Pastore, and Judy Althoff

Prologue

◆

The execution was over.

The fires had died down, emitting now only snakes of gray smoke. Sparks of orange flashed sporadically from the bits of charred wood, lying in a soft mound that the salt wind of the bay would soon sweep away.

As appalling as it was, as unjust as it seemed, the scene had been repeated so often that the onlookers were only mildly affected by it. They had seen it before, the girl, screaming of her innocence. The priest, praying softly and not really caring what happened to the girl's soul.

And the executioner—his face a mask as he brought the torch down to her feet.

When it was over, the women gathered their children and the men set about returning to work. Soon, they would forget the scene. Soon, when they were busy with their daily tasks, no one would guess that they had cried so viciously for such young blood.

One man remained behind today. His tall, caped figure cast a long shadow over the smoldering pile. He dropped to his knees before the blackened skeleton, reaching his hand out to wrap his fingers around what had once been a soft, pink hand. He had held that hand. . . .

When the town constable walked up behind the man, the constable heard a faint snapping sound, like the breaking of a twig. But when he tapped the man on the shoulder, the constable did not notice how tight the man's fist was when he rose. Or that the skeleton was no longer whole. The man held a treasure in his fist, and he brought it home to wrap it forever in a cloth of blue and gold.

1

Gary VanBuren turned his station wagon into the gravel driveway of his new home and pulled up to the front door. He sat there for a moment, taking in the property around him and the house that loomed enormously in the center of it. Even though he had seen it a dozen times before, slamming doors and kicking radiators before signing the contract, he was so awed by the size and beauty of something he could now call his own that he was barely conscious of his hand twisting the key from the ignition. He felt very good about this place, as he had from the first time the real estate people took him on a tour of it. How could he resist it, with its old-fashioned charm? And best of all, a good deal of the old furniture was miraculously still intact. Gary, a lover of antiques, had bargained with the realtors to buy the pieces. Without them, the house would have lacked something. It certainly didn't lack dust, but a good cleaning would make it a wonderful place to live. Or so Gary thought.

It was just magnificent. A leaf-lined porch stretched across the front, broken at the center by four steps, leading to carved double doors. There were bay windows on either side, and an old-fashioned swing hung from the wooden board ceiling.

He raised his eyes to see a window of amber stained glass in the center of two larger windows. At the peak of the roof, a weather vane turned lazily, as if it couldn't decide which way the wind was blowing. The original Colonial mansion was largely hidden by Victorian additions.

Gary turned around to ask the children what they thought of the place, but the seat behind him was empty. As soon as the car stopped, his wife Melanie and their three children jumped out to explore their new home. Gary smiled, imagining the children's reactions. This mansion on Starbine Court Road, in the Long Island town of Belle Bay, was a far cry from their six-room apartment on East 79th Street in Manhattan. They had lived in the apartment since the birth of their oldest child, twelve-year-old Gina, and it was about time the kids had a back yard to play in.

Gary went to find them, stepping carefully on the slate stones so that his footsteps would not crush the thick grass of the front lawn. Gary respected its clipped and trimmed beauty, even though the lawn had long before turned to the beige of early October.

Around the side of the house, he caught sight of Melanie, holding hands with their son. Kyle was eight years old, and the very image of his mother. He had her small nose and her freckles, and a mouth that seemed to take up his whole face when he smiled. His only resemblance to Gary was his curls, and even then he got their blond color from Melanie. Gary's own hair was dark and tightly curled, as if he had just stepped out of a pool.

Kyle was rambling on in an animated way, waving his arms and jumping up and down.

"It's so big!" Kyle cried, making a sweeping gesture that took in the entire grounds. "Do we really own it right down to the beach?"

"Halfway into the woods," Gary said. He looked at the trees that bordered two sides of the hill on which the white mansion sat. "But we can use the beach any time we want. Now, how about helping me carry some things inside?"

Kyle followed his father back to the car, still holding Melanie's hand. He climbed into the back and pulled at a lamp. With a grunt, he jumped down.

"Kyle, isn't that too heavy for you?"

"No, Mom," Kyle insisted. He took one arm away and bounced it on his hip as proof. "See? It's not heavy at all."

Melanie sighed. "You're right, honey. I guess I was just being an old nag."

"You're not a nag," Gary said distantly.

"Gary?" Melanie asked, a surprised lilt in her voice.

Gary didn't answer her. He rarely spoke to her at all these days—ever since he had found out she'd had an affair with another man. It was too hard to talk to her. It was hard to even *look* at her. When he did, all he could think was that her lips had kissed another man's, that those slender legs had felt another's against them. He had hoped the excitement of moving would change his attitude toward her, but the wounds were still fresh enough to resist the remedy of even this major change in their life-style. He had to admit it was a blow to his ego, but he made no apology.

He looked up at Melanie, briefly, and felt something jump inside him. My God, she was beautiful. Her hair was the color of golden honey, falling thickly over her shoulders in soft waves. That face, with its blue eyes and delicate nose, could have been carved by a great master. And her smile . . .

Melanie caught his look and started to say something. But just then, their two daughters appeared at one of the bay windows, giggling and waving. Framed by the white curtains, they were a sweet picture, and the artist in Melanie saw a portrait in the scene. Gina, with her long hair falling in dark waves over her shoulders, was a night-and-day contrast to five-year-old Nancy's fair-skinned, golden-curled looks.

"It's the most beautiful place I've ever seen!" Gina gasped, her eyes bright with the enthusiasm of a twelve-year-old experiencing something very new.

"I knew you'd like it," Gary said. "Wait till you see your room."

"First help me carry some things inside," Melanie said.

For the next half hour, the family moved the few odds and ends they had brought with them in the car. Gary and Melanie had spent the previous weekend at the house setting up all the furniture and belongings that the moving van had brought out from the city.

"Ready for a tour?" Gary asked.

His two older children agreed in unison. They walked to the end of the hall, Kyle counting the doors as he passed them. At the end, some six feet above the floor, was a stained-glass window. The sun was shining through its amber panes, and the elongated shadows cast by the stairway's carved posts were almost grotesque. As Gary led the children up the steps, Kyle rubbed his fingers up and down the double twists of the railings.

"Oh, Daddy, look!" Gina cried, pointing to the brass sphinx that decorated the post at the top.

"I know what that is!" Kyle cried. "We learned about them in history. It's a finks."

"*Sphinx*, you nutty kid!" Gary said with a laugh.

"It's from Egyptian stories, isn't it?" Gina said. "Half-woman, half-lion. But there's really no such thing."

"I know that," Kyle said, with a twist to his lips.

Gina and Kyle each took one of Gary's hands, and the three of them walked down the long hallway. Halfway down, it was branched by two smaller halls, each of which was decorated at the end by an amber window similar to the one downstairs. Each hall had doors spaced in military rows.

"There's so many doors!" Kyle cried.

"Some are closets," Gary said. "Here, this is going to be your mom's art studio."

He took them into a huge, brightly lit room. Its windows stretched from just a foot above the floor to nearly touch the ceiling. Gary knew they would take some cleaning, but once the film of dirt was removed, the sunlight would shine in beautifully. The room was empty except for a single, worn-out couch and a pile of cardboard boxes.

"There are closets just like this one in all the bedrooms," Gary said, opening a door. "These shelves are good and strong."

He pounded his fist against one of the four shelves. Kyle stepped in beside him and imitated his actions.

"I hate to use a cliché, but they don't make these like they used to."

"What's a cliché?"

"A sentence people use so many times it gets to be a drag," Gary told his son. "C'mon, get out of there."

"Can we see our bedrooms?" Kyle asked.

"Gina's is right across the hall," Gary said.

The little girl gasped in amazement when Gary opened the door, her eyes immediately focusing on the bed. It was a huge, canopied thing. Melanie had discovered a beautiful white quilt in the attic and had had it cleaned for her daughter's new room. It was a perfect match for the heavy velvet curtains that hung around the bed. They had been drawn back with new gold tassels to reveal posts carved in the same spiral design as that on the staircase.

"Oh, I love it!" Gina squealed, throwing her arms around Gary's neck.

"Take a look at the other furniture," Gary said, hugging her.

There were two tall bureaus, each covered with antique lace. Though the lace had faded to yellow, it was still delicate. Gina touched it, very lightly, as if it were a magnificent piece of art. She then moved across the room to find a desk, carved with intricate scrollwork. The two glass doors of the desk were etched with a simple boat design. On one door, the boat was initialed with the letter *L*, on the other, with the letter *B*.

"L.B.," Gina read. "That must be the lady who first owned this."

"I'd guess so, honey," Gary said. He bent down to open a few of the little drawers. "You can keep lots of treasures in here. And the bottom drawer has a lock that still works!"

"I just love it so much," Gina said, shaking her head in disbelief.

"Hey, when are we gonna see my room?" Kyle demanded.

"Right now," Gary told him.

Kyle's bedroom didn't come near the splendor of Gina's, but it didn't bother him. He was delighted that his bed was high enough to require a step.

"Do you think the guy who lived here was a sailor, Dad?" he asked, staring up at a painting of an eighteenth-century ship. Similar paintings hung on the walls of every room they had inspected.

"I suppose," Gary said. "In fact, there's a post in my study that I think might have had a telescope on it once. Come on, I'll show you."

Both children gasped at the huge, faded map that completely covered one wall. Kyle followed the paths of arrows that had been inked on it, moving his finger from Long Island to Wales. Gary showed them the telescope stand, its brass fittings green with age. There was a stone fireplace in the room with nautical designs carved in it, and a huge painting of a storm at sea hung above it, remnants of the early days of the house. Gary wondered how all these antiques and paintings had survived during the years the house had remained empty. Especially recently when the prices on antiques had skyrocketed, the house must have been a tempting target for burglars. "Why should I try to solve the mystery?" Gary thought. "Whatever the reason, I've got a house full of antiques. And at a good price."

"Can we see the downstairs now?" Gina asked.

"Later today," Gary promised. "We have some chores to take care of after lunch."

"Ooohhh," the children groaned together.

"Never mind 'ooohhh,'" Gary said. "Everything needs a good cleaning, and we still have to unpack!"

The children babbled among themselves at lunch, barely tasting the food in their excitement. The kitchen, bright in the late afternoon sun, was an anachronism, with its polished Formica counters and modern stove and refrigerator. When they stepped from it into the adjacent dining room with its heavy oak furniture, it was like walking through a time tunnel.

The downstairs had the same nautical, dark-wood decor as the upstairs. There was a bay window in the dining room, just like the ones at the front of the house, and an enormous fireplace. Gina stayed in there with her mother and Nancy, folding tablecloths and napkins to put them in the hutch. Melanie found a box marked *dining room* and pulled out plates and glasses, rearranging them on the hutch shelves. She unpacked various knickknacks and stood looking around the room. She had rearranged them a dozen times before deciding everything was in its proper place.

Kyle and Gary had taken charge of the living room. Gary had brought a rug from the apartment and wanted to cover the bare wooden floor with it. He and Kyle pushed it as far as it would go, then Gary held up pieces of furniture as Kyle kicked it along with his foot.

"Oof!" he groaned. "This is heavy, Dad."

"Don't wear yourself out, son," Gary said. "We've got other things to do." Kyle worked busily, whistling along with Gary; father and son were delighted with their new home.

After a day of hard work, everyone was ravenous at suppertime. When Gary realized that no one had remembered to pack salt and pepper, Gina started to giggle and soon everyone joined in her laughter, unaware that a pair of hungering eyes were staring through the bay window, fixed on Melanie.

2

———◆———

Melanie drove Kyle and Gina to school that Monday to introduce them to their new teachers. St. Christopher's was on the other side of town, and the three of them had a chance to get a good look at their new neighborhood. Belle Bay was a peaceful little place, its one main road lined with small shops. Melanie made a note to tell Gary about the antique stores she had spotted.

People were walking along the road, browsing in front of store windows even at this early hour. An occasional group of children skipped down the sidewalk, and a big black dog laced its way through the few parked cars.

Gina's teacher was an elderly nun, a very kind woman with a bright smile. She sat down and talked to her new pupil, including Melanie in the chat. Watercolor paintings by budding Renoirs decorated the walls of the classroom, and the names of the winners of the previous day's spelling bee were displayed in the corner of one blackboard. Melanie was brought back to her own grammar-school days, some two and a half decades ago.

"Where do you live?" the nun asked.

"Starbine Court Road," said Gina. "On top of a big hill."

The nun's smile faded, then returned quickly, but not so quickly that Melanie didn't detect the change. Gina, on the other hand, was too interested in hearing about her new class to pay attention. At last, the nun stood up and walked Melanie out into the hall.

"Do you like your house?" she asked.

"It's lovely," said Melanie. "But it needs a bit of fixing up."

"Well," said the nun, "best of luck in it. God bless those who live there."

She reentered her classroom before Melanie could ask what she knew of the house.

*　　*　　*

The rolltop desk Gary had ordered for his study finally arrived after a ten-day wait. He followed the movers up the stairs, guiding them so that they didn't scratch the walls or the desk. He tipped the two husky men and then set about arranging his papers in the new desk. The paperwork he brought home from the office every night gave Gary a good feeling. To his mind, the volume of work to be handled was proof that he and his partner, Warren Lee, had a thriving legal practice.

Gary had found an antique lamp in the city that week. Removing it from the box, he carried it across the room to the desk, its long cord dangling.

Then, suddenly, the cord became taut—as if someone had stepped on it. Gary tripped and went flying forward. His body struck the window with a loud thud, then fell back to the floor. Dazed, he stared up at the panes of the window, watching them vibrate in almost perfect unison with the beating of his heart. It set his head spinning. Around him the dark walls of the room swirled, until the paintings on them seemed a blur. Gary touched his head and drew back a finger spotted with blood.

"What in the hell?" he asked himself. But the blood was not quite so frightening as the realization of just how hard he had smashed against the window.

Just a little more force, he thought, and I would have gone right through the damned thing.

He tried to stand up, to see if the lamp plug had snagged on anything. That would explain how he had tripped. But dizziness overcame him, and he sank back down to the floor. Sitting Indian-style, he rubbed his arms, fighting off a sudden chill.

"*Leave her!*"

Gary looked around when he heard the voice. Across the room, the lamp sat upright, its cord lying innocently along the floor. The room was quiet except for the hum of the radiator. Gary told himself he was hearing things. He thought he heard a faint shuffling noise, like footsteps, and called, "Kyle, are you hiding in here?"

No voice answered. There were no giggles to give his son away. The children weren't up here at all. Gary pulled himself to his feet and walked slowly out of the room. He heard someone on the stairs and met his wife at the door to the bathroom. She stood watching him as he popped two aspirin in his mouth.

"I heard something fall up here," she said. "Are you all right?"

"Fine," Gary said. "I just stumbled."

He was glad the side of his head that had been cut was turned away from her.

"Gary, we're in a new home," Melanie said carefully. "Can't we talk about starting a new life?"

"Later," Gary said, heading back to the study.

Before Melanie could answer him, he disappeared into his room.

Infuriated, Melanie called after him, "Stop being so stubborn! I've forgotten Terry! Can't you?"

But Gary wasn't listening. Melanie repeated the words again, softly to herself. She really had pushed Terry Hayward from her mind. He meant nothing to her now. But two months ago, he had been a very important part of her life. By God, it was nice to have a man open doors for you and toast the color of your eyes.

They had met in March. Melanie had been shopping that day. Absorbed in finding a sophisticated dress for the opening of her first one-woman art show, she hadn't been watching Nancy. Bored, the little girl had wandered off in search of more interesting pastimes. When she couldn't find her daughter, Melanie had panicked. Soon she had all the salesgirls helping in the search. Then a young man appeared; Nancy was clutching his hand and chattering away to her new friend. As Melanie threw her arms around Nancy, alternately scolding and kissing her, Terry stood by patiently until Melanie remembered to look up and thank him. Terry looked like something off the cover of an old-fashioned romance novel. His face was deeply tanned and his hair was coal black and curly.

As they waited for an elevator, they exchanged social pleasantries.

"Tell me what you do," Terry asked.

"I'm an artist," Melanie said. "In fact, I'm having a show up at the Merkin Gallery. On West 54th. Will you come to the opening party? It's the least I can do to thank you."

"You can bet on it," Terry promised.

He did show up that day, and every day during the show's week-long run. Melanie brought Nancy a few times, and the little girl was always delighted to see Terry. To her, he was "Uncle" Terry, who brought her little toys and played games. Melanie loved to see her child so well entertained—it was rare that she or Gary found the time to play make-believe and other preschool games. Watching the two together, Melanie began to form a strong feeling for this handsome young man. So when he asked her to lunch, she accepted— telling herself it was as a friend. But when the meal was over, she knew it was more than that, and it frightened her. She tried to convince herself that only Gary mattered, but Terry made it so difficult when he brought her roses and candy—something Gary hadn't done in years.

After their fifth lunch, Terry kissed her warmly before they went their separate ways in front of the restaurant. The warmth of his lips forced her to open her eyes—somehow she had fallen in love with Terry Hayward.

In the cab ride back to her apartment, Melanie said to herself over and over that the kiss was meant to be Platonic. But every denial of Terry's affection was contradicted by the knowledge that she truly liked his attentions. And the feeling was strengthened even more when she walked into the apartment to find Gary so busy with his papers that he barely gave her a "hello," let alone a kiss.

She stayed awake most of the night, feeling a delicious sense of anticipation when she thought of Terry, and yet feeling a tug of warmth and love to see Gary lying next to her. She would stop this. Tomorrow she'd tell Terry that everything was over. My God, she thought, she'd been seeing him for two months now! It was time to end whatever it was that was happening between them.

And so she attempted to tell him her feelings at lunch the next day, when they sat on the steps of the 42nd Street library. Terry took her hand in his, but she pulled it away.

"Please, I know people in this city," she said.

"So what would they do? Tell your husband?"

"He'd kill me."

"That isn't the first time you've said that," Terry said, taking her hand again and holding it more firmly. "What kind of man is he?"

"He's just wonderful," Melanie said. "The sweetest man on earth."

"You still love him?"

"I do," Melanie insisted. "That's why I don't think we should see each other any more. Terry, let's stand up right now and go our separate ways—before we do anything more than hold hands."

"Off into the sunset," Terry joked. "C'mon, let's go for a walk. We can talk about this."

Somehow, the walk led down into the IRT subway, and Melanie found herself riding with him to his Greenwich Village apartment. She didn't say a word to him, but fixed her eyes on an ad for a secretarial school. Three people riding on a pencil into the future. Melanie thought it looked silly, but still she stared at it.

Terry brought her upstairs to his apartment. Even though he was always neatly attired, his rooms were in disarray. He had thrown his suits over the back of a chair when they came back from the cleaners, and they still had their plastic bags on. Shirts and socks hung from every available doorknob or covered the floor. In the bathroom, where Melanie had immediately retreated, wet towels slopped over the floor. Looking for a glass for water, she was surprised to discover a dozen bottles of pills in the medicine cabinet. Was her handsome lover sick?

"That's his business," she said, closing the door softly.

Melanie trembled throughout their lovemaking, at first from guilt, and then from a strong passion that this beautiful man brought out in her. He was so terribly gentle that she found herself sinking in ecstasy—forgetting Gary, forgetting the children. And it was just like that every time they came here for the months after that, just one or two days a week, when Melanie could get a sitter to stay with Nancy. Melanie thought heaven would last forever.

Their dates were only marred by Terry's occasional irrational outbursts of temper, usually at slow waitresses or reckless cab drivers. Once he'd even gotten into a fist fight with a burly man on the subway. But, as Melanie tried to tell herself, "no man is perfect."

The end came on a warm day in Central Park.

Terry and Melanie were sitting on a bench, while Nancy played nearby. Nancy came over and put her head in Terry's lap.

"Can I have fifty cents for ice cream, Uncle Terry?"

"It's too close to your dinner time, Nancy," Melanie said.

"Please? Oh, please?"

"Here, kiddo," Terry said, pulling out two quarters.

"Damn it," Melanie said after Nancy had left, "I told her she couldn't have it and you deliberately defied me!"

"Look, what's the big deal?"

Just then the sun came from behind a cloud and shone brightly in Terry's face. For the first time during the hour they had spent together, Melanie got a good look at his eyes. They were glassy and distant, not Terry's eyes at all. Melanie recalled the bottles of pills at his apartment and asked, "Are you taking some medication?"

"Just some pills to keep me going at work," Terry said. "It's getting really bad there."

"I'm sorry," Melanie said. A moment later, she added, "I thought you said you jogged to keep yourself in shape. What happened?"

"Jesus friggin' Christ!" Terry yelled, standing abruptly. "Since when are you my damned mother?"

The very first thought Melanie had when he stormed away was that she had really known very little about this man. She should have sensed something was wrong with him. But he had always managed to be kind and considerate toward her—at least until today. Melanie shivered, and not from the cool wind.

Nancy came back and climbed upon the bench. She wrapped her arms around Melanie's neck. Her mother's hair blew forward and brushed over the soft ice cream. Melanie didn't move to clean it.

"How come you're crying, Mommy?"

"I'm not crying, honey."

"Yes, you are!" Nancy cried, pointing to her mother's red-rimmed eyes. "Where's Uncle Terry?"

"He's gone," Melanie told her. She stopped short and knelt down to her daughter's level. "Nancy, Uncle Terry was a bad, bad man and I don't want to hear you talk about him ever again."

They didn't say a word to each other for the entire subway ride, and when they got home Melanie told Gary she was sick and went straight to bed. Gary, unable to talk to his wife, immediately questioned the children about her behavior. Nancy, wanting only to help, told Gary all about Melanie's fight with her Uncle Terry.

Gary listened incredulously. Later, alone in their bedroom, Melanie confessed everything, hoping Gary would forgive her. But he was too shocked to do anything but move his pillow and blanket to the living-room couch, where he would sleep for the rest of their stay in the apartment.

Melanie cried herself to sleep that night, her emotions a mixture of guilt, self-pity, and horror. But when morning came, so did her strength, and she steeled herself to go down to Terry's apartment. When he opened the door to her, she couldn't stop her hand from flying to her face in horror. He was dressed in the same outfit he had worn the day before, although now it was soaked wet. He hadn't shaved yet. His hair, usually combed so neatly, hung in his eyes. Those eyes were glazed.

"Come in," he said, pulling her arm when she hesitated.

"I only came to tell you goodbye," Melanie said, trying to keep her eyes fixed on his. She shuddered.

Suddenly, Terry grabbed her by the flesh of her upper arms and shook her. This wasn't the polite gentleman who had rescued Nancy; this wasn't the handsome lover who bought her roses and paid her compliments. Melanie could smell liquor on his breath. She struggled to break away from him, crying out.

"I will have you again," he seethed, pushing her against the wall, "if I have to kill you first."

Melanie reached up and scratched him with her long fingernails, drawing blood. When he let her go, she ran from the apartment on numb legs. Somehow, she managed to reach the street before he started after her, and miraculously, a taxi pulled up to the door. She jumped inside just as Terry raced out of the building. Her heart pounded loudly, and she shook with nausea. She tried to calm herself by thinking that Gary would be waiting for her at the apartment with forgiving, open arms. But when she walked in the door, Gary didn't even look up at her. For a week, he refused to speak to her, not even to ask her to pass something at the dinner table.

"Gary, please?" she asked plaintively.

"Don't 'Gary, please' me," her husband said coldly. "It's your own fault. Don't talk to me, damn you!"

The children cast sidelong glances at each other and picked nervously at their food. They watched their mother's eyes widen, then close with tears as she jumped from her seat to run to the bedroom. Her sobs filled the apartment. Except for that, the rooms were so completely silent that the sound of the phone ringing made Gary jump. He sent Gina to answer it.

"Hello?"

Heavy breathing. Gina frowned and repeated her greeting.

"Hello? Is anyone there?"

"Hello, kiddo!" someone with a loud, bright voice said. "I'm coming to your place tonight to have fun! Ha! Ha!"

"Who's this?"

"Gina, hang up," Gary ordered.

But the little girl was too nervous. From the other end, the laughing man whispered a string of obscenities, naming parts of the body that Gina didn't yet know about. But she was bright enough to know this man was no friend and that his words were wrong and filthy. She began to cry, until Gary wrenched the phone from her.

"Listen to me, you mealy-mouthed faggot," Gary snapped. "Don't call here again!"

He slammed the receiver. "It's okay, Gina, just a stupid crank. It won't happen again."

But it did happen again, the next night, and the next, and the next, until they were afraid even to lift the receiver. When they brought their problem to the police, they were told to get an unlisted number.

They didn't have to. A week later, Gary found the house in Belle Bay, and they began to make preparations to move. By late September, after three months of listening to the crank calls, they were out of the apartment and far away from Terry Hayward. Everything was safe and easy now.

* * *

It was late. Melanie rolled onto her side and stared at the spot of light that filtered through the lampshade. The lamp cord hung in a series of tiny metal beads and ended in a sculptured lily. *Gary used to bring me flowers,* she thought.

She picked up a paperback novel and threw it with all her might. It struck the door with a loud bang. Melanie held her breath, waiting for the steps that would come running to see what had happened. But the steady tick of the grandfather clock down the hall was the only sound in the sleeping house. Melanie drew aside her covers and put on her robe and slippers; maybe a strong cup of coffee would help.

The yellowing bulb of the kitchen chandelier gave the room the peacefulness of an empty church. Melanie felt herself relaxing. She set the pot on the stove and leaned against the counter to wait for the water to boil, ready to catch it before the whistle woke up everyone in the house. Then she made herself a cup of instant coffee and took it to the table. She drank it black tonight, not because she liked it that way, but because she was too tired to care. She sipped at the coffee, feeling the warmth rush into her chest. Soon her entire body eased. She looked straight ahead through downswept lashes as she drank. In the light of the chandelier she saw something on the counter that she hadn't noticed before. It was a tiny package.

Melanie lifted the parcel in her hands, examining it, feeling like a child who shakes a Christmas box to guess its contents. It was wrapped in a blue and gold brocade cloth and tied with a strip of the same fabric. She untied the ribbon. When the fabric fell away, she found a pearl ring in her hand.

"Oh, Gary," she whispered, slipping the ring over her trembling finger. She held it to the light and bit her lip, tasting a mixture of coffee and salt tears. For the first time since their fight, Gary had given her a sign of his love. This proved she still meant something to him!

"I love you, Gary," she whispered, leaning her head back against the cupboard. She sighed. She wanted him now, more desperately than ever before. She needed to be with him.

She dumped the rest of the coffee into the sink, watching the brown liquid wash over the porcelain. The tail of the cat-clock swung rhythmically, its luminous eyes watching now the door, now the window. It was 3:42 A.M.

Melanie walked up the stairs and gave the sphinx a pat. It stared hard at her. She half-walked, half-skipped down the hall, trying to keep herself from whistling. She stopped at the door to Gary's room —to her husband's room, she thought with a grin—and knocked softly. When no answer came, she leaned closer to the door and called softly. Silence.

She wrapped her fingers around the knob, but it turned only a fraction before jamming against the lock. Melanie's elation drained away to confusion. Why had Gary locked the door? Didn't this ring mean he wanted her tonight? Melanie raised a fist to her mouth and bit hard on her knuckles. She ran to her room, her slippered feet scraping softly on the floor.

Her foot caught on a string of worn carpeting, and she stumbled forward in the darkness. Oh God, she thought. Can't I feel rotten in peace?

There were voices coming from somewhere. Melanie looked around, blinded by the pitch darkness. It sounded so like a crowd, like people were talking just outside the house. Or just inside.

Melanie chided herself. "Voices! That's the radiator hissing! You're just tired, Melanie. So damned tired. . . ."

She let her head drop back down on the rug and began to slam her fist against it. Her tears had turned to sobs, and she buried her face in her robe to muffle them. Her body heaved up and down in furious spasms and she growled in her anger.

Then she felt a touch on her back. She quieted herself, but she didn't turn around. The touch stayed with her. She mumbled, "Gary?"

The voice that replied was sensuous, edged by the slightest accent. Accent? Had she really forgotten what Gary's whispers were like?

"I want to be with you now," he said.

"Oh, yes," Melanie sighed.

She let him lift her in his arms and carry her back to the bedroom. He laid her down softly and climbed in next to her, stroking her blonde hair with large fingers. His hand slid down her neck and over her shoulder, then pulled at the tie to her nightgown.

His fingers followed every contour of her body, moving slowly over her breasts and down to her hips. He let them linger there, making odd spiraling patterns. Melanie began to notice how cold his fingers were. She put her hand over them and squeezed tightly. She loved this gentle way he was approaching her. It was so unlike their usual rough-and-tumble scenes.

He stopped massaging her and crawled down the bed to kneel over her. Again, he remained in the same position, until Melanie pulled him down to her and sought his lips in the darkness. They were full and passionate, but he kept them tightly closed. This strange way of kissing bothered her, but she didn't stop him. Strong arms encircled her, squeezing her. For a split second, Melanie thought of Terry Hayward, for this was almost exactly the way he had treated her during their lovemaking. But when she heard her lover's voice, Terry passed from her mind.

"You're here again," he said, kissing her neck.

"I always was," Melanie whispered.

"Don't leave again," he begged.

"Never," Melanie promised, stroking his hair.

She didn't notice when he left the room that night, for she fell into a deep sleep soon after their brief exchange of words. When she woke up the next morning, she lay with her eyes closed, thinking of the beautiful night they had had. Everything was going to be fine, she knew it now.

But if she had known that Gary had slept soundly throughout the entire night, in his own bed, and that it wasn't he who had locked the door, the beauty she remembered would have rotted away to horror.

3

◆

Melanie was in such a giddy state that morning that she hardly paid attention to the food she was cooking. She absentmindedly poked her long fork at the bacon, humming to herself.

"It smells so good," Gina said. "Daddy, how come we can't have bacon every morning?"

"Don't they teach you about health in school?" Gary asked. "It isn't good to eat bacon that much."

"Mommy, I don't want my sunny eggs to run all over," Kyle said.

Melanie didn't answer him. She was thinking dreamily of the night she had spent with Gary.

"Mommy, my eggs!" Kyle said, louder now.

"Huh?" Melanie asked, waking up to the real world. "Oh, yes—no runny eggs for Kyle."

Gina reached over the table and tugged at her father's sleeve.

"I'm going to be in a play at school, Daddy!"

"Really? What kind of play?"

"All about Halloween," Gina said. "I get the lead role 'cause I'm the tallest in my class. I'll be a witch!"

"Oh, you're too pretty to be a witch," Gary said.

"No, I'm going to wear a pointy hat and a black gown. And I'm going to be real mean!"

"That'll take some acting," Gary said. "How many lines do you have?"

"Twenty-two, Daddy!" Gina answered, as if that were the most magnificent thing in the whole world.

"Well, you've only got two weeks to practice," Gary said. "If you want, I'll help cue you."

"Okay!"

Melanie came over to the table and set the plates down. Kyle stared at the yolk that oozed all over his plate, then looked up at his mother with a screwed-up nose.

"They're all runny," he complained.

"Oh, Kyle," Gary said, switching plates. "Take mine instead. Melanie, do we have any salt?"

"I think Mommy's got something nice on her mind," Gina said when Melanie didn't answer.

"Melanie," Gary said again. "How about some salt?"

"The world for you," Melanie said, laughingly handing him the shaker.

"Thanks," Gary said, shaking his head at her.

"Daddy, I'm going to be home late from school today," Kyle said then, around a mouthful of eggs and bacon.

"You're not in trouble, are you?"

"No," Kyle answered. "I'm gonna play football with some of my friends."

"You made lots of new ones?"

"Uh-huh, Billy, Kevin, Roger, Brian," Kyle said with a nod.

"Hey, we're gonna be late if you don't move it," Gina said.

"Kyle, finish your eggs," Gary told his son. "There's only a few bites left."

Kyle stuffed everything he could into his mouth.

"Oh, gross!" Gina cried.

"Kyle, sometimes . . ."

"You said to hurry, Dad," Kyle reminded him.

"Well, get your coats on," Gary said. He accepted goodbye kisses from his two older children.

"Mom, where's my lunch?" Gina asked. "MOM!"

Melanie responded to her name only after Gina had called it three times. She made a weak comment about not being awake yet, rising from her seat. Lunch bags were put in small hands, and her two oldest children were ushered out the door.

Melanie watched them through the glass door of the kitchen until they stopped down the hill to wait for the bus. Kyle pointed to a squirrel and said something that sent his sister into waves of laughter. We're lucky, Melanie thought. We never had that proverbial attack of sibling rivalry. If only Gary and I could be like the kids!

"Soon," she said out loud.

"Did you say something?" Gary asked, folding down his paper.

"No," Melanie answered, waving her hand as if to prove the air was free of her words. "How are you this morning?"

"Just fine," Gary said, frowning.

Melanie turned to fill the sink with breakfast dishes, smiling to herself. Behind her, she heard the scrape of Gary's chair against the floor and the click of his briefcase as he locked it.

Had this been just a day earlier, she would have also listened for the door to shut when he left the house. But after last night, she wasn't about to let him get away without kissing her goodbye.

"Gary," she said quietly. He turned around and took a step backward when she moved to kiss him. But she caught him squarely on the lips and held hers against them for a long moment.

"I'll see you tonight," she said, drawing away.

"Yeah, sure," Gary said. He turned his head and walked from the house, wondering why Melanie was behaving so strangely.

Melanie went back upstairs, humming the current disco hit. She wanted to paint now, even though the restless night had somewhat fatigued her. The studio was icy, and she pulled the drawstring on her robe until it wrapped her like the shroud of a mummy. She looked at herself in a mirror and was pleased with her figure. No one would guess she was thirty-eight, and today she *felt* younger.

She set out her paints and turned to the easel that held her current masterpiece. It was the portrait of Nancy and Gina that she had envisioned the first day they had arrived at the house. Gina was a blur of blues and greens and browns, while Nancy remained a penciled sketch. The two girls were waving and Gina had a knee up on the window seat. Melanie dabbed her brush into white paint and began to highlight the folds of her daughter's jeans.

"I want you!"

At the sound of the voice, Melanie's brush dropped to the floor, leaving a streak of sticky whiteness where it rolled over the boards. She could feel her heart beating, knowing Gary had pulled away from the driveway. She had seen him pass the bus stop!

The voice cried out again, so very near the door. It didn't sound like Gary, but it was similar to the whispers she had heard the night before. That strange accent—English?

"What are you saying?" Melanie asked herself. "Of course it's him! He sounded just like that last night!"

But logic was fighting against her. Gary hadn't had enough time to get back to the house. And if he had somehow managed that, surely she would have heard him. . . .

"*Gary?*"

Nobody answered her. There was a rustling along the rug outside her door, and Melanie watched for the knob to turn with her breath caught in her throat.

She could stand there all day, watching that doorknob, expecting it to turn, as if this were one of those silly old haunted-house movies. Doorknobs always turned in haunted-house movies, heralding knife-bearing prowlers. And a young woman would watch and wait, ready to let out a piercing scream as the camera lens zoomed down her throat.

In a quick, now-or-never motion, Melanie reached out and jerked open the door.

There stood Nancy, a sleepy-eyed cherub in a pink nightgown. Melanie closed her eyes in relief and laughed at her fears. Today was the day Nancy started afternoon kindergarten! She had been so busy that morning that she had forgotten the note she had tacked to the refrigerator with a pineapple-shaped magnet: *Nancy: PM Kinder Monday.*

"Melanie," she said softly, "you're a romantic turkey. Prowlers!"

"Prowlers?"

"Forget it, honey," she said.

She noticed her daughter wasn't carrying her favorite toy this morning. Instead, Nancy clutched at a large package wrapped in the same brocade material as the ring had been.

"What's that you've got?" she asked.

Nancy handed the package to her mother. She brought one of her thumbs to her mouth, then the other, and sucked at both noisily. Melanie turned the package in her hands, ignoring her daughter's bad habit for once.

"Did Daddy give you this for me?"

"It was on the rug," Nancy said around her thumbs.

"On the rug?"

"In the hall on the rug," the child explained, with a yawn that stretched her mouth into a tiny oval. She rubbed at her cheeks, flushed pink where the chill of morning fought with the warmth of her skin.

"Well, why don't we see what it is?"

"Yeah!" Nancy cried eagerly.

Melanie tugged at the ribbon, which was tied in a fancy knot. She wasn't sure where Gary had learned to tie a bow like that. Melanie let the fabric drop to the floor and held up a beautiful gown that seemed to be made of pure silk. It was yellowed with age, with sleeves that were tight to the midarm, then belled in rows of lace. It had a low-cut neckline and was delicately embroidered over the bodice.

"It must have cost him a fortune!" she gasped, wondering what antique shop he had found it in.

He hadn't mentioned the ring that morning. Most likely, he wouldn't mention this either. It was all part of a game they had played long ago, when they would leave little gifts around the house for each other. No thank-yous would be exchanged, but good-night kisses would be longer and warmer.

Let's play that again, Gary, she thought to herself, almost praying it.

She stooped down and hugged Nancy. This was proof Gary had finally forgiven her. And would she make him glad he had!

She lifted her daughter and carried her toward the stairs, singing. Nancy giggled. And a lonely being watched them, unseen, loving Melanie, needing her, and cursing the child who had come between them that morning.

*   *   *

Gary watched the man across his desk with eyes that barely took in his features. He only heard what the man was saying because it was second nature for him to pay close attention to his clients. That was what made him a good lawyer, he told himself. It kept all these high-paying people knocking at his door. Divorce Headache Number 297, he thought sourly.

Number 297 was making accusations about a wife who didn't understand him. Gary nodded and *hmm'd* where it seemed necessary. But today his thoughts wavered between his client's lamentations and Melanie's unexpected display of affection that morning.

Gary raised his hand to his mouth. He ran a finger over his lips, as if to prove to himself that Melanie had really kissed him. Even though she had surprised him, he liked it. Since the day he had met her fifteen years ago, Melanie's kisses had been something to write home about. Gary, momentarily forgetting his client, recalled the afternoon he had walked into a store that sold prints, intending to buy one for his newly opened law office. Melanie was standing behind the counter, her blonde hair pulled up in a high ponytail and her eyes made up with the heavy liner of the sixties. Gary recalled that she was wearing a miniskirt. She looked much younger than 23, but when she spoke to him, it was with an impressive maturity. He had walked out of the store with five prints and the promise of a date the next Saturday night. Six months later, they were married.

Gary felt himself trembling inside to remember all the good times they had had together, all down the drain because of one stupid mistake. But he could have them back again, just by bringing flowers to her that night. He wanted them back again! Damn it. He missed her in bed. It had been so long. He started to smile, but his lips froze at the sound of his client's voice.

"You'll get me my fair share, won't you?" Number 297 was asking.

Gary nodded. The man eyed him suspiciously, guessing his lawyer wasn't paying much attention to him. But before he could say anything, the buzzer sounded. Gary punched the lit button and found himself talking to a frantic Melanie. Nancy had been hurt that morning and Melanie couldn't calm her down. Could he *please* come home?

"I'm on my way," Gary said, letting the receiver drop.

When he stepped out of the office, Warren Lee looked at him with questioning eyes, and Gary quickly explained what little he knew from talking to Melanie.

"Let me know if she's all right!" Warren called as Gary left.

Gary was into the elevator before he got both arms through his coat sleeves. At the parking lot, the attendant didn't seem to care that he was in a hurry. And, of course, Gary's car was on the top concourse. Gary tapped his foot impatiently, and when he saw the car ease down the ramp, he felt a surge of anger. The attendant was purposefully taking his sweet-loving time! Lazy bastard . . .

He shoved a bill into the man's hand and climbed behind the wheel. The station wagon slid back onto 50th Street and turned onto Madison Avenue. For ten or twelve blocks, it seemed everything would go smoothly. And then the traffic lights began to torment him. Each turned on its brilliant red just as he approached, making him wait on edge for endless seconds.

By the time he made it to Long Island, Gary was shaking with nervousness. Visions of Nancy bandaged from head to toe passed through his mind. What was it Melanie had said? That Nancy had somehow spilled hot water all over herself? (What a thing to happen to a five-year-old!) At last, he pulled up the hill to the house. He jumped from the car and ran inside, calling for Melanie.

Melanie was waiting for him in the kitchen, her eyes red from crying. Gary pulled off his coat and tossed it over the back of a chair, then sat down beside her. As gently as he could, he asked what had happened that morning.

"I just don't know," Melanie blubbered. "I had brought her down to breakfast—she had waffles. Then I had been upstairs working for just a few minutes when I heard her screaming! She somehow spilled boiling water all over herself from that teakettle."

Gary looked to where she pointed and saw the kettle on the floor by the stove. He went to it and picked it up, turning it in his hands. His reflection blurred where the metal had been dented. The mark was two inches long and so deep that only a tremendous strength could have bent it. Gary shook his head.

"We didn't even use that this morning," Melanie said. "I just don't understand. . . ."

"Is Nancy upstairs?"

"She's been resting since I brought her home from the hospital," Melanie said. "Gary, you should have seen her little legs! I can't imagine how much it hurt her!"

"What did the doctor say?" Gary asked.

"Just to keep her quiet," Melanie told him, "and that the real danger is infection. We have to keep her clean, and let it heal on its own. He says it probably won't hurt after today. He even gave her some pills to calm her down."

"I want to see her," Gary said.

She followed her husband up the stairs to the child's room. The little girl was curled up around her pillow, clutching it to her stomach. Her mouth moved steadily, chewing at her tiny thumbs.

Gary was stunned to see those tiny legs swaddled in bandages, hiding the ugliness of the skin beneath. He had seen burns before, and tried to fight a vision of redness and blisters that formed in his mind. He closed his eyes and swore silently. Then he walked closer and leaned over her.

Gary greeted her softly. At the sound of his voice, she threw her covers over her head and began to scream.

"MMMMOOOOOMMMMMEEEEE! ! ! !"

"I'm here, baby!" Melanie cried.

Nancy tightened her blanket protectively, terrified that the masculine voice she had heard belonged to the man who had hurt her that morning. Gary, not understanding that his daughter was afraid of him, tried to pull the blankets away to show her who he was. He gently touched her cheek where the blanket didn't cover it, then brought his finger away with a cry of his own. She had bitten him.

"What is *wrong* with her?" he demanded.

"I don't know, Gary," Melanie said over the child's loud sobs. "She keeps saying something about a *man* hurting her. But we were alone all morning!"

Melanie bent over her daughter and put her arms around her. Nancy was crying so hard that she wouldn't listen when her mother tried to tell her that Daddy was here. But Gary had had enough. He pulled Melanie gently away and sat down with Nancy. He couldn't help her if she wouldn't tell him who hurt her, he said. Daddy had to know who it was before he could make him not do it again.

It took some effort, but at last Nancy calmed down. She stared up at him with soft, bloodshot eyes.

"Daddy," she said softly.

"It's me, sweetheart," Gary said. "Want to tell me why you screamed like that?"

"A mean man hurt me, Daddy," the child told him. "I thought *you* were the mean man!"

"A man hurt you?" Gary said. "But Mommy says there wasn't any man here. Maybe you should tell me what he looked like."

"Make him go 'way, okay?" Nancy pleaded.

"I'll do that," Gary promised. He thought for a moment, then said, "Nancy, he wasn't your Uncle Terry, was he?"

Melanie gasped.

"No, Daddy," Nancy insisted. "He wears his hair like Mommy, in a 'tail. And he's big and tall."

She stretched herself up to show his height. Gary formed a picture in his mind of a latter-day hippie and asked Nancy if she remembered the man coming into the house. Nancy shook her head. She closed her eyes for a moment, seeing him in her mind. She told her daddy how the man was wearing a blue cloak and funny blue pants. His mouth was turned down in a scowl. He reached for the teakettle. . . .

"I'm scared, Daddy," she said, turning to bury her face in Gary's coat. Gary kissed her head and laid her back down on the pillow.

"Try to sleep now, baby," he said. "Mommy and I will stay here until you do."

"Don't let the mean man come back again," Nancy said sleepily.

Melanie and Gary stood by their daughter's bed until they were sure she was asleep. Then they quietly left the room and went back downstairs to the kitchen.

"Gary, you don't think I had Terry Hayward here, do you?" Melanie asked.

"Not on purpose," Gary said. "But he was threatening you for a long time."

"But he doesn't know where we live!"

"He could have found out easily enough."

"Nancy said it wasn't him," Melanie reminded him.

"She was frightened and upset," Gary answered. He sighed. "Well, okay. Maybe it was a delivery man."

"We didn't get any packages," Melanie said.

"Did you check to be sure the kitchen door was locked?"

"It was," Melanie said. "When I took Nancy to the hospital, I remember having to unlock it. But that's not the only mystery. Gary, I'll swear on my life we didn't use that teakettle this morning!"

"It might have been left on overnight," Gary suggested.

"Great way to set the house on fire," Melanie replied. "Oh, Gary! I'm so upset!"

"Do you suppose you'd feel better if you helped me move your things into my room?"

Melanie's smile was all the answer he needed.

4

The next morning, Kyle and Gina were waiting at the bus stop at the bottom of the hill. Kyle grabbed the signpost and spun around it, then went to pick up a rock to throw at the metal.

"Cut it out, Kyle," Gina said. "You're making too much noise!"

"Who's gonna hear?"

"Maybe the old lady," Gina suggested.

Kyle looked at the big gray house that sat a few hundred feet back from the road. All the lights but one were out, and in the square glow he saw an old woman staring out at them. He waved. The old woman smiled and waved back.

"She's awake," he said. "She won't care about the noise."

"Why do you suppose she stares like that?" Gina asked. "Every day she's up at that window!"

"I don't know," Kyle said. "But she sure gives me the creeps."

He hoisted himself up onto the low stone fence that wound around the old woman's property and started to walk along it. Gina walked beside him.

"I hope Nancy feels better when we get home," she said.

"Yeah, she sure hurt herself!"

"Someone hurt her," Gina told him. "I heard Mommy and Daddy talking about it."

"You were eavesdropping!" Kyle gasped. "I'm gonna tell!"

"If I tell you everything I heard, will you keep the secret?" Gina bribed.

"Well, okay," Kyle said, stopping to sit on the fence.

"Daddy says that someone threw hot water on her," Gina began. "And he thinks it might be that weird guy who used to call us up at the apartment all the time."

"He scared me," Kyle admitted. "I hope he doesn't know where we live! What else did they say?"

"Nothing," Gina said. "I had to move away 'cause I heard someone coming toward the door."

"Are you scared, too, Gina?"

"A little," his sister said. "But Daddy'll take care of everything. Hey, here's the bus!"

Kyle hopped onto the bus and took a seat beside Gina. The driver pulled away, and he looked out his window to see the old woman, just as he had seen her every day since he had started picking up the VanBuren kids. Probably a lonely old soul, the bus driver thought as he turned off the road.

*   *   *

The VanBurens' only neighbor on Starbine Court Road was an elderly woman named Helen Jennings. After bringing her through 85 years of life, fate had rewarded her by refusing her a family with whom she could spend her last years. She lived alone in her big gray house, with only a cat for company.

But Helen didn't suffer in her loneliness. Her life had a purpose—and that purpose was followed to the point of obsession. For Helen had made herself the unofficial guardian of the VanBuren family.

It was an obsession that had begun some eighty years earlier, on a day in her childhood, just a few months before her fifth birthday. It was a day made for children, with blue skies and sunshine beckoning them to climb trees and chase kites. Helen found her own little niche on a swing that hung from her favorite tree.

She stretched her bloomer-clad legs taut as she swung high, tucking them under the seat as she drew back again. At the height of each arc, she could catch a brief glimpse of the white house on the hill. It was empty—it had been for as long as she could remember. Mama said it was because the place was evil and people were afraid.

Up went the swing, almost as if it wanted to throw her over the hill, only to pull her back again at a teasing, dizzying speed. Each time she went up, she saw the house and its empty grounds.

Then, on one trip up, she saw something else. Moving as softly as the wind blowing through Helen's hair, a young man walked from the house to the stables. Helen, surprised, let her legs relax and scuffed her feet along the ground to stop the swing. She was curious—had someone new moved into the house? Perhaps he had a little girl she could be friends with!

She walked behind the swing to climb up the tree. Without effort, her feet found each knob and hole until she had reached a thick branch some six feet above the ground. Wrapping her arms around it, she snuggled against the wet bark and watched the strange scene.

The man, moving as unhurriedly as before, came out of the barn again. He was shaking his head at something, running his fingers through his thick black hair. Helen watched him, fascinated, as he paced across the path. But when her young eyes adjusted to their focus, she saw something that caused her to let out a startled cry.

She wanted to climb down, but something had frozen her to the limb. If the scene she watched was unreal, Helen, at an age when fantasy becomes reality, was much too young to know it. For when the man passed the rock fence, his legs did not obscure it! Helen could still see the stones—right through him.

And then, as if he had heard the thumping of her heart, he turned around and stared hard at her with cold, dark eyes. With a scream, Helen fell from her perch, landing on the ground with a bang. She turned her swimming head and breathed in the sweet, strong smell of . . .

. . . carpeting.

Helen opened her eyes and looked at the arm that had flung itself over the grass. The hand, a moment ago pink and chubby, was stretched thin now, spotted brown. She put it on the couch for support and pulled herself to a sitting position. She had been dreaming again.

*   *   *

Helen let herself return to complete consciousness, sitting on the carpet with her eyes closed. Then she pulled herself up onto the couch from which she had fallen and reached for her walker. She had long since learned to use it without assistance, and she had become so adept with it that she could even manage the stairs up to her bedroom.

Helen had thought once of calling someone to come move her things to the first level—at 85, stairs were an encumbrance—but when she realized that her bedroom window offered the best view of the house on the hill, she decided to stay put. Helen needed to watch the house. It had been her one obsession since that first day she had seen the man walking past the stone fence.

She had, after her first glimpse of him, told her family what she had seen. That was when the comments began, starting with her father, who patted her on the head and called her "daft." Her brothers and sisters called her a liar, but Mama didn't say a word.

Helen was undaunted. When no one was looking, she would sneak up to her sister's bedroom (later her own) and watch the house through the big bay window. On very rare occasions, she would see him. But he never appeared when someone else was there to witness the scene with her.

Until she was ten years old, the house stood empty. Then one day, as she was watching it, she saw a carriage pull up the hill. A man and his wife stepped out, followed by their daughter. But Helen never met the girl—never knew her name. Within a month, the man had packed his family's belongings and taken them away. In a brief conversation with Helen's father, he had said the house made his daughter nervous.

Another forty years passed, and though Helen's hair had begun to fleck with gray, the man who walked the grounds of that house remained young. By this time, another family had moved in—a young couple with four little sons. And for a while, everything seemed fine.

But a scream reached Helen one night, so loud that it was carried all the way down the hill to her house. She put on her robe and slippers and went downstairs, where she was told by an older brother to wait until he went to the house to investigate.

When he returned an hour later, his face was ashen. In a shaking voice, he reported that the father had somehow fallen from his bedroom window, headfirst. He had broken his neck.

Half a year later, his sons were dead too.

Helen tried to push that memory from her mind—four tiny bodies wrapped in sheets. It had been over thirty years ago, she told herself. But if time heals all wounds, it hadn't yet, after all those years, healed the pain she felt inside when she thought of those four little boys.

She walked over to the window and gazed out at the big white house. Two lights were lit, and through a ruffle-curtained window she could see the silhouette of a child. There was a new family in the house now.

She would not let him have this one.

5

Melanie felt Gary's lips against hers. She responded dreamily, sighing with the feeling of warmth he gave her. In her somnolent state, his hair seemed thicker, his lips fuller. When he whispered, it was with a passion that seemed out of another time.

"I do love you so," he whispered.

His grip on her body tightened as he lifted her a bit off the bed to kiss her. She felt her body heat rise as he rocked her, her breathing deepening into sleep.

Then she opened her eyes for a moment to see a man who wasn't Gary. The figure disappeared in the few seconds it took for Gary to roll over in his sleep. Melanie's heart began to pound with fear. It would be hours before she fell asleep again.

* * *

Gary woke at two o'clock in the morning to the sound of his own coughing. His eyes began to tear with the sting of cold as soon as he opened them. He sat up and looked at Melanie, sleeping soundly under a huge mound of blankets. It was no wonder he was freezing, he thought, reclaiming his own covers.

Outside in the hallway, the ancient metal radiator banged loudly. But when Gary put a trembling palm against the one standing near his bed, he felt no heat rising from it. He threw aside his covers and climbed out of bed to take a closer look. Somehow, the valve had been turned off in the night. He twisted it, heard a spitting sound, and started back to bed again. Damn these old houses and their faulty heating systems. Maybe they should have bought a brand-new house—less atmosphere but everything would have worked.

Now there was a draft coming from somewhere. Gary scanned the room for its source, squinting to stretch his vision through the darkness. He spotted the opened closet door and guessed that the small window above the top shelf had blown open. In the darkness, he pushed away suits and coats and picked up his foot to place it on the first shelf.

But instead of landing quietly on the wooden plank, his foot fell heavily to the floor. It was as if he had miscalculated the number of steps on a dark stairway. But Gary had miscalculated nothing. There was simply no shelf for him to step on. Confused, he swung his hand over his head until he touched the light cord, then pulled it.

The bulb swung a bit, casting dramatic shadows over the shelves Gary had, only a few weeks ago, called solid and sturdy. Now they were broken neatly down the center, as if someone had karate-chopped them from top to bottom in one clean stroke. The few items that had been placed on them had fallen to the floor. The closet reeked of aftershave.

Not believing what he saw, Gary reached out and grabbed one of the shelves. He had misjudged them, of course. They were merely plaster, or cheap imitation wood. If he tried, he could break off a piece as easily as if it were peanut brittle.

But the shelf, in spite of his efforts, remained intact. He gritted his teeth, put all his weight against the wood, and still couldn't crack it. By now, his shock had turned to anger, though logic told him there was no one to whom he could direct it. No one else in this house could have broken these shelves like this. It would have taken an axe—and someone a lot stronger than any of them.

Gary thought about searching the house but finally decided that whoever had done this was long gone. If it had been done tonight, he would have heard something. No human could destroy something so thoroughly without making noise.

He looked at Melanie, debating whether or not to wake her. He decided against it, reasoning that nothing could be accomplished now. If law school had taught him one thing, it was never to take as truth what one saw in the dark. In the morning, Gary thought as he shut the closet door tightly to keep out the draft, he would ask questions.

* * *

Melanie walked into the kitchen to find Gina and Kyle huddled on the same chair. Gina had an arm around Kyle, and the little boy was rubbing a finger under his red nose. Melanie frowned.

"Are you two feeling all right?" she asked. "You look like you're coming down with something."

"We're just cold, Mom," Gina said. "It was freezing in my room last night! Kyle's, too. I think our radiators got turned off in the night. Did yours?"

"I don't think so," Melanie said. "I was warm when I woke up. We'll have Daddy fix them when he gets up, okay?"

She lifted the teakettle from the stove and started to fill it. It was still hard to imagine how water had come from this empty pot a day ago to burn her little daughter. An aluminum teakettle, innocent on its own, had somehow turned into a thing of evil. . . .

She suddenly threw down the kettle with a yowl. The scorching hot water from the tap had leaked through a hole in the dented metal. She gave her hand a hard shake to take the pain away and watched a bright red mark appear where the water had splashed her hand.

She felt a hand press her shoulder. Gina's so quick to comfort, she thought. But when she reached up to place her hand on her daughter's, she felt nothing but the plush of her bathrobe. The pressure was constant, but there was no hand.

Melanie turned and looked at Gina, who still sat with Kyle. The girl returned her mother's gaze with a befuddled one of her own and started to get out of the chair.

"You okay, Mom?"

"Huh?" Melanie faltered. "Yea—yes. I'm fine. I just spilled water on my hand and hurt myself a little. The kettle's broken—we'll do without oatmeal today."

"Yay!" Kyle yelled. "I hate oatmeal!"

Gina clapped a hand over his mouth and sternly reminded him that Nancy and their father were sleeping. Kyle shrugged, but lowered his voice when he said, "I'm still cold, Mom."

"Me, too," Gina put in.

"I'll make some cocoa," Melanie offered, sucking at the red mark on her hand.

She was thinking of the touch she had felt on her shoulder. It was such a strange thing—like that vision she had while in bed with Gary. If someone asked her, she would have sworn on a Bible that the man bending over her was real. But she had heard somewhere that dreams sometimes go on for a few seconds even after the eyes are opened. Some dream, she thought with a quiet laugh. Gary would appreciate the competition! Well, she never went for tall, dark men—like the one she had seen.

"Hi, Daddy!" she heard Gina say. The reply was a grumble, and Melanie turned to see a frown where Gary usually wore a good-morning smile. He sat down heavily in a chair and stared at the coffee cup Melanie put in front of him.

"The kids say their rooms are cold," she told him.

"My radiator's off," Gina said.

"Mine, too," Kyle put in.

Gary looked up. "Really? I had to turn mine on last night."

"I was warm all night," Melanie said.

"I'm not surprised," Gary answered. "You stole all the blankets."

"I did?" Melanie asked. "I've never done anything like that before. I wonder what made me do it last night?"

"I couldn't tell you," Gary replied, "but you were certainly bundled up."

"Well," Kyle drawled, "*I* froze my toes!"

When he discovered the poem in his last sentence, he began to tap his spoon against the edge of his cup, chanting it.

"Froze my toes! Froze my toes!"

"Quiet, Kyle!"

It wasn't Gina, but Gary who silenced the boy this time, reminding him that Nancy was still asleep.

"Gary," Melanie said quickly, "could you just check on her? I don't want her room cold."

"Will do," Gary said, taking a quick sip from the still-full coffee cup.

He walked up the stairs, thinking to himself that he'd tell his wife about the shelves when the kids were gone. No use frightening them. But it had been a trial to hold in his anger.

Kyle's room was nearest, so he entered it first. It was simple enough to turn on the radiator. But he had a strange feeling about the closed door to his son's closet. He reasoned that he was doing it "just out of interest" when he opened the closet door. His casual air faded when he saw the shelves, broken exactly as his had been. On the floor, every toy model he had worked on with the boy for so many hours was smashed.

He slammed the door. He didn't want to think about this now. He knew that no matter what explanation he came up with, nothing would make sense.

He walked into Gina's room and picked up a stuffed animal that had fallen on the floor. Still holding it in his arms, he went to the radiator to turn it back on. Then he turned to the closet, expecting to find the same thing he had found in Kyle's. His suspicions were justified. Up above the broken shelves, the tiny window flapped in the breeze, banging against the tree that stood just outside it. An icy wind seeped into the room.

Gary threw the stuffed toy across the room to vent his anger. In Nancy's room, he again fixed the radiator, moving softly around the sleeping child's bed. When he opened her closet, it was only the worry of waking her up that kept him from crying out.

Those shelves, too, were broken.

6

Melanie drove her car down the long road that led into Belle Bay, tightly clutching the steering wheel. Halfway between her house and the center of town, the road took a swing to the right and ran along the beach for a half mile. The morning wind of late October stirred little chops of waves from the nearby water and sent the soothing aroma of salt water into the half-open car window. She sucked in the air, letting it refresh her, but still kept a tight grip on the steering wheel. She clutched it in terror, because she was certain something strange was going on at the house, and that morning she had had to run away.

The road turned back again and met the main highway. Melanie followed this until she saw a sign announcing that Belle Mall was to the right. She turned, then drove past the line of stores until she came to the end of the road.

At the duck pond, she turned off the engine and got out of the car, heading for a green bench that sat at the water's edge. As she settled herself, a half-dozen mallard ducks came swimming over, expecting her to feed them. When she didn't move, they quacked in anger and swam away.

Melanie watched them, staring at the iridescent green head of a drake. She had come here to think, hoping the peaceful emptiness of the park would help her. She closed her eyes and pieced together the events of the morning.

She couldn't recall a time when she had seen Gary so upset. Within minutes after he had gone upstairs to check on Nancy, he had returned to the kitchen with an unusual spark of anger in his eyes. Someone had axed the closet shelves in all the bedrooms, he seethed.

"What?" Melanie whispered in disbelief.

Gary stood in the doorway with his chin tucked into his neck. His jaw was clenched and his face was red. The arms that had held Melanie so gently the night before hung stiffly, ending in clenched fists.

"Daddy?" Gina said carefully.

Gary let out a long sigh at the sound of her worried voice and shook his head. He assured her that he wasn't angry at any of *them*, but at the stupid senselessness of the whole thing.

"What would anyone gain by doing a thing like that?" he demanded.

"Shouldn't we call the police?" Melanie asked.

"I don't know," Gary said. "Let's get the kids out of here first. Nothing seems to be missing, and I'm sure no one's hiding here."

He slammed his fist on the table in a resurgence of his anger when Melanie gently reminded him that the house was big and had a lot of empty rooms.

"Damn it, Melanie!" he roared. "Will you let me do the thinking!"

"Gary," Melanie retorted, "I have as much right as—"

Kyle was suddenly on his feet.

"My models are in my closet!" he cried, racing to the stairs.

"Kyle, wait a second!" his father called after him.

Gary didn't want his son to learn about the broken models in such an abrupt way. But Kyle was already shuffling back down the stairs, clutching the remains of a plastic army tank and sinking his teeth into his lower lip to bite back tears. He handed it to his mother.

"Dad and I made that on my birthday," he blubbered. "All my models are buh-buh-broken!"

"Kyle," Melanie said soothingly, kneeling down to hug him. She looked up at Gary over the curled head and demanded: "Who would do such a sick thing?"

"I'm scared," Gina said then, very softly.

"Don't be, honey," Gary said. "Daddy'll straighten this out. Kyle, I'm sorry about all this. It was a crappy thing to do and I'm going to make somebody pay for it."

"Yeah," Kyle sniffled, pulling away from Melanie.

"I'll tell you what," Gary suggested, "we'll go over everything when you get home today. I'm sure most of them can be fixed."

Kyle studied the army tank carefully, wanting to believe his father's words. He looked at Gary and said, "Really?"

"Really," Gary said. "Now get your coats before you miss the bus."

He bent down to hug his son and planted a kiss on Gina's dark hair. He and Melanie watched them walk down to the bus, each waiting for the other to speak. But neither was ready with a theory. Perhaps Nancy's "mean man" had something to do with it. . . .

"Excuse me!"

Melanie's eyes snapped open, and she saw a young woman staring at her. She straightened herself and rubbed her eyes, then looked up. The young woman held out a set of keys. "I found these on the path and wondered if they were yours," she said.

"I—I think so," Melanie said, taking them. "Yes, they are. Thanks."

"Sure," the young woman said. She started to walk away, but when she saw Melanie put her head down in her lap, she stopped. "Are you all right?"

Melanie nodded, then shook her head. She wasn't all right. She felt dazed, as if she had just waked up from a deep sleep. She rubbed her eyes again.

"I just feel a little dizzy," she admitted. "I had a rough morning."

"I believe it," the woman said, taking a seat beside her. She was a good head shorter than Melanie, with fine blonde hair that reached down to her thin waist. She took Melanie's hand.

"I'm Janice Lors," she said. "Local librarian. I work just down the block from here, so I decided to come outside for my coffee break. It's always so quiet in there on weekday mornings!"

Melanie laughed. "I'm Melanie VanBuren," she said.

"You know, I recognize most of the faces in this town," Janice said. "There are so few of us here in Belle Bay. Why don't I recognize you?"

Melanie started to explain, "We just moved here a few weeks ago," when Janice interrupted her.

"The *Times!*" she cried, snapping her fingers. "You did an illustration for the cover of the *Times* magazine section last year. I remember it because it was a story on the singles scene."

"Am I really worth remembering?" Melanie asked with a laugh.

"Oh, yes," Janice assured her. "If you're ever in town, drop by the library. I want you to sign our copy of that issue. Maybe we could do a display on a Belle Bay 'Artiste Extraordinaire.'"

"That's a first," Melanie said. "I've never been asked for an autograph before. As a matter of fact, you're the first person I've met in this town."

"What?" Janice asked with surprise. "What have you got for neighbors—snobs?"

"We have only one," Melanie told her. "An old lady who the mailman says is senile."

She felt stronger after this chance meeting. Janice Lors' cheerfulness was catching. The young woman sat for a half hour with Melanie, oblivious to the time, and told her all about the parts of Belle Bay that she had not yet seen. "There's an art club that meets on Tuesday night in the basement of the church," Janice said. "You might be interested in that."

"I would," Melanie said. "Sometimes I just like to get out of that big old house."

"Where exactly do you live?"

"We live on Starbine Court Road," Melanie answered. "At the top of the hill. Our property line is halfway into a forest on one side, and that's just a half mile from the beach."

"You must mean the old Langston place," Janice said. "I'd love to live in a place like that. I'm surprised it took this long to sell it. How'd you get so lucky?"

"I guess we—"

"Don't answer that," Janice said. "I didn't mean to be nosy. If you ever want to find out more about the house, just ask. We've got newspapers and magazines on microfilm to way back when at the library. There's even a collection of diaries and letters about the town."

"It sounds fascinating," Melanie said. "I'll take you up on the offer some day."

"There have been stories about the place," Janice told her. "But any house built way back in the 1700s is bound to have some tales behind it."

"What kind of stories?" Melanie asked, trying to sound casual. But Janice immediately picked up her uneasiness. She gave Melanie a questioning look.

"I'd like to hear about them," Melanie pressed.

"Well, why don't we make a date for lunch tomorrow?" Janice suggested. "I don't know much about the old place, but what I do know, I'll tell you then."

"Are you in a hurry to get back to work?"

"Look," Janice said, "maybe I shouldn't have said anything. There isn't much to the stories, just gossip that's been passed down for generations. The more a story is told, the more farfetched it gets." She smiled. "Isn't that a bit of neat philosophy from an old-maid librarian?"

"Old maid?" Melanie laughed. "How old are you?"

"Twenty-nine," Janice answered, "which is too damned old to be playing the singles scene in a town like this, if you ask me." She sighed. "Oh, hell, it's fun. Come on, I'll walk you back to your car."

As they walked, Janice pulled out a pack of cigarettes and offered one to Melanie. When Melanie shook her head, Janice said, "No one else likes 'em either."

She shoved them back into her pocket. "I got these in the city. They were handing them out free a few days ago. These girls with boxes tied around their necks and dumb straw hats. I went around the block four times just so I could get more of them. They must have recognized me after a while." She stopped to laugh. "And I can't stand these! Sure I can't unload a pack on you?"

"I don't smoke," Melanie said. "I quit."

"The worst kind," Janice mumbled.

They had almost reached their cars when a voice called out from behind them. Melanie and Janice swirled around to see a stooped old woman, aided by a young nurse, emerging from a nearby car. The nurse held fast to her arm until she had steadied herself against her walker, and walked slowly beside her, keeping pace with the woman's slow gait. Although she was weak, bent over and wrinkled with age, there was a fierce determination in her eyes that mesmerized both Melanie and Janice and held them fast until she reached them.

When she did, she looked Melanie straight in the eye and said:

"There is danger in your home, young woman. He's a murderer. He'll destroy your family!"

Melanie was taken aback by the fanatical insistence in the woman's voice. The man's face that she had seen over her in bed the night before flashed in her mind, with the echo of Nancy's words "mean man." She couldn't speak. It was Janice who came to her rescue.

"Say," she snapped. "What do you mean, scaring her like that? Just who are you, anyway?"

"Please," the young nurse said, "she's just an old woman. I take her out once a week for fresh air, and, well, sometimes she forgets herself."

"I most certainly do not!" the old woman hissed.

The old woman eyed Janice and ran a pointed tongue over her lips. She knew this woman. Had seen her grow up. Why, she was one of that high-school gang that used to pelt her house with eggs on Halloween. Why should Helen Jennings tell this brazen young thing her name?

"Well?" Janice pressed. "Who are you? And what do you want with my friend?"

The words "My friend" had a strange effect on Helen. Her eyes softened, and she smiled slightly.

"Helen Jennings," she said at last. "I live next door to Mrs. Van-Buren."

"Fine," Janice said. "Now why don't you go home and leave her alone?"

At that, Helen's calm front fell away. She leaned over the front of her walker and grabbed Melanie's sleeve.

"Please, you must listen," she pleaded. "For years I have cried out in warning, but not a soul will listen to me! I've seen innocents like your own children die by his hands! I've seen them suffer hideously because he hates them so!"

"Stop that!" Janice cried. "Just get lost, will you?"

She took Melanie by the arm and pulled her away, cursing softly. She headed toward her own car, ignoring Helen's cries. She could feel Melanie stiffen and pulled her a little closer. Melanie stared ahead, still absorbing the words hurled at her by the old woman.

Who would kill her children? Why would Gina, Kyle, and Nancy have to "suffer hideously"?

. . . Screaming on a miniature rack designed just for them, painted with teddy bears and tin soldiers. Turn the handle and out comes . . .

"Hey!"

She thought she heard Janice's voice in the distance. Her eyes stared blankly at a face that was close to hers. Melanie felt someone shake her.

"Wake up!"

With a start, she blinked and looked at Janice.

"Have you landed yet?"

"Huh?"

"Are you all right?" Janice said. "You looked like you were off in space."

Melanie let out a long sigh. She shuddered quickly in one jerking movement, and she wrapped her arms tightly around her body.

"She upset me," Melanie answered.

"Who, that old bat?" Janice said. "Ignore her. She's as senile as they come."

"But there have been some strange happenings in my house," Melanie said.

"Which are probably very easy to explain," Janice said.

Melanie nodded in agreement, but she secretly wanted to talk to the old woman. She seemed to know something about the house that no one else did.

"What say you and I meet for lunch today?" Janice suggested.

"I couldn't," Melanie said. "Not today, anyway. I've got a million things to do—go to the supermarket, stop at the laundry, pick up a package at the post office. . . . How about tomorrow?"

"Sounds fine," Janice said. "I'll see you then. Meet me at the library, okay? Now go home and get yourself busy with a painting and forget your nutty neighbor."

Melanie watched Janice walk to her car. With each step her long blonde hair swished back and forth, just barely touching the bottom of her rabbit-fur jacket. From the back, Melanie thought, she looked just like a teenager. Why would a pretty unmarried girl like Janice stay in a small, dull town like this?

As she drove home, Melanie was certain this chance meeting with Janice had given her some sort of strength. But that strength didn't prepare her for what she found inside the house. Her courage drained away at the sight of Gary twisted at the bottom of the stairs. His head was bent at an odd angle, revealing a bruised neck.

7

When Melanie left, Gary had gone upstairs to reexamine the shelves. He was no longer angry, but more worried about his family's safety. God help them if it was that easy to vandalize this place without being seen . . . if there was some maniac running around who enjoyed destroying things for no reason. They were using only half the rooms in the vast house. There were plenty of empty rooms and closets for anyone to hide in.

He picked up the two halves of one shelf in his bedroom and tried to fit them together. From above him, the window moved in the wind to tap against the outside of the house, as if to remind him it was still open. The branches of the tree outside touched the window ledge, as if they were grabbing at something inside the closet.

He went to the linen closet in the hallway and pulled down a small stepladder. From over his head there came a low whine, and he looked up at the square indentation in the ceiling that led to the attic. The noise began as a thin wail, then sounded incredibly like a child crying.

"Squirrels," Gary said, spitting it as if it were a curse word.

The first window to be locked would have to be Nancy's. She didn't need those late-autumn gusts drafting in her room to add to her problems. Gary rested the ladder against the small yellow dresser next to her door and walked softly to the bed. Although she was usually awake and playing at this hour, she was still sound asleep, sucking at both thumbs. Gary thought to himself that sleep must help her forget the frightening experience she had had.

Gary opened the closet door slowly, so that the creaking wouldn't wake her up, and placed the ladder inside. He climbed to the top and reached for the window to pull it shut. Satisfied that it wouldn't blow open again, he climbed down and headed for Kyle's room.

He stopped for a moment to pick up one of the models and remembered his son's tearful face that morning. Well, he thought with a sigh, they would build new ones, and Kyle would forget all this.

When he finally returned the ladder to the hall closet, he listened for the sounds of squirrels. But this time no sound came from the attic above.

He walked out and headed for the stairs, where he gave the sphinx a pat on its brass head.

"I suppose that after all these years you've seen a lot of weird things happen in this house," he said. "This must all seem pretty ho-hum to you."

The shining Egyptian statue did nothing. It stared forward into forever, unable, or unwilling, to respond. It was another voice that Gary heard, low and gruff, filling the empty hall behind him.

"*Leave her!*" it demanded.

Gary turned around and looked down the hall. Though he could see no one, the voice seemed to be only a few feet away. It roared again.

"*This time she is mine!*"

Gary shook his head and took a step forward, certain it was some kind of a trick. He thought with excited anticipation that he was about to confront the person who had broken the shelves.

Suddenly, icy fingers wrapped around his throat. He gasped for air, ripping at his collar. But he could not stop the pressure of the unseen fingers against his neck. His arms flailed against the air, trying to push away something they could not feel. He choked, whooping in high-pitched breaths.

"*You shall give her to me!*" the voice cried. "*You will not hurt her again!*"

Gary tried to speak, but his words were clipped short when his tongue involuntarily pushed forward, as if to lick up any small bit of air it could. His eyes rolled back and he let out one long sigh. Then, as suddenly as they had grabbed him, the fingers fell away, and Gary felt his knees bend beneath him. With dulled reflexes, his arm swung out too late to grab the twisted rung of the banister before he fell down the stairs. The last thing he saw before he hit the bottom was a milky-white cloud at the top of the stairs.

His assailant watched him, his long-dead heart almost beating with his fury. The strength that had hurt the daughter and broken the shelves hadn't been enough to frighten him away, the being thought. Perhaps this would serve as a better warning. . . .

* * *

March, 1818

The stains just wouldn't come out. The young maid leaned forward heavily on her scrub brush, scouring and scouring. Yet when she rinsed the suds away, the mark was still there. She rubbed her hand under her nose, tucked a stray hair back into her cap, then challenged the task once again.

Mrs. Baxter had been adamant that the stains be removed from the rug. So Adele worked until her fingers were raw, ready to burst into tears when she rinsed the rug to find the spot again. How could Mrs. Baxter make such an impossible demand? Adele Collins was only thirteen, and it just wasn't fair to expect this of her.

"Hush," she told herself firmly. "Papa sent you here to work, and work you shall. You aren't paid 50 cents a week to complain!"

Two black slippers and the hem of a long black gown suddenly appeared before her. Adele looked up to see her mistress. The woman returned Adele's smile with a cold stare. Adele tried not to frown at the sight of Mrs. Baxter's pale tired visage; but it was difficult, especially when it was so easy to recall how rosy and alive those cheeks had once been.

"Is it coming out?" Mrs. Baxter asked, her voice far away.

"No, my lady," said Adele. "I'm sorry, but I'm trying."

It was the fifth time she had asked that question in the last half hour. Adele had shown a good deal of patience with her mistress, but even her kind spirit was beginning to fray. She thought for certain that if Gwendolyn asked it once more, she'd hand her the brush and make her try to clean up the mess herself.

Mrs. Baxter sat awkwardly down on the steps and leaned her head

against the carved post. Her hair glistened in the light of the chandelier the girl had lit. Adele knew there was no use starting a conversation, for Gwendolyn's mind had lost itself somewhere in the short
time since her husband's "accident."

Adele shuddered. *Why is it*, she thought, *that horrible things happen only to good people?*

She had only been with the Baxters since they had moved into this
house three months ago. This big white house on the hill had been
in a terrible state then, thick with dust and dirt from two decades of
neglect. Adele couldn't understand why no one had bought the place
after the first owner passed away; it was big and roomy and very nice
to look at. Oh, her father told her stories about evil there, but since
it didn't stop him from sending her to work, she had paid no attention to them.

It was just two weeks after she first moved into the house that she
began to wonder if the stories might be true. She had waked up one
night to the sound of footsteps shuffling across the rug to her bed.
But when she opened her eyes, no one was there. And the door was
tightly closed. She felt incredibly cold and decided to go to her bureau for another blanket. The cold became worse as she moved
across the room, groping forward in the pitch darkness. She knew
that all she had to do was walk a straight line and she would touch
the smooth oak of the dresser. But instead, her hands touched the
bare chest of an unseen intruder, who stood in her path. Adele let out
a small, startled cry and backed away.

"Who's there?" she demanded. "Say, or I'll scream. I swear I
shall!"

The only answer was a low, evil laugh. Then, before Adele's
scream could emerge, it was blocked by a strong hand. She felt herself being pushed back to her bed. Her feet stumbled up the step
backward, and she fell, her body at an angle over the side of the bed.
She heard the sound of lace ripping from her nightdress. Adele had
no knowledge of sex, but she knew he intended to hurt her, badly.
She trembled, not struggling. She couldn't—the man was too heavy
on top of her. He pressed close to her ear and whispered.

"You shall not have your mother's life again, witch-child," he said,
in a faint British accent. "She is mine now! She has returned."

And then he wasn't there. Adele, sprawled against the side of the bed, couldn't move for her fear. Was he there in the darkness, waiting? She kept perfectly still, listening. Then all was black.

The next morning she found herself under her covers, as if she had been there all night. Still shaken, she rolled from the bed and went to splash water on her face. Looking in the mirror, she studied the lace of her nightdress. It hadn't been ripped.

"You dreamt it," she told herself. "What a silly! And besides, who would accuse you of hurting your mother?"

Yet there were other bizarre events. Adele, not a superstitious girl, could live with books that disappeared and candles that blew out when there was no wind. But when Mr. and Mrs. Baxter fought because of it, she felt she couldn't go on working here. Who would believe they had been so loving once, when they first moved into the big house?

And they had been. Adele had seen the signs of their love. "I love you so much," Adele had often heard the handsome Dane Baxter whisper to his wife.

"And I love you," Gwendolyn would sigh.

They had said it. Adele had heard them. So she knew they meant very much to each other. That's what made it so terribly frightening when they began to fight. It was over little things, like disappearing vases, figurines that neither could find. Then the little spats became violent arguments, initiated when Dane found a piece of sharply glistening glass under his pillow. Gwen denied ever having seen it and expressed shock that her husband might have been seriously hurt. Three months ago, Dane would never have thought such things of his wife, but now he accused her of attempted murder.

But Gwendolyn hadn't left the glass there, and Dane's would-be murderer was angered to find that his trap had failed. One thing did work in his favor, however. Dane moved out of the bedroom, leaving his wife to sleep alone. Gwen tossed and turned in her sleep, praying fervently that her husband would believe her and return to her bed. That night, her prayers were answered, but not in the way she had hoped.

She pretended to be asleep when she felt the bed sink under Dane's weight. But when he kissed her softly, she reached up to hold his face in her hands. How cold he felt! Even his lips. But Gwendolyn didn't care. He was here again, and that was all that mattered.

"Please stay with me forever," he said.

"Forever," Gwen whispered.

"I love you so!"

"And I love you," Gwen answered. "*Je t'adore.*"

Someone was pounding at the door. Thinking it was Adele, Gwen whispered that they should ignore her. But the voice behind the door belonged to a man. As soon as she heard it, she felt the burden of weight on her body disappear. Confused, she lit the lamp and looked around the room. It was empty.

She went to the door and opened it wide, her heart beating loudly. Dane was standing there, a look of anger on his face. He was completely dressed. He didn't look at all like someone who had just made love.

"Why did you lock that door?" he demanded.

"It was not locked!"

"Then why could I not open it?" Dane asked. "You are hiding someone in here—I heard you!"

"Dane," Gwen said, "I must have been talking in my sleep. There is no one here!"

"I heard a man's voice."

Dane pushed her aside and entered the room, throwing open the closet, checking under the bed, and moving dressers aside. Gwen wasn't lying—there was no one in here. But he had heard a voice, and the door had been locked!

"There is a secret passage here," he shouted. "You have hidden him!"

"How ridiculous!" Gwen cried. "To think you could accuse me of such a thing!"

But Dane was already pounding at the walls and tugging the chandelier. Nothing moved in the walls, yet still he was convinced his wife was hiding a lover. Of course, that would explain her lies about the missing articles. She had stolen them to give to her lover! Dane turned to look at her, his eyes wild. How could she dare to stand there like that, haughtily mocking him while another man listened from a deep shadow?

"Stop laughing," Dane said.

"I am not laughing."

"Silence!"

Gwen fell backward when her husband's fist reached her eye. She touched it gingerly, shocked, and drew back a finger spotted with blood. How could Dane do such a thing to her? She opened her mouth to call to him, but he had already left the room.

He spotted the man standing at the top of the stairs, one hand resting on the golden sphinx. He was dressed in a naval uniform that was at least two decades out of date. Was this the man his wife had taken to her bed? Dane couldn't understand why. This fellow looked downright ridiculous in that costume. But Dane didn't laugh at him.

"What were you doing with my wife?"

The man didn't answer. Dane reached out to grab his throat, but when he reached him, his hands sliced through the neck and touched each other. There was nothing there—nothing but a blast of cold that ruffled his hair.

And then something grabbed at his own throat. He backed up, terrified, trying to get away. What was this? Was he mad? But if so, then why did he feel the pain? He choked and gasped, struggling, helpless.

But he wasn't helpless! He had put a dagger in the pocket of his robe. His hand reached for it. But what would he do with it? How could he stab something that wasn't there? He was desperate. The blade sliced through the coldness. The fingers around his neck loosened, but the pain was only lessened for a brief instant. Suddenly, Dane felt something cuff him under the chin, hard. He fell backward, tumbling, falling head-over-heels. The dagger was still useless in his hand. When he hit the bottom landing, he fell on its sharp point. Blood gushed from the wound in his heart, staining the rug. Both Adele and Gwendolyn had watched the scene in shock. By the time they reached the bottom of the stairs, Dane was dead.

And so Adele found herself scrubbing to remove the stains. Who could believe such a thing would happen to Master Dane? Who could believe the beautiful, spirited Mrs. Baxter had turned into something akin to a walking corpse? Adele shivered.

Once again, she poured clean water over the area. This time, her efforts were rewarded. Sighing, she stood up and wiped her forehead. Then, lifting her bucket, she went to dump the water, leaving Mrs. Baxter to sit on the stairs.

"She won't be lonely much longer," Adele said out loud, as she threw the water out the back door. She turned into the kitchen and replaced the scrub brush and bucket just inside the cellar door. "When her mother and father arrive, they will certainly cheer her."

The day after Dane's death (she still couldn't bring herself to call it murder), Adele, in desperation, had written to Gwendolyn's parents in her childish hand, telling them their daughter needed them. They lived all the way in Philadelphia, but she expected they would come as soon as they received the letter. That had been five days ago.

She heard the sound of horses' hooves and ran to the parlor window. Someone had pulled a horse and carriage to the side of the house. Adele ran back into the kitchen, out the back door—the only door servants were allowed to use—and around to the front drive. She led Gwendolyn's parents into the house, where her mistress still crouched on the stairs.

Gwen's mother gasped at the sight of her daughter. Gwen didn't move an inch when her mother approached, but still kept her eyes fixed on the chandelier. When her father passed a hand in front of her eyes, she didn't blink.

"Dear Lord," he whispered, crossing himself with a wrinkled hand.

"She talks sometimes, sir," Adele told him, "but very little. Usually she sits and stares, just like that."

"Has she had a physician?" George Kingsley asked.

"Yes, sir," Adele replied. "I called one here when we found Mr. Baxter. Oh, sir! It was awful! Just awful! Do you see that wet spot on the rug? I spent hours cleaning the blood!"

"Oh, George, what are we to do?" Hedda Kingsley wailed.

She sat down beside Gwen and pulled her close, smothering her in her ample breasts. She rocked her daughter, who at last had turned to acknowledge her presence. Gwen stared at her for a few moments, then said, "Mama? Where is Dane?"

"Hush," Hedda cooed.

"We must get her away from this house," George insisted, "and under proper care. What physician could leave her like this?"

"Doctor said it was nerves," Adele said, "and that it would pass in time!"

"Paugh!" George cried. "We are taking her away tonight."

"I already packed some of her things," Adele said. "Someone can return for her other belongings."

"And what of you, child?" Hedda asked.

"Oh, my father visits me every Saturday," Adele replied. "When he comes tomorrow, I will ask him to take me home."

"But you will be here alone!"

"I'm not afraid, ma'am," Adele said, smiling. "And it's only for one night."

"It's only for one night." How often did she repeat that in the hours that followed. Soon after the Kingsleys had left with their daughter, Adele began to feel unnerved. She was the only soul in this house. The only living soul, she thought. She listened attentively for any sounds. Finally, late that night, she slid down under her quilt and fell asleep.

Some time later she was wakened by a voice—the very same voice she had heard months earlier, accusing her of wanting to harm her mother. She answered sleepily, insisting that she loved her mother dearly.

"You have sent her away!" the voice hissed. "You have sent her to her death!"

"You're just a dream," Adele mumbled, turning over and falling asleep again.

She never felt the pain. She slept through the blaze that shot up from her pillow, then licked over her hair and down her body, destroying only what it had to destroy and nothing more.

When her father arrived the next day, he found her lying in a fetal position—or what was left of her. With a cry, he picked up the grotesque shape, so like a dead tree in winter. Her legs were stumps, and bones jutted from the tips of her fingers. There was nothing left of her face, no mouth, no nose, no eyes. He shivered to think he was holding his daughter, wrapped inside a heavy blanket. In spite of what he saw, he prayed this wasn't his little Adele. But he knew the truth.

Someone would pay. He searched every room. No one was there. He felt tears welling in his eyes, and he fled the house. Behind him, he heard the distinct sound of wild laughter.

*   *   *

Melanie hated waiting rooms. A sort of tense heat always filled the air, making them unpleasantly stagnant. The uneasiness was almost choking. That uneasiness enveloped her for the second time this week, and she could feel it sucking away at her nerves. She paced the floor for a few more minutes, then dumped herself into a chair to stare at the wall.

Across the room, Nancy leaned toward a fish tank, unable to kneel because of the bandages around her legs. She traced the slow path of a little goldfish with a chubby finger. Then, she turned and hobbled over to a pile of magazines, walking like a tiny mummy. She inspected the one on top, yawning widely. It was so quiet in the little room that she was beginning to get drowsy again. She had been sound asleep when Melanie woke her to take her daddy to the doctor, and still didn't feel very playful. Nancy wanted her mother to read to her but she had such a sad look on her face that the little girl went over and sat with her instead. Melanie had to help her up onto the bench, and she wriggled until she settled herself between her mother and the armrest. Melanie put an arm around her and Nancy studied her mother's pale visage with large, blue eyes.

Melanie sprang to her feet when the door opened, nearly knocking her daughter to the floor. But the man who entered was only a janitor who had come to feed the fish. He chirped at them, calling them by name. Greedily, the fish swam to the surface, sucking at the food in small, jerking movements.

The janitor looked over at Melanie, who had disappointedly sat down again, and eyed her with understanding. He seemed to be telling her that he had seen many others here too. He knew, he knew. He nodded slightly and left.

Melanie looked at her watch. Somehow that little shake of the janitor's head had calmed her. She finally spoke to her daughter.

"It's two-thirty already," she said.

"Can we go eat now?" Nancy asked.

Melanie hadn't thought of food since she had brought Gary to the hospital, and she realized that she was as hungry as her daughter. Poor kid, Melanie thought. The banana she had been handed to eat in the car on the way here wasn't enough to satisfy a five-year-old's appetite. Melanie knew she would have to get them both something to eat before they wore themselves out.

"Let me see what the doctor says," she said. "You wait here, and Mommy will be back in a minute."

She went to the nurses' station and asked the RN to contact the doctor who was in charge of Gary. She pointed out that it had been nearly two hours—surely they were finished by now! With the smile of a professional, a meaningless smile, the nurse complied, and in minutes a plump, red-faced man appeared.

Dr. Padraic O'Shean smiled at Melanie. "Your husband is sleeping well, Mrs. VanBuren. We've given him a mild sedative."

"How is he?" Melanie wanted to know.

"No bones were broken," O'Shean said. "His wrist is sprained, badly enough to need a cast, but I think it will heal quickly. But there are bruises on his neck that I . . ." He stopped to think, pulling at the lapels of his brilliant white jacket.

"Mrs. VanBuren, I have some questions I'd like to ask you. Won't you come with me to my office?"

"Well—" Melanie mumbled, faltering under the powerful authority of this man. "I was kind of thinking of having lunch. You see, my little girl—"

"Of course!" O'Shean said with a laugh that reminded Melanie of an old engraving of Santa Claus. "We'll have something sent up."

Melanie went into the waiting room again and brought Nancy out into the hall. Hand in hand, the two followed the doctor to his office. Inside, Nancy ran up to his desk and stood on tiptoe to examine the biological statue there. She poked a finger at a plastic heart and gasped when it popped out and bounced across the floor. She scrambled after it, just barely reached it before Melanie snatched it up from the floor.

"Sit down, you," Melanie ordered, smacking her daughter's little arm. Embarrassed, she handed the plastic organ to the doctor.

"I'm sorry," she said. "I think it's broken."

"Nonsense," O'Shean replied reclaiming the heart and pushing it back into the figure's chest. "It's supposed to come out. Do you know what it is, little girl?"

"Her name is Nancy," Melanie told him.

"Nancy," the doctor repeated with a grin. "Do you know what this is?"

The little girl tightened her lips and shook her head. Her round blue eyes stared at the little thing that had made her mother angry. She didn't care what it was! It was such a hateful thing!

"It's a heart," O'Shean explained. "You've got one, too. Right here."

He poked a fat finger gently at her chest. Nancy frowned and squirmed away from his touch. Amused, the doctor straightened himself.

"Don't you believe me?"

Again, Nancy shook her head in silence. That wasn't a heart! Hearts had two round bumps at the top and a point at the bottom and they said "I Love You." This couldn't be a heart. There was no love in it!

"I'm sorry about her," Melanie said. "She had a bad experience a few days ago and she's been a little nervous since then."

Dr. O'Shean sighed, looking down at the pouting child. He unhooked his stethoscope and handed it to her.

"Would you like to hear your own heart?"

Reluctantly, Nancy reached out and took the instrument. She stood perfectly still as the doctor placed it in her ears. She heard the *boom-bum-boom* of her heart and thought of a drum. She loved drums, with their loud, rhythmical beats. Was her heart shaped like a drum? Or was it like that hated thing in the plastic man?

"Now," the doctor said, "you play with that while your mother and I have a talk."

Dr. O'Shean directed Nancy to a big couch far across the room. He turned from her and walked to his desk. Hoisting himself up onto it, he rested a well-padded hand on his knee and leaned forward. Melanie sat in the chair he indicated.

His tone all at once became serious. "Were you alone with your husband this morning?"

Melanie started, not expecting such a blunt question. She explained that she had been out shopping for about an hour and a half, and Gary had been just fine when she left. A bit angered over something, but . . .

"A bit angered?" O'Shean echoed. "Why?"

"What does that have to do with this?" Melanie asked, not impolitely.

"Perhaps in his anger he stumbled," O'Shean hypothesized, "and fell. But that doesn't explain the bruises on his neck. Somebody must have tried to injure him."

Suddenly infuriated, Melanie stood up abruptly and glared at him. It was bad enough that he asked questions that really didn't concern him. But to insinuate that she had had something to do with Gary's accident was more than Melanie would take.

"I think I know what you're saying," she told him. "But I swear *I* never hurt him! For God's sake! I've got two witnesses to prove I was out of the house this morning!"

Dr. O'Shean widened his eyes and slid back on his desk, away from Melanie's gaze.

"Mrs. VanBuren," he said, with reassurance raising the tone of his voice, "I never said you injured your husband. I only wanted to know if you had been there when it happened. Your husband refuses to discuss this with anyone. But you might be able to help us find out what happened, exactly. The police will want to know."

"Oh, God," Melanie groaned. "I forgot to call them."

"As soon as you get home," O'Shean suggested.

Melanie nodded. At that moment a nurse came into the room with their lunches. Dr. O'Shean suggested that she take Nancy into the pediatrics playroom.

"Anyone could see those bruises didn't come from you, Mrs. Van-Buren," O'Shean went on, taking such a huge bite of his sandwich that Melanie was certain he'd take his finger with it.

"The fact that you wouldn't want to hurt him is beside the point," O'Shean said. "The distance between the thumb mark and the finger marks indicates a hand much bigger than yours. And your husband certainly could have fought back if you were the assailant. The sprained wrist, however, probably happened in his fall."

"I'm glad you haven't marked me as a suspect," Melanie said with unconcealed relief. "Well, since you've started this, I'll tell you the entire story."

She began to recount the morning's events, from the broken shelves to Gary's twisted form at the bottom of the stairs. O'Shean didn't comment, but took it all in with interest and finally offered his own explanation.

"Perhaps," he suggested, "someone had broken into the house, knowing of the fine antiques to be found there. A house that size might have secret passages and hiding places with priceless items in them. So, in order to find them, the thief broke the shelves."

"Without Gary or myself hearing?"

"I can't explain that," O'Shean admitted. "But perhaps the thief didn't find what he was looking for. Suddenly, he realized he couldn't leave the house without being caught. So he hid in one of the spare rooms. When he tried to escape the next morning, Gary found him, and a struggle followed."

"When you were a child," Melanie asked with a smile, "and people would ask what you wanted to be, did you say a doctor or a detective?"

"You guessed," Padraic O'Shean laughed. "I haven't lost the touch of sleuthing. Forgive me if I've gone too far, but I cannot help being concerned about my patients."

"Don't apologize," Melanie said. "Yours is the most logical answer to what happened this morning. I appreciate it."

She put a slender hand to the side of her head and leaned back against the chair.

"Oh, God," she sighed. "You know, I stayed out all morning on purpose. And to think Nancy was alone in that house with Gary knocked out cold!"

She closed her eyes in thought. It was *hideous*. Though she tried to fight it, her mind was connecting the events of the past days. That voice she had heard in the hall the morning she found the beautiful gown. Had some maniac been hiding in one of the house's many rooms? It would be easy enough. Perhaps the man who had tried to kill Gary was the same one who had attacked Nancy!

She thought for a brief moment of Terry Hayward. He was the only person she knew who could do anything so sick, and yet she felt strongly that it *wasn't* Terry. The fact that he didn't know where they lived was enough to make her dismiss him as a suspect, but still she was certain *someone* had been in the house.

"I don't know what we're up against," she said. "I think, though, that I heard a man the other day."

"I'd guess that much," O'Shean said. "The finger marks . . ."

"No, no," Melanie interrupted, shaking her head. "There was a man in the house a few days ago. I heard him."

"If that happened," O'Shean asked, "why didn't you tell your husband?"

Melanie opened her eyes and looked at the doctor. She couldn't answer his question.

8

Both Gina and Kyle had been itching to get home that day to find out more about the broken shelves. They sat on the bus together, the center of attention among a group of children, who had heard the tale that morning. One little girl made Gina repeat the story four times, listening wide-eyed.

"I'd sure be scared if I were you, Gina," she said.

"I *was* scared," Gina told her. "My daddy was really mad, and he never gets mad like that."

"My father yells all the time," Lorrie said.

"Well," Gina said, "Daddy was mad because he cares about us. I mean, whose father wouldn't be upset to find all the closet shelves broken?"

"And my models," Kyle put in. He took Gina's hand. "You know what? I couldn't think of a thing all day but my models. Dad and I worked on those for hours and hours!"

"It was a mean person that did that," a little boy said. "I hope your dad gives him a bop on the nose when he catches him."

Kyle nodded at him, then leaned very close to whisper in Gina's ear.

"Do you think it was the same guy who hurt Nancy?"

Gina shrugged, trying to hide her fear.

"Hey, it isn't fair to tell secrets!" a boy across the aisle cried.

"Quiet down back there!" the bus driver snapped.

"Hey, Gina—there's a cop car at your house!"

From this point on the road, the entire mansion was visible, and parked at its front was a black-and-white police car. Gina and Kyle glanced at each other, both wondering why the police should show up so late. Their father had called them first thing in the morning.

"Gina, something else happened," Kyle said.

"They've just come back to talk again," Gina insisted.

But she too was anxious to get up to the house for an explanation. When the bus driver pulled to the bottom of the hill, both children jumped off without saying goodbye to their friends.

"Hope everything's okay!" the bus driver called.

They ran up to the house, covering the ground with leaps and bounds. As they reached the porch, a handsome young policeman came out of the door to greet them. His name was Tony DiMagi, "Officer Tony" to the kids who knew him. Gina blushed under his smiling gaze, feeling a brief twinge of puppy love. But her face soon became solemn again and she frowned. She wanted to know what Officer Tony was doing here.

"Your mom can explain that better than I can," Tony said. "She and your dad had a crazy morning, but everything seems to be all right now."

Gina rushed into the house to find her mother, but Kyle remained behind to talk to the young cop. He liked Officer Tony, who let him wear his cap and touch—just a little—the gun strapped to his waist.

"Did you ever shoot anyone?" Kyle asked.

"No!" Tony said. "And I hope I never have to, either. I like people too much to kill anyone."

"Say, are you here because of those shelves?"

"Sort of," Tony said. "And also because your dad had a bad accident and we want to know why."

"Is my dad okay now?"

"Well," Tony said, "you'll have to ask your mom to explain everything. She's inside."

At that moment, another cop came from inside the house. Jack Hughes, Tony's partner, was a good fifteen years Tony's senior, with graying temples and a rugged face that spoke of a long, tough career. He was as bulky as Tony was slender.

"I didn't find a thing," he said.

"Me neither," said Tony. "The downstairs is clean."

"What're you looking for?" Kyle asked.

"Some things," Tony said, "have to be a secret, Kyle. Police work, you know." He turned to his partner. "He's the VanBurens' son."

"Hi," Hughes said.

"Listen, Kyle," Tony said. "Go inside and talk to your mom. She needs you, I think."

Kyle ran into the house with a quick "goodbye" to both cops.

"You've always been great with kids," Jack said.

"I wish Mandy and I had had a few," Tony said.

"Don't think about that now," Jack answered. "Brooding over your divorce isn't going to make it better. Forget it. Out of sight, out of mind."

"Except for alimony," Tony joked.

"Alimony," Jack Hughes repeated. "C'mon, kid, let's forget about Mandy. You're young. You've got a zillion sons in your future."

"God," Tony laughed. "You make me sound like Henry VIII!"

Inside the house, Kyle had found his mother in the living room, a tearful Gina in her arms. He didn't cry when he heard what had happened to his father—he was by nature an optimist—but his mouth turned into a deep frown. He asked if they were in trouble now.

"No, we're safe," Melanie told him, though she wasn't quite sure herself. "There's no one in the house now, or the cops would have found him."

"Maybe he's a murderer and he's hiding in one of the rooms," Gina said dully.

Melanie looked down at her daughter, shocked that this beautiful twelve-year-old could voice the same theory that she herself had thought of. She tried in vain to deny the possibility. But there were such feelings of doubt in her own mind that she couldn't keep them from getting in the way as she tried to reassure her children. It was Officer Tony who came to her aid.

He had let himself into the house after talking for about fifteen minutes with Jack Hughes, and now he knocked at the door to the living room. They had found nothing at all, he told Melanie. No footprints, nothing disturbed.

"I think your doctor was right," he said. "This fellow was a prowler who happened to get caught. Your husband was in the wrong place at the wrong time."

"So he tried to kill him," Melanie said.

"I'm not sure," Tony said.

"But," Melanie wanted to know, "if that's the case, why won't Gary discuss it with me?"

"He doesn't want to frighten you, I guess," Tony said.

"It frightens me more when he broods like that," Melanie said. "Gary and I have had some trouble communicating. But he usually doesn't clam up this much when we aren't having a fight!"

"This whole thing is pretty bizarre," Tony said. He looked at Kyle. "Who knows, this may be my first real case. And you can bet Officer Tony'll get his man!"

Even Gina began to smile. They talked to Tony for a while longer, as they waited for the detective squad to come and dust for fingerprints.

Kyle walked with Tony and Jack through the house, listening eagerly as they explained what the detectives were doing. He watched them dust the banister and photograph the stairs, and he made a decision there and then that he wanted to be a cop when he grew up. Just like Officer Tony.

*   *   *

"I warned them, Belle," Helen Jennings said to the cat that rested in the bend of her arm. "I warned them, but they never listen to me."

She had seen the ambulance two days ago, and this morning the husband had been brought home. His head hung, as if pulled forward by the sling around his neck, and his wife, the girl named Melanie, supported him as he walked up the porch stairs into the house.

Helen opened her arms and let Belle jump to the floor. "He got the father this time," she said.

The cat turned its head and yowled in reply, then twitched its tail and ran from the room. Helen reached for her walker. She moved slowly to the telephone and eased herself into the chair next to it. Settling her head back against its worn upholstery, she reached for the receiver. This was her chance. Maybe now Melanie would be willing to listen.

"Operator," she said when a faceless voice answered, "give me the number of a VanBuren family in Belle Bay. The address is Starbine Court Drive."

"Hold, please," the woman said. The line buzzed for a few moments, then clicked. "VanBuren?"

"Yes, that's it."

"I'm sorry, the number is unlisted," the woman said.

"Nonsense," Helen retorted. "Look again."

"I am sorry, madam," the woman snapped back. "The number is unlisted."

"It can't be!" Helen cried. "You're lying! I must have it!"

"I-don't-have-the-number," the operator said in clipped tones.

The line went dead.

Close to tears, Helen replaced the receiver. She would have to go in person to the house, to warn them of the danger. She had an obligation to save them from the man who walked the grounds of their house.

She got up again and went over to the window. She could see the hill that went up to the VanBuren home. It was so steep! Helen was uncertain if her heart could take the stress of pumping energy to her legs so that she could reach the top.

"I must do it," she said with determination.

She pulled on a fur coat that had long ago been in fashion and fastened its remaining rhinestone buttons. Clutching the neck closed, she went out the back door, holding an ancient diary under her arm. The air was cold, laced with the scent of wet leaves. The soles of her shoes collected fallen leaves as she headed for the Van-Burens' house. The very slight rain chilled her.

With a deep breath that pulled the cool air of autumn inside her and revitalized her lungs, she began her slow climb up the hill. Every few feet, she stopped to rest, a gloved hand pressed against her chest to massage away the dull pain. When at last she reached the top of the hill, Helen, her weakened legs a badge of honor, wanted to cry out in triumph.

She stopped in front of the door, teetering on the bulging floor-boards of the porch. When she rocked, she heard them creak beneath her, and the thought occurred to her that when *he* had walked here, when he had had weight to bear down on these boards, they had not creaked.

But the thought of him did not depress her as much as the thought of facing Melanie again. The woman (woman? girl!) hadn't listened to her the other day. Why now?

Helen reached up and tapped the U-shaped knocker against the wood. She held her breath, expecting the door to be slammed in her face before it had been swung completely open. But to her surprise, the greeting she received was a pleasant one. Melanie's smile was warm, but her eyes were as distant as they had been that day in the park. Helen looked into those dull eyes and was certain *he* had already taken his toll on this family. With a friendly greeting, she followed Melanie inside.

Helen accepted the younger woman's offer to take a seat in the living room and settled herself to wait patiently while Melanie went to the kitchen for tea. Helen chose a plush velvet chair; her small frame was nearly lost in it. The antique furniture brought back memories of her childhood, but Helen couldn't feel nostalgic about this place. There were too many bad thoughts connected with it. She looked at the huge stone fireplace and wondered if *he* had leaned against it once, an arm resting on its mantel, a glass of port in his other hand. Looking oh so handsome . . .

And those bay windows. How many times had she seen faces looking out of them, faces that would be no more within a few months' time? She had seen the VanBurens' faces at those windows, and she intended to see them there for many years to come. She looked up when Melanie entered the room and smiled.

"You have some lovely antiques in here," she said.

"My husband collects them," Melanie told her, handing her a teacup. "Most of the furniture you see was in the house when we came, and Gary bargained with the realtors to buy it. Why the last owner left all this valuable furniture I have no idea, but it was fortunate for us; I just can't imagine modern furniture in a house with seven fireplaces, can you?"

"Never," said Helen.

Melanie sat across from her and waited for the old woman to speak. But Helen merely sipped at her tea, silent. At last, Melanie thought she understood what was expected of her.

"I was a bit rude the other day," she said. "But there was so much on my mind. You see, my husband had found . . ."

"I know, dear," Helen soothed. "Things happen here that we don't understand. Every other family went through it, too, but they wouldn't see. Funny how we're all so willing to admit danger only when we're right in the middle of it. But you'll see, I'm sure."

"You spoke like that the other day," Melanie said. "And it frightened me. Please, don't start about those things again."

"Those things?"

"Murdered children," Melanie said quickly. She watched Helen raise her cup. When it was set down again, it looked as if she had only touched her lips to the liquid. The cup was still full.

"Oh, of course," Helen clucked. "Here, I brought this for you." She handed the book she had brought with her to Melanie.

"My own great-great aunt wrote that," she explained, "in 1797. If you read it, you may understand some of what has been happening around here."

Melanie looked up, startled, but Helen quickly reached out a hand and placed it gently on her knee. She had been watching the house, she said, and she had seen the ambulance take Gary to town. And, she added, she had heard the screams the morning the little girl was hurt.

"I do hope the child is all right?"

"She's fine," Melanie said, unnerved that this woman had been spying on her family. She looked down at the book in her lap and opened it. The name *Nora Jennings* was written across the top of the first page, over the date January 1, 1797. Melanie thumbed through the record of the first few months and saw that every yellow page had been filled with elaborate script.

"They didn't have much to do in those days, did they?" she commented. "I couldn't keep a diary like this myself!"

"Indeed," Helen said, "there is a lot of information. My family has lived next door to this place for over two hundred years. She talks of this house a great deal. For instance, she wrote that the first man to live here was a British naval captain."

"We guessed that," Melanie said. "It's obvious. The house was filled with maps and nautical paintings when we moved in. I'm an artist—I've decided to paint a seascape for my next work."

The two women smiled at each other, Helen genuinely interested, Melanie trying to be polite. She wasn't quite sure if she welcomed this woman's visit. But if it meant finding out what had caused Gary's and Nancy's accidents, then she did welcome her. She rose to her feet and went over to the mantel, lifting a piece of scrimshaw in her hands and pretending to study it.

"It's beautiful," Helen said. "But it seems wrong that such a delicate piece is in such wicked possession."

Melanie eyed her in such a startled way that Helen lost no time explaining herself. She reached over to the coffee table and set down her cup.

"My dear," she said, "I meant the original owner of this house, of course. He was a truly evil man."

"Oh?" Melanie asked with forced interest. She sat down and looked at Helen, her eyes sober.

"Mrs. Jennings," she said.

"Miss, dear," Helen corrected.

"Miss Jennings," Melanie repeated. "You seem to know a good deal about this house. About its history, I mean. You said the other day that there was danger in my home. I was inclined not to believe you then, but so many things have happened since that I'm willing to at least hear you out."

"Thank God," Helen said with a sigh. "I'll put it simply. This house is haunted by a man who has taken the lives of many. His most recent cruelty is still so vivid in my mind that I simply can't discuss it. But believe me—you are in danger in this house!"

"Haunted?" Melanie echoed. "Really! I might believe the place has a jinx on it, but—"

"Can you explain these things in a better way?" Helen asked.

"Well," Melanie said after a pause, "anything is possible, isn't it? When my husband is better, I'll discuss it with him."

"Has he told you anything?"

"No," Melanie said. "He needs to rest first—he'll tell me when he's ready."

"Whatever he tells you," Helen entreated, "believe him. You must believe him."

"I believe everything Gary tells me," Melanie replied. "Mrs.—Miss Jennings, it's nearly time for din—"

Before she could finish, Helen took the hint and pulled herself up on her walker. In one last effort to convince Melanie, she looked at her and said, "Read the diary. It will tell you everything."

She looked around, almost trying to spot an apparition. Outside, a loose wire that ran from the television up the side of the house tapped against the window. Helen turned her head to the sound, expecting to see a face in the window. But no one looked through the panes into the living room.

Melanie walked with her to the door.

"Can you get home all right?" she asked. "I, uh, hate to leave the children, with Gary sick."

"I'm fine," Helen said. "You will read the diary, won't you?"

"By all means," Melanie promised. "Antiques fascinate me. I'll return it as soon as I'm finished."

After a quick goodbye, Melanie opened the door for Helen and watched her move down the porch stairs with the skill of someone much younger. Then she closed the door and leaned against it. The whole meeting had been a waste of her time, she thought. For some silly reason she had hoped Helen might know of some hermit who hid out in the woods—and that the *he* Helen spoke of was some kind of maniac. And all that Helen had meant was a ghost!

Melanie went into the living room and picked up the diary. She opened it to the first page and sat down with it on the couch. She became so wrapped up in it that she didn't lift her head—didn't see the horrid little scene being played down the hill.

When she had nearly reached her front gate, Helen felt someone tug roughly at the long gray braid that ran down her back. With a gasp, she tried to turn around, but a strong arm clamped her neck and held her fast.

"Please," she begged. "I have no money!"

There was no answer. Reaching an arm that had suddenly pulled free, Helen swung it over her head in self-defense. But her hand sliced through the air and felt nothing but a strange, icy cold. This was it, she knew. He had found her out. The grip around her neck tightened. She screamed.

"Nnnnnooooo! Please let me g—"

A sparrow turned its head toward the ugly cracking sound.

A split second of eternity had passed when a single leaf fell from the tree above her to land on her sightless eye.

9

***

Melanie hadn't planned to read the diary at all. She had wanted to start in on the pile of art magazines stacked up by her chair. But here she was now, at midnight, still absorbed in Nora Jennings' writings.

Gary was lying with his head half-buried under a pillow when she walked into the bedroom. He slept like that now, since the accident. To Melanie he looked as if he were hiding. She slipped her dress over her head and climbed into the bed next to him. She pressed herself against his back and threw an arm around him.

Was he hiding from something? Had his accident really been so terrible that he couldn't talk about it, even after three days? Even to his wife? She thought of Helen's warning that she should believe everything Gary told her.

"Anything," she whispered. "I'll believe anything you tell me."

Gary's eyes sprang open. He turned his head and stared through the dark at her, pushing his pillow toward the headboard. For a moment, he didn't speak.

"I'm sorry," Melanie said. "I woke you."

Gary shook his head, his hair making a faint sound against the sheets.

"I was awake when you came in. How come you're up so late?"

"I'd been reading a diary our next-door neighbor brought over," Melanie said, hoping to draw him into a conversation. "She's a really nice old lady named Helen Jennings, but she's nutty as a fruitcake. Anyway, the diary has some things about this house in it that she thought we'd be interested in."

"I'd like to hear about it," Gary said, sitting up.

He pulled Melanie into his arms. She sighed, settling herself, and began to recount what she had read in the diary. Gary listened attentively, alert for the first time in days.

"The first owner of this house was a man named Jacob Armand,"

Melanie began. "He was a captain in the British Navy in the late 1700s. The girl who wrote the diary is Nora Jennings. She's Helen's great-great aunt, and she's fascinating! She wrote the diary in 1797!"

"That's something," Gary said, impressed. "Does she say much about this house?"

"A lot," Melanie replied. "She's definitely Helen's relative—they're both busybodies. Do you know that old lady has been spying on us? She says this place is haunted—by some fellow who's out to kill us all. I think she was talking about this Jacob Armand. She must be loony."

"You're right," Gary said, trying to hide the look of fear in his eyes by turning his head. "She must be crazy."

Great act, Gary, he thought. Call the old lady crazy to keep that title away from you. Maybe you can forget those hands the other day. The ones you couldn't see. . . .

"So," he said suddenly, cutting off his thoughts, "tell me what she said in the diary."

"She spent a lot of time writing about some girl Jacob had," Melanie said. "She wrote that she had seen her in town with two little girls. But Jacob was definitely not her husband. So either she was a widow, or maybe she was having an affair."

"Nora Jennings wrote that?" Gary asked. "I always thought those Colonial girls were such prudes. You know, 'pure of mind and body.'"

"She was," Melanie said. "She started to write something like that, but she stopped. She said it would be un-Christian. But it's obvious what she meant.

"Anyway," she went on, "Jacob Armand seems to have been an interesting person himself. Nora listened in on her father's meetings with his friends a lot, and she wrote about what she heard. Jacob paid a sort of protection fee that was collected by a servant of the Jenningses. I guess it was to keep the neighbors from burning his house down, since he stayed loyal to the King of England."

"Sounds like the Colonial mafia," Gary said. He lowered his voice in an imitation of Marlon Brando. "You has come to see da Godfadder?"

"That's terrible," Melanie said with a giggle.

"Well . . ."

Melanie gave his arm a squeeze and smiled up at him. She much preferred this happy Gary, with his bad imitation of Brando, to the introverted man she had brought home from the hospital. With him cheerful again, she wasn't sure if she cared to ever know the truth behind his accident. The only thing that mattered now was that he was happy again.

"You're terrific," she said, kissing him.

He let go of her to slide down under the blankets next to her. He could feel her warmth, hear the breathing that passed through her nostrils deeply and slowly. His tongue found hers, his hands the richness, the smooth silk that was her skin. He held her close, caressed her. When he made love to her, it was with an animal force that wore them both out. He told her again and again how he loved her. For only a brief moment, Melanie noticed that the strange accent she thought she had heard when they had made love before, was gone. Then the moment exploded and the thought was split in two.

"I love you so much," she sighed, clutching him tightly as her heartbeat began a descent to its normal pace.

"Don't ever stop," Gary said, rubbing his face over her neck. She was so warm. . . .

*   *   *

Melanie leaned over the breakfast table and looked at Gary with smiling eyes.

"I've got a great idea," she said. "Let's go down to the beach for a picnic today."

"In the middle of autumn?" Gary asked. "I don't think that's such a hot idea."

"Why not?" Melanie wanted to know. "It's not that cold yet. Do you know we've been in this house for almost two months, and we haven't done a thing together as a family?" In the city, before Terry, they'd always done things as a family—trips to the zoo, boating in Central Park, going to see the dinosaurs in the Museum of Natural History. Perhaps, Melanie thought, they should plan an excursion back into the city some weekend. She felt so cut off from her previous life. She missed shopping in Bloomingdale's, walking along Fifth Avenue, visiting the art galleries. A weekly call from her agent kept her up to date on what was happening in the New York art world, and occasionally friends would call to gossip and tell her about the new plays and restaurants. But back in the city she'd be afraid of see-ing Terry's face in every crowd, on every park bench.

"Okay," Gary consented. "It sounds good to me."

"It sounds *great*," Melanie said. "We'll take the hibachi down to the beach."

"What're we going to use for charcoal?" Gary asked. "I doubt if I could get any now."

"So," Melanie said, "we'll use firewood. That would be okay, wouldn't it?"

Gary shrugged. "I guess so. The kids can help carry it."

"Then we're set," Melanie said with a smile. "We'll leave after lunch—so we can have dinner on the beach."

The children were bundled up more than usual for the picnic, since Melanie was sure the beach would be extra cold. Kyle, with his blond curls and very rosy cheeks, looked like a picture of his Dutch grandfather. Melanie decided that she would have to do a portrait of him, looking exactly as he did now.

The three children were walking ahead of their parents, and Kyle and Gina's arms were laden with wood. Kyle was whispering to his sisters from the corner of his mouth. Melanie smiled when he looked back at them from time to time.

"Mommy and Daddy sure are nice to each other now," he whis-pered.

"That's because they made up, silly," Gina told him. "And I'm glad they did, too. They're nicer to us, even! You know what? I'm going to ask if I can have a slumber party for my birthday this year!"

"Oh, really?" Nancy asked with enthusiasm.

"Uh huh," Gina replied, nodding her head so that the pompom on top of her hat bounced. "I never asked to have a big party before. I hope they say yes."

"They will," Kyle reassured.

"Well, don't say anything yet," Gina said.

Kyle twisted his fingers over his lips as if he were turning a key. Nancy made a quick cross, with the wrong hand, over her heart. Then the three of them began to giggle.

"What's so funny?" Melanie asked.

"Can't tell you," Gina said, looking back at her mother and trying to hide a smile.

"Oh, I get it," Melanie said. "Trade secret."

"Huh?"

"Never mind, Kyle," she said. "Gina, that wood isn't too heavy, is it?"

Gina shook her head and ran back to join her parents. Her father was carrying the hibachi so awkwardly, she thought. His bandaged wrist jutted out beyond it, and she leaned closer to read where she had signed the cast.

"Do you remember that time we were cooking burgers out on the balcony of our old apartment?" she asked.

"And the neighbor's dog went crazy barking because of the smell?" Melanie said.

"What you don't remember," Gary added, "is that I threw him one. That's the one I said fell over the side."

"Gary!"

"He's kidding, Mom," Gina said. "Aren't you, Daddy?"

"Sure," Gary replied. "But I was going to before it dropped. He was a cute little fellow."

"Can we get a dog?" Gina asked hopefully.

"I was waiting for that," Melanie said.

"Maybe," Gary said, "once we get a little more settled."

"Wow!" Gina cried, running ahead to tell her brother and sister the news.

"That's not such a bad idea," Melanie said. "Maybe a nice German shepherd."

"You mean an attack dog," Gary said, reading her mind.

Nancy suddenly sat herself down on a flat rock and began to pout. They'd been walking for a while, and the beach was nowhere in sight. When, she wanted to know, were they going to get there?

"Yeah," Kyle said. "It must be a hundred miles from here!"

"In just a few minutes, honey," Melanie said. "It *is* a long walk from our house."

"Can't you hear the gulls?" Gary asked.

Nancy sat silently for a moment, listening. Then she nodded her head. Yes, she said, she could hear the gulls.

"Well," Gary told her, "the gulls are right on the bay."

Encouraged, Nancy got to her feet again and rushed ahead. Her little legs, the burns now healed, moved quickly, and she was soon far ahead of the others.

Something moved behind the trees next to her. She turned toward the sound, to see something blue and flowing disappear into the thick of the pines. Nancy blinked, waiting with her heart pounding for the mean man to appear. But the woods were empty.

When Gary caught up with her and bent down to hug her, he didn't know her slight scream was one of terror.

"Daddy!"

"A penny for your thoughts, Nancy," Gary said.

"Can I have a dime instead?" Nancy asked with a grin, all thoughts of the mean man gone.

"I'd give you all the dimes in the world," Gary said, "if I had them. But all I can offer now is chicken. Sounds yummy?"

"Real yummy," Nancy said. She clutched at her father's coat and walked with him the rest of the way.

On the beach, Gary set the hibachi down on a flat rock. Melanie suggested the children gather shells to decorate later while they waited for Gary to cook the chicken. She would even let them use some of her paints.

With that promise, the three children ran down toward the water and walked along its edge. Shells were lifted and examined, only to be thrown down again when a chip or break was discovered.

Gina wandered ahead of Kyle and Nancy, humming a tune to herself and putting shells into her sweater pockets until they bulged. Each was designated for a different friend, and Gina had the idea to make Christmas presents of them. She was certain her mother had so many paints that she could color each one differently.

Something hooked her ankles just then and sent her flying forward into the sand. Her teeth slammed into her lower lip.

"Witch-child!" she heard a low voice growl.

She started to turn around to yell at Kyle or Nancy for tripping her. But the two children were yards behind her, running. She sat on the sand rubbing her lip. The bay was calm. Gina stared out over it, to the thick beige grasses on its other side. She had heard a voice, had felt strong hands shove her from behind. And yet she was all alone.

"Just like Daddy's accident," she whispered, still staring at the marsh.

Oh, she had thought a good deal about that. How Daddy had been nearly strangled, then pushed. How he couldn't remember who the man was. Gina shivered, remembering the terrible phone calls from that man Nancy called Uncle Terry.

Hello, kiddo! I'm going to . . .

Gina shook her head, trying to clear her mind. She didn't understand a word the man had said, but she didn't have to. She had been afraid then, and she was a little afraid right now. But then, Mommy and Daddy were right down the beach. And here came Kyle and Nancy. She erased the solemn expression from her face.

"Gina!" Kyle cried, helping her to her feet. "What happened?"

"I tripped over something," Gina said breathlessly. "Is my lip bleeding?"

Kyle stood on tiptoe to get a closer look. "Just a little. Wanna go back?"

"Okay," Gina said. "But don't tell Mom and Dad, okay? They'll think I'm a klutzo."

"I don't think you are," Kyle said.

"Did you hear someone say something just before?" Gina asked.

"No, I didn't hear anything," Kyle admitted. "There isn't anyone else here, Gina. Maybe you heard a gull."

Gina nodded, although she knew it was no gull she heard. Perhaps, she thought, it had been her father's voice. It had seemed so close, yet she might have been imagining things. It had sounded like "witch-child," but could her father have been asking her mother "which side?"

"Race ya!" Kyle cried suddenly, running up the beach.

"I don't want to race!" Nancy cried.

"I'll walk with you," Gina said. She called up the beach to her brother: "We're not included!"

"What are you going to do with all those shells?" Nancy wanted to know.

"I'm going to make Christmas presents out of them," Gina told her. "I'll help you make some, if you want."

"Okay!"

"You know what?" Gina said thoughtfully. "I'm going to hide

them in a special place. There's a really deep drawer in my old desk, and if I push the shells back really far, no one could ever see them!"

Gina made Nancy promise she wouldn't say a word about her secret drawer. The two girls skipped up to the rest of the family, giggling. The fire Gary had made was roaring, filling the air with a delicious scent. In a few minutes, they were eating, talking, and laughing. It was easy to forget anything bad had ever happened to them.

10

Gina arranged her shells on her dresser in size order and chose the best ones for her parents' gifts. She would use some of them to outline a little hand mirror to give to her mother. For her father, she'd paint the biggest shells so that he'd have a nice place to put his paper clips and rubber bands. And, as she had told Nancy, she'd keep them hidden in her desk.

One of the cubbyholes was deep enough to push the shells back into without their being seen. But the little door refused to open when she tugged at it.

"Oh, come on!" Gina cried, pulling hard. She didn't expect it to snap open so quickly and she gasped, knocking the side of her hand against the trimming on one side of it. It flipped aside, and a panel in the desk slid open. Gina poked her hand inside the dark hole, delighted to have found a secret compartment. The tips of her fingers touched something cold, and she pulled at it.

"Oh, neat!" she cried, seeing a pearl-handled pistol. She ran from the room. "Mom! Mom!"

Melanie's first reaction upon hearing her daughter's cries was to pray nothing had gone wrong again. When Gina stepped into the studio, she gasped. The little girl was aiming a gun at her.

"My God, Gina!" she cried. "Put that down! Where did you get it?"

"I found it in my desk," Gina told her, handing over the pistol. "There's a secret compartment in it, Mom!"

"Really?" Melanie said. "How'd you find it?"

"The little door got stuck and I hit against the side when I pulled it. There's a panel that looks just like it's part of the desk, but it slides open."

"Another mystery to add to our list of funny happenings," Melanie said. It sounded more casual than she meant it.

"Yeah, but this isn't as creepy as other things that go on here," Gina said.

"Do those things bother you?"

"Sometimes I worry in school," Gina told her. "The other kids want to know what's happening, but I don't want to tell them any more. And sometimes I have nightmares."

"Oh, honey!" Melanie cried, putting an arm around her. "I never realized you kids paid any attention to all this. If you have nightmares, come into bed with Daddy and me."

"I can do that?" Gina asked.

"Sure," Melanie said, kissing the child's dark hair. "It's a big bed." Gina snuggled against her mother and touched the gun.

"Why do you suppose it was hidden away like that?"

"Oh, just to keep it safe," Melanie said. "Just the way we keep guns in drawers and not out in the open."

"But if it was a secret compartment, how could anyone know the gun was there?"

"It wasn't always a secret, Gina," Melanie said. "Whoever had this gun knew how to get to it."

* * *

Perhaps the owner had known how to open the panel, but this knowledge had been of little use to her when she wanted to use the gun. The last person to see it was a woman named Jesse Prentice, who had lived in the house just after the end of the Civil War. She had hidden the gun in the panel, not daring to leave it in plain sight. She was afraid the raiders would come back to her house again. On a day she had been to town, they had come to her house to kill her husband and kidnap her baby son. And Jesse was certain they'd be back to steal the treasures of the house.

But she would wait forever for them, because they didn't exist. There were no raiders planning another attack on the house. In fact, the same man who murdered her husband and took her child away meant to protect her from any harm. He loved her. He would take care of her. But in order to take care of her, he had been forced to murder not only her husband, but her infant son.

Jesse stood perfectly still as the news that her baby had been found in the bay was gently broken to her. Then, dry-eyed, she closed the front door and walked up to her bedroom. The pistol she had hidden was loaded. One bullet would be enough.

Jesse pushed against the molding around the secret panel and waited for it to ease open. Nothing happened, although she had pushed the trimming as far as it would go. The strip of wood remained tightly shut, sealing the gun away from her.

A cold wind blew up behind her, and she turned to see if she had left the window open. But it was closed, and the curtains were still. She turned back to the panel and pounded at it, the tears she had held back gushing now in torrents. Jesse Prentice wanted to die. Why wouldn't they let her?

She buried her face in her arm and slammed her fist against the desk top, again, and again, and again . . .

. . . until it hit something hard and cold. The letter opener! She stopped crying only for a few moments to look at it before slashing it over her wrists, again and again.

Her lover watched her, unseen, confused. Why was she doing this? Didn't she know she was safe now, that he would protect her?

He threw himself over her body and began to scream.

*   *   *

Melanie placed the gun on the table and asked Gina to find her father. Gary and Kyle were outside in the barn. Both looked up when Gina opened the big doors and walked inside. She headed for the light of her father's flashlight.

"Guess what?" she asked. "I found a secret compartment in my desk!"

"Oh, wow!" Kyle cried. "I want to see!"

"First guess what I found inside," Gina said.

"A book?" Gary suggested.

"Uh-uh."

"A doll?"

"No, a gun!" Gina told him.

"C'mon, Kyle," Gary said. "Let's go inside and see."

When he was nearly to the door, Kyle's foot caught on something protruding from the dirt floor. He stooped down to pick it up. But what he thought was a rock turned out to be the corner of a small box that had been buried there. He dug at the earth around it, pulling the treasure from its hiding place.

It was a tin box, very small, and when he opened it he found a tiny package with a note tied to it.

He realized that the barn was suddenly very dark, and he looked up to find his sister and father gone. He stood up and walked outside, opening the package.

"Why would anyone bury a stick?" he wondered, confused.

He took it up to his mother's studio and handed it to his father. Gary was holding the pistol, and he frowned when his son gave him what seemed to be a bent twig. But on closer inspection he found it was, in fact, the slender bone of a human finger. It had been charred black.

"This note was with it," Kyle said, handing him a slip of paper.

"I'll bet it has an interesting story behind it," Gary said, showing it to Melanie. "It's a bone."

"Oh, yecch," Gina groaned.

"Read the note, Gary," Melanie said.

Gary unfolded the yellow paper. He lifted his glasses from his pocket and slipped them on as the children fidgeted anxiously.

"The writing's kind of faded," he said. He began to read. "This is all that remains of my beloved Lydia. By this and by God I swear my eternal love for her, and by this I shall avenge her death. JNA, September 10, 1797."

"JNA," Melanie said. "Jacob Armand?"

"It could be," Gary said.

"The year is right," Melanie said. "Remember the diary? I guess Jacob really did have a girl, just like Nora Jennings wrote. And he loved her a great deal."

"Enough to keep part of her with him for all time," Gary said.

"Who's Jacob Armand?" Gina asked.

Her question was ignored. Melanie had caught sight of something
Kyle was holding in his hand, and she let out a cry of astonishment.
She pointed at it, too shocked to explain why it terrified her. Confused, Kyle tightened a chubby fist around the blue and gold brocade
that had wrapped the charred bone.

11

Jacob Armand had built his home far from the town, for privacy
and as a safety precaution against those who would destroy his property. As a result, very few people traveled up the hill to his home.
The VanBurens had been the first to use the road regularly in some
thirty years. With them came the milkman, the mailman, and the
newsboy.

But not a soul had been on the road since Helen Jennings left the
house that Saturday afternoon. On Monday Gina and Kyle set off
for school as usual, gloves and hats added to their coats to protect
them from the bitter winds that had blown up overnight. Though it
was only two days before Halloween, winter promised to arrive, at
least with respect to temperature, within a few days. Gina held
tightly to a box containing her witch costume for the school play, for
whatever extra warmth she could get from it.

They found Helen in a crumpled pile. At first there was no reaction from either child. They had seen death before, in the face of a
wino who had fallen in the gutter in front of their city apartment.
They hardly knew Helen Jennings any better than they had known
that bedraggled old man.

Though the icy air had preserved the body to a degree, it was still
an abhorrent picture. Her puffy cheeks were split in the center by
thin, blued lips that stretched into a ghastly smile. Eyes like prunes
had fallen back into her head, staring. One thin arm had been
thrown over her head, and now its skin was stretched and pulling.

Reality stopped against something in both Kyle's and Gina's

minds that was there to protect them from this horrid sight. And then Gina let out a gasp and grabbed Kyle's hand. The two ran back home, bursting into the kitchen, both shouting at once.

"Okay! Okay!" Melanie cried, taking each child by one shoulder. "Gina, tell me what happened."

"We found an old lady on the hill," Gina said breathlessly. "She's —uh—dead, Mom."

"Oh, God," Melanie whispered. "Did you know who she was? Did she look bad?"

Gina shook her head. "She wasn't as bad as the wino, Mom."

"I don't know who she was," Kyle said. "I think maybe that Mrs. Jennings you were talking about."

Melanie, not taking her hands away from the children's shoulders, called to Gary.

"The kids say they found an old lady on the hill," she explained when he appeared in the doorway. "I think it's Helen Jennings. Gina says she's dead."

"Christ," Gary mumbled. "Where is she, exactly?"

"Right near the bus stop, Daddy," Kyle said.

"For God's sake, Gary," Melanie said, "get her out of there before that bus comes with all those kids on it." She turned to the children. "Do you want to go to school?"

"I do," Gina said quickly. "For once I've got something neat to talk about."

"Me, too!" Kyle put in.

Nodding, Melanie sank down into her chair. Gary had already gone out, carrying a large piece of canvas that had been used to wrap furniture when they moved into the house. Gina, without a word, ushered Kyle out the door.

By the time the bus pulled away, with the two children on board gasping for breath, Helen Jennings was wrapped and in Gary's arm. He held her awkwardly, his injured wrist pushed out beyond her body so that she rested more on his upper arms. He was happy that he had reached her in time; he had seen the children on the bus craning to look out the window after Kyle and Gina got on board.

He carried her up to the house and laid her in a trough in the barn. It seemed a callous thing to do, but he wasn't about to sit her at the kitchen table.

Melanie, after a few moments of respectful silence dedicated to her eccentric neighbor, had phoned the police. By nine A.M., Helen Jennings was packed into a tiny cubicle to wait in darkness while her next of kin was sought.

From the discovery of her body to her delivery into the hands of the coroner, every act was performed dutifully and with little emotion. The VanBurens had little reason to mourn her death. As far as they knew, she had never done anything for them.

*   *   *

Janice brought her rubber stamp down hard on the last book of the night and pushed it toward the man who stood in front of her desk. Ten minutes later, she was bundled up in rabbit fur and suede, heading out the door. She laughed at her reflection in the glass display case, thinking she looked a bit too much like a refugee from Antarctica.

She had been thinking of Melanie VanBuren that day. For some reason, she wanted to befriend her, even though Melanie hadn't kept their lunch date. Perhaps, Janice reasoned, it would be fun to get to know a near-celebrity. It wasn't everyone who got an illustration in *The New York Times.*

The rain that had been falling lightly had changed and was now coming down in heavy drops. Janice turned up the speed of her wipers and watched them swish back and forth noisily, throwing off the rhythm of the song she was trying to sing. She said out loud, "The Starship disco'll probably be empty tonight." She lit a cigarette. "Oh, hell," she sighed, "maybe the creeps'll stay in out of the rain and I'll meet somebody decent."

She turned her car onto Starbine Court Road and headed toward the hill. She switched it into low gear so that it could comfortably take the steep climb to the top. When she brought it around the driveway, she stopped it with a gentle pressure to the brake. But in spite of her care, the old thing coughed and shook before settling down to wait for her.

Melanie registered surprise when she opened the door to find Janice Lors standing on her porch.

"Janice, hello!" she cried. "Come on in—I didn't expect to see you after I didn't call about having lunch. I've been so busy . . ."

"Hey, don't worry," Janice said, slipping out of her jacket. She handed it to Melanie. "I'm sure you've been caught up with moving-in chores."

"That and other things," Melanie answered. "You don't know how glad I am to see someone who isn't wearing a uniform," she said.

"Oh," Janice answered. "I left mine at the library. You know, the bun and glasses."

"I can't see you in that," Melanie said with a shake of her head.

"Neither can I," Janice answered, looking around. "My God, look at this place! What's behind all the doors?"

"Oh, most of those are closets," Melanie said. "And empty. I suppose we'll fill them as years go on, but since we moved out of an apartment, there really wasn't much to bring."

"Oh, jeez," Janice said, "I'd have them filled in five minutes. Can I see the rest of the house? I've never been in a mansion."

"Sure," Melanie answered, leading her down the hall. "I'll give you the grand tour. Anything to get my mind off this day."

"What's wrong?"

"Oh, let's not discuss it right now," Melanie said quickly. "This is the first chance I've had all day to relax."

She led Janice through all the downstairs rooms, delighted to hear her friend gasp at the beauty of it all. Janice had to take a closer look at the fireplace in the dining room and couldn't help touching the pieces of antique furniture.

"And look at those neat nautical paintings!" she cried. "In every room! Did you do them?"

"Oh, no," Melanie said. "Those came with the house. The first man who lived here was a sailor, Jacob Armand."

"Romantic name," Janice said. "So, let's see *your* work."

Melanie took her to the upstairs studio, where stacks of her paintings remained covered with sheets. Unlike the rest of the house, which was walled in dark wood, this room had been painted white, and when Melanie turned on the light, Janice squinted in the brightness that bounced off the enameled walls. She went to the canvas on the easel, a painting of a lighthouse.

"Pretty," she said. "Do you ever display?"

"I've had several shows," Melanie told her. "My last one was way back in May. But we've just been too busy with the house." She walked to another easel. "When I get a chance to finish it, this is my current project."

Janice smiled at the portrait of Nancy and Gina, nearly finished, but left without its last touches for weeks. She shook her head, smiling at the pretty faces.

"My daughters," Melanie said proudly.

"You're kidding!" Janice cried. "Aren't they adorable!"

Melanie pointed to each. "My youngest, Nancy, and this is Gina."

"God," Janice sighed. "What dolls."

"I have a son, too," Melanie said. "His name is Kyle. I'd introduce you, but they're sleeping now."

"I'll have to come here some Saturday afternoon to meet them," Janice said, "when they're not in bed." Suddenly, she looked up at the huge floor-to-ceiling windows and chuckled: "Do you sunbathe in here?"

"I suppose I could," Melanie laughed.

"In the nude, no less," Janice suggested.

"Oh, God!" Melanie cried. "I don't think so! Come on, let's go downstairs."

Janice ran her finger over the brass sphinx at the top of the stairs, declaring it was kind of cute. Then she went down with Melanie, admiring the carved banister. She felt relaxed in the warm amber glow that bathed the bottom landing.

"This place has *romantic* stamped all over it," she said when they walked into the living room. "My God! Another fireplace! And look at the bay windows! Oh, geez, Melanie, this place is beautiful!"

"Beautiful, maybe," Melanie agreed, "but I think it has a jinx on it. Since I saw you last week I've lived through a murder, an attempted murder, and God only knows what else. The police were here all day."

"You weren't kidding about the uniform then," Janice said. "Poor thing. Tell me about it."

"The day I was with you," Melanie began, "I came home and found my husband lying on the floor at the bottom of the stairs. I think he was pushed."

"Pushed?" Janice asked. "You aren't sure?"

"He hasn't said so," Melanie told her, "but there were bruises on his neck that the doctor said might have come from fingers. We think he ran into a burglar and there was a fight. But we don't really talk about it. Gary doesn't seem to be too inclined to tell me the whole story, and I don't believe in pushing."

"But is he all right?" Janice wanted to know.

"He sprained his wrist," Melanie said. "But the doctor said it'll heal quickly. But here's the other strange thing that happened—remember that old lady we saw at the parking lot?"

"Yeah?"

"She was at my house Saturday," Melanie said. "She told me stories about this place—that it was haunted."

"She told you that in the park," Janice pointed out, "and I think you were ready to believe her."

"*Now* I might be," Melanie admitted, "after what's been going on here. Helen—that's her name—gave me a diary to read that her great-great aunt had written in 1797. It gave me a good deal of information on this house."

"So," Janice said, "does it have any weird stories behind it?"

"I don't know," Melanie said. There was a hint of disappointment in her reply. "The darned thing disappeared the day after I started reading it. And I'm afraid I can't ask Helen to fill in the blanks. She was killed Saturday, on her way home from here."

"Oh, no!"

"Oh, yes," Melanie said. "My children found her on their way to school this morning. She'd been lying there since Saturday afternoon."

"How did they take it?" Janice asked, leaning forward in her seat.

"Better than I could," Melanie admitted. "They couldn't wait to run off to school to tell everyone. Anyway," Melanie went on after a pause, "the police were here for a few hours today. I couldn't give them much information, though. But they're convinced that there might be a connection between my husband's accident and Helen's death."

"How did she die?" Janice asked.

"They weren't too willing to talk about it," Melanie said, "but one of them—Tony DiMagi—confided that her neck might have been broken, judging from the finger marks. Of course, since Gary has his wrist bandaged up, he's not a suspect."

"Thank God," Janice said for her. "It sounds like someone wanted to strangle both people—bruises on both their necks, I mean. Gross! Who could it be? Some very respectable local figure who's a psychopathic killer? Spooky." Melanie stood up. "Can I offer you a drink?"

"No, thanks," Janice said. "I'm saving my stomach for the Starship."

"Starship?"

"A disco," Janice said. "Not that I care for the music, but once in a while somebody worth bringing home shows up."

"I remember the singles scene only vaguely," Melanie said. "It must be fun."

"Well," Janice said with a sigh, "when you get to be twenty-nine and you don't have a man, it's kind of a drag. But in this day and age, I guess I could go it alone. I did it for four years at Ohio State University." She clapped her hands together and leaned back. "So! Tell me what else has been going on here. It might do you good to get it off your chest."

"Oh, it would take me all night," Melanie said. "But the most recent thing—a little thing—was a gun my daughter found in her drawer. Gary says it might date back to the Civil War! And there's something else, too. My son, Kyle, found a human finger bone buried out in the barn. Somebody wrapped it up in a blue and gold cloth."

"Sounds pretty sickie," Janice said.

"I think so," Melanie agreed. "The thing that got to me was that cloth. About a week or two ago, I found a pearl ring, and a silk gown, wrapped in the same cloth. That was two separate occasions. I thought the gifts were from Gary, but now that I think of it, they couldn't have been."

"Why didn't you ask him in the first place?" Janice inquired.

"We used to have a game we played when we were first married," Melanie explained. "We'd leave little gifts around the house for each other and not talk about them."

"That's sweet," Janice commented.

"After I saw that cloth Kyle was holding when he brought in that terrible thing," Melanie said, "I asked Gary about it. He didn't have the slightest idea what I was talking about."

Janice shuddered. "That's creepy!"

"Creepy isn't the word for it," Melanie sighed. "My family is in some kind of danger, and that damned cloth has something to do with it."

"Does Gary think so?"

Before Melanie could reply, Gary appeared at the door with Tony DiMagi. The young cop had returned to the house to give back a law book he had borrowed earlier that day.

"Can you believe he finished it already?" Gary asked. "Two hundred pages!"

"I'm impressed," Janice said, smiling at the handsome young cop.

Introductions were followed by another offer of drinks by Melanie. Tony declined, saying he had to get the car back to the station. He started for the door, buttoning his coat. But as he moved to open it, a scream came from upstairs.

Gary looked at Melanie for only a split second before running, with the others, up the stairs. At the door to Kyle's bedroom, they were stopped by great, dark curls of smoke. Tony pressed his hand to the door, then pushed it open.

Kyle was sitting on his big bed, screaming, in the midst of roaring flames.

12

Kyle was crouched on his knees in the center of his bed. All around him, the light of the fire danced, making brilliant flecks of color in the tears streaking down his face. It was a fierce blaze, flowing angrily around the bed and digesting everything in sight.

Tony's trained mind took only a split second to assess the situation: the fire was concentrated and could be put out easily with an extinguisher. He turned to shout at Melanie to find one.

"Aren't you going to radio headquarters?" Gary demanded.

"No time for that! Move it!"

Under the authority Tony had suddenly assumed, Gary jumped

and ran from the room, announcing he would call the fire department. He coughed in the smoke and held his bandaged wrist up to
his mouth until he reached clear air. At the bottom of the stairs, he
leaned over the banister and lifted the receiver—for nothing. There
was no sound through the wire.

"Shit," Gary mumbled, slamming it down. Now what would he
do?

Pounding the banister on his way back up, Gary gritted his teeth
in anger. What the hell was this? How could the phones be out?
There hadn't been any storms.

The thought was cut off when something shoved hard against his
back and sent him flying forward. He hit his lip on the top stair, and
the faint taste of blood rose on his tongue. He tried to stand to continue his ascent, rubbing at his cut lip and cursing in his impatience.
And then he heard the voice.

"*You cannot stop me!*"

Gary's mind raced back to the day he was attacked, when he had
heard this same voice. His heart thumped in anticipation of the cold
grip. (*Oh, God! Oh, God! He's trying to keep me from Kyle!*)

He rested his head on the step for only a second, breathing in
heavily for strength. Then he attempted to continue, only to be hin-
dered when something hooked around his ankles and painfully
dragged him to the bottom of the stairs, *thump, thump, thump.*

"*You cannot stop me!*" the voice hissed again.

"Eat shit, you sadistic bastard!" Gary screamed, not knowing at
who or what his anger was aimed. He shot to his feet and ran up the
stairs, something deep within telling him speed was his only means
of escaping the fearsome presence. When he reached Kyle's room
again, the combination of running and breathing the heavy smoke
made him gag. He stumbled to the bed and took the wool blanket
Tony held out to him.

"The phone's dead," he shouted, choking.

"It's all right," Tony screamed. "I think we can put it out when
your wife brings the extinguisher! Just keep smothering the flames
with the blanket!"

Gary did as he was told, moving around the bed in a constant motion, trying to find one spot where the flames were low enough that
he could reach his son.

"Why can't we pull him out?" he shouted.

"The bed's too high to reach him!" Tony yelled back. "And our weight would collapse it! Even one man is too heavy for that thing."

"Damn it, it's solid oak!" Gary told him.

"You think so?" Tony asked, aiming below the bed. Two of the crossbeams had split and were angled toward the floor.

"But what do we do?"

"What we're doing," Tony said, trying to reassure him.

"Bull!" Gary cried. "I want to get my kid out of there!"

"I told you . . ."

"Then I'll do it!" Gary yelled, moving closer to the inferno. He reached a hand through it, hoping to quickly grab his son—the way one might pass a finger through a birthday-candle flame in order not to be burned. But the moment his arm began to reach, the flames shot up, as if something were working a bellows at them.

"What was that?"

"I don't know!" Tony admitted. "Come on, we can still put it out! Keep at it!"

As he heard his son coughing and crying, Gary felt terribly helpless, wondering why Tony didn't do more, wondering what more he *could* do. The flames were higher, nearly blocking his vision of his son. Kyle was screaming his head off, sitting in the middle of all this, for the moment untouched. The flames seemed to be avoiding their prey, and yet Gary knew he was being teased, that something planned to hurt his child when it felt the time was right.

"You sadistic bastard!" Gary seethed again to that unknown malevolence.

While the men were working at the fire, trying to get through the flames and arguing about how to rescue Kyle, Janice was frantically trying to find Melanie in the dark hallways. The main hall was glowing from the fire, but the two branch halls were pitch black. Finally she managed to discern an open door. She went through it and found herself in a closet. She also found Melanie, standing very still, staring up at the ceiling. In the dim light of the closet's single bulb, Melanie looked like a corpse. Her eyes were bloodshot, and her face had lost its color.

"Oh, my God!" Janice cried. "What's wrong with you?"

She tried to pull Melanie from the closet, but her friend's feet were rooted.

"What happened?"

Melanie found her voice.

"Someone kissed me!"

"Oh, don't be silly!" Janice cried. "There's no one here but me, and I didn't see anyone leave the closet. Did you find the fire extinguisher?"

At that question Melanie seemed to wake up. "It's on the wall behind you," she said, pointing. Janice turned, yanked the extinguisher off the wall, and led Melanie back out into the hallway.

"Come on," Janice said, "they need it. The fire is getting worse." The two women hurried back to Kyle's room. Janice shoved the extinguisher at Tony and took his blanket.

Just then a bedpost fell. It collapsed in such a swift movement that it left a dark blur through the air. Inches away, Kyle shook with screams. Melanie began to cry.

"Stop it, Melanie!" Gary snapped. "Get to work on the fire! Here!"

He tossed her his blanket and went to find another. He tore apart drawers, finding nothing, then at last finding an old wool jacket. It was small, but good enough. He turned around in time to see a flame attach to Kyle's sleeve. The child frantically pounded it away, and it left a black mark on his blue flannel pajama top.

(*He's starting, Gary thought. He's had enough fun and games, and he's going for my kid!*)

"But *who's* going for my kid?" he asked out loud.

"Gary?" Melanie asked.

"Nothing!" her husband insisted. "Hey, why isn't that extinguisher working?"

"I'm *trying*," Tony yelled, almost impatiently.

He knew enough not to show it, but Tony was as frightened about this whole thing as everyone else. He just couldn't understand why the fire wasn't going out. It had been a good five minutes. He felt his throat growing sore from the smoke, and his body was chilled by sweat. Suddenly foam spurted from the extinguisher. Tony worked at the flames until they began to subside. He sighed heavily and moved the foam over the remaining spots of fire.

And then it was gone. Tony stared at the blackened bed. Something was very wrong here. Not the child whimpering in his mother's arms, not the smoke that still hung in the air, nor the stifling heat. It was there. And then he saw it.

"Funny," he said.

"I don't think so," Gary snapped. "My son was nearly kill—"

Tony cut him off, pointing. "No, look. Don't you see that the fire didn't spread? It seems to have been concentrated around the bed, and that carpet is too old to be fireproof. I've never seen anything like it!"

"Very few things surprise me in this house any more," Gary said. Then, feeling the emotional aftereffects of the ordeal, he turned to confront his son. "Kyle, were you playing with matches?"

"Gary!" Melanie gasped. "Kyle would never do a thing like that!"

"Don't butt in," Gary told her. He wrestled the child from his mother's grip and held him firmly by his small shoulders, leaning down to meet him eye-to-eye. "Tell me the truth, Kyle—were you playing with matches?"

"I-I was sleeping, Daddy!" Kyle wailed, his eyes brimming.

"Then how did that fire start?" Gary, horrified by the strangeness of the event, wanted terribly to place the blame on something simple —like a little boy with matches.

"I-I don't know!" Kyle insisted, looking up at his father with pleading eyes.

"Gary, stop it!" Melanie cried, taking the boy into her arms again. "Kyle's never told a lie in his life, and you know—"

Whatever she was about to say was cut off by the sound of new screams from down the hall. Melanie let go of Kyle and ran toward Gina's room, only inches in front of Gary and Tony. When they burst through the door, Melanie gasped. Like an instant replay on a Saturday football game, the scene of a few minutes ago was being repeated. Only now the victim was Gina, and the fire was twice as bad as the one in Kyle's room. Tony didn't have to consider long to realize it would take more than an extinguisher and blankets to put it out.

"I'll call in," he shouted over the din of the flames. "Get some blankets and work at it until I come back up!"

He ran from the room, the light of the fire guiding him through the dark hall. Halfway down the stairs, he felt a touch on his shoulder and turned to face Janice. When she asked if she could help him down here, he told her to look for more wool blankets. Janice turned into the first door she came to and entered the dining room. It was dark now, and across the room, the fireplace loomed like a gaping black hole. Janice kept her eyes turned from it, even after she turned the light on. Something about the void bothered her.

"Crap," she said when she had pulled open three drawers to find only silverware and linen tablecloths. And there was no rug she could pull up—it was all wall-to-wall.

Over her head, she could hear the sounds of running footsteps. A moment later, they were drowned out by nearer ones, and she walked out to the hall to meet Tony. He shoved an extinguisher in her hand and said, "Take this right upstairs, then come down again. I'll need you!"

Janice hurried up to Gina's room, where Melanie and Gary were pounding the flames with blankets. The fire shot all the way to the ceiling, helped by the heavy canopy. Gina was sitting upright, alternately coughing and choking. Janice pushed the extinguisher at Gary, then ran downstairs again.

Outside, she found Tony fumbling with his police radio, trying to pull some reaction from it. But it was as silent as the phone inside.

"Something's gone wrong with this thing," Tony said. "Can you drive to town to get help?"

"Sure," Janice said, turning to run to her car.

She got inside, turned the key—and nothing happened. Giving the dashboard a punch, she tried again, pumping the gas. In her rearview mirror, she could see the orange flames in Gina's bedroom window and the shadow of someone running.

"Move it, you old bomb!" she yelled, pumping the gas harder.

With a sputter, the engine finally revved, then hummed. Janice rolled it forward, watching Tony's reflection in the mirror. Then something up ahead caused her to lower her eyes. A swift movement of shadow. She squinted and pushed her head forward, trying to discern what it was. As she moved closer to it, she saw the shape of a tall man moving along the edge of the hill.

She honked her horn to flag him down and ask his help. He moved right past her without turning. When he neared her window, she tried to get a good look at him, but in the darkness and light rain his face was obscured.

She looked up at the mirror again. Tony had lifted the hood of his car and was leaning over the engine. The strange man came up behind him, slowly. Janice did a double-take at the scene. How in the hell, she thought, did he get there that fast?

"Stop worrying about dumb things and move your body out of here," Janice said to herself. "If he's a weirdo, Tony can handle him. He's got a gun."

Under the hood of his police car, Tony was using a rare string of curse words, holding a bundle of cut wires in his fist. They had been sliced, carefully, then tied together to make their reassembly all the more impossible.

"Arson," he said plainly, suddenly wishing Jack Hughes were here. If only his senior partner hadn't had the flu!

He was thinking just that when a strong, cold wind blew up behind him, and the hook of the car hood came crashing down on his spine.

*　*　*

Up in Gina's bedroom, Gary and Melanie were still trying to put out the fire. Melanie was crying, and by now Gary felt like joining her. He was confused, and yet he knew exactly what was going on. The unseen thing was out to kill his kids, and there was nothing he could do about it.

"Melanie, give this a try," he said breathlessly, handing her the extinguisher. He wiped the sweat from his forehead. "I'm exhausted."

Even so, he took a blanket from her and pounded at the flames. They shot as high as those on Kyle's bed and even higher where the canopy was draped. And, like Kyle, there was no way to get to Gina. Gary shuddered. This damned thing was just too weird.

Melanie struggled with the extinguisher, finding it awkward at first. Gina screamed and screamed, her skin bright red from the heat, and yet still untouched by the flames. Melanie didn't wonder about that, but Gary knew.

On the other side of the house, Nancy slept soundly, exhausted after a very busy day. Something dark loomed over the little girl's bed, holding her stuffed yellow rabbit dangerously close to her face.

Nancy did not feel the softness of the plush that touched her cheek. She mumbled in her sleep and turned away, dreaming. The figure pressed the rabbit closer and then suddenly threw it across the room. It sensed something.

At that very moment, Melanie became so frustrated with her helplessness that she forgot the danger and crossed the flames to Gina's bed. She wrapped her arms around her daughter and looked for a chance to escape. The flames began to hypnotize her, and she became oblivious to what was happening.

"Are you out of your mind?" Gary demanded.

She said nothing.

"Melanie, you'll be hurt!"

But that wasn't what was intended for the fire. When the dark presence in Nancy's room realized what Melanie had done, it knew its plan to kill the children had failed. Melanie must never be harmed.

"Daddy, I'm cold!" Gina screeched.

Suddenly, it *was* cold. In fact, the whole damned room was *freezing*. Gary felt a shiver rack his body, and goose bumps formed over his skin. As he worked at the fire, still calling to Melanie, his teeth began to chatter. It was as if the temperature in the room had dropped fifty degrees.

An incredible wind blew up just then, ruffling the curtains and blowing Gary's hair into his eyes. In the half second it took for Gary to brush it away, the fire disappeared completely. Gary looked at it in amazement, for only the blackened bed gave evidence of what had happened here just a second ago. He let the extinguisher fall to the floor and passed his bandaged wrist over his forehead. His body, alternately heated by the flames and chilled by the mysterious cold, shook violently. He walked over to the window to open it and let the rain blow cooling spatters over him. The sound of a siren reached him from down the road, growing louder as the truck approached the house.

"I wonder what happened to Tony," he said then.

He turned back to the bed, where Melanie was hugging Kyle and Gina. Gary went to her and stroked her cheek, his eyes asking what had happened. But she had nothing to say.

Gina leaned her head back and looked up at her canopy, or what was left of it. A tear rolled down her cheek and caught on the edge of her lip. She unconsciously reached her tongue around to lick it, staring up in confusion at what had once been her beautiful bed.

But no more. The rich white velvet had taken on the sickly gray of the smoke, and the canopy now hung like the leaves of a weeping willow. The rug around the bed was pitch black for about two feet, then was completely unmarred. Gary thought about what Tony had said when they had put the fire out in Kyle's bedroom. Here again, the fire seemed to have concentrated in one small area, as if someone wanted to destroy only the bed. (*Or the children.*)

He dropped to his knees and crawled to where the pink floral design of the carpet stopped against the black. He rubbed his fingers over the area, then leaned down and sniffed at it. But he couldn't tell if anything had been put on part of the rug to make it fireproof. It was as if someone had wanted to harm the children, but not the rooms around them.

A man dressed in a fire chief's uniform burst into the room, followed by two other men.

Gary stood up. "We took care of it. I-I can't explain what happened."

"The children are all right?"

"I think so," Gina mumbled. Kyle nodded slowly.

"Thank God for that," Melanie said. She turned to the chief. "What took you so long?"

The chief looked at the two men with him and frowned.

"It seems something went wrong with officer DiMagi's radio," he said. "A woman named Lors came to us in person."

"Why didn't anyone call us on the phone?" A fireman asked.

"It was dead," Gary answered.

The fire chief went over to the window to signal that everything was under control. Down in the driveway, where Police Chief Bryan Davis had found the body of Tony DiMagi, a rookie cop stood staring at Tony's car with enormous, sickened eyes.

The chief started out the door, saying to his two men, "Check this place out—every inch of it."

"Gary," Melanie said, "we'll let the children sleep in our room tonight, okay? Then we can move them into the rooms across from Nanc—"

The remembrance of her youngest child jolted through Melanie and set her running. Gary understood. He followed his wife around the hallway, leading the two firemen. They burst into the little girl's room, where the child lay sleeping under a mound of blankets. Melanie went over and touched her lightly. She was fine, she was just fine.

The two firemen returned to Gina's room to talk to the children. Gary gave his wife a hug to encourage her and ran downstairs to answer a furious pounding at the door. He opened it to let in a husky cop.

The man snapped out a badge that identified him as Police Chief Bryan Davis. He moved further into the house, a sober look making him appear quite stern. His voice, though deep, was quiet.

"Do you need an ambulance?" he asked.

"No one was hurt, thank God," Gary said. After a moment, he added, "I'm Gary VanBuren."

"I know who you are," Davis said.

"Where's Tony, by the way?" Gary asked.

Davis ignored him. "Tell me everything that happened here tonight."

Gary related the events of the past hour, up to the start of Gina's fire. He explained why Tony had been up at the house in the first place and how the two of them had believed the fires were no accident. He saw Davis' expression change at that statement, but went on with the story.

"When the fire in Gina's room started," Gary said, "Tony ran down to his car to radio for help. I haven't seen him since."

"The Lors woman came down with him, didn't she?"

"I don't really remember," Gary admitted. "Everything was happening too fast. You understand."

"Yeah," Davis said softly.

A policeman opened the door and asked, "Ambulance requesting leave, sir. Anyone else?"

"No, go ahead," Davis said with a wave of his hand. "Tell them to get the hell out of here."

"What does he mean 'anyone else'?" Gary demanded.

He heard the motor being revved, the sirens. He put a hand on

Davis' shoulder and turned him around. In the man's eyes he could see tiny speckles of tears.

"What the hell is going on out there?"

"Officer DiMagi is dead," Davis whispered, pushing his hand away.

"What?"

"He was caught under the hood of his car," Davis said quickly, as if the words were poison to be gotten rid of. He eyed Gary's cast. "How long have you had that on?"

"About two weeks," Gary said. "Jesus, I can't believe this night!"

Davis squeezed his eyes shut and pounded his fist on the table. Those cut wires under the hood—still in Tony's hand. *Tony!* The best damned cop that ever came to Belle Bay.

He could see it. He could see it. Two blue-trousered legs dangling over the grill of the car, like a scene from a Japanese horror film. The car like one of those plastic monsters. And the hook . . .

He snapped open his eyes and gave his head a sharp shake. Duty. Calm and collected—that's right. Always keep your head. Even when you lose one of the best men you ever knew. They never explained this at the police academy. They never explained the hurt.

"I'll have to take fingerprints," he said. "You'll come down to the station."

"Why?" Gary demanded. He thought for a few seconds, then said, "That was no accident, was it?"

Davis shook his head slowly. "I don't know."

"I can't leave my wife and children alone," Gary said.

"We'll talk tomorrow," Davis said. "I'm posting an all-night guard on this place."

"Thanks," Gary mumbled. He wasn't really certain if the guards were to keep others out or them in.

13

◆

When at last sleep came to her, Melanie's dreams were shrouded in a cloth of blue and gold. Her children screamed for her, but no matter how many halls she turned down, no matter how many doors she opened, she couldn't find them.

Open the door—inside there is a package wrapped in blue-and-gold brocade. Huge, hundreds of times bigger than real life. They seem to float in an invisible pool, packages in every room. Huge white clouds loom behind them, like a Dali painting.

She opened another door. This time, the cloth began to move away from the treasure it wrapped. (*There is nothing there to see.*) It was coiling itself, tight, and moving like a sidewinder toward a man who stood with his back to her.

He couldn't see the rope standing on end, reaching for his neck. Melanie opened her mouth. No screams. The man turned to her, as if he had heard her silent plea. It was Gary, pop-eyed, a blue tongue dangling from his mouth. . . .

Melanie bolted upright, awake. Her heart pounded in the silence of the room. Next to her, Kyle and Gina were sleeping soundly. Her movements hadn't disturbed them.

Melanie rolled off the bed. She felt somewhat smug, because she had at last discovered the culprit behind all the things that were wrong in this house. A cloth of blue and . . .

"You're really going crazy," she whispered, stepping out into the hall.

It was dark. One day soon, she thought, she would have to ask Gary to put some fixtures in here. She opened the door to the room he had taken across the hall, just to have a look at him. It was good to know he was here.

She wanted to read the diary again, to learn more about the house. It had to be *somewhere* downstairs, because Melanie was certain she had put it on the coffee table that night and hadn't read it since.

Since she couldn't sleep, she would try to find it. To read it might ease her tension, she thought. It would answer questions.

She started toward the stairs, moving quickly, wanting to be down them and into the light. But as she neared them, a strange sound came from above her. It was like the crying of a child. She stepped closer to the linen closet, and the cries became clearer. What was up there?

She opened the door and looked inside at the dark shelves. The cry stopped for a few moments, then started again. It seemed to be saying "Mama, mama. . . ." Then it choked and died away.

Melanie looked up at the ceiling. It was a trick, she told herself. Someone's hiding up in the attic and trying to lure me up there by sounding like a child. He is waiting for me.

"The police tore that place apart," she reminded herself out loud, "and they found nothing."

Then she remembered the guards who were posted downstairs. She went quickly down the steps, but saw no one. She headed for the darkened living room.

"Ma'am?"

Melanie nearly hit the ceiling. With a gasp, she turned around to see one of the guards standing behind her. She smiled at him sheepishly and said, "I thought I heard something upstairs. Can we check?"

"That's what I'm here for," said the policeman.

Melanie let him lead the way up the stairs, and up the narrow steps to the attic, following close at his heels. The attic was dark and musty, not a place she liked to be in so soon after her horrible dream. But she felt secure with the young cop, who kept his hand ever in reach of his gun. The two poked through the clutter of boxes and old furniture, finding nothing. At last, the guard said, "Maybe it was squirrels."

"My husband mentioned them a while back," Melanie recalled. "Oh, you must be right. Besides, there isn't a place here where anyone could hide."

"I should be going back down now," said the guard.

"Go right ahead," Melanie told him. "I'd like to stay up here for a few minutes. I can't sleep anyway, and it might be fun to rummage through a few old trunks."

"I'll be right downstairs, then," said the cop. He disappeared through the square hole in the floor. Melanie looked around, then picked up an old leather case lying on top of the nearest pile of boxes. The initials JNA sent chills through her.

She put the case down again and walked around the room. The cries had stopped completely now, but still she kept her ears and eyes open. It didn't matter that the guard hadn't found anything. Just the thought of it made her shiver.

Something sparkled in the beam of her flashlight, and she moved forward to investigate. Her fingers touched cloth.

It was the blue-and-gold brocade, yards and yards of it wound around a bolt. It leaned against an antique wooden mannequin. There was a picture pinned to it of a young girl dressed in a lovely gown, done in the simple style of a Colonial artist—all out of proportion in uneven ink strokes. Melanie guessed that the fabric had originally been intended for making the gown that the figure was wearing. She picked up the end of it and saw that two pieces had been cut away. Pieces just the right size to wrap the gifts she had found.

She started to look further around the room, driven by an excitement that protected her from fear. Then the crying began again. Melanie turned toward it, aiming her flashlight. The beam hit the metal of a doorknob that was barely visible above a big old trunk.

Even as she walked toward the door, Melanie was telling herself she could be walking into the hideout of a madman.

She couldn't stop. She shoved the trunk away from the door, thinking it was strange the police hadn't seen this in their long, detailed search. A strange, comforting thought hit her. How could there be anyone in there, with this trunk here? It couldn't have been pushed from the inside, naturally. (*Perhaps unnaturally . . .*)

The noise was mice, of course. But Melanie had to be sure. She lifted a small telescope from the floor to use as a club. Holding it up, ready to strike, she entered the room.

She saw no one. She walked further inside, keeping her back to the wall and looking right and left in a constant motion, to be certain no one was hiding there. She took in her surroundings. The room was papered with a toy soldier motif. A teddy bear, its ancient plush rotting away, lay forlornly at the foot of the small bed. Melanie smiled for a moment, realizing she was in a nursery.

But the gentle sweetness that had once been in here was gone now. There was something terrifying and ugly about its emptiness. It made Melanie wonder to God what she was doing here.

Go down and get Gary. . . .

Still holding her telescope up, ready to strike, she went over to the dresser and pulled at drawers, finding an array of little boys' clothes. A piece of wood broke off in her hand and fell to the floor. A streak of ice shot through her. The dresser had been burned. And the bed?

She walked over to it, and found that the mattress had been set on fire. All that was left of it now was blackened springs. It stood there before her, something to tell her that the evil in the house wasn't natural. It told her that someone had succeeded long ago in doing what they hadn't done tonight. Murder.

Suddenly frightened, she turned to run from the room. But the cries came again, pulling her back. She stopped short, just a foot in front of the door, feeling her heartbeat. She didn't want to turn. . . .

In the bed, four little boys screamed silently, reaching out to her. Light danced in the tears on their faces, the light of fire. But there was no fire.

"I'm not seeing this," Melanie said with determination.

Her eyes focused on the youngest of the boys, a tiny child who couldn't have been more than two. His big blue eyes were wide with terror. She read his lips, moving slowly as if he were eating sticky candy.

Ahhhhh . . .

Mahhhh . . .

MMAAMMMMAAAA!!

He wanted his mother! Melanie took a step toward him, the innocence of a child crying for his mother making her forget that there was something very wrong, very evil here.

One of the older boys collapsed, knocking the little one down. His hair began to shrivel away, his skin suddenly blistered. As if the scene were being run on a too-fast old-time movie camera, the pajamas blackened and disappeared in invisible flames.

"NO!" Melanie screamed, running to the bed.

She reached out to pull them away—and found Helen Jennings in her arms. The woman pulled away and slapped her, her long nails grazing Melanie's cheek.

Fool! You did not listen to me and now he'll kill them all!

"You're dead!" Melanie screamed.

He'll kill them all! Aaaahhhh!

"NNNNOOOOOO!!"

Melanie screamed as she ran.

This is only a dream, she told herself. *Please, dear Lord, make it a dream!*

Her badly shaking legs carried her, too slowly, down the stairs and into the hallway. From above her, she heard an angry, masculine voice, then a woman's screech. But she didn't stop to hear more of it.

Her arms groped forward to guide her when her tears blocked her vision in the darkness. Then she couldn't run any more. She sank to her knees and began to cry in her terror. She wanted Gary.

She suddenly felt strong arms around her. She bent her head to bury it in Gary's shoulder, trembling in the darkness.

Her body shook violently, and she cried until there were no more tears left inside. Whimpering like a little animal in a trap, she pushed herself closer to him and said in a choked voice, "I'm so frightened!"

"I know, my love," the voice said. "I'm so sorry you were hurt."

She felt herself being pulled up to him, his grip around her tight. It was a strange feeling in this pitch-black hallway, where not even the light of the moon cast any illumination on them. The lips she touched were cold, yet they responded to her with an unusual warmth. His hands massaged her back. Something, Melanie thought, was wrong with that. The hands were too smooth, not like a plastered wrist should feel.

"Gary?" she asked, backing away. She didn't trust what she couldn't see.

"My love," the voice whispered, "there is no need for fear now. I shall protect you from those who mean you harm."

A bright light caught her eyes just then, and she squinted to see one of the guards standing behind it.

"Mrs. VanBuren?" he asked. "I heard you call out."

"I-I'm all right," Melanie mumbled, edging closer to Gary. "My husband can take care of me."

"I'll take you to him, then," the guard offered.

Melanie eyed him strangely. What did he mean? Then she turned to look at Gary, to ask if he understood what the guard was saying. But Gary wasn't behind her. There was no one there at all. Melanie screamed.

"Here, here," the guard said, helping her to her feet. He led her to Gary's room, where her husband was tightening the belt of his robe. Gary took her in his arms.

"My God," he said, "what happened?"

"I found her on the floor of the hall," the guard told him. "Mrs. VanBuren, please tell me what happened. Did you see anyone?"

Melanie nodded, then shook her head.

"I don't know," she whimpered.

"I'll check it out," the guard said.

"Helen Jennings was right," Melanie said softly.

"Come inside and lie down," Gary said. "What happened to you?"

"H-Helen Jen-nings was right," Melanie said again. "There's someone in this h-house!"

"Yes, I know," Gary soothed, brushing the hair from her eyes. "The guards will find him."

Melanie shook her head, hard.

"N-no," she said. "He's-he's . . ."

She buried her head in Gary's shoulder and mumbled, "I-I couldn't see anything. He was in the hall and I thought it was you and it was-wasn't. . . ."

Gary pushed her gently down on the bed and stood up. He removed a gun from the drawer next to his bed and walked into the hall. Melanie, seeing him go, started to rise, but Gary told her firmly that she would be safest right here. He wanted to find that bastard, and he wasn't about to let two guards get the best of it.

He could hear the sound of doors being opened and closed as the guards inspected the upstairs. He had a strong feeling, a hunch that nothing would turn up. It was more than a hunch—he knew for a fact that the search was fruitless. How can you find what you can't see?

Gina and Kyle were sleeping quietly, just as they had been when Melanie left the room a while earlier. Gary recovered them, thinking it was no wonder they slept that way—locked together. The poor kids were probably nervous wrecks by now.

In Nancy's room, he found the little girl sitting up in her bed, tears rolling down her cheeks. She took one look at the pistol in his hand and began to cry loudly.

"Oh, honey!" Gary cried, putting the gun behind his back and walking to her. "Did all the noise wake you up?"

Nancy nodded. "I heard crying upstairs, Daddy."

Gary kissed her and promised that everything was quite all right. Nancy didn't know about the guards, or even about the fires. Gary put her covers on and kissed her lightly.

"Daddy will take care of everything," he said. "Now, you go to sleep, sweetie. I'll check on you again later. Okay?"

"Okay, Daddy," Nancy said, closing her eyes.

He left the room to check on what she meant by "crying upstairs." That meant the attic, of course. Was it the squirrels he had heard a few weeks earlier? (*Or the sound of a bodiless voice.*) He went to the closet and opened the door, looking up at the ceiling. The square panel had been moved.

He climbed awkwardly to the top. But the investigation of the attic wasn't to be his own. One of the guards had already seen the moved panel. He flashed his light in Gary's face, ready to pull out his gun. Gary said, "My little girl said she heard someone crying up here. Did you find anything?"

"Your wife and I were up here earlier," the guard told him. "We didn't see a thing. But there's something over here that looks like a nursery."

"The landlord told me about a sealed-up room," Gary recalled. "I meant to have the door opened to use it for storage."

"It's still furnished, for some reason," the guard said, stepping inside.

Gary followed, eyeing every inch of the floor and walls. The dressers were pressed flat against the now-peeling wallpaper, and the closet was child-sized, too small to hide an adult. The bed? Gary walked over to it.

"I've checked under it already," the guard said. "But, uh, I think you should take a look at the bed itself."

"Oh, Christ," Gary said when he saw the burned mattress. "Do you know if that was done recently?"

"I don't think so," the guard said. "A fire big enough to destroy half a bed wouldn't get by unnoticed. If it had, this whole house would have burned down."

"Then it's—uh—possible that this has nothing to do with the fires tonight?" Gary suggested, wanting it to be so.

"I really don't know," the guard said. "I'm not a detective. But I suggest we tell Captain Davis about this."

"I'll do that," Gary promised. "Look, don't tell my wife what we found, okay?"

"I won't," the guard promised.

Gary took one last look at the nursery before leaving it to go downstairs.

"What an idiotic place for a nursery," he mumbled.

In the hallway, he and the guard were met by the other cop. The report from all sides was similar—nothing had been found. It was suggested that Melanie had been sleepwalking and had had a bad scare. That was the only explanation that made sense right now. There was no way anyone could have left the house without being seen.

Gary, because he wanted to believe the guards' words, agreed with them and returned to Melanie. He told her what they had said, that she must have been seeing things.

"I didn't see anything," Melanie whispered.

"Or hearing things, I mean," Gary said. "We've looked everywhere. Even the attic."

"You didn't see the little boys?"

"What little boys?"

"They were burning," Melanie said plainly.

Gary rose from the bed, not taking his eyes from her. She was in some kind of shock, he thought. He took a sleeping pill from the medicine chest in the bathroom adjoining the bedroom and handed it to her with a glass of water. She took it without asking what it was.

In a few minutes, her breathing evened out. But there was no sleep for Gary that night. He stared through the darkness of the bedroom, listening until he could no longer hear the guards' voices downstairs. If they were discussing the possibility that there had been someone in here, they were right. But Gary knew they would never find him. He also knew that his wife had had a frightening run-in with the very force that had tried to kill him.

14

Janice swung her arm at the alarm clock to silence it and pulled her covers tightly around her shivering body. She drew her knees up into her chest and tensed her muscles, trying to drive away the cold.

She didn't want to get up this morning. Shaken by the fires at Melanie's house, she had gotten a little too drunk at the Starship disco. Well, she was in charge of the library, and it could damn well wait until she was good and ready to open it. Right now she just wanted to sleep.

But the alarm was ringing again. No, the telephone. With a groan, Janice turned over and lifted the receiver.

"H'llo?"

"Miss Janice Lors?"

"That's my name," Janice replied, yawning widely.

"This is Captain Bryan Davis of the Belle Bay Police," the voice said.

Janice was suddenly wide awake. She straightened herself against her pillow and took on a more serious air. She didn't wait for Davis to finish his introduction.

"It's about last night, isn't it?" she asked, smoothing her mussed hair as if Davis could see her.

"Yes," Davis replied. "We tried to reach you later in the night, but couldn't. Where were you?"

"Out," Janice snapped, letting him know she thought it was none of his business. Then, after a moment's thought, she added, "I went to a disco."

"Tell me about it down here," Davis said. "When can you get here?"

"I have to open the library," Janice said. "Say eleven, okay?"

"Eleven," Davis repeated. He hung up.

Janice slipped off her warm nightgown with regret, as the cold air of her apartment was painful. She stepped into a warm shower and let the hot flow massage her thoughts away. Janice enjoyed the fun side of life and hated anything that stood in the way of it. So now, she thought, breathing in the warmth of the steam, she was being called in by the police. All the times she and her crowd had gone out together, from their days of underage drinking to more recent escapades of singing through the streets at late hours, Janice had never been pulled in. Today, she would finally know what it was like to be questioned. And somehow that scared her more than if she were going there to answer a summons for one of her earlier misdemeanors.

*   *   *

The drive to the police station took Janice through the heart of town, then around the duck pond and up another road. Belle Bay was a small community, easily covered in ten minutes. But Janice was so lost in thought that the drive took her nearly twenty. She didn't notice the Thanksgiving decorations on the house doors or the great piles of leaves that had been raked off dozens of front lawns. All she thought about was the upcoming confrontation with the police.

She went over the events of the previous night, wondering if it would sound too much like a rehearsed speech when she rattled it off to them. She hoped Tony would be there. He seemed like such a nice guy, and she wouldn't mind getting to know him.

"Officer DiMagi died last night," Captain Davis informed her ten minutes later when she asked where he was. He turned his eyes for a moment, so that he would not have to take in another look of shock. Janice looked at him, and then at the officer who sat on a bench on the other side of the room. This other man was Jack Hughes, who had ignored his aching throat and head to come down here today. Both men wore black armbands, and Jack Hughes was holding something in his hands. A cap—Tony's?

"I can't believe it," Janice managed to whisper. "I just met him last night!"

"Miss Lors," Davis said, in a voice that cut through the quiet hum of the room, "did you see anyone leaving or approaching the house when you came to report To—Officer DiMagi's failed electrical system?"

"I'm not sure I want to answer anything," Janice said carefully. "Do I need a lawyer?"

"You're in no trouble," Davis reassured her.

"Well," Janice said, pulling herself up tall. "Go ahead. I just won't answer if I don't want to."

"Please," Davis said with professional politeness, "the more cooperative you are, the sooner we'll find out who killed Tony."

"Killed?" Janice echoed. "Jesus."

"Answer my question," Davis pressed.

"Let me think," Janice said. "I did see someone at the house, but it was after the fires. He was walking on the road up that hill."

Davis sat up straighter. Across the room, Hughes leaned forward and looked at his captain with widened eyes. Before Davis could speak, he asked, "What did he look like?"

"Big," Janice said, holding her hand up to indicate the man's height. "I'd guess about six foot six."

"Did you see his face?" Davis asked.

"It was too dark," Janice said. "But I know he was wearing a cape of some kind. I saw him from the back when I looked in my rearview mirror. He had very dark hair and the cape was blue. He was talking to Tony, I think. I don't know what happened after that."

Now Hughes was on his feet. Davis gave him a quick look, then ran his eyes over Janice. The blonde woman sat cross-legged in high boots and a well-fitted jumpsuit. Common sense told him she couldn't have made up her story. The only reason to do so, he reasoned, would be to cover for herself. And, as slim as she was, she couldn't have pushed the car hood down so strongly. Was she covering for someone else?

"Did you report this?" Davis asked, a bit more sternly than he had intended.

"I suppose," Janice said with a shrug, "that I forgot about it in the confusion. Getting help to Melanie and those little kids was more important."

"Yeah," Davis said. "Look, I want to talk with Officer Hughes. Could you wait outside?"

"Sure," Janice said pleasantly, though she was unnerved that they had something to discuss that she wouldn't be allowed to hear. What did they think of her?

Hughes walked over to the captain's desk and leaned against it, watching Janice close the door behind her. He noted that her hands had begun to tremble.

"What do you think, sir?" he asked.

"We have a choice," Davis said, looking at the end of his pencil, ragged where his teeth had chewed it. "Either she's guilty, or she isn't."

"Why would she kill Tony?" Hughes said, trying to fight the feeling of enmity his mind was forming toward her.

"Somehow," Davis said, "I don't think she did. Logic fights against it. Look at her, Jack! She couldn't be taller than four eleven and a half—maybe five feet. She'd have trouble reaching up for the hood without Tony knowing it."

Hughes nodded. It made sense. Everything Captain Davis said made sense, he thought with a mixture of admiration and jealousy. Davis always had a perfect explanation for everything. That was how he became captain.

"Then what do you think about her caped man?" he asked, wondering if Davis, for once, didn't have an answer to a certain question. That was, who had killed Tony?

"Maybe someone else at the VanBuren house saw him," Davis suggested. "We'll go down there right after lunch. I've had a guard on the place all night."

"What about Gary VanBuren?" Hughes suggested.

"It doesn't seem right to think he did it," Davis said. "He's a wisp of a guy, and besides, he's got one of his wrists in a cast."

"I know that," Hughes said. "But that doesn't mean he isn't a prime suspect."

"I'd go easy with him, though," Davis said. He explained himself. "Jackie, you weren't there. You didn't see it. I know it must have taken a tremendous force to push that hood dow—"

Hughes cut him off. "Please, sir. I don't want to hear again about how Tony died. It makes me vicious."

Davis sighed and thought for a long moment, turning his pencil in his fingers. He began to bounce it on the desk.

"Something bothers me," Davis said. "In all that rain last night, there should have been footprints. There were Tony's, and Janice Lors'. But no third set. It doesn't fit right."

He went on bouncing the pencil, one of his ways of steadying his thoughts. Then he leaned forward and said with an all-knowing voice, "Then again, we weren't looking for footprints last night. I'm sure they were there and we didn't take notice."

"I'm surprised you admit a thing like that," Hughes said evenly. "I mean, failure in the line of duty. Footprints would be the first thing to look for."

"Don't forget who you're talking to before you go making accusations," Davis said, though not as austerely as he should have. He couldn't bring himself to bully Jack Hughes. The man, though rebellious at times, was one of the best in the department. A rare, good cop.

He softened the look on his face. "I'm going to take Vic Towers down there with me this afternoon. We'll let you in on everything that happens."

"What do you mean, 'let me in'?" Hughes demanded. How could they dare to leave him off this case? "My God, Captain, Tony was my *partner!*"

"I don't think," Davis said carefully, breathing in a sigh that spoke of his many years as a cop, "that you're up to it. Jack, you couldn't even come to the *phone* yesterday, let alone go out on a case. You look terrible—you look like you ought to be in the hospital. I need all the men I have, and I'd rather keep you off for a few days than have you laid up for weeks. Don't you understand?"

"No, I don't," Jack said evenly. "But you're right, sir. You're right."

"I know I'm right," Davis said. He took on a firm tone. "You're to keep off this case and in bed. That's an order, Officer Hughes."

"Yes, sir."

The reply was respectful, but there was no mistaking the look on

Jack Hughes' face. It was a look of untapped anger. Davis knew the man was defiant enough to disobey the rule.

* * *

Daylight often works like the best medicine to ease a mind troubled in the night. When sunshine lights a room, an ugly face on the floor becomes a sweater carelessly thrown there, and an apparition turns into a robe hung a bit crookedly on a door hook.

Daylight had been shining for hours when Melanie reacted to it. The room seemed innocent in this bath of sunshine. Melanie's first thoughts were of the previous night. Did the nursery look this innocent now?

Gary came into the room with a cup of coffee for her. He handed it to her, and with a slight smile asked how she was. Melanie's smile was just as slight. She didn't answer him, but asked instead, "How're the kids?"

"Fine," Gary told her. "I kept them home today. Last night was a bit much. Just so things look smooth, Nancy's here, too. I said I'd take them out somewhere. Maybe we'll drive into the city to see the Rockettes."

"We can't do that," Melanie reminded him. "The police are going to be here, aren't they?"

"To hell with them," Gary said.

"Never mind," Melanie answered. "You can't avoid this issue, Gary. My God—a young man was killed here last night, and you want to go off to New York City!"

"Just to help us forget," Gary told her. "To help calm the children."

Melanie reached out for his arm and pulled him toward the bed until he sat down.

"We've got to talk about this," she said. "Ignoring the things that have happened here isn't going to do the children—or us—any good. *Please*, Gary, let's get this all in the open so we can figure out a way to handle it! I'm much too worn out from last night to take another minute of this!"

Gary noticed the desperation in her voice. She was still upset about running into that "someone in the house." Someone she couldn't see, as he had been unable to see the hands that had nearly strangled him just a couple of weeks earlier. He sighed, as if released of a great burden. He was finally able to tell Melanie the exact truth of his "accident."

"But," he said when he finished, "it happened very quickly. I can't even say for certain that I *was* attacked. It just felt that way. I want to believe that the voice was my imagination, and that I had just tripped over a rip in the stair carpeting. I've been trying to convince myself, Melanie!"

"Gary," she said with a sigh, "why did you think I'd make fun of you for that? Why wouldn't I believe you?"

Gary shrugged, unable to explain himself. But far from being embarrassed, he was quite happy. At long last the secret that tortured him was out. And Melanie believed him. He leaned over and kissed her hard, giving her a silent thank you.

"I have things to tell you that I've kept to myself," Melanie admitted, "little things that meant nothing until last night. I think they're connected in some way with your mishap."

She told him again about the little gifts she had found and how she had been shocked to see that bone tied in the very same fabric that had been used to wrap them. She explained how she had heard a voice in the hall, and that when she opened the door to find the package, she believed Gary had sneaked back up there to leave it for her.

"But you didn't, did you?" she asked.

"I don't think so," Gary said.

"Don't be so careful with me!" Melanie snapped. "I'm not a child, you know."

"I'm sorry," Gary said, pulling away from her. "No, I didn't." He thought for a moment. "Melanie," he said, "what about Terry Hayward? It makes sense—he threatened us, so that would explain the accidents, even the fires, if he knew a way to get in and out of here that we don't."

"I can't believe that," Melanie said. "First, there's no way Terry could know where we live. And second, how could he know more about this house than we do?"

"Somebody does," Gary answered. "And there's something else that makes me think of Hayward—the gifts. Obviously a token of love."

"No, Gary. I *know* it isn't Terry. So much has happened here lately that can't be attributed to anything human. First, little Nancy, then you, and the fires. Why haven't we seen a culprit yet?" Melanie sighed. "But something else happened last night that horrified me more than anything that's happened to us. I saw and heard things—evil things. Gary, I'm convinced that Helen Jennings came here with a warning for us that day. She said there was evil in this house!"

"She was a crazy old woman," Gary insisted.

"No," Melanie said evenly. "She was sincere. And I believe her now. Helen tried to caution us before these things happened last night. If we had listened to her, there would never have been a fire last night at all. And poor Tony . . ."

She cut herself off, thinking deeply.

"Melanie," Gary said, "all this talk of 'evil' is insane. I refuse to believe that the things that went wrong here were caused by anything other than nature and some mortal. A damned insane one—and I can tell you I'm more afraid of him than something I can't see."

(*Can't see—those words again. Gotta stop saying that.*)

"Hear me out, Gary," Melanie requested with a wave of her hand. "Last night, I ran into *someone* in that hall, even if the cop didn't see him. I was running from the attic, and I was so terrified I couldn't think straight. Gary, I saw something in that attic that turned my stomach. I saw four little boys in a bed, screaming in a fire! And I couldn't save them! When I went over to the bed, they were gone. Helen Jennings was there!"

"For God's sake, Melanie!" Gary cried, as if he were losing patience. "You were sleepwalking. Helen Jennings is dead."

"I know that," Melanie said with a click of her tongue. "But who were those little boys? If you don't believe they existed, go up and look in the attic. There's a nursery there, and the bed's half burned away."

"I've been up there," Gary said. "I can understand why you were so frightened, considering that spooky old place. Don't you see, Melanie—when you saw the burned nursery, you thought of Kyle and Gina, and you imagined those little boys as a representation of our kids."

"Why do you always sound so much like you know it all?" Melanie snapped, getting out of bed.

She stormed into the small bathroom, her blonde hair flying over her face. Gary sat on the bed, hearing her turn on the faucet. She was whistling something, an angry tune that made no musical sense. She cut herself off suddenly, and came back into the room, her hair tied back.

"Helen Jennings scratched me last night," she said triumphantly, indicating her jawbone. Gary saw three evenly spaced scratch marks there. "If I imagined everything, where did these come from?"

Gary didn't bother to attempt an answer. He had none.

15

◆

Gary didn't go to work that day. The explanation to his secretary, who said his week-long absence was causing quite a stir among his clients, was as brief as he could make it. He said only that something had gone wrong at the house the night before and he was staying home to take care of it. He made a perfunctory promise that he would be in the office the next day, if only to go over his papers with her.

A twinge of guilt led him to his study, where he pulled out his briefcase to put in a little at-home work. But the telescope stand and map and all the naval pieces kept pulling his eyes from the papers in front of him. What he had once admired now made him nervous.

There wasn't much time for thoughts like this, though. By one o'clock the locksmith he had called arrived. Gary planned to have every window and door lock changed, at any cost, to keep his family safe. It didn't matter that he couldn't even see what endangered them. The locks were Gary's way of solidifying what Melanie called an "evil." They made that bodiless voice something tangible, something he could touch and fight.

He toyed with the theory that someone had a way of getting in and out of the house in spite of the locks. If anyone had a key, he was out of luck now. But his second idea would take a little more effort than just calling a locksmith—a secret passage. Why not? Gary reasoned that in a house this old there might very well be a secret tunnel that led from the cellar out to some cave on the beach.

He was on his way to Melanie's studio when he heard Gina call upstairs that the police were here. At first Gary was annoyed with the intrusion. But logic told him it was better to get the questioning over with now. As Gary headed back downstairs, he saw the guard who had stayed during the daylight hours leading Captain Davis and another cop (not Hughes, Gary was surprised to see) into the living room.

He followed them into the room and sent Gina to bring her mother down. Gary noticed that Davis had a more relaxed, professional look on his face now. It was a far cry from the saddened face he had seen the night before, a face ready to twist with tears and anger. But Bryan Davis had finished with his grief. He now displayed the cool manner that he used in every situation that involved a serious crime, speaking as if the victim were someone he didn't know.

"Did you see anyone in or near this house last night, with the exception of your family, Janice Lors, and Officer DiMagi?" Davis asked, wondering if they had come in contact with Janice's caped man.

Gary shook his head and answered in the negative. Melanie, who had just stepped into the room as Davis was asking the question, told him they had been upstairs the entire time Tony was out in the driveway. Davis replied that Janice Lors had seen someone.

"A tall man dressed in a cape," he said.

Melanie gasped. Gary took her hand in his and tried to avert the policemen's attention from his wife's face. Her wide-eyed stare told them she knew something of this. Gary hoped she wouldn't start talking about ghosts and things.

He had no cause to worry. Melanie knew as well as he that talk of evil and haunted houses would only turn the police against them. It would sound too much like playacting, as if they were both pretending to be insane, so that if Gary were accused of killing Tony, he could use that as an excuse.

Instead, she said calmly, "My little girl, Nancy, had boiling water

thrown on her by some strange man. We thought she was imagining
it when she said he was tall and wearing a long cape. But she wasn't
seeing things, was she?"

"Where is she now?" Davis asked.

"I'll get her," Gary said, leaving the room.

"Something else happened here last night," the guard reported.
Melanie held her breath, praying he wouldn't tell of her running
through the hall.

"We went up into the attic again," he went on. "We must have
missed it before, but there was a child's nursery up there. I think the
door must have been hidden by a trunk or something. But Mrs. Van-
Buren had been up there, and she came down to—to tell us what she
had found."

"What were you doing up in the attic?" Davis asked.

"I don't have to have a reason for walking through my own
house," Melanie said stiffly.

Before Davis could answer her, the guard went on with his report.
"The thing that's strange is that the bed was half burned away, just
like the kids' beds last night. But I doubt if there's a connection.
That room hasn't been used in thirty or forty years."

"It could be," Davis said, "that someone set fire to the bed recently to make it look like the bed had been burned that long ago."

"Why would anyone do that?" Melanie wanted to know, trying to
push aside her thoughts of the little boys.

"Well," Davis explained, "then it would make it look like the
fellow who's been doing all this is very old. A younger man couldn't
have been alive at the time the fire in the attic might have been set,
if it was set in the nineteen-forties."

Gary walked into the room, holding Nancy. He was accompanied
by Kyle and Gina, who had been prepared for this interview. They
knew that they had to tell Davis everything that had happened.
Davis smiled at Nancy and asked, "Do you remember that man who
hurt you?"

Nancy's smile faded. "Uh-huh!"

"Well," Davis went on, being as gentle as possible with this tiny
child in spite of his need to get quickly to the truth, "want to tell me
what he looked like?"

"He was real tall," Nancy said in a fascinated tone.

"Tell Captain Davis what he was wearing," Melanie prompted.

"A cape," Nancy said immediately.

"A cape?" Davis echoed. "What color, honey?"

"Blue," Nancy replied.

Davis looked at Melanie and Gary. Had this child been rehearsed? Had Janice Lors been rehearsed? He still didn't know if the man really existed.

He tried to trap them. "He had blond hair, didn't he?"

"No," was Nancy's firm reply, followed by a shake of her blonde-curled head.

Davis was convinced. He knew the little girl was telling the truth. Honesty was easier to see in the eyes of children than in the eyes of adults. He went on with the questioning, speaking with Kyle and Gina.

"I don't really know what happened," Kyle said, thinking hard about Davis' question. "I was asleep. The smoke woke me up."

"You didn't see or hear anyone?" Davis asked.

"No, sir," Kyle said. "I was sleeping."

Gina could give no more information than her brother. Finally, Davis asked them to run off and play while he spoke with their parents.

"I don't have much to go on," he said. "Except a vague description given to me by a little girl and a young woman. I'm not even sure it will be believed in a court."

"I guess I'd be the first suspect," Gary said.

"I'd just be sure I could prove how badly that wrist is hurt," Davis said.

"There is one other person you might consider questioning," Gary said. "A fellow named Terry Hayward. He lives in Greenwich Village."

"Gary, Nancy's description doesn't fit him," Melanie said softly.

"Are you sticking up for him?"

"No, but why lead the police on a false trail?"

"I'll take any lead at this point," Davis said. "What makes you talk about this Terry Hayward?"

"He was harassing my family with crank phone calls when we lived in the city," Gary said. "And he even threatened to kill my wife."

Bryan Davis listened carefully as Gary related the story, then took down the man's address from Melanie. He pulled on his coat and stuffed his note pad into his pocket.

"If you see anyone, give me a call. I'll check this guy out and let you know."

"I have to have the phone fixed," Gary said. "The phone company is a bit slow about that."

Davis stopped. "The phones were dead last night?"

"I didn't tell you?" Gary asked.

"Maybe," Davis said. "I don't remember."

"That's why we didn't just call you," Gary said.

"I'll send a team down here to check it out," Davis said. "I'll talk with you again."

When he left, Melanie sighed heavily and put her arms around Gary.

"I'm sick of 'teams,'" she sighed. "Locksmiths, cops, everybody!"

"But they might help us out," Gary insisted. "Then we can find this maniac and be rid of him."

"I wish it were that simple," Melanie said wearily. She broke away from Gary's embrace and walked upstairs. When she was out of sight, Gary opened the door to the playroom. He brought Kyle out into the hall.

"We're going to play a game," Gary said. "I want to see if there are any secret passages under this house. Want to help?"

"Wow!" Kyle cried eagerly. He took the flashlight Gary had pulled from a utensil drawer in the kitchen and followed his father down the cellar stairs.

"Now, here's what you do," Gary explained. "Run your hands over this wall and pat it. That's to see if there are any loose bricks."

With an excitement that can only be experienced by a little child, Kyle slapped his palms over the cool cement, covering every possible inch. When four walls were inspected with no results, he suggested pulling at the posts on the stairway to see if they were fixed with a trick wire. Gary looked at him with surprise and said, "Smart boy, Kyle! Why didn't I think of that?"

"I saw it on TV once," Kyle said.

But nothing in the basement hinted there might be an entrance down there. The ornaments on the old wooden stairs were fastened securely, as were the various gas lamps and torch holders.

As disappointed as his son, Gary went back upstairs and returned the flashlight to its drawer in the kitchen. Kyle was sent back to play with his sisters, after being promised that Gary would tell him if he found anything.

Gary pulled on his jacket and went outdoors. Something about the crisp autumn air helped set his thoughts in order. It was dark outside today—the gray clouds blocked the sun and threatened snow. Snow! Gary thought. That would really fix things. No one could possibly get into the house then without his footprints being seen.

Gary leaned against a tree inside the woods and stared back at the house. It was still beautiful, in spite of the fires and chokings and boiling water. How was he supposed to feel about all that? He felt anger that someone had dared to hurt his children. And disgust. And fear . . .

. . . but he felt fear a lot lately.

He shook his head and started to walk back to the house. A dry leaf crunched behind him and a voice ordered him to stay right where he was. At its command, Gary raised his hands into the air and turned around—slowly, to find a .22 in perfect line with his heart.

But not for long. Its owner dropped it to his side quickly and mumbled an apology. Gary took a step toward Jack Hughes and demanded to know what he was doing here.

"I—I couldn't get Tony off my mind," Hughes said hoarsely. "I just had to come here to have a look for myself. I thought I'd find something the others didn't."

"Your captain and another cop were here earlier," Gary said. "I'm sure they would have looked in the woods if they thought they'd find anything. I don't like the idea of you sneaking around my property with a loaded gun. I've got little children."

"So do I," Hughes said, sheathing the pistol. "I'm really sorry."

"Sure," Gary obliged. "I guess you're just doing your job."

"No, I'm not," Hughes admitted. "I'm not on this case. Davis left me off because of my health." As if to verify this, he coughed.

"I won't tell anyone I saw you," Gary promised. "This time. But please don't be wandering about my property any more."

"I won't," Hughes said, knowing it was a lie.

Gary turned to walk away. When he entered the house he found Melanie in the kitchen, preparing dinner. He offered to do it himself, to let her rest, but she insisted she could do fine. Besides, she said, he had that sprained wrist to worry about. She pulled a bunch of carrots from the refrigerator and began to peel them.

"Say, Gary," she asked, "have you seen that diary around? I've looked for it over and over and it just doesn't seem to be anywhere."

"No, I haven't," Gary replied. "Did you look in the library?"

"Yes," Melanie said. "Gary, I've been thinking about what I read. Helen Jennings brought it over for a purpose—so that we'd know more about the first owner of the house. I think she was using it to give us the answer to what's been going on here. The evil she spoke about—the clue to it is in that diary. I think I understand what she was trying to tell us."

"Melanie," Gary said carefully.

"No, Gary," Melanie said. "It makes sense. I think this place is haunted. Maybe by Jacob Armand, the man mentioned in the diary. Do you think it could be?"

Gary widened his eyes at Melanie's statement. A ghost! It would make things very clear, wouldn't it? It was the perfect explanation for the unseen hands and bodiless voices. But Gary shook that thought from his head. He was becoming too drawn in by a simple explanation. He couldn't just say he agreed.

"I don't think so," he said finally. "I'm sure as ever that we'll find this crazy idiot and he'll be as real as you and I."

"I wish you'd give me the benefit of the doubt just once," Melanie griped.

They heard the sounds of the children giggling in the playroom and looked at each other in wonder. No one would guess what had happened here last night if they saw Kyle and Gina now. Gary and Melanie were amazed at the spring-back power they had.

Kyle, Gina, and Nancy were playing explorer. Kyle had told them what he had done in the cellar with Gary, and now his two sisters wanted to share his fun. The fireplace was toyed with; every wall was patted. Nancy climbed onto the window seat and was checking the windows. She stopped for a moment to look at the shining new lock there. Then she shrieked in laughter at Kyle's funny imitation of Sherlock Holmes.

But it took only one sight to stop her laughter—one quick glimpse, through the glass of the window, of the man who had hurt her so many days ago. She stood there, so still she might have been a statue, her chubby body pressed against the glass, her round eyes staring in awe at the stern face that considered her. Then she jumped from the seat with a scream and ran to Gina.

"It's him!" she cried. "It's him, he's outside!"

Gina and Kyle looked up at the window and saw nothing.

Nancy pulled away and ran toward the kitchen, screaming for her mother. She ran into Melanie's arms, sobbing, screaming that the "mean man" was outside. Melanie looked at Gary.

"Maybe you should get the gun. . . ."

But Gary had already had that thought. He was running down the stairs and toward the front door now, breathing heavily. He all but pulled it from its hinges in his haste to get to the front porch before the intruder got away.

The night had a kind of deadly silence that makes one fear something is going to drop unexpectedly from one of the trees above. A slight wind, heralding a storm, blew the leaves around the porch floor. Gary stepped carefully into the darkness, able to see only as much as the porch light allowed. There was no moon tonight.

He kept trying to tell himself that he was a grown man and that he was the one who was armed. He tried not to think that the man he was stalking was some kind of maniac who thought nothing of terrorizing little children.

(*Who could make himself invisible and hurt those who crossed him.*)

He went back inside after a few minutes, reasoning that the new locks would keep them safe. The children were sent from the kitchen, but Nancy still clung to her mother.

"How could he have disappeared so quickly if he was human?" Melanie demanded. "Neither Kyle nor Gina saw him. Gary, that was Jacob Armand out there—I'm sure of it!"

"I can't believe that yet," Gary said softly.

Melanie watched him close the door, then turned to the refrigerator for a treat to divert Nancy.

* * *

In spite of Melanie's bizarre "dream," and in spite of the fact that he couldn't remember seeing the man who attacked him, Gary was still willing to put the blame on a mortal. Nancy had very definitely seen someone at the window, and it was a good guess that that someone was Terry Hayward. Without telling Melanie, Gary went to work the next morning with plans to visit the man's apartment and confront him, to put a stop to this once and for all.

"I'm glad to see you back," Warren Lee said when Gary walked into the office. "How're the kids?"

"They're doing okay," Gary said. "I would be making the understatement of the year if I said they were shaken up a bit. But they're calming down."

"Kids are great about those things," Warren said with a smile. "How's your wrist?"

"Scratchy," Gary told him.

Warren grinned and handed him a pile of papers. "This ought to take your mind off it," he said. "And you'll be glad to hear we've gotten a millionaire divorce. That'll mean big bucks, if we do right by the old lady."

"Oh, damn," Gary moaned. "Look, Warren—I've got so much on my mind that I couldn't think about these right now."

"But this is a big case," Warren pointed out. "And I can't handle it by myself. Gary, you'll have to leave your home problems at home, no matter how awful they are!"

"It's a little difficult to push your children's safety out of your mind," Gary said, shuffling through the papers. "Warren, would you take a ride downtown with me at lunch today?"

"What's downtown?"

"Remember that guy Terry Hayward?" Gary asked. "The weirdo who made all those crank phone calls? I think he might be the one who's been pestering my family."

"How'd he find out where you live?"

"I don't know," Gary admitted. "Nobody's been asking questions here, have they?"

Warren shook his head.

"Then Terry's the most likely suspect," said Gary.

"You told the police, I take it."

"Yeah," Gary answered. "They're going to question him. But I want to get to him first."

At noon Gary and Warren hailed a cab for the twenty-minute drive downtown. Along the way, Gary told Warren all the details of the bizarre events. Warren listened carefully, then said, "It sounds like you've been invaded by a poltergeist, instead of a real person."

"A what?"

"A poltergeist," he repeated, "sometimes called a 'noisy ghost.' They usually show up in houses with adolescents and cause lots of trouble. Gina's about that age, isn't she?"

"She'll be thirteen on Thanksgiving Saturday," Gary said. "God, Warren, Melanie would love you. You both think along the same lines."

"She's talking about ghosts?"

"Something to that effect," Gary said, pulling out his wallet to pay the cabbie. When they were on the sidewalk, he went on, "But I want to see a human culprit."

They walked into the Christopher Street apartment building, and up to the fourth floor, looking around until they found the apartment number Melanie had given Davis. Gary pounded at the door.

"No answer," Warren said.

Gary tried again. This time, an old man opened the door and peered over the chain. He scowled at them.

"You cops?" he asked. "I seen enough cops for one day."

"We're lawyers," Gary told him. "We want to see Terry Hayward."

"How come everyone's looking for that guy?" the old man said. "He don't live here."

"Looks like the cops got here first anyway," Warren said when the old man shut his door.

"I want to talk to the landlord," Gary said, heading for the stairs.

The landlord was a landlady, a fat woman who puffed at a string of cigarettes. There was a smell of cats in her apartment, and the place looked as if it hadn't been cleaned in months. Warren was hesitant to sit on the dusty couch, but Gary was too interested in learning about Terry to care. Both men declined when offered a drink.

"So you're a friend o' Hayward's?" the landlady asked. "He's popular these days. Two cops was here askin' about him."

"Do you know where I can find him?" Gary asked.

"Just like I told them cops," the woman answered, "you might try Potter's Field. He's been dead for three weeks."

"Dead?"

"You heard me right," the old woman said. "I figured it was coming. You never know these days, do you? I took him in 'cause he was nice and clean-cut. I don't take weirdos in. Anyway, all of a sudden he turns into Mr. Nasty. Musta been mixed up with pills and booze —so many people do that now."

"How did he die?"

The fat woman took a slow drag from her cigarette, then leaned forward, squinting her eyes.

"Electrocuted himself," she said. "I wouldn'ta found him at all if I didn't go up to collect rent. When he didn't answer I used my key to get in—and Jeee-sus! The smell! Like if you burnt meat and left it sitting for a week. It almost killed me."

Gary shook his head. "That's a hell of a way to die. How'd he do it?"

"The cops said he was blow-drying his hair," the woman explained. "They said the cord was really worn down, and the wire was exposed. But the weird thing is that there was an inch of water on the floor when I found him. I was sick, I tell you. The way his hair floated it was like he wasn't real."

"I'm sorry that happened," Gary said, standing. A cloud of dust rose with him.

"Well," the woman said, "you can't keep the weirdos away, no matter how hard you try."

Gary thanked her for her time, and they left quickly.

"Well, you've done what you can," Warren said. "Let the police finish it."

Gary nodded, but the fear stayed with him. Melanie's conviction that they were dealing with the supernatural unnerved him. He desperately needed someone to pin the blame on—someone human. And his only suspect was dead.

16

In a time that was very far into his past, yet still clinging to his inner soul, Jack Hughes had been a gang member. The Deadly Knights. At the time, he was only thirteen, but he was already adept at beating the system. He knew that he just had to roll his large brown eyes and feign innocence to melt almost any judge.

Until one day, the system beat him. He and the rest of the gang had been caught in the middle of a rumble with their rivals, the Knives. (Hughes still clenched his fists when he thought of the name.) But he was one of the luckier ones. He was placed in a foster home, and for the first time in his life he was made to feel he could stand on his own. By the time he was eighteen and ready to start his life over again, the gang had dispersed—death, jail, execution. One or two went straight. And Jack Hughes went to college. The police academy followed, with Hughes in the top third of his class at graduation.

But his distaste for authority never left him. His stubborn, defiant character made him the "bad boy" of the department. But it was also one hell of an asset on the streets. His first assignment was the Upper West Side, and his name soon became a household word there. His superior work in tracking down and arresting a gang of hoods that had been terrorizing old people got him a medal and a promotion. And a transfer—to quiet, gentle Belle Bay.

It had once been gentle, anyway. Quiet? Yes, it was still quiet. Quiet like this damned squad car was now that Tony wasn't sitting beside him.

Hughes had made a mistake the night before by pulling his gun too quickly. Like a damned fool, he had almost put a bullet through Gary VanBuren. He wondered if he had come face to face with Tony's murderer. Could it have been Gary?

But the man had kept his promise to keep quiet. Tonight, Hughes would be more careful, because in spite of everything he'd said to

Gary, he didn't intend to stop coming here until he was satisfied no more could be done. He owed it to Tony, he told himself.

It was that thirteen-year-old hood that still lived inside him that made him do it, made him disobey a direct order to stay off the Tony DiMagi case and ignore the fact that he should be back home in bed with his flu.

This time he left the car at the bottom of the hill. He couldn't help glancing back at the old woman's house, all boarded up now with a "For Sale" sign posted on its front lawn. Davis had been down here with a search warrant, only to report he had found nothing. But, Hughes thought, maybe tonight . . .

Hughes pushed his door shut and walked toward Helen's house. Every window was covered with a wooden slab. At the side of the house, the untrimmed ivy grew over one window—a window that for some reason hadn't been boarded. Hughes pulled at the vines, ignoring their stinging needles, and ripped them away from the house. Without looking to see if anyone was watching, he lifted his gun from its holster (worn under a blue civilian jacket) and smashed the window.

He was in the kitchen. For some reason, the food Helen had last placed on the table was still there, waiting for her. Hughes saw a piece of rotting chicken, and next to that a loaf of bread that had gone green and fuzzy. There were small insects crawling over it, having an enormous repast.

The thought tugged at his stomach, hard. He hurried from the room, trying to convince himself that it was only the flu that still held fast to him that was making him feel so sick. He passed through what seemed to be a short hall and entered the first door he came to. Hughes felt along the wall until he touched a light switch, then clicked it. The pitch black stayed in the room.

"Damn," he said, "they've got the electricity cut off."

He turned back to the kitchen and climbed through its window. The run to his car was a short one, and he was back inside the house in minutes with a flashlight.

The living room looked like something out of the eighteen-nineties, except for a television set and a recliner. But the rest of the furniture was quite old, and the stuffed chairs, leaking now, even had little lace doilies placed over their backs.

You could almost hear them talking in here. Hughes didn't quite know who "them" was, but he guessed that at one time Helen had sat here with her family, chatting and laughing while the women sewed and the men smoked fat cigars.

His flashlight caught the mantel, and he walked over to it, lifting each of several tiny portraits in his hand. The gold plate on one said "Helen, Aged 3, 1899." Hughes set the picture down again, carefully.

He walked into a hallway, stepping inside every room. His hand was always ready to grab his gun, but Hughes had a feeling there was nothing to be found in the house. It was almost impossible to keep from being charmed by the place. How could a killer hide here?

"He could," Hughes told himself.

He found himself in a sewing room, and he nearly fell when his foot caught on a pile of fabric that had been thrown on the floor. He kicked it aside and looked around. The sewing machine, still with a piece of fabric inside it, was an ancient foot-pedal model. It was strange—it seemed as if the house would wait like this forever for Helen to come home again.

Upstairs, he found five huge bedrooms, though only one looked as if it had been used in recent months. He went inside and pulled open Helen's closet door. She had had only a few dresses, each hung carefully on a padded hangar. The closet was so big he could stand comfortably inside.

An indentation in the wall, near the floor, caught his eye when he aimed the flashlight down. Hughes kicked at it, and it gave way to reveal a storage space. He guessed it might lead to the closet in the adjoining bedroom.

But it could also be a hiding place. He bent down to look through it. He was pushed roughly away by an odor that was so strong it reached him even through his stuffed nose. It was the smell of death.

Hughes flattened himself on his stomach and pushed a hanger into the tunnel to pull out whatever it was that had been caught in there. When he turned his head to the sight, it was one so horrible that even the street-wise cop flinched. It didn't belong in this lovely little house. It was a cat, dead from starvation. Her mouth was still open, with tiny bits of wood stuck in her teeth. She had tried to gnaw her way out of the trap.

Hughes jumped to his feet and ran from the room. It seemed impossible, but he somehow managed to reach the kitchen window and climb through it before losing the lunch in his stomach.

"You damn idiot," he said to himself when he stood straight. "You've seen worse than that. What if the bastard *is* in there?"

If he was, he could be caught another time. Right now, Hughes decided to check the woods again. Perhaps, he thought, he would go down to the beach to look for a cave, where someone could hide.

He still had cat hairs on his coat. He noticed them when he got back to the car. His already sore throat had become unbearably painful from the vomiting. Jack Hughes, usually a very strong man, was embarrassed that the sight of a dead cat had made him so ill. But sick or not, he wasn't about to go home.

He opened the glove compartment of the car and took a box of cough drops from it. Popping one into his mouth, he leaned against the door and debated whether or not to keep the flashlight. There was a moon tonight, but the trees would no doubt cast shadows that would confuse him and hide the enemy. The enemy! Hughes thought wryly. It sounded like the damned army.

Hughes moved into the woods without the light—reasoning it could be seen too easily from the house. His hand was ever ready to grab his gun. It was not only ready, it was hopeful. Hughes wanted more than anything to be able to use it.

He suddenly bent over and had a coughing fit. Maybe there was something in the wind that didn't want him to find Tony's murderer. It seemed everything was against him tonight. The cold was his worst enemy, chipping away at his lungs like an ice pick. He felt dizzy.

He had a frantic urge then to scream. The cat hairs were still there; he brushed them away again with vigor.

His eyes started to droop, and there was nothing he could do to keep them completely open. There was something pulling at his head—no, pushing it from the inside. It made the trees fly around him. Hughes put a hand to his forehead and felt the warmth of sweat and fever.

"Who are you?"

The voice seemed far away and angry. It was British, a faint accent. Hughes turned around and found himself looking up at a huge figure. The man was a good six inches taller than he, and he stared down at Hughes with no expression. Then Hughes noticed the cape and remembered what Janice Lors had said. He pulled out his gun.

But when he finally found the energy to pull the trigger, there was nothing to shoot. The clearing before him was empty.

"Fever," Hughes told himself as he crumbled to the ground.

*   *   *

There were no lights on in the house when Hughes finally returned to consciousness. He glanced at his watch and cursed out loud when he saw the time. 12:51.

He walked on legs that barely seemed there, wishing to God he hadn't been out cold for two hours. He had looked right at the guy. He almost had him!

17

———◆———

It had been a quiet week. Melanie was thinking that as she hung the last of the balloons she had bought to decorate the playroom for Gina's birthday party. A few things had happened, such as toys and books disappearing. Melanie had combed the entire house (except the attic) to find the diary—to no avail. She had been able to spend several peaceful hours a day in her studio. They had enjoyed a nice Thanksgiving, with Gary's parents as their guests. Melanie had almost expected them to say the house felt strange to them, the thing people usually said about haunted houses. But Mr. and Mrs. Van-Buren had only good things to say. And it was fine by Melanie, who wanted to enjoy every minute of this holiday.

"What do you think, Gina?" she asked, stepping down to the floor. She bent her head back to survey the ceiling. The decorations she had put up there had turned it into an array of brilliance. Green, pink, blue, and yellow balloons completely covered the gray paint.

"Oh, it's gorgeous!" Gina gasped, her eyes smiling. "I love it, Mom! I love you!"

She turned around to look at the entire room. Gina was convinced her mother was the best party-giver in the world. Across the back of the room, a long card table had been turned to line the wall under the windows. A pink tablecloth with three-dimensional daisies (Gina's very favorite color and flower) had been laid carefully over it. To its left was a small table that held the stereo, on loan from her father for this special occasion.

Gina went to it and slowly lifted the cover, then knelt down until the needle was at her eye level. She looked down her nose at the tiny chip of diamond. The turntable was a black one that contrasted greatly with her own little plastic portable. Wouldn't her friends be *impressed?*

"I hope Doreen remembers her Billy Joel records," she said, walking over to Melanie.

She gave her a hug, then turned and walked from the room. With her eyes closed, she could have walked the path from the playroom to the living room. She had done so a dozen times since the mail had arrived that morning. There were eight birthday cards from assorted aunts, uncles, and friends and an enormous package, one that contained a stuffed animal, she guessed, from the way its brown wrapper gave with pliable ease when she poked a finger at it. She couldn't wait until her parents would give her the okay to open it.

Finally, needled by her constant requests, Melanie said yes. The gift, from Melanie's parents, who were away on a cruise, was a stuffed mother kangaroo with a baby in her pouch. Gina squealed with delight when she unwrapped it, since she had never had a toy as big as herself. She hugged her mother and father and said, "I'm going to name her Happy, because that's how I feel right now."

"What about the baby?" Kyle asked.

"His name is Joey," Gina said.

"That's appropriate," Gary commented.

At that moment, a crashing noise sounded from upstairs. Conditioned by the events of the past weeks, Gary and Melanie did not hesitate to run to its source. At the top of the stairs, Melanie gasped to see Nancy sprawled head over heels on the floor. She was crying, pointing to the statue. The sphinx was lying on its side, not two feet from her. It had been torn from its mount.

Gary dropped to his knees beside her and helped her to stand up. Melanie had dressed her in her best outfit that day for Gina's party, but now the velveteen dress was crushed and dirty. Gary smoothed it as best he could and checked the little girl for bruises. But, except for a bad scare, nothing seemed to have happened to her.

"Do you hurt anywhere?" he asked.

"Uh-uh," the little girl said.

"Nothing a little ice cream wouldn't fix," Melanie said, lifting her.

"What happened, sweetheart?" Gary asked.

"The lion jumped on me," said Nancy.

"Jumped on you?" Gary echoed. "Honey, it's a statue!"

"It did, Daddy!" Nancy insisted. "It said, 'vissus waif,' and jumped!"

Her tears began to fall again, and Melanie said quickly, "Nancy, I think you mean 'vicious.' So you see, you must have dreamed it. My little girl is sweet, not vicious!"

He threw it at her.

Melanie took her down the stairs with promises of ice cream. In a short while, Gary heard giggling from the kitchen. He turned to the statue, to put it in the closet until he had time to remount it. He tried to lift it and was surprised to find it was solid brass.

His wrist, free of its cast for only a few days, buckled under the weight of it. Gary couldn't understand how anything so small could be so heavy, even if it was solid brass.

The statue suddenly thrust forward into his chest, as if the sphinx had decided he was prey to attack. The blow was so quick that Gary was stunned by it, and he forced his way back from the stairs, terrified he would be pushed down again.

He tried to call out to Melanie, but shock and the incredible pressure of the statue were fighting too hard against him. All he could muster was a faint, long gasp. His face began to turn red as the pressure increased against his lungs.

He was pushed roughly against the grandfather clock, and, under the weight of the statue, he slid down to the floor.

I can't breeeaaattthhhe.

He felt as if he were caught in a vise, wedged between the smooth oak of the clock and the relentlessly pushing statue. But the hands that worked the vise were invisible. And that voice didn't come back to him again. The thought crossed his mind that he was being murdered. And there wasn't a thing he could do to stop it.

He tried, again, to push the statue away. But something (nothing) was holding it fast against him. Gary's hands flew into the air in front of him, feeling that cold. *He* was here!

Must-get-Mela . . .

The sound of laughter reached him, sounding near and far away at the same time. Knowing he was no match for what he couldn't see, Gary tried in vain to scream for help. He heard a faint cracking sound from within his chest cavity. The laughter stopped.

Gary clenched his fist and began to punch at the glass door of the clock behind him. It was awkward, but his fist finally smashed through the panes. The sound of shattering glass brought Melanie running upstairs, and the statue pulled away from him.

Melanie found him hunched over, breathing like a runner at the end of a strenuous marathon. Some two feet away, the sphinx stood silently.

"Gary!" she cried.

When she stooped down to touch him, he looked at her with terror in his eyes. He closed them and tried to breathe evenly.

"Where are you hurt?" Melanie demanded.

"I—I think I cracked a few ribs," Gary wheezed.

Melanie was on her feet. "I'm going to call an ambulance."

Gary tried to stand, leaning heavily against Melanie. But the pain forced him back down to the floor again. He tightened his jaw against it, feeling like he wanted to cry. He never knew anything could hurt so much.

"It attacked me," he whispered.

He fell down into blackness.

18

◆

Gina stared through the diamond panes of the living-room window at the ambulance that was carrying her father to the hospital. She was filled with hurt and confusion. Why did this have to happen tonight? Though the young woman in her knew it was only right to forfeit her party and lament over her father's mishap, the child she still was wanted to enjoy the party she had dreamed of for so long.

Her mother hadn't said very much, except that Daddy had fallen while carrying the sphinx. Gina didn't buy a word of the hasty explanation. It was another one of those strange accidents, like the night her and Kyle's bedrooms had caught fire. And like the time she had fallen on the beach, when a voice had called her a name. Gina had forgotten just what it was, and she was glad. She didn't want to think about bad things like that. She had tried to steel herself to the situation, remembering that her mother had said she could spend the night in their room. She had been glad to right after the fire, but she soon moved back into her own redecorated room. She didn't want her parents to think she was a baby, yet she longed to be always in their presence, protected from whatever it was that so frightened her.

She felt a hand on her shoulder. Looking up behind her, she saw the understanding eyes of Mrs. Calder, her friend Beverly's mother. The woman had been the first to bring her daughter to the party—it had been much too late to call it off—and had volunteered to stay with the children until Melanie could get back home again. Melanie, who had met her at PTA meetings several times, was relieved by her offer.

"Your daddy's going to be just fine," Bonnie Calder said. "I'll bet your mom calls any minute now."

"You're wrong," Gina started to say, but she nodded and replied instead, "I guess so."

From outside there came the sound of a car and then the squealing and laughter of a new group of guests. Beverly took Gina by the hand and led her to the front door. It was thrown open, and the girls were welcomed with a halfhearted smile by Gina.

"What's up, Gina?" Lorrie Moulin wanted to know.

Gina shrugged. "My dad had an accident and my mom had to take him to the hospital."

"Wow, really?"

"In an ambulance?"

"Uh-huh," Gina said.

"Gina, what happened?" Doreen Wiley asked.

"My dad hurt himself," Gina explained, "when he was carrying a really heavy statue. He hurt his ribs."

"Yecch," Lorrie said with a grimace.

"One time," Doreen said, "my dad fell off our roof. *He* cracked his collarbone, and he was out of the hospital in a few hours."

"So cheer up, Gina!" Beverly insisted.

Gina's eyes lit up for the first time in an hour. Then her lips parted with a smile, and she said, "So, let's have a party!"

Beverly turned to her mother with her mouth open to speak, but Bonnie didn't have to be told her presence was quite unwelcome among these teenagers. She slipped quietly from the room and went upstairs to check on the other children. She found them in Kyle's room, watching television. Even though he had met her earlier, Kyle's eyes narrowed with suspicion when she walked into his room.

But his friendly personality took over quickly, and he offered her a seat on his bed. Bonnie sat with him, leaning against the back. She asked, "Don't you want to go downstairs to see what's happening?"

"No," Kyle said. "That's my birthday present to Gina. I promised not to bother her or her friends all night."

"That was nice of you," Bonnie praised. She turned to the little girl curled up next to him. "How are you doing, sweetheart?"

"When's my daddy coming home?" Nancy asked, in a voice so tiny that Bonnie grabbed her and hugged her to give her comfort.

"Oh, sweetie, soon," she cooed.

The telephone rang then, and Kyle sprang to his feet to run to it. But when he lifted the receiver, he found to his dismay that Gina had beat him to the extension.

"Hi, birthday girl," he heard his father say.

"H-hello, Daddy," Gina replied, ready to burst into waves of laughter at his voice.

"Enjoying your party?"

"Well, I wish you were here."

"What?" Gary asked. "If I were, you'd want me to hide in a closet. Any boys there yet?"

"Daddy!" Gina cried with a giggle.

"Don't worry, Dad, the boys at school are too smart to—"

"Hiya, Kyle," Gary said. "What's up?"

"Nothing," Kyle replied. "But when are you coming home?"

"I don't know," Gary said. "Not tonight. It's too late to leave here. But tomorrow, I promise."

"Are you okay?" Gina asked carefully.

"Kind of," Gary lied. "I did crack my ribs, but the doctor says I'll be okay soon. I just have a bruise on the outside. But I'm okay. So enjoy that party, will you?"

"Okay, Daddy," Gina said.

Melanie was on the line now. "Gina, honey? Tell Mrs. Calder that I'll be home in a few minutes. I'm bringing a treat for everyone. How many girls are there now?"

"Eight now," Gina said, "and five more are coming."

"Good," Melanie said. "I'll see you later, sweetheart. Bye, Kyle."

"Mom?" Gina asked.

"Yes, Gina?"

"Hug Daddy for me?"

"Me, too!" Kyle put in.

"Sure," Melanie said. "Love ya."

Gina put down the receiver and jumped up and down. The party was saved! Daddy was all right, and so was her birthday! It was great!

It would have done Gary a great deal of good to see how happy his phone call had made Gina. He had fallen against his pillow after he handed the phone to Melanie. He was amazed at how cheerful he could be when every part of him hurt.

"Okay, now," Padraic O'Shean said. "You've saved your little girl's party. Lie down and rest. I'm going to give you something to help you sleep."

Gary watched the needle go into his arm and said, "I don't want those kids alone in that house."

"Gary, I wish—"

"Shh," he said, "we'll talk about it ano . . ."

He was asleep.

"What did you give him?" Melanie demanded.

"Just a sedative," O'Shean replied. "He'll need it. He's going to hurt for a while. May I walk you to the elevator?"

"Please," Melanie said.

Dr. O'Shean got right to the point. "Your husband is rather hapless, isn't he?" he said.

"I don't know," Melanie said. "I can't explain this one off as easily as the last—what should we call it, an accident? This time, there was no way anyone could have attacked him without my knowing it. I was right downstairs!"

"Don't worry," O'Shean said. "If you need help, I'm on duty all night."

"I appreciate that," Melanie said. "Really."

The elevator door slid open.

"Please," she said, "I've got to go home now."

All Gina's guests had arrived when Melanie carried two pizzas into her house and set them on the table. She was happy to see that even Gina was laughing and enjoying herself. And, like the perfect hostess, Gina asked each little girl what she wanted to drink with her pizza. She headed for the kitchen with her mother to fill the order.

"Is Daddy really all right?" Gina asked, as she poured soda into pink-and-white cups.

The question stunned Melanie. When she responded, she didn't look her daughter in the eye, for fear the little girl would know she was stretching the truth. Yes, she said, Daddy was just fine. Dr. O'Shean said so.

"Let's take these out," she said, lifting the tray of cups.

Bonnie Calder declined when offered a piece of pizza. She said goodbye to her daughter and left. Melanie suddenly wanted her to stay, but when she found herself unable to explain why, she kept silent and watched the woman close the front door.

"Let's have a séance!" she heard one of the little girls suggest from the living room.

"Yes!" someone else agreed.

Melanie stepped in the room. "No!"

"Why not, Mom?" Gina asked. "It's just fun."

"It isn't safe," Melanie said. "Who knows . . ."

"It's no big deal," Doreen interrupted. "We do it at my parties all the time."

Melanie looked at the pairs of eyes watching her and realized how ridiculous she sounded to these teenagers. So, although her fears didn't subside, she gave her consent.

"I'll be upstairs," she said. "If you happen to conjure up George Washington, let me know. I want to find out if he ever slept here."

The jokes passed over the girls' heads, and, with a sigh, Melanie left the room. Gina went over to the stereo and turned it off, handling it as if it were a priceless antique.

"I have to go to the living room to find a candle," she said.

"The candle's supposed to be black," Judy Young said when Gina returned.

"It's red," Gina answered. "That's good enough."

The table was emptied and the candle placed in its center. Carefully, Gina lit it and turned off the lights.

"Who should we call?"

"I know," Christine Haynes suggested. "Jimmy Carter!"

"He's not dead," Doreen said with a click of her tongue. "Let's try —umm—Boris Karloff. He's good and creepy."

"Yeah," Gina said. "I watch all his old movies."

"I'll do the chant," Beverly said. "Hold hands."

She breathed deeply. "Booorrrrissssss!"

Lorrie giggled.

"Shut up," Beverly snapped. "Boorrrissss!"

There was a scraping noise along the table, but none of the girls would open her eyes to inspect. A few tittered nervously, and Beverly told Lorrie to keep her hands to herself.

"I didn't touch it," Lorrie said softly.

"I know you did!"

It was Doreen who first opened her eyes to see that the candle had been moved. Then she saw, in almost slow motion, Christine's long, braided hair snake toward the flame. . . .

"Chriiissss!!" she screamed, jumping up.

Whatever happened next could not be recounted by the girls without confusion and contradiction. Gina saw Doreen—or was it Judy? —toss a half cupful of cola at the tiny flame on Christine's hair. She lifted another cup herself, and soon Christine was a sobbing, soaking mess.

Melanie burst into the room and demanded to know what had happened. Christine stared up at her, her dropped lower lip quivering. Her tears, which flowed in abundance from hurt brown eyes, mixed with the orange and brown of the soda and painted her face like a clown's.

"Gina?" Melanie asked. "What happened?"

"I just don't know, Mom," Gina admitted.

Except for the whimpering of Christine Haynes, no sound filled the room. The little girls stared around, not quite knowing what to do now. Finally, Melanie touched Christine's shoulder and led her into the kitchen to clean her up.

"Don't you worry, Christine," she said. "As soon as I get that soda wiped off your face and dress, you'll look fine."

She wasn't certain herself if there was reason for optimism. So he had harmed one of the children. God only knew what he would do later in the night. But Melanie had this little child to take care of right now. She set herself to comforting her, checking to be certain the little girl's skin hadn't been harmed. To her relief, she saw that there was no red mark on Christine's cheek and that her hair had barely been singed.

Christine burst into new tears and fell into Melanie's arms. She didn't understand what had happened to her, and she was terrified.

The kitchen door opened.

"Mrs. VanBuren?" asked Doreen.

"What?"

"I—uh—saw it all happen," Doreen said.

"You did?" Melanie asked, standing. "What did you see?"

"It kind of looked like the *wind* blew her hair at the candle," Doreen said. "I felt a really cold draft right before it happened."

"Sure," said Melanie.

He's after them. He's after them and Gary isn't home tonight. She thought about calling the police. But what could she tell them? They'd write her off as a neurotic housewife.

"Do you want to go home, honey?" she said to Christine, pushing bad thoughts from her mind.

Christine nodded. Melanie took her by the hand and led her to the telephone in the foyer. The other children were waiting in the hallway, and they immediately set about putting Christine at ease. Melanie eyed Gina for a moment, debating whether or not to send the others home. She decided against it. So much had happened to ruin the little girl's birthday that such a thing would be nothing short of cruel. No, the party would go on.

"I'm sorry, Christine," Gina was saying. "I don't get it."

"S'okay," Christine sniffled.

"It'll grow back soon," Gina went on. "I got my hair cut once and it grew back in just a few weeks."

"You only lost a tiny bit of it," Judy put in.

"Yeah," said Beverly. "You look fine."

"I do?"

"Sure," Beverly said. "Heck, you'll look terrific by the time we get to Belle Bay High. Who cares now? There aren't any boys worth impressing at St. Anne's!"

"Yeah," Lorrie said. "When we get to high school next September, you'll probably knock out the seniors!"

"Yeah?" Christine asked. She fingered her hair and began to smile at last. It wasn't so short, after all.

Melanie hung up the phone. She hadn't really heard a word the woman screamed into the phone. Her ears were sharpened for the sound of that familiar British accent.

When Christine had left, and the party started to return to its happier, pre-séance state, Melanie left the girls and headed up the stairs. At the top, she noticed the light spot where the sphinx had been torn from the banister. She placed a hand on it and, looking up to the ceiling, seethed, "Why don't you leave us alone?"

19

◆

Melanie's eyes stayed open late into the night, her ears sharp for any screams or gasps from the group sleeping downstairs. The house was still, so still that when the radiator banged suddenly, Melanie jumped, startled. It was well into the early hours of the morning when she finally found sleep.

She had a dream that night. Not the terrifying nightmare that found her opening doors, but a loving nightmare. For in fact, what Melanie was experiencing as a dream was too real. But she wasn't frightened by it—she was lost in that ecstatic state between sleep and consciousness where everything seems very slow and warm.

She was in the arms of a man, an incredibly handsome man who kissed her with a warmth and passion she had never known. When her conscience tried to remind her of her promised faith to Gary, she ignored it. This was too beautiful, too beautiful—this encounter with a fantasy lover, a lover who hadn't appeared in her dreams since the days before her affair with a man who had turned her affections from Gary. And now he was back, to comfort her when Gary had gone away from her. Where was Gary tonight when she was so, so frightened?

She felt those full lips against hers and pressed her mouth hard to them. Her fingers ran through silken hair and down over a warm, powerfully muscled neck. He spoke, in the strange whisper she had heard that night when the meeting with Helen Jennings had sent her running through the halls.

"My darling," he said. "It's almost over now. I've almost saved you."

"I love you," Melanie breathed.

"All that remains now are the children," he went on, his voice stiff with determination.

"The children are asleep," Melanie said, as if she were reminding Gary that they wouldn't be interrupted in their lovemaking.

"They shall never again harm you," the voice swore. "I shall destroy them. I shall do it soon."

Destroy? Destroy?

The word jolted Melanie to full consciousness. It was wrong—it didn't belong here in this dream of love. With a long sigh, she tried to steady her heartbeat and calm her jittering nerves. She kept her eyes closed, trying to let all thoughts pass until she felt serene again.

The bed was too hard. She could feel springs pushing through the mattress—in a mattress that had no springs.

Melanie bolted upright. Her mouth dropped open at what she saw. She wasn't in her bedroom at all. This was the attic (oh, my Lord, what am I doing here?) and she was in a small cot, with heavy wool blankets laid over her. At the bottom of the bed was a little dresser with a lit oil lamp on it. Its golden flame made the room seem warmer. It had a strange scent that reached Melanie's nostrils and reminded her that someone must have come to light it.

She threw the covers aside and stood up. So this was it—wasn't it? The *pièce de résistance*. She had been lured up here and taken advantage of in her sleep. She wondered, in a strange way, if he had enjoyed it as much as she. And she *had* enjoyed it. But right now she wanted to erase the memory of that dream forever. It was ugly. She had made love to a man who had tried to kill her husband and children—and she had enjoyed it!

"I'm so sorry," she whispered out loud, in a plea to her family. She started to say "if I had known," but the thought was cut off when she put her arms around herself for comfort.

Her hands felt the smooth coolness of silk. She looked down to find that she was no longer wearing her own flannel nightgown, but was dressed in the silk gown she had found outside her studio door that morning so long ago. The fit was almost perfect. The arms fit tight to the elbow, then belled in rows and rows of lace. The neckline was low, so low it showed a good deal of cleavage. Self-consciously, Melanie covered herself. She wanted to rip the gown off. She wanted to use it to smother the man who had dressed her in it.

"I want out of here," she said aloud, looking around at the chests and crates and old pieces of furniture. Someone had cleaned them up and set them in neat order.

She started to run toward the trap door, but was stopped by a flow of sweet, gentle music. She whirled around and caught sight of the dancing figurines on a small music box.

"I guess my walking set it off," she told herself nervously. Her voice echoed strangely in the empty room.

She went over to the music box and took it in her hands. The tiny porcelain figures were of a man dressed in knickers and a white wig and his lady, her skirts swirling as the sculpture froze them in time at the height of their breathtaking waltz.

When Melanie turned the box upside down, she read an inscription that verified everything she had believed of the haunting of this house. It told her that the existence of Jacob Armand the ghost was as real as Helen Jennings had said. And that he had a strange, fanatical purpose in all that he was doing.

"To our first month together, my Lydia. In love or death I am yours. I shall protect you, forever.

> Yours in love,
> Jacob Nicolas Armand
> April 23, 1797"

Melanie slammed the figurine down. That was it! He was haunting the house because he was keeping this vow to protect her. Hadn't he said to Melanie that he would do so? But why?

"Who do you think I am?" Melanie asked.

She had to go downstairs. She *had* to go now. She pushed boxes and crates out of her way in her haste to get to the children. They shouldn't be alone down there.

The crying in the nursery started up behind her. Melanie was ready to ignore it, thinking it was those little boys again. She didn't want to see them. But she couldn't ignore the strong smell of smoke that was coming from the room.

She picked up a wooden beam from the floor and walked into the room. She should have known it—there was no smoke in the nursery. It was quiet, exactly as she had left it the other night, with its half-burned bed and its dresser drawers pulled out. She started to back out of the room and felt something tug at her gown. She looked down to see the silk fabric around her knees pinched and folded. She tried to wrench away from the unseen hand that clutched it. That was when the child appeared to her.

"Who are you?" she demanded of the small boy who looked up at her, his eyes pleading. "Who are you?"

The tiny boy sniffled, but no tears ran from his eyes. Then, suddenly, there were no eyes. There was no face.

Melanie screamed and bolted from the room. The terror inside tightened her every muscle, slowed down her ability to run. She wanted out of here, now. She wanted Gary. Oh, God, how she wanted Gary!

She stumbled down the last steps into the hall and reached out to steady herself against the wall. She pushed the closet door shut and rolled herself along the wall until she was pressed against it. Upstairs, she could hear the faint music of the sculptured box. It had started up when she slammed the door.

I shall protect you forever. . . .

"But why?" Melanie demanded in a choked whisper. She tasted a sourness in her mouth and swallowed hard.

Protection meant hurting her husband and children. God only knew how far this sick mind would go in that promise of protection. Would he kill? Innocent children? An innocent man?

"What do you want of me?" Melanie asked. "If you love me, please leave my children and husband out of it!"

But there was no one there to respond. Melanie stood against the door like a statue, the only sign of life in her the heaving of her breasts as she breathed deeply for strength. The more time passed, the more she relaxed, until she was ready to declare it all a very bad dream, something that never happened.

But she was still wearing the silk gown. . . .

A thought occurred to her: just how long had she been upstairs? Minutes? Hours? Enough time for something terrible to happen to the . . .

Melanie didn't let the thought continue through the word *children*. Lifting the skirt of the gown (it was much too long), she ran through the hall until she came to Nancy's room. Carefully, she opened the door and walked over to the child's bed.

(*Let her be all right, please God.* . . .)

The little girl stirred in her sleep and sighed. Melanie bent to kiss her, thankful she was all right.

Kyle was sound asleep, clutching his pillow as if it were a teddy bear. Melanie kissed him, too, and covered him up again. On her way out the door, she stubbed her toe on a toy truck and sent it rolling across the floor. She stared at it, wondering if she would look at it one day and remember Kyle at age eight. But she didn't want to dwell on such morbid thoughts. She wanted to look at Kyle in the future to remember the Kyle of eight. What a beautiful child he is, she thought suddenly. A surge of love made her vow that no one would ever hurt him—or his sisters.

Melanie was on her way downstairs when a scream fractured the stillness of the night. Her walk turned into a run, and she took the steps two at a time. Her arm reached out to the doorknob of the playroom, and she wrenched open the door. It was a deafening sound, like the blast of a hundred rifles.

Inside, the girls were cuddled in terror in each other's arms. Wide eyes fixed themselves on the ceiling, ignoring Melanie. She followed them and saw the source of the noise. The balloons she had used to cover the ceiling were bursting in quick succession, as if an unseen torch were being run under them. A few of the girls covered their ears in terror at the deafening noise. Melanie was frozen to the floor.

Across the room, the cover was knocked from the stereo. Gina and Beverly ducked out of its path as it came flying toward them. Then the turntable switched on and the record was touched by the needle. The volume dial turned until the record was playing at full blast.

When she saw Gina running toward her, Melanie found her voice. "*Stop it!*" she demanded, screaming the words. "*Stop!*"

The needle came off the record player with a scratching sound that sent chills through Melanie and the children. The room was quiet once again. Then the sounds of whimpering began. Melanie hugged Gina hard, stroking her brown hair. Her daughter looked up and asked, "What's wrong here, Mommy?"

"I don't really know, sweetheart," Melanie admitted in a strained voice. "I don't know."

She looked at the young faces across the room, some stained with nervous tears, others wearing stunned expressions. She tried to comfort them.

"Strange things happen in a house this old," she began, finding the words difficult. "I—I think the room was too hot, and the radiator made the balloons burst like that. It was just that there were so many that it was so loud."

"What about the stereo?" Doreen wanted to know.

"Maybe," Melanie suggested hopefully, "someone fell against it and it started up."

Some of the girls nodded at the possibility. But others, including Gina, knew they hadn't seen anyone near the stereo at all.

But it was so much easier to accept Melanie's words.

"No one's hurt?" she asked. When the response was negative, she offered to make hot chocolate for them. But no one wanted it.

"I'll be upstairs if you need me," she said finally. "You can stay awake and talk if you want—it's already four-thirty."

Halfway up the stairs, Melanie heard the sound of her daughter's voice. She leaned over the banister and acknowledged the call. Gina looked up at her with worried doe's eyes.

"Mom," she asked, "you do know what happened, don't you?"

Without answering, Melanie shook her head and stared hard at her daughter. She knew, she thought she knew. But she didn't understand.

20

Toby Langston toddled across the grass in his back yard after the tall man. Toby had often seen him, but the child hadn't yet learned the words to tell his older brothers about it. All he could explain was that he had seen a man, but they shook their heads at him in wonder, knowing there were no men living here.

They were in the house, helping with chores. On occasion, one would look out the back door to be certain Toby wasn't into any mischief. They saw him skipping around the barn, calling to someone they couldn't see. Poor Toby! they thought. He doesn't understand that Father is gone now.

Toby walked into the barn, looking for the man. He wanted to play with him, but the man ignored him. Toby peered into the darkness and hesitated to step further inside.

"Where you go?" he demanded in a three-year-old's squeak.

Herbie, his ten-year-old brother, appeared at the barn door. Limping on a weak ankle that had been, until yesterday, encased in a plaster cast, he walked over to Toby and took him by the arm.

"Toby Langston," he said. "What are you doing in here? If Mama saw you, she'd skin you alive!"

But Toby wanted to play. He threw himself on the ground and began to kick the air, screaming all the louder when Herbie insisted he be quiet. Exasperated, Herbie pulled him to his feet and swatted him hard.

"Want man!" Toby insisted, crying from the pain of Herbie's blow.

"You be quiet or I'll use a belt on you," Herbie snapped. Since his father had died, he had assumed the role of authority, and it was wearing him down. Ten years old was much too young to bear a weight like this.

Audrey Langston looked up from the basket of laundry she had set on the kitchen table. Her eyes had no expression, and her voice was dull when she asked, "Why is Toby crying like that?"

"Oh," Herbie sighed, "he's mad because I took him out of the barn. He keeps talking about some man out there—but I didn't see anyone!"

The blank expression on Audrey's face changed momentarily, and her eyes became wide. But she quickly erased the look and sent Herbie out of the kitchen. She shoved a cookie into Toby's hand, and for a while his crying stopped.

So Toby was seeing it, too. She thought she had seen someone walking through their back yard the day Justin died, a wide smile across his dark face. But when she ran out to have him help her—to tell him Justin had fallen from a window—she found the back yard empty. There were no footprints on the soft dirt.

She passed it off as imagination, until one night she felt a strong hand on her shoulder and heard a voice say, "Fear not, for I shall not let them hurt you again."

She remembered now that she had been too terrified to cry out.

Half a year had passed since that day when she had heard Justin's scream. Audrey had tried to be both mother and father to her four sons, and the burden was taking its toll. Though she tried to be cheerful and patient, exhaustion chipped away at her nerves, making her stern and distant toward her sons. But more than that, her growing, irrational fear of the dark frayed her sanity. Each night, as she lay in bed, she wondered if she would feel that strong hand and hear that voice again.

"Toby have 'nother cookie?"

"No," Audrey said, snapping out of her daydream. "Mama's going to fix our dinner now."

When Toby started to cry, she pushed him roughly out the door and sent him to play with his brother Frank. Toby walked into the playroom, where he found his favorite brother coloring. Frank handed him a crayon and the little boy set about scribbling on the piece of old newspaper Frank gave him.

He held the crayon in his fist and began to scratch circles and lines. Finally, he pushed it toward his brother and said, "Man looks like that?"

"What man, Toby?" Frank asked, leaning closer to study the picture. He clicked his tongue. "That's not a man! He's got a pony tail! Men have short hair like you and me."

"My man has a pony tail," Toby insisted.

"Well, okay," Frank consented. "If you want him to. Say, Tobe—why don't you draw a picture for Mommy?"

With a smile, Toby tackled another sheet of newspaper and drew a lopsided flower. Frank wrote his name across the bottom and told his little brother to put it on Mama's plate at dinner.

"It will make her smile," he explained.

And it did. Audrey picked up the drawing and grinned broadly, then leaned over and kissed Toby on his jelly-stained cheek. He giggled. Soon his brothers joined in, and Audrey, who couldn't be sad when her children acted this way, started to laugh merrily.

She even read to them before they went to bed that night. She kissed them gently, hugging each little body to her. Even Justin Jr., who hated to be coddled, did not protest when she leaned toward him with a goodnight kiss.

For several hours, the boys slept quietly, filled with content. But later in the night, that content was broken, and Audrey woke to the sound of her children's screams. She ran from the room, not stopping to put on a robe or slippers. To her horror, she saw that smoke was gushing out of the linen closet.

She yanked the fire extinguisher from its holder and started to climb the stairs, squinting against the stinging smoke. But her feet would not make contact with the steps.

She moved her hands through the space in front of her and felt nothing. When she thrust her hands out sideways, her fingers touched the ragged edges of what had once been a set of shelves cut like stairs to lead up into the attic. They had been smashed to bits.

The screams went on upstairs, tearing at her. A thick curl of smoke seeped into the closet, grabbing her by the throat. Without wasting a moment, Audrey ran out of the closet to go to the cellar for a ladder. Even down there, in the remotest part of the house, she could hear the screams of terror.

She tore the wooden ladder from the pegs that held it up, keeping her eyes on what was straight ahead of her. She was too afraid to turn around—there might be something waiting for her in the darkness of the basement.

If the ladder was heavy, Audrey was too intent on getting to her children to notice. She slammed the ladder against the shelves and, tearing the extinguisher from its holder, climbed to the top.

"Oh, my Lord," she prayed, "let me get to my boys—please, oh God, just do this for me!"

The smoke was so thick that she could barely make out the door to the boys' room. The horror of this moment made her remember the argument she and her husband had had when he chose this location for the nursery.

She had argued that it was unsafe for four little boys to sleep up here. And now her fears had come to pass, and her husband was not there to make things right.

A prayer began to run through her mind: *Now and at the hour of our death, now and at the hour . . .*

She groped toward the door. Just a few feet away from it (she could see the tiny faces now), her foot caught on a beam that had fallen across the floor, and she stumbled to the ground. Her head smashed against the wooden floor, cutting off her senses.

Herbie caught sight of the extinguisher, rolling out of her hand, and braved the flames to get to it. The sound of his sobs increased as he ran from the room, beating at the flames on his pajamas. He had never used an extinguisher before, but that fact didn't stop him. He aimed it at the fire and shot the white foam, trying not to look at Justin Jr. Why was he staring like that?

Something pushed hard against his back, sending him stomach-first onto the blazing mattress. The extinguisher flew from his hands, its hose spurting wildly.

The very last thing he saw was a man, dressed in a strange costume, lifting his mother in his arms. The man fell to his knees and threw back his head with a loud, triumphal laugh.

"She is saved!" he screamed insanely. "She is saved!"

*   *   *

He kept her in her room for days, undisturbed by calling neighbors. Since school was closed for summer vacation, no one called to find out where the boys were. And few people contacted Audrey Langston, a quiet, shy woman who kept to herself.

She woke once, and he touched a glass of wine to her lips. She drank, sucking in the liquid as if it were a life-giving nectar. Nothing mattered to her. Nothing.

He lay in the bed next to her, in his most human form, and held her in his arms, stroking her hair. To Jacob Armand, this was the moment he had pined for over the past two hundred years. He had his beloved again. He kissed her and caressed her, and in her delirium Audrey found his body warm and comforting. She didn't care about Justin any more. She had found another man to love.

But one morning, her mind came back to her.

She awoke, alone. The sun was beating through the windows and the air was already humid. Audrey lay there for a few moments, lost in a limbo where nothing could reach her—from either side of her mind.

Then she was fully awake, feeling as if she had slept on and off through a rough night. She thought she had to get up and fix break-fast for the boys, who must be bickering with each other over the morning paper by now. Audrey rolled out of bed, not aware that she had been lying there for days.

He came up from behind her and put a strong arm around her shoulders. He bent to kiss her neck, whispering of his love. But Audrey was no longer his love. She swung around, abruptly putting up her arms to defend herself. She stared into the handsome face and gasped.

"Who are you?" she demanded, her voice shrill.

"Fear not, my love . . ." he started to say, moving to pull her into the folds of his cape.

Audrey struggled to get free and ran from the kitchen. Her boys! Why weren't they down here? She ran up the stairs, crying out for them. But the only answer was silence.

Audrey pulled open the door to the linen closet, and at the moment she saw its interior, her mouth dropped in a soundless scream. As her eyes took in the broken shelves and the soot-covered towels that had fallen to the floor, it all came back to her—every moment of that terrifying night.

She fell forward against the splintered shelves and held fast to them, a long scream thrusting from her lungs.

"*Oh my Gooooooodddddddd!!*"

She ran from the house in her robe and slippers, screaming and ranting. She had to get to the Jennings' house. . . .

21

———◆———

Melanie sat before a microfilm projector at the library, carefully turning forward the filmstrips of Belle Bay's newspaper. To her left, she had stacked up a pile of reels that had proved worthless, evidence of her hours of sitting here. Since eight-thirty, when Janice had opened early for her, she had been studying these pages.

She set this spool aside, then wound another, and another—until her wrist stopped suddenly to freeze an image that had come up on the screen. She looked at the headline, then down at the picture beneath it—a photograph of four little boys. Calling to Kyle to send for Janice, she sat mesmerized.

"Melanie, what's up?" Janice asked, following Kyle into the reference room.

"I've found something," Melanie said, pointing to the screen. "I've had a recurring—" she paused for the right word—"nightmare, where I see little boys dying in a fire up in our attic. I'm sure that's a picture of the same children."

"It couldn't be!" Janice said, bending to take a closer look.

"Read the headline, Janice."

"Four Boys Die in Mystery Fire," Janice read. She advanced the film and went on. "A mysterious fire took the lives of four young boys here in Belle Bay some time earlier this week. Due to an extreme case of shock, Mrs. Justin Langston, mother of the children, could not be reached for comment. The Langston children, who lived at Starbine Court Road,"—Janice looked at Melanie with wide eyes—"ranged in age from three to ten. Terence, nicknamed Toby,

Francis, Herbert, and Justin Jr. shared an attic bedroom. An anonymous source reported that Mrs. Langston's husband died from a fall this past winter."

"You don't have to go on," Melanie said. She wiped her fingers over her eyes. "I've known for a long time there was something evil in that house. Janice, how could I have imagined those boys when I had no idea until today that they even existed?"

"I don't really know," Janice admitted. "What do you think this means?"

"It has something to do with the first owner of our house," Melanie said thoughtfully. "With Jacob Armand. I think I've come in contact with him a few times."

"I read you, Melanie," Janice said. "Are you saying the place is haunted? What fun!"

Melanie's startled look was almost a glare.

"Well, it isn't fun," Janice said quickly, realizing her mistake. "But it is interesting. I usually don't go for those things, but if you look at all the weird things going on in your house, well . . ."

"I want to tell Gary about those boys," Melanie said. "Will you come over tonight and back me up?"

"Do you think he'll be willing to listen to all this just after he's out of the hospital again?"

"The sooner the better," was Melanie's reply. "And I'm going to tell him something else—that no matter what goes on in that place, I'm going to fight it. It's our house and I want to keep it!"

"Bravo, Melanie," Janice said, giving one quick clap of her hands. "I'm glad to see you're not giving in to the pressure. Sure, I'll come over tonight."

Kyle was tugging at Melanie's sleeve.

"It's time to go get Dad," he reminded her. He was already in his coat.

A few minutes later, Melanie walked out the glass doors with her two youngest children. They picked Gina up at a friend's house, then drove in silence to meet Gary at the hospital. Even talkative Kyle, reading his mother's solemn mood, kept quiet.

The checkout was quick, all papers were scribble-signed, and Gary leaned lightly on Melanie to walk out the door. She noticed his hands rubbing where his chest had been bruised. Her eyes told him it was all right to talk about his pain, but he said nothing. When they had driven some five minutes, he pointed to a small store and said:

"Pull over there, Melanie. I want to get the paper."

He slid out of the car, turning his head so that Melanie couldn't see his grimace, ignoring her offer to get it for him. "It" turned out to be one copy of every paper in the store. He tossed them onto the seat and climbed into the car.

"Gary?" Melanie asked.

"We're moving," was the simple reply. "I'm sick and tired of that place. I'm going to spend the next week looking for another house."

"But I like our house!" Kyle cried.

"Shhh," Melanie said, pulling up the driveway. "The decision is between your father and me."

Inside, Gary carried the papers into the house and spread them out over a table in the library. His finger ran up and down columns in a smooth motion, until it stopped and tapped one small box.

"Here," he said. "6 rms, bath, ¼ acre. It's in Garden City."

"Six rooms!" Melanie cried. "Why don't we just move back to the city? No way am I going to live in six rooms with three kids! Gary, we're going to give this a fight. We have to! It's our home—not his! And don't argue with me about that. I've got proof something is strange about this place."

"So do I," Gary said. "And it's all I need to want out."

"But Gary," Melanie pressed, "I'm beginning to understand things now. I think I know what we're fighting."

"Melanie . . ."

"No, Gary," she said quietly.

He looked up from the paper, surprised. So the roles were reversed. He was ready to run scared, and Melanie had stopped running. He could tell by the look in her eyes that she loved this house and that it would take hell to move her from it.

"I was down at the library today," she said. "Looking through microfilms of the town paper. Do you remember those little boys in the attic that I saw a few weeks ago—when you thought I was dreaming? They existed, Gary. I saw a picture of them. They died in a fire up there forty-odd years ago."

"It's just those things that make me want to get out of here damned fast," Gary said. "After the things I've seen in these past weeks, I don't need to hear that my children may be murdered."

"Not if I read my ghosts right," Melanie said. "I don't quite know what I mean by this, but I think Jacob Armand has some strange feeling of love for me. I think he might be jealous of you and the kids, and that's why he's trying to drive you out. But if I can communicate with him, I think I can end it. Gary, I'll say it again: this is *our* house, and I'm going to fight to keep it!"

Gary knew there was no use fighting her. She was steadfast in her belief, and damn it all, she was right. The best he could do was cooperate, to make sure nothing else went wrong. But he did not know that there would be no time to make plans and dream up a line of defense against the evil in his home.

22

The snow was falling lightly when Janice drove up the hill to the VanBuren house. The silence of this late November night was somehow calming, easing the tension she felt. There was something eerie and chilling about going to a man's house to testify that a ghost existed there, when she herself hardly believed it.

She could see flecks of snow falling into the beams of her headlights. A dark form blocked the whiteness with its massive shape, and Janice leaned on her horn. The figure didn't quicken its pace—but turned for a brief moment to look in her direction. Janice gasped when she caught a glimpse of the face she had seen the night Tony DiMagi was murdered.

"It's him," she whispered.

He moved out of the headlight beam and into the darkness of the woods. Janice brought the car to a full stop and climbed out, all the while telling herself she should really speed up to the front door and scream like crazy. But Janice was too excited by this moment of terror to run away from it.

The man was no longer on the road, but she guessed his footprints would be some distance ahead. If she hurried, she could find them before they were covered. She ducked her head against the snow and walked forward, looking for tracks. There were none.

"How do you like that?" Janice said aloud. Her breath formed tiny clouds, and her body gave one hard shudder.

A gathering of clouds moved in front of the moon, and the roadway was suddenly very dark. Janice had left the headlights on, and she moved quickly in their direction. Behind her, a dead branch fell from a tree, and she turned on her heels with a gasp. In the shadows, the limb was twisted in a shape that grotesquely resembled a human form. She quickened her pace to the car.

She put her fingers around the handle and pulled at it, swinging the door just far enough to let her slide inside. But as she stooped to get in, something pulled her away, and she fell clumsily into the snow. The car door slammed shut, and Janice saw her automobile slowly lose its traction.

"Hey!" she cried, jumping to her feet as it quickened its pace down the hill.

There was no use running after it. She looked around, half expecting to see that tall man again. She moved a step forward, and then another . . .

. . . and then she was running wildly toward the house. Why did it seem so damned far away? If she cried out, would anyone hear her?

She wheezed as she ran, years of smoking taking its toll. But Janice was too frightened to pay attention to the pain in her chest. A shadow blocked her vision suddenly, and she veered into the woods just in time to avoid the outstretched hands.

She didn't turn when she heard the sound of her car as it crashed at the bottom of the hill. She ran back toward the road, knowing it was the safest and quickest way to make her escape. Up ahead, a light suddenly came on in the upstairs. They had heard the crash! They would be out in a second or two to check it out!

But there was little time for relief. Janice felt something tug at the fur of her jacket. She turned, her arm raised to strike, and in the bright light of the moon she saw his face for the first time. She dropped her arm and gasped in awe. He was the handsomest man she had ever seen in her life.

"Oh . . ."

There was something in those eyes that began to drain whatever will power she possessed. They were so solemn, filled with centuries of pain. Janice could feel something happening to her under their spell, yet she could not make a move to run away. His fingers moved to encircle her neck. Even through her thick scarf, she could feel their iciness. Something was happening. . . .

He drew her up close to him, his cape falling around her. She breathed deeply and closed her eyes, lost in a hellish ecstasy. He pulled her close, still clinging to her neck, and moved to kiss her. She did not protest. But before his lips touched hers, he pulled abruptly away and tightened his fingers.

"You're not my Lydia."

When he said this, Janice snapped out of her spell. She was immediately struck with the realization that she was about to become a victim like Tony, and she had to think quickly to get out of it. If she knew his name . . . it was a biblical one, she remembered. Something very romantic. Jason—Joshua—Jae—Jae . . .

"*Ja*COB!" she cried out suddenly.

The grip around her neck loosened. His hands fell to her arms and he held her fast, staring at her with those sad eyes.

"Jacob," Janice said again, softly.

The eyes fixed themselves on her in that draining way. She felt herself being drawn inside him, being pulled with such a force that she couldn't fight against it. She was losing herself in that passion again, overcome by his mysterious sensuality. She no longer felt his cold.

"Jacob Armand," she breathed, hearing a voice that sounded far away. "I want to help you."

*   *   *

Gina leaned closer to her mirror and studied the freckled face that stared back at her. So this was what it was like to be thirteen? She certainly didn't feel any different. For all the change in her, she might as well still be twelve. She studied her childish figure, wishing she had Doreen's build. Lucky kid, Gina thought. She isn't flat like I am.

She stood up and walked over to her desk, where she turned on her radio to the sound of Christmas carols. Christmas! Gina threw herself on her bed and thought of the holiday. Just then, a crashing noise reached her bedroom from somewhere outside. But she ignored it, too wrapped in her thoughts.

A while later, her thoughts were again interrupted, this time by the sound of tapping at her window. Was it the tree outside, swaying? Or perhaps the snow had turned to sleet. She watched the glass and saw a handful of pebbles come flying at it. She went to the window to investigate.

At first she saw nothing, then she looked down to see Janice standing in the snow, signaling for her to open the window. Gina twisted the latch and gave the window a hard push. As it scraped over the sill, a fluff of snow fell to the ground.

"Hi, Janice!" Gina cried, leaning out.

"Shh!" Janice hissed, bringing a finger up to her lips. Gina noticed she wasn't wearing gloves.

"What's up?" she asked.

"Uhm," Janice said, taking a step backward in the snow. She looked uncomfortable. "I brought a welcome-home gift for your father!"

"Should I get Mom?"

"No!" Janice cried, in an almost frantic tone. "No, don't do that. It's a surprise for her, too. Can you come down and help me carry it inside?"

"Sure," Gina said. "Be right there!"

She pulled the window back in place and clicked the lock shut. Then she sneaked downstairs to the kitchen, where she pulled on her coat. No one saw her leave the house. She slipped out the back door and felt the snow crunch under her feet. It was covered by a thin layer of ice.

Gina walked to where Janice had been, but no one was there. Of course, Janice had already gone to her car! Her footprints were in the snow. Gina put her feet down next to them, measuring her stride to match Janice's.

She had taken three steps like this when someone grabbed her from behind. She felt a heavy arm around her, and struggled to turn around. She stared up into a face she had never seen before, a hard, cruel face. Her thoughts screamed for her.

DDDDAAAAADDDDDDEEEEEE! ! ! !

The man, his eyes cold, flung his cape around her and pulled her close to his body. Gina felt her legs give way and was barely conscious when he lifted her into his arms and headed into the woods.

23

◆

The kids were giggling about something. The sound of their laughter had waked Gary, and he sat on the edge of his bed with his head in his hands. He looked through the weave of his fingers at the clock and jumped to his feet. He had been sleeping for *hours.*

His ears sharpened to the sounds coming from downstairs. He heard the dishwasher starting up, then Melanie calling to the children to settle down. Kyle's cheerful voice announced they were playing "Wild Kingdom" with Gina's new kangaroo. It was nice to hear them laughing. It made him think Melanie was really right about staying in this house.

He walked out of the room to head downstairs for a late dinner. When he reached the stairs, he instinctively reached out his hand to pat the sphinx. His hand touched the air, and he remembered what had happened to the statue.

He was halfway down when he heard the doorbell ring, then the sound of Melanie greeting Janice. With a shake of his head, he went back upstairs to watch TV in Kyle's room. He was in no mood to socialize. He even turned up the volume when he found he could hear Janice's voice.

Downstairs, Melanie was listening with amazement as Janice told of her car's mishap. The two walked into the living room and sat across from each other. Melanie tried to remember when she had seen her friend look like this. She was positively *forlorn.* That gorgeous blonde hair, usually swishing cleanly over her shoulders, had been drawn up sloppily in a knit hat and wet strands hung around her face. When Janice raised her hands to brush them away, Melanie looked with dismay at the lobster-red skin.

"You lost your gloves," she said.

"Yes," Janice said. "Guess I dropped them when I was running after my car."

She leaned against the back of the chair. "I thought I saw one of your kids walking up the hill, so I stopped the car and got out to offer her a ride."

"It wasn't one of ours," Melanie said. "They aren't allowed out after dark."

"Well," Janice said with a laugh, "it really wasn't anybody. My eyes were playing tricks on me. Some trick! Next thing I knew, my car was rolling down the hill!"

"Funny," Melanie commented. "I didn't hear any crash."

"I did, for sure," Janice said with a frown. "It's in a heap in front of a telephone pole."

They sat in silence for a few moments. Melanie brought her legs up and tucked them under her, feeling uneasy in Janice's presence. No matter how cheerfully Janice spoke, there was something in those eyes that was out of character—something very frightening. Melanie started to ask her about it.

"Janice . . ."

"Melanie," Janice said distantly. "I saw him tonight."

"Who?"

"I understand him now, as you would if you had listened to him. I know everything now."

"Janice, I don't understand," Melanie said softly, though the rapid beating of her heart told her exactly what Janice meant.

"He tried to recapture what he had lost that day," Janice went on. "And every time, he failed. But he won't fail again, for I have given myself to his service."

"Janice, who are you talking about?" Melanie demanded.

"Jacob Armand."

The reply was a scream. Janice was on her feet and moving toward the couch where Melanie sat. Melanie brought her legs closer to her body, like an armadillo wrapping itself for protection. Janice came over and sat beside her. Melanie didn't move, except to pull a throw pillow to her chest.

"In 1797," Janice said, "Jacob witnessed the execution of the only woman he had ever loved."

"Lydia?" Melanie asked, recalling the music box.

"Lydia Browning," Janice said. "She had been married to a merchant, and she had two little daughters. Jacob told me that her husband was a cruel man."

She spoke of Jacob as if he were a longtime friend. As if he were still alive. Melanie felt her skin creep.

"He met her in the market one day," Janice continued. "There was an ugly bruise under her eye, where her husband had hit her. Jacob offered to take her home to give her a salve for it, and she accepted."

"Then they fell in love?" Melanie asked.

"Yes," Janice replied. She closed her eyes in thought. "For weeks they met secretly at his house, at *this* house. He even had a room made for her."

"The room with the four-poster bed," Melanie put in.

"Then her husband heard of their meetings," Janice went on, ignoring Melanie. "He deeply hated the British, and when he heard of his wife's lover's nationality, his anger at her sharpened to a hateful edge. He had her brought to trial for adultery and threw in a charge of witchcraft. Do you know what that beast did? He made the two daughters testify against Lydia!"

"But what about Jacob?" Melanie asked. "Wasn't he brought to trial?"

"He wishes he had been," Janice said. "But he brought a good deal of money into the town when he decided to live there, and the people were more ready to forgive him than to give up having him as a patron for their shops.

"He did *try* to save her," she went on in a low voice, "by bribing the jury. But they took his money and found her guilty anyway. He had been tricked, and there was nothing he could do about it."

Janice's eyes were slits now, and her cold hand reached out to latch onto Melanie's leg. She heaved her shoulders once and clenched her teeth with bitterness. She was feeling for Jacob Armand.

"They found her guilty," she said again. "They put a rope around her and dragged her along the streets. He was there—he saw it all. And he couldn't stop it! Do you know what it's like to see someone you love dragged like a dog along a dirt road? Can you imagine what it's like to see the mouth you had once so lovingly kissed fill with dirt and pebbles? She had nearly choked to death before they propped her against the stake."

"Oh!"

"She screamed for mercy," Janice said, "but they turned a deaf ear to her. They were in the mood for a good execution that day—the burning of a witch adulteress. Jacob told me they had trouble starting the fire because of the mist rolling in from the bay."

"It happened on the beach?" Melanie asked.

"Yes," Janice answered. "The salt water sprayed them as the flames went up around her. It took only a few minutes. Jacob stayed after the crowd had gone home. He broke off a piece of her fingerbone to keep it with him, always."

"That explains why our ghost is so unhappy," Melanie said. Janice's hands, still clinging to her leg, had begun to turn frostbite gray. "But I still don't see what it has to do with us. I mean, that happened so long ago!"

"Do you think a memory dies when a body dies?" Janice demanded. "When Jacob died, his heart was loaded with guilt. He couldn't live with the memory of what had happened to Lydia, something he couldn't—didn't—prevent. He's carried that burden for nearly two hundred years."

"But we weren't there when it happened," Melanie protested. "Why should he take out his problems on us?"

The graying hands tightened. "Don't you understand, Melanie? In you he sees Lydia Browning. In Gary, her husband. And in your children, hers. He needs to defend you against Gary and the children, because he thinks they're out to send you to the same fate as Lydia's!"

"That's just ridiculous," Melanie insisted.

"Is it?" Janice asked, her voice husky. "Can you really say that after everything that's happened in this house? *You* are the cause of his anger. Each family that ever lived here experienced the same things. Each time a woman moved in, he saw his Lydia, and the obsession to save her drives him to want to destroy her family."

"But can't anyone make him understand what he's doing is wrong?"

"It isn't wrong," Janice snapped. "It's very right. He loves with a great passion. He loves you!"

"He loves what he thinks I am!" Melanie cried.

The women were standing now, staring at each other. Melanie was unable to understand why Jacob tormented her family. Why didn't he take out his revenge on those who really killed his Lydia?

"The children in the attic," she said then.

"Bastards," Janice spat. "They've been trying to warn you. He set their nursery on fire to save another Lydia—the Audrey Langston we read about on the microfilm. He almost had what he wanted then. He had her in his arms. Do you know ghosts can cry? I swear there were tears in his eyes when he spoke of her. They carted her off in a straitjacket. She had gone crazy when she found her sons' bodies."

"He killed her little boys," Melanie said, shaking her head. "And he says he loved her?"

"Burned them," Janice reminded her. Her head cocked to one side, and she smiled sweetly. "Children burn sooo easily. He's going to kill yours tonight."

Melanie's fear was suddenly overcome by anger. This was insanity! Before her stood the personification of evil in her home. She threw herself at Janice with a growl, lashing her hand out, catching tiny bits of flesh in her fingernails.

She picked up an ashtray and swung it forward, with an animal-like cry. Janice fell to the floor, throwing up her arms in defense. Melanie struck her again and again, her anger making her blind to the blood that flowed from the temple of the girl she had once called her best friend.

"No! No! No!" she screamed with each blow. "I won't let him have my children."

24

Something was tugging at her arm. Melanie stood staring at Janice's unconscious form, the ashtray dangling from her fingers. The tugging became more firm, and a voice reached her mind from very far away. She dropped to her knees and touched Janice's forehead, feeling the stickiness of blood on the blue, swelling skin.

That voice was persistent. Melanie looked toward it and saw a child. A little boy—the little boy she had seen in the attic? He was screaming at her, his blue eyes moist. She didn't want him here. She pushed . . .

"Mommy!" Kyle cried, sprawling backward. He steadied himself and went back to her.

"Please, Mommy!" he yelled, wondering if she could hear him. "You hafta come upstairs!"

"Oh, Janice," Melanie whispered. "I don't know why I did that!"

"Mommy," Kyle pressed, "Daddy's acting funny!"

He was so confused. Why had Mommy knocked Janice down? Why wouldn't she talk to him? Worst of all, he couldn't comprehend the strange scene he and his younger sister had just left upstairs. It had looked as if their father was fighting something—but there was nothing there. Kyle needed his mother to help, but she was in a daze.

Nancy started to wail and joined Kyle in pulling at their mother. At last, Melanie snapped out of it and stared in confusion at the two. Then she touched her swimming head and said softly, "Kyle, honey, don't look. Nancy, don't look at this."

"Come upstairs, Mommy," Nancy said. "Daddy's doing funny things."

(*Funny things—mime? comical? clown?*)

The two children took each of her hands and led her up the stairs. Melanie heard the crashing noises now, coming from her studio, and the sounds of two angry male voices. When the three reached the studio, Melanie gasped to see Gary go flying against the portrait of Nancy and Gina, breaking its wooden frame in half with his weight. She let go of the children and ran to him.

"Leave him alone!" she screamed at someone the children couldn't see.

Gary looked at her with eyes that spoke of fright and pain. He opened his mouth to cry out to her, revealing blood-stained teeth. His lower lip had swollen to twice its size.

"Dear God," Melanie whispered, choking on her tears. "Please help him! Please make Jacob Armand stop!"

But Jacob Armand would not stop. Suddenly, Gary let out a gurgling scream that spattered blood from his mouth and sprawled backward with a violence that sent him crashing through the window. Melanie caught her breath, watching the diamond-shaped pieces of glass fly, hearing the sound of metal reverberating as her husband hit the trash cans on the ground below.

But there was no time to stand here in shock. She turned quickly and grabbed the children, leading them from the room.

"Where's Gina?" she demanded.

"I don't know, Mommy," Kyle said tearfully, tightening his grip on her hand.

Melanie ran down the hallway to the child's room, but found it empty. She screamed her daughter's name through the halls, hearing nothing in reply. Did he have her already? Was Gina dead? *Oh God, oh God.*

It's happening to us, she thought frantically. He's destroying my family and I can't stop him! Just like the Langstons . . .

"GIIINNNAAAA! ! ! !"

Nancy reacted to her mother's frenzy and buried her face in the folds of her skirt. Melanie was frantic. The child wasn't up here. Where should she look next in this enormous house? She had to get to Gary. She had to find Gina soon, before Gary . . .

(*Don't think of that!*)

She knelt down to Kyle and kissed him on the forehead.

"My baby," she said. "I want you to do something for me. Can you run outside *really* fast and see if Daddy needs help?"

Kyle nodded. "I'm scared, Mom."

Melanie pulled him close and hugged him, kissing his curled hair.

"Please, Kyle," she said. "I'm going to try to find Gina down-stairs."

Kyle mumbled something about the "crazy night" they were hav-ing and ran from the room. His mother called out that he shouldn't speak to anyone out there. If he saw someone, he was to come back inside, *immediately*. In the kitchen, Kyle pulled on his coat and boots and, without bothering to buckle them, went out the door.

An iciness shot through him as he walked toward the trash cans. His daddy was lying there, twisted strangely, one arm hung over a metal can. A leg was so misshapen it seemed not to be part of Gary's body. It bent over his back and touched a toe against his neck.

"Dad?" Kyle whispered cautiously. His father didn't look—*real*.

He had seen firemen on his favorite TV show lift a man's arm when they wanted to see if he was alive. Kyle did the same, but it told him nothing.

He bolted to his feet and ran away from his father, stooping over to vomit in the snow. He was crying now, tasting the bitter bile that had gushed over his tongue. He was frightened, but he had to look again. He had to see if his father was all right.

He looked down at the snow, at his footprints that covered the ground. And at another set. He stepped inside them, finding his feet were only an inch smaller. He knew at once to whom they belonged and started to run toward the house. Gina had been out here!

He stumbled into the kitchen, falling down on the newly waxed floor in his haste. As he pulled himself to his feet, he heard someone come into the room, and looked up to see Janice Lors, leaning heav-ily against the door jamb. Her long blonde hair hung in strings around her face, spotted and streaked with blood that dripped from her forehead. Kyle backed away from her, his childish instinct telling him she wasn't to be trusted.

"Kyle," Janice said, licking her lips. She laughed—a drunken laugh that chilled the little boy. "Kyle, let me help you."

"Go away!" he cried. "*Mommy!*"

"Aww, c'mon Kylie," Janice drawled. "You know I'm a nice lady. I've got someone I want you to meet. He's a *real* nice man. . . ."

"*Mommy!*"

"He just *loves* little boys like you."

For every step she took, Kyle took one away from her, until he was against the sink. Carefully, his arm sought the utensil drawer. His fingers grabbed at it, and he pulled it open. Even as Janice watched him, moving closer, his hand pulled out a knife and pointed a gleaming blade straight at her.

"*Mommy!*" he screamed again.

"Don't you cry for your mommy!" Janice snapped. "She's crazy! She hurt me, see?"

She was getting too close. Kyle didn't want to hurt her, he was afraid of the knife, but he had to defend himself. She looked as if she meant to kill him with those outstretched hands.

"Coooommme oooonnnn, you naughty boy," Janice singsonged. "Give Auntie Janice the nasty widdle knife."

"Go away!" Kyle warned.

Then she was so close he could feel her breath. Without thinking, he lashed out at her. The tip of the blade caught her just above her right breast. Janice looked down at the two tiny droplets of blood on her blouse and let out a monstrous scream. She gnashed her teeth and knocked the knife from the boy's hand. Her hands grabbed his upper arms, and she pulled him up close to her face.

"You vile beast!" she hissed. "You've been spoiled too long. I'm going to bring you to that man. Jacob will see that you don't turn your mother in to the authorities again. He'll see that she's saved this time!"

Kyle kicked her hard. "Let go of me! *Mommy!*"

"Calling your mother," Janice said, in a disbelieving tone, "so you can turn against her again, so you can call her witch? No, my dear brat!"

Kyle struggled and spit in her face. Hissing in anger, Janice grabbed his arm and dragged him to a chair. She sat down and threw him over her lap.

"You need to be taught a lesson," she said hoarsely. Her voice was deep, not her own. "Yes, to tame you once and for all!

"Jacob, I am helping to save her!" she screamed. "You deserve worse punishment than this, piglet. You deserve to die as your mother did!"

Kyle tried to get up, but Janice's hand was too firm against his back. He wasn't afraid of being hit, but he was afraid she might do something worse. Her hand raised high in the air . . .

. . . but stayed there. Janice felt something cold and round against the back of her neck. She didn't move.

"I have a gun on you," she heard Melanie say. "If you lay one finger on him, I'll kill you."

"You don't understand," Janice insisted. "The children want to have you executed!"

"You're out of your mind, Janice," Melanie said. "He's got you under some kind of power. Can't you see that?"

"No power," Janice insisted. "I do this on my own. Let him destroy the children and save you. Let him love you Melanie. Mela-melydia. Lydia! Lydia!"

Kyle felt a momentary lull in her grip and jumped off her lap.

"I saw Gina's footprints in the snow," he said. "She's out there somewhere. I don't know if Daddy's . . ."

"Shh," Melanie whispered. She still held the gun to Janice's head. "Where's my child, Janice?"

"It's too late now, Lydia," Janice replied, the insane giggle spitting from her lips again. "He's taken her down to the beach. She should be honored. He's going to kill her on the very spot where they executed you that first time. Oh, yes, Lydia, the child should be honored."

Janice suddenly jumped at Melanie. In a reflex reaction, Melanie swung the gun out and struck her, hard enough to knock the life from her. Janice's body sagged to the floor, catching the chair.

Melanie was trembling. It wasn't fear—it was fierce determination. She was suddenly filled with the instinct common to so many animals, the need to protect her young. There was no time for fear and crying now.

Quickly, she handed Nancy a coat and pulled on her own. She helped the little girl buckle her boots, but when the three ran from the house, her own feet wore nothing but house slippers.

They weren't alone, Melanie knew. He was watching from somewhere. But she also knew that as long as the children were in her sight, they were safe. She took one look at her husband and felt a cry choke her.

No, don't do that! If there's any hope to save Gina . . .

But she couldn't resist a short prayer.

"Oh, Lord, please help her! Please help my Gary, too!"

Then she turned and walked quickly into the woods. The trees loomed above them, some naked, some with pine needles covering them. Their branches looked like arms ready to grab.

It seemed as if time were endless. The walk was long, longer than it had seemed the day they had gone down to the beach for a picnic. She scooped Nancy up into her arms and started to walk-run. When they reached the beach at last, the three of them were breathless.

The snowy, icy sand clicked under their feet. The bay was silent, stretching black and forever. Against its horizon, Melanie caught sight of her daughter, several hundred feet away. She was leaning against a pole. But when Melanie got closer, she saw that Gina wasn't standing at all. She was tied to the pole!

And around her feet was a pile of dried wood chips.

25

"Can you believe this, Tony? Two inches of snow on the ground and it's only Novem—"

Jack Hughes sank about three inches into his car seat. Damn, he thought, cringing, he'd done it again. That made the fifth time this week. He'd have to face facts: Tony was *dead*. And no amount of hoping would ever bring back his talkative, smiling partner.

But Jack Hughes still hoped. He thought: if I turn right now, Tony will be sitting next to me. And he'll have his hat pushed back like always. And he'll be . . .

"Are you going crazy, Jack?" he asked himself. "Are you so damned obsessed with Tony that you think he's still alive?"

He'd have to stop talking to someone who wasn't there. And he'd have to stop going to the VanBuren house every chance he got. Lord only knew what Davis would do if he found out he'd been here.

"Just once more," he vowed. "Just tonight, and if I don't find anything, I'll give up."

He started to sing "White Christmas," hating the silence. Some Christmas it would be, without Tony.

He turned off the main road and drove slowly toward Starbine Court Road. The clusters of people shopping for Christmas thinned out, until he was alone. In this section of town, where the Van-Burens lived, there were few people and no stores.

Up the hill, he could see that magnificent white house—and the grounds that had kept his mind in their power for days on end. The VanBurens obviously had money, he thought.

Tony had once made a comment that he'd love to be so rich he could buy the place. But nobody really wanted to live there. Every-one would gasp about how beautiful it was, but even the ones who could afford it refused to live there. There was some story behind the place. He had heard it once when he was much, much younger, when he had first come to this town. Something about the place being haunted. But Jack Hughes just thought it was a bunch of bull. Give anyone an enormous old house and he'll write the spook story of the decade.

But Tony had still been charmed by the place. Hughes remem-bered how his younger partner saw the good in everything. He had even said one day, "Wouldn't it be nice, Jack, to live and die in a place like that?"

It was ironic, Hughes thought, but Tony had gotten his wish, in part. He had never lived there, but dying there was easy. Hughes bit his lip. He was crying again.

He turned off his lights as he approached the house. The moon was behind a cloud now, and just about the only things visible were the house and snow, both stark white against the total darkness. He stopped the car some hundred yards away and got out, ready with his flashlight.

It was cold. The quilted blue jacket he wore did its best to keep him warm, but its best wasn't good enough. Hughes sneezed, still feeling the aftereffects of his flu.

He heard a metallic noise from the side of the house. Trash cans, he told himself, rolling in the wind. But when he moved closer, he found it wasn't the trash cans at all. It was the back door, opening and slamming in the wind.

He hesitated, wondering if someone would catch him sneaking

about these premises when he was specifically warned not to do so, then pushed the back door tightly closed. With the cessation of the noise from the slamming, the night was suddenly very still. Still enough for Hughes to pick up the sound of an animal whining. Making terrible noises.

A picture of the putrefied cat suddenly came up too clearly in Hughes' mind. He shook his head to clear it, then took a few steps toward the sound. He saw an arm flung over a trash can, hugging it as if it were a capsized boat. His fingers moved to touch his gun.

"My God," he whispered when he saw Gary. "Can you hear me?"

Gary's eyes fluttered. "Uuuhhh."

"Okay, take it easy," Hughes said quickly. "Just don't move, and I'll get an ambulance."

Hughes took off his jacket and tucked it around Gary's shivering body. He could see the bare hands and the feet going gray with frostbite.

"Mel . . ."

"I'll find Melanie," Hughes said, thinking he understood.

"Nnnnoo!"

Gary's cry stopped Hughes midway up the stairs to the kitchen door. He turned and saw the man trying to struggle to his feet, finding his feet quite unwilling. Hughes ran down to him and wrestled him back to the ground.

"Just stay put," he said firmly. "You might be hurt worse than you think. Don't make it worse!"

"Mel-a-nie . . ."

"I'll get Melanie!" Hughes promised.

Gary settled again. Hughes looked down to see that he had fainted. He got to his feet again and went into the kitchen, wondering out loud where in the heck Melanie was and why she hadn't found her husband. How long had he been out there?

The kitchen light was on. Hughes took in the opened utensil drawer, the knife (blood on the tip, he noted) on the floor.

And a lump on the floor like a woman's body.

Hughes walked over to it, his breath caught. He expected to see Melanie lying there, the leg of an overturned chair pulling up the back of her sweater.

Had something finally come of his obsession, he wondered? Had the bastard who killed Tony come back again to finish off witnesses?

He stooped down and carefully touched the mat of bloodied blonde hair at the back of the woman's neck. He was on his feet in a flash when he saw the ashen face of Janice Lors. He walked into the hallway in search of a phone and found one at the bottom of the stairs. Something made him recall what Janice had said the day after Tony was killed—that the phones had been dead in here. He let out a sigh of relief when he heard the dial tone.

"Captain Davis?" he said when his officer answered. "Hughes here. Look, I'm down at the VanBuren house. I *know* I wasn't supposed to be here! But I am, sir. There's been some bad trouble. I'll need backup and an ambulance. I found Mr. VanBuren outside— looks like he fell out a window. And the Lors woman, too. I can't find the wife and kids—I'll need a search party."

When he hung up, he started to call out names. But there was no one in the house to hear him. Where in the hell were Melanie and the children, he thought? Were they hiding somewhere?

He found the bloodied ashtray in the living room, where Melanie had dropped it on the rug. A cushion that had been pulled from the couch sat too near the fire, still burning, and Hughes moved it as carefully as he could, without changing the actual scene in the room. He had a feeling there was much more here than he could see.

He heard the ambulance coming up the road and went out to meet Davis. Once his captain had heard the story, he set about assigning people their duties. Two young paramedics tended to Gary, moving with an efficiency that Hughes could only admire. Of the three remaining officers, two were sent out into the woods and one accompanied Jack Hughes and Bryan Davis into the kitchen.

"You didn't see Melanie and the children anywhere?" Davis asked, crouching down to get a better look at Janice.

"No, sir," Hughes told him. "The house seems undisturbed, except for the living room. There's evidence of a struggle in there. I found an ashtray with blood on it—I think it might have been used to hit her. I haven't been upstairs yet."

"Get on it, Towers," Davis said to the younger cop who had come inside with them.

"Tear the place apart!" Davis yelled after Towers. "They may be hiding somewhere, scared to death! And keep near your gun; we might have some nut on our hands!"

He and Hughes walked back outside and examined the grounds. When a slight wind brought the smell of Kyle's sickness to them, neither man grimaced. They had experienced worse. And they were too interested in the strange footprints they found in the snow.

"I would guess these belong to Melanie and the kids," Hughes said, pointing to the sets of prints, two small and one large. "But I don't know what happened to the third one."

"If she's in the house," Davis said, "Towers will find her."

Hughes walked further around the house, keeping his eyes to the ground. Then he called to Davis, seeing a row of a dozen or so footprints that stopped—*just stopped*—dead in the middle of the snow.

"The other child," Davis said knowingly. "It looks as if she were picked up about here. See the way the snow is fluttered—as if it'd been kicked?"

"But where's the footprints of whoever did the picking up?" Hughes asked. Davis shook his head.

"Chief," Hughes said, after a long silence, "I think we ought to get another team out here. It might take us all night to find them."

26

◆

If they had turned at that moment, they would have seen a bright flash of light shoot up from the mile-away beach. It was a flame that had leaped to devour the stake Gina had been tied to only seconds earlier. Now, the little girl was being squeezed tightly in Melanie's arms. Melanie closed her eyes and sighed with relief, rocking the semiconscious child.

Thank God, thank God . . .

The knot had been tied carefully, but Melanie had worked quickly and patiently as the flames began to crackle at her feet and a bodiless voice roared at her. By the time the knot gave way, her freezing fingers were bleeding. But she had gotten her daughter safely in her arms before any harm at all was done. For the time being, Gina was safe.

She watched the flames now, trying to push from her mind the thought that if she had been a few seconds late . . .

In one hand she held the gun, but she knew it would do little to help her tonight. She debated throwing it away, but decided to keep it. It would be her security blanket. When she heard the cries again, her finger moved to the trigger. Still holding Gina, and feeling Kyle and Nancy clutching at her, she began to cry out in anger.

"Just leave my kids alone, you son of a bitch! Just because you screwed up your life you have to take it out on innocent people? You couldn't make things right when your Lydia died, so you have to hurt little children? You *coward!*"

His cries became louder, sounding as if he were standing very near to her. When she felt his touch, she shrugged it off roughly and tightened her grip on the children.

"You *bastard!*"

"Nnnnnoooooooo ! ! !"

"You didn't like that, did you?" she asked, smiling. "Did you, coward?"

"Nnnnnooooo! !"

"COWARD!"

"Lydia, my love—what lies have they told you?"

"I am not your Lydia!"

"Why do you turn against me now?" he whimpered. Though Melanie could not see him, she could imagine the look on his face— pouting, ugly.

"Leave us alone," Melanie said darkly.

"Know you not the danger?" he asked, appearing to her in a hazy form that did not reveal his features.

Melanie spat at him, and he roared, dropping to his knees. He began to howl, rocking back and forth. He slammed a massless fist against the snow. Then he was gone again.

There was dead silence. Melanie didn't dare move from her place, watching the beach in front of her. Where was he now? And now? He could easily move anywhere he wanted within seconds, couldn't he? Couldn't ghosts do that, she asked herself?

Without warning, Gina was tugged away from her. The shock brought her daughter to complete consciousness, and the little girl began to scream in terror, not understanding why she was being jerked back and forth by nothing.

"I shan't let them hurt you again, my Lydia!" he cried. "I-shan't-let-them-my-Lydia!"

"Can't I make you understand?" Melanie cried, rushing desperately toward her daughter. "I am *not* your Lydia! Lydia is dead! She's *dead!*"

But Jacob Armand wouldn't understand. He thought his Lydia was under the spell of these three children. Angered that he couldn't persuade her, he threw the child he held across the sand. Her head struck a piece of driftwood that jutted like a broken bone through the sand and snow. There! The daughter was gone, and the father. The younger two would be easiest. *Samantha and Sarah Browning. Two evil-wench children. Sarah so dirty she looked like a little boy* . . .

"Mommy, I want to go home!"

Nancy's pitiful cry snapped Melanie from her staring spell. Was that Gina—her beautiful Gina—all crumpled on the snow? Was she alive? Was she alive?

"Oh, God," Melanie whimpered. "Oh, God—my baby!"

But Nancy and Kyle needed her now. Melanie lifted her little daughter in her arms and started to run up the beach. If she had lost her husband and her oldest child, she still had to protect her youngest. The shock of the insanity of this night was cushioning her mind against the terror of realizing what really had happened to Gary and Gina.

(*Let it be a mistake.* . . .)

"Just try to get them from me," she snarled as she ran along the sand and snow. "Just try, you bastard!"

He was standing in front of her in his most solid form. Melanie did not hesitate to look him straight in the eyes, challenging him to dare to pull the children from her arms. Though he was grimacing in anger, his features were still breathtaking, but Melanie was so filled with hatred that she wasn't taken in as Janice had been. He stepped toward her, his eyes reflecting his purpose. He said firmly, "You mustn't trust them, my Lydia. Come with me now!"

"*Stop calling me that!*" Melanie snapped.

She turned from him and stumbled up into the woods. She couldn't hear him behind her, and it frightened her. She couldn't fight what she couldn't see. And Nancy was so heavy!

"Kyle," she said breathlessly. "Run as fast as you can. *Hide* somewhere! Mommy's right behind you!"

The little boy picked up his speed and shot forward. Still grasping Nancy, Melanie followed as closely as she could, until she lost traction in the snow. She fell backward, Nancy on top of her. The little girl rolled off and the two helped each other up. But when they were standing again, Kyle was gone. Completely.

"*Kyle?*" Melanie cried.

No answer came.

"*Kyle, answer me! ! !*"

But the night was silent. Had her child already reached the house? But it was a half mile away! On a straight path! Kyle couldn't have run that fast!

"*Kyle, where are you?*"

"Hey!"

The voice that answered her was masculine, but not young. It wasn't Kyle, but it wasn't Jacob Armand either. Gary? Could it be Gary? *Oh, please, God, let him be unhurt!*

"Hey!" the voice called again, closer now. It was Jack Hughes. Melanie didn't stop to ask him where he came from.

"Did you see my little boy?" she asked.

Hughes shook his head. "What's going on here?"

"Please find him," Melanie implored, ignoring the man's question. "That maniac's killed my husband and my dau-dau—"

She fell to her knees, the terror of the night finally reaching her. As Nancy hugged her neck, her body shook with great sobs. Nancy cried with her.

"Mrs. VanBuren," Hughes said gently. "Your husband is alive."

Melanie looked up.

"Please, did you see the man who hurt him?" Hughes asked.

Melanie nodded.

"Was he armed?"

"He's a ghost," she said quickly.

Hughes looked at her strangely, then pulled his walkie-talkie out.

The captain was summoned, and in minutes he arrived with Towers. When he heard what had happened, he told the younger cop to take Nancy back up to the house and to find Kyle. Two other policemen arrived in a few moments and were sent to join the search for the little boy. And if they spotted the suspect, they were to take him alive.

"I want to have the pleasure of seeing him suffer," he explained. "As much as you, Jack."

"I was right about this," Hughes said softly. Before Davis could agree, he said, "The woman is hysterical, sir. She says he's a ghost."

"That would explain his knack for disappearing, wouldn't it?" Davis replied, not meaning it as a joke. "Let's get a move on here. We'll find him tonight."

"I hope I get him, sir," Hughes said, anger in his voice.

They heard a shot fired some distance ahead and were running to it before it had time to echo. Frank Croyens was pointing to a clearing in the woods with his gun. He had just seen a tall, caped figure run through the trees. Hughes caught Davis' eyes, and the story Janice Lors had reported was brought back to them.

"It's him," Hughes said softly.

Melanie, who had followed them here, suddenly broke into a run, heading toward the beach. The policemen followed, their guns drawn. But Melanie was as confused by her action as they were. She had no idea what made her suddenly rush toward the bay, but when she arrived, she saw her daughter standing up. Gina was rubbing the bump on her head, crying. Croyens rushed to the little girl's aid. But before he reached her, something struck him from behind and he hit the sand in a dead faint. Stunned, Hughes and Davis looked around for the assailant.

"*Nnnnooooo! ! !*"

The cry was a horrid, dragging sound. Jacob Armand was here again, Melanie knew. But Hughes and Davis saw nothing. They watched Gina running to her mother, then saw her stop in midflight, as if someone had grabbed her. They watched, unmoving, as she screamed and flailed her arms through the icy, empty air.

Davis shot his pistol in the air, but the child's unseen tormentor did not let go. Gina began to gasp, her face bloating like an overripe tomato. Hughes rushed forward and grabbed her, pulling with all his might. She fell, limp in his arms, and he laid her on the sand. He began mouth-to-mouth resuscitation.

"*She must die!*"

Someone was trying to tear him away. But he fought, hard, to save this little girl's life. Somehow, Hughes felt that saving one life would make up for the loss of Tony DiMagi. He wouldn't let the bastard who had killed his partner have a child too.

Something like a foot connected with his head, and Davis saw a string of blood trickle from Hughes' head. Down the beach, Croyens had picked himself up, and he limped to his captain.

"Who hit me?" he asked.

"I don't know, damn it," Davis admitted. "You okay? Get up to the house and help Towers find the little boy."

Jacob Armand had stopped his fighting for only an instant to study this situation. Why wasn't the girl dead? What was this man doing to her, and why didn't he fear what he couldn't see?

"Aaaaaahhhhhhh!"

Davis looked around. Hughes kept working with Gina, pressing his mouth to hers, listening for her breath. Davis clicked on his walkie-talkie.

"Towers?"

The airwaves crackled.

"Do you know what that was?"

"Negative, sir," Towers answered. "It came from down there."

Jacob was desperate now. He hadn't believed the children could possibly deceive him again, as they had done every time he had tried to save his Lydia. These were the men who would see her burn! He had to stop them!

He grabbed at the back of Hughes' jacket and pulled with an unnatural strength. The little girl beneath them opened her eyes and blinked a few times at the men standing over her. Two men. Three . . .

Both Hughes and Davis tried to pull him away but suddenly found themselves grabbing at empty air. The man who had been there only a split second earlier had completely vanished. Gina kicked up at nothing, her cries mixed with her efforts to breathe. He was strangling her.

At that moment, another voice cried out. It was Melanie, who had stood watching the scene in terrified silence. She walked toward her struggling child, an angry look set on her face.

"Stop it, Jacob Armand," she insisted.

"No!" the bodiless voice shot back. "She must die so that you may live!"

"Stop it now!" Melanie screamed.

"She must die! She must die, my Lydia! ! ! !"

"I! AM! NOT! YOUR! LYDIA! ! !"

He started to screech viciously. And then, hell came to the night. . . .

27

It began with the sound of faraway voices, a muffled noise that Melanie had, so many weeks ago, blamed on a hissing radiator. No one had noticed it at first, so occupied with Jacob Armand were they. But now the beach was so quiet that the sounds could be plainly heard.

It was like the sounds at a crowded party—definitely voices, but unintelligible because each utterance masked another. Here and there, one would hit a loud intonation, and a full word or phrase could be understood.

"Armand!" a woman's voice cried.

"To hell with Armand!" bellowed an unseen man.

"Revenge! Revenge!"

Mumbling. Then more voices. Davis and Hughes moved carefully forward, alert to spot anyone who might come leaping from behind one of the large rocks on the beach. Melanie had taken the now-conscious Gina in her arms. She bit her lip to steady its quivering.

"Who's out there?" Davis called. "Come out—the game's over!"

He shot his pistol once into the air, but the voices did not cease. Instead, they grew ever louder and closer. Davis and Hughes looked at each other and knew the thoughts in each other's minds. There was something very wrong here—more wrong than anything either man had encountered in all their years as cops. It was something they couldn't deal with, and they began to empathize with each other's helplessness.

Jacob Armand had started screaming again. But they were no longer the cries of anger and determination. This time, he screamed for help. It seemed as if he were in terrible trouble.

"*Help me! Don't let them hurt me! Oooohhhh please!*"

"Who was that?" Davis cried. "Come out where we can see you!" But he already knew no one was hiding from him.

"To hell!"

It was a child's voice this time! Shadows appeared to the living humans. A flash here, a man with his fist raised—then a cluster, so much like a group of children. Faces in the ghostly crowd became visible for fleeting moments. Melanie gasped to see Helen Jennings among them. The woman looked over to her and smiled with an eerie sweetness.

She saw the four boys, the massless forms shifting from wholeness to the hideous state of their deaths. A man was with them—the father? His head lolled from side to side on a deformed neck. His opened mouth roared the name of Jacob Armand.

They were all visible now, moving straight forward on feet that left no marks in the snow. There were some fifteen of them—almost half were children. Jesse Prentice was there, with her infant son in her arms. The child's head was still wreathed in the seaweed that had caught him at the bottom of the bay.

"We shall send him back to hell!" a man cried.

"*To hell! To hell! To hell! To—!*"

The cries took on such fervor that they soon became one massive noise. The crowd moved ahead.

Jacob appeared again, no longer standing tall and proud, but hunched over and pleading mercy. He knew he was finished. His victims had at last arisen to send him back to the hell he had avoided for nearly two hundred years. He tried to find safety with Melanie.

He threw himself to his knees and buried his face in Melanie's coat. Startled, Melanie did not attempt to pull away from him. But her grip around her daughter tightened.

"Don't let them hurt me, my Lydia!" he moaned. "I only wanted to save you!"

"But I'm not your Lydia," Melanie said again, softly now. "Nor was Audrey Langston, or any of the other women here. The people you killed were innocent victims of your need for revenge."

The words Melanie spoke set the crowd into a new fervor, and the chant was taken up again:

"To hell! To hell! To hell!"

"*Stop it!*"

The scream came from Melanie's lips. The crowd turned their glazed eyes to her. Feeling a trembling starting inside her, Melanie took in a deep breath and tried to reason with them.

"I can't stop you from doing what you feel is necessary," she said. "But I don't believe you're doing the right thing. Jacob Armand is guilty—*yes*—but only of being insane. He's mad! But what does it make you if you destroy him? Doesn't it reduce you to his evil level?"

"We must have revenge!" a little girl cried.

"And I want this finished!" Melanie cried angrily. "I'm sick of the things that have happened to my family! I want to be guaranteed they won't ever happen again! Who will promise me Jacob Armand won't find his way out of hell to come back and hurt us again? My God—look at my daughter! She's just a child! I don't want her to suffer like this!"

"We *shall* end it, my dear," Helen insisted. "Now move away from him. Let us have him, and it will be over!"

"To hell! To hell!"

Helen stepped closer. A few yards away, Hughes grabbed his captain's arm and pointed to Tony DiMagi. The cop turned around at the sound of their astonished calls and smiled a deadly smile.

But Helen wasn't smiling. She moved closer to Melanie, until her cold hand touched the young woman's face. Melanie was in a state of shock now, not understanding the words she had just spoken, but not afraid. She didn't back away when Helen stroked her cheek.

"My dear girl," she cooed, "there is only one way to deal with him. He must be sent to hell, to the punishment he deserves. Now, dear, we don't want to hurt you—you've done nothing to us. But don't try to stop us."

"Save me, my Lydia, oooohhh!" Jacob whined. "I don't want to be hurt by them!"

The crowd had had enough. Jacob was wrenched from Melanie's side and dragged down the beach. He was beaten—his massless body struck again and again by equally massless fists. Bloodless veins gushed red. Shapeless mouths screamed.

They disappeared, but the cries were still full on the wind. Jacob Armand pleading his innocence. That terrible chant: "To hell! To hell!"

Hughes and Davis ran to Melanie.

"She's in shock, sir," Hughes said, snapping his fingers in front of her eyes. They did not blink.

"I'm near to it myself," Davis admitted. "Come on, let's get these two back up to the house."

"What about them?" Hughes asked, looking down at the now-empty beach.

"It isn't for us to handle," Davis said. He lifted Melanie into his arms.

She was dead weight, in spite of her small frame. Her arms hung limply, her eyes still staring. If not for the slight rise and fall of her chest, Davis would have thought she was dead.

Then her eyes blinked once. Melanie's arm shot backward, striking Davis so hard that he was forced to drop her. Before she could be stopped, she was running down to the beach.

The two policemen blinked in disbelief. As Melanie ran screaming down to the bay, her clothes seemed to vary from a dress to a gown, at times so briefly that they seemed to blend. Her hair went from blonde to dark, dark to blonde.

"What the hell is this?" Hughes whispered, holding Gina tightly.

Melanie was no longer there. In her place stood a young girl. Melanie VanBuren had become one with Lydia Browning.

Jacob Armand's lover had waited these years, as the women of her day had waited for their men to return from the sea. She did not understand his cruel deeds, but she did not question them. He was a man—and she had been taught not to question men.

But he needed her now, and she could not let her prudish upbringing keep her from him. She cried out his name and ran to him, toward a crowd that was once again visible. Jacob straightened himself at the sound of her voice and turned swiftly to face her, his great height knocking down the two men who held him. The two lovers ran and embraced each other. Their whimpering over the joy of finding each other was like the sound of animals. For the moment, the crowd left them alone.

Jacob closed his eyes and ran his fingers through Lydia's curls. He buried his face in their softness, shaking his head. Lydia threw back her head and let out a cry.

"You were so different these times," Jacob whispered.

"No, my darling Jacob," Lydia said. "I have always been the same. I have always waited for you."

Jacob bent to press his lips of nothing to hers. But the ghostly kiss was brief, for Jacob was suddenly ripped from her arms. Two brawny men held him fast and started to drag him away again. A little child began to chant (to hell! to hell!) and Toby Langston giggled in evil delight as the crowd pushed forward. Jesse Prentice's baby screeched.

"You cannot have her now!" Helen said.

"Yes," Justin Langston agreed. "This child is not for hell."

Jacob struggled.

"Please, oh please!" Lydia begged. She moved toward them in a motion so smooth it seemed she was made of liquid. Her arms, Melanie's arms, reached out.

"I only did it to save you, my Lydia," Jacob whimpered.

"Then *I* am the cause of this!" Lydia insisted. "You must punish *me*, not my Jacob! Oh, mercy, not my Jacob!"

Helen Jennings smiled at her. She knew what this woman wanted. And if it meant getting it, Lydia Browning was willing to burn in hell with her lover. That they would do, she thought. That they would do.

"Stay with him then, child," Helen said. "Not for his sake, but for yours."

"Why should he win his prize after his deeds?" a man wanted to know.

"I feel it is best," Helen insisted.

"Silence, woman," the man shot back. "Only a man could know what is best!"

Helen let out a wail. "I lived longer than any of you!" she cried. "And I was the most recent to die! You must understand me—if

Jacob is kept from his Lydia, he will come back! He'll destroy more like us!"

"Lydia!" Jacob moaned.

The young woman threw herself at Jacob. And as she did so, her spirit passed from Melanie's body, giving back its form. Melanie watched the scene in a daze, seeing, not seeing. Helen Jennings reached out and stroked her cheek with a cold hand.

"He shall not bother you again, my darling," she promised. "It is in our hands now."

Melanie was suddenly alone, staring down at the water at her feet.

Hughes snapped from a disbelieving stupor to see Davis running down to Melanie. He caught her just before she collapsed.

"I was dreaming," she whispered.

"Yes," Davis said. He took her gently by the arm and led her to the others. "Jack, get that little girl up to the ambulance."

"I want to stay with my mother," Gina said.

"We'll go up together," Hughes said.

"Where's Kyle?" Melanie demanded. "Did you find him?"

"Right here, ma'am," someone behind her said. She turned to see Kyle, his face streaked with tears, in the arms of one of the policemen.

"Where were you, my baby?" she asked, pulling him close to her.

"I hid up a tree," Kyle answered, a choke in his voice. "I was so scared when I looked back and couldn't see you any more! I just closed my eyes and got so scared!"

"I heard him crying up there," Towers said.

It was Melanie's turn to cry now—an insane sobbing mixed with wild laughter, muffled into the plush of Kyle's jacket. She had talked to a ghost, ha! ha! She had talked to a lot of ghosts!

"Gary?" her face went straight again.

"He's already at the hospital," Davis said. "We'll take you to him now. Towers, take them up to the house."

Hughes was staring down the beach, thinking hard. He had solved his mystery, and he knew Tony lived forever. He would no longer weep for him.

Towers escorted Melanie and Gina back up to the house. Hughes and Davis stood on the beach, not speaking, not knowing what to say. At last, Davis leaned his head back and let out a long sigh.

"When I get home," he said, "I'm going to drown myself in Bud."

"Ditto," Jack Hughes promised himself.

"I might even retire," Davis said thoughtfully.

"You're kidding?"

"Of course," Davis answered.

Hughes shifted on his feet. "How're we going to write this up?"

"We aren't," Davis said. Catching the surprised look in Hughes' eyes, he said, "Look, Jack, if we did, everyone in Belle Bay would treat us like madmen. This town would go crazy! Be realistic, Jack— who would believe a story like this?"

"Then what about Janice Lors?" Hughes demanded. "Who killed her?"

"Janice Lors," Davis said carefully. "Janice Lors was killed by a man who later set himself on fire down at that pole. It's charred, see? That's proof enough. And there'll be a promotion for every man here tonight who can remember that."

"But, sir," Hughes pressed. "When they make the investigation, they won't find any human ashes!"

"Of course not," Davis said, reaching out a hand to catch the bits of snow that were falling. "That's a damned strong wind blowing out to the bay, isn't it?"

Epilogue

◆

Gary would walk again, with a bad limp. The children were just fine—by some miracle, there was no sign of frostbite. Their natural resiliency would heal the trauma of the night before. Melanie, knowing it was over and that her family was safe again, would adjust to a normal life in a short time.

"I hope I'm not in here too long," Gary said, feeling cheerful in spite of his body cast. "How can I train a dog in this getup?"

"We don't have a dog," Melanie said, thinking her husband was delirious.

"We'll get one," Gary said, winking at his oldest daughter, who sat with her brother and sister at the foot of his bed. "I promised Gina, didn't I?"

"A puppy!" Gina squealed. Nancy and Kyle began to bounce up and down, laughing with delight.

Soon they were all laughing. They laughed because they were certain life in their new home would be as it should always have been. But there would only be a short time for that laughter. Their lives would just be settling down to normal when the evil of the house would rise again—in the hateful, disturbed form of Janice Lors.

Ghost House
Revenge

———◆———

Prologue

---◆---

Summer, 1975

The little girl clung to her father's hand, feeling a warmth that made her happy and secure. It was a beautiful afternoon to be seven years old, and Alicen Miller was very happy. Her father smiled down at her, seeing the anticipation in her brown eyes. She was such a cheerful little girl!

They were standing on a corner, a block away from their apartment building, watching the cars that sped down the highway. Alicen and Derek were looking for one car in particular, a blue sedan that belonged to Alicen's mother, Elaine. She had spent the last week in Maryland, attending the funeral of her only relative, Alicen's great-aunt. Both Derek and Alicen missed her terribly.

"Now, listen," Derek said. "Mommy might still be very sad, losing her aunt like that. After all, your great-aunt practically raised her. Now all she has are you and me."

"I'll be extra-special nice to her," the little girl said in a sing-song tone.

Just then, they spotted Elaine's car. Alicen jumped up and down, waving excitedly. Derek raised his arm to wave, too, but he never completed the gesture.

There was another car behind Elaine's, about thirty yards away. It was weaving erratically across the highway and coming up on Elaine's car—fast, too fast.

Desperately, Derek tried to signal her off the road. Reading his gestures, Elaine looked up into her rear-view mirror and saw the car behind her. Quickly she tried to turn out of its path, but it was too late. There was a loud crash, a screech of tires, and a scream.

Elaine's car flew over a road divider, tumbling down a deep embankment. Derek felt his legs pull him forward. His arms stretched out as if he could grab his wife and save her.

"Elaine!"

This couldn't really be happening. . . .

Derek's legs gave way from under him as Elaine's car went up in flames, and he fell to the sidewalk. His mouth dropped open, and his palms pressed hard against the warm sidewalk as he gazed at the inferno. He vaguely heard sirens, barely registered the sight of the fire trucks and water-gushing hoses. He was too busy watching the fire and praying.

Please let it be a mistake. Please don't let it be Elaine.

He pulled himself up onto his feet, his legs as heavy as tree trunks. Derek hardly felt the sidewalk underneath him as he walked toward the car. He heard humming in his ears—was it the whispers of the curious bystanders or the shouts of the paramedics? Or maybe it was the hacksaw they were using to get Elaine's door open.

That's not my wife, he thought.

Two hoses at last managed to still the flames enough for firemen to get inside the car and pull out Elaine. Or what was left of her. What had once been a beautiful woman was now a blackened mass. Not a woman. Not his Elaine.

Then he noticed the blackened hand. On one finger was a diamond ring—the ring Derek had given Elaine the day he had asked her to marry him.

He threw back his head and screamed. And then he felt a small, cool hand in his. He looked down and to his horror saw his little daughter standing at his side, staring at the flame-engulfed car.

"Oh, my God," he whispered.

He grabbed Alicen into his arms and turned her away from the sight, hugging her tightly as if to protect her. If only someone would protect him . . .

He heard laughter. Sweet, childish laughter that rose above the sirens and screams. It was Alicen's laughter.

"Oh, daddy," she said, "I made a mistake. Mommy isn't coming home today at all. She's coming home later on."

She's in shock, Derek thought. Thank God she's being spared from all this. Thank God we both don't have to suffer.

"Mommy will come home when she's ready," Alicen said. "When she wants to see me again, mommy will come for me."

1

———◆———

When the noon sun struck the mansion at the top of Starbine Court Road, its whiteness seemed to glow like a holy vestment, and anyone seeing it might have thought: "There is a good, beautiful old house." And on this April Saturday, it seemed everything *was* good about the 185-year-old structure. Nothing set it apart from dozens of other Long Island mansions. Its large front porch faced the town of Belle Bay. Magenta azalea bushes ran from either side of the wooden steps to the rounded towers at its sides. These towers, added over a hundred years after the original Colonial mansion was built, made the house all the more breathtaking.

But those who had the powers to see beyond pretty flowers and inviting front porches would have known the house harbored a terrifying evil and that those who lived within its walls faced unspeakable dangers.

For now, though, all was well. Behind the house, two children were working on a corner of the back yard, which stretched for an acre to the thick woodlands that surrounded the house on three sides. Kyle and Gina VanBuren tugged hard at weeds and dug up rocks in preparation for a spring garden. Kyle found a fat grub and dangled it in front of his sister's nose.

"Daddy, make him stop!" Gina cried, her mouth turning down in a grimace.

Their father looked up from the legal papers he was reading. Kyle was giggling, but he had put the worm down again. Gary smiled at him.

"You're a rip, Kyle," he said. "Be nice to your sister."

Gina decided the incident had been funny after all and started to laugh. Both children rolled around merrily on the newly cut grass. Gary grinned at them, forgetting his work long enough to watch them play. He felt a surge of love for his two oldest children and decided that in the long run it had been a good idea to move from the city into this house. They would have to put last year out of their minds. It was over, and now it was time to enjoy their new home.

Gary looked up at the house. Although the front was somewhat gingerbready, the back was more true to the original Colonial style. His eyes roamed proudly across the back of the house. Suddenly they stopped at one particular window, which stood out because of its modern construction. The odd window brought back memories that made Gary shudder, and he forced them out of his mind. He quickly raised his eyes higher.

The weather vane at the peak of the roof needed straightening, he thought. Someone would have to come and fix the whole roof. The shingles were all curling up at the edges. Gary sighed to think that less than a year ago, he could have been the one to climb up there and do the job. But that was impossible now. He couldn't even climb stairs.

Gary looked down at his legs, muscular after so many painful hours of exercise, and yet useless. His fingers wrapped around the arms of his wheelchair. He'd been confined to it for four torturous months, ever since an—*intruder*—had pushed him out of that hated upstairs window. That November night, when he had become a cripple, had been so horrible that he and his family never talked of it.

He shivered, then pushed the accident from his mind and went back to his paper work. Gary refused to let the wheelchair hinder him. Maybe he couldn't go to his office in the city, but he wasn't about to give up on the law practice he had had for fifteen years. He had arranged with his partner to have all paper work sent to the house. Clients were handled over the phone and were invited to the house to discuss divorce settlements in his upstairs office. But he still longed to get back to his Manhattan office.

Well, Gary thought, sighing, that was impossible right now. As part of his rehabilitation program, he had to go to physical therapy sessions four days a week at a distant medical center. Gary worked himself hard and amazed the doctors by his progress. His bones were mended by now, and they said he would soon be able to walk on crutches. Nothing would make him happier.

"Daddy," Gina said, interrupting his thoughts, "would you hold the bag open for us?"

"Sure," Gary said.

He closed his briefcase. Lad, the Weimaraner puppy at his feet, jumped up from his nap, and Gary patted the puppy's smooth, silver-brown head, then unlatched the brake of his chair. He wheeled himself toward the children. "When's Mom coming home, anyway?" Kyle asked, obviously hungry for lunch.

"In a while," Gary said, looking at his watch. "It's just noon now."

Gina had something else on her mind as she filled the plastic bag with debris. "Daddy, the school glee club is singing next Wednesday afternoon," she said. "Can you come?"

"Oh, honey, I'm sorry," Gary said. "I have therapy that day. I can't miss it."

"It's okay," Gina mumbled, though it was clear she was disappointed. A moment later she looked up and asked, "Do you mind going to the hospital so much?"

"I'd much rather jog on the beach," Gary said, playfully flicking the long dark braid that hung down his thirteen-year-old's back. "But therapy helps me, and the sooner I get out of this wheelchair the better."

Having finished cleaning up the debris, Kyle put a twist tie on the bag and carried it to the barn. Gary couldn't help smiling to see the grim expression on his son's face. Though he was barely nine, Kyle was already a go-getter who considered no job too big. God bless my kids, Gary thought. They make it so much easier.

As Kyle turned back to the house, he saw someone move past the bay window of the dining room. She stopped, and through the lace curtains Kyle made out her blond hair. He waved. She did not wave back.

"Mom's home!" he cried, racing toward the house. Lad ran after him, barking and wagging his tail.

Gary, wondering why he hadn't heard his wife's car, wheeled himself around the side of the house. The driveway was empty. For a few moments he stared in confusion at the strip of gravel.

"Hi, honey!" someone cried.

Gary jumped a little when an arm wrapped around him from behind and a kiss landed on top of his head. He turned so abruptly that his wife, Melanie, backed away from him.

"I'm sorry," she said. "I didn't mean to startle you."

"It's okay," Gary said. "I was lost in thought. Where's the car?"

"You wouldn't believe the trouble it's been giving me. It stalled three times this morning, and then it died completely down on Houston Street. Nancy and I had to walk up the hill."

"I'm glad you were close to home," Gary said.

"Well," Melanie said, shrugging it off, "the station wagon's an old car. It was bound to start giving us trouble some time."

"We'll have the garage check her over," Gary said. "Tell them to do a complete overhaul. I don't want my wife driving a dangerous car."

With that, he reached out and slid his hand around Melanie's small waist, pulling her onto his lap. Before she could protest, his fingers weaved through her hair and squeezed the back of her neck. He brought her face to his and kissed her warmly.

"Love you," he said.

"I love you, Gary," Melanie replied. "Now, let me up. I'm much too heavy for you."

Gary snarled playfully but let her go. He wouldn't admit that under the weight of her body pain had shot through his legs. No less a man because of his wheelchair, Gary winked up at his wife.

"Never mind, Romeo," Melanie said, turning him around. She pushed the chair toward the ramp. "I know that look in your eyes, but I've got three hungry kids in the house and a car full of groceries down the road."

In the kitchen Melanie poured Gary a glass of beer, then steered Kyle and Gina out to help fetch the abandoned groceries. Gary grinned at his five-year-old, Nancy, who sat on the floor playing imaginary games with a stuffed yellow rabbit. "You've got a mustache, daddy," she said, pointing a chubby finger.

Gary erased the offending stripe of foam with the back of his hand. Then he opened his arms, and Nancy ran to him.

"I want a ride!" she squealed, wriggling onto his lap.

Gary laughed, kissing her golden curls. He wheeled the chair toward the kitchen door, into the dining room and down the hallway.

Nancy laughed with delight, trying to touch each brass doorknob as they raced past. Neither Gary nor his daughter knew they were being watched by a pair of malevolent eyes. A beautiful young woman stared at them, her heart almost set aflame with desire to destroy their happiness and their lives.

On Monday Melanie dropped Nancy off at kindergarten, then headed toward the medical center with Gary. She hummed softly as she drove, enjoying the scenery.

"Long Island is so beautiful in the spring," she commented. "I'm so glad we moved here from the city."

Gary mumbled a reply, staring out the window. He was thinking how much he hated these long drives. In truth, he hated them less than the fact that he himself was not doing the driving. Melanie recognized his frustration and tried to cheer him up.

"Dr. Norton says you're doing remarkably well," she said. "Pretty soon you'll be able to stop coming here."

"Nothing would make me happier," Gary said.

At the clinic Gary was greeted by his doctor, a middle-aged woman with a perpetually sunny disposition.

"My colleagues and I had a meeting about you this morning," she said. "We're all very impressed by the progress you've made. Looks like you'll be out of this wheelchair in a few weeks, Gary. And there isn't anything you're doing here that couldn't be done at home, under the care of a private therapist."

Gary smiled broadly and said excitedly, "When do I start?"

Dr. Norton laughed. "Next week, possibly. I know a fine therapist who is available. His name is Derek Miller, and I recommend him highly."

"Then he's the one," Gary said. "Uh, what sort of setup will it be? Does he live near Belle Bay?"

"He's from New Jersey," Dr. Norton said. "I'm sure he could find an apartment near your house."

"When we've got lots of extra bedrooms? He'd be welcome to stay with us."

"I haven't finished telling you about him," she cautioned.

"Why would I have any objections?"

"Because Derek hasn't done private work in three years," Dr. Norton said. "You see, he's a widower with a teen-age daughter. If you were to board Derek, you'd have to take in Alicen, too."

"That's okay," Gary said. "There's nothing wrong with the kid, is there?"

"No, nothing really. She's rather shy. She wouldn't be any trouble."

"I'm sure," Gary said. "Listen, I want to discuss this with Melanie before I give my final answer. But I can't see any problems."

The entire family was sitting around the dinner table that night when Gary announced his news. The children were delighted. Now their father would be able to spend more time at home. They asked dozens of questions about the therapist and his daughter. Melanie, however, remained silent. Gary looked at her, not understanding the worry in her eyes. But he decided it was best to discuss her objections in private.

Later that night, as they lay in bed, their arms entwined, Melanie told Gary of her fears. "I just don't think it's safe to bring people into this house," she confessed.

"Why not?" Gary asked. "We certainly have enough room. And if the extra housework is too much for you, we'll hire a maid."

"I can get along fine without a maid," Melanie said. "Gary, you know what I'm talking about. You know what happened last year! What if it happened again? What if . . ."

"That is over, darling," Gary said. "We promised not to talk about it, remember?"

"Perhaps we *should* talk about it," Melanie said. "Let's get the statement out in the open, Gary. Our house was haunted. And not by nice harmless ghosts flitting around in white sheets. What's our guarantee that the ghost won't come back again?"

"I just don't think it will," Gary said firmly. "You know, lightning doesn't strike the same place twice."

"Yes, it does," Melanie protested.

"What do you expect me to tell the man?" he demanded. " 'You're taking this job at your own risk, Miller. We once had a ghost in our house who may come back again'?"

"Stop making fun of me," Melanie said, "I think my fears are justified."

Gary's expression softened as he bent to kiss his wife. "I'm sorry," he said. "But don't you see how much this means to me? I *hate* going to that medical center. It would be easier for me—and for you. Just look at all the time you take out of your painting just to drive me."

"That never bothered me," Melanie said.

"Look, Melanie," Gary said. "Nothing is going to happen. I want this so badly that I'll go ahead and do it in spite of your objections. But please say it's all right with you!"

His eyes were so like a little boy's that Melanie felt herself melting. She nodded slowly.

"All right," she said. "All right, do what you want. I'm just being ridiculous."

"No, you're not," Gary said. "But don't worry. Everything's going to be fine."

2

---◆---

"Are they here yet?" Gary asked as he wheeled himself into the living room.

"Not yet," Melanie said. She was standing near the bay window, her slender hands resting on the back of an antique chair. Gary came up beside her.

"Are you still worried?" he asked.

"No, I've gotten used to the idea of house guests," Melanie said.

"They'll turn out fine," Gary insisted. "You'll see."

"From the looks of that rain," Melanie said, "they may not make it here today."

But just then, through the heavy downpour, they heard the sound of an engine. A few minutes later, a green Volvo came over the top of the hill and stopped in the driveway. Melanie and Gary watched as Derek Miller got out. He was wearing a raincoat with an upturned collar, which hid his face. He opened his daughter's door, and the two shared an umbrella up to the porch.

Derek was shaking the rain from his umbrella when Melanie opened the door. He looked up and smiled.

"I'm Derek Miller," he said.

"I know," Melanie answered. "Come in out of that rain, will you?"

Derek immediately introduced his daughter, then bent down to shake Gary's hand. Doctor Norton had told him about his patient, and Derek was impressed by the firmness of Gary's grip. Gary, in turn, was scrutinizing his therapist. After Derek removed his coat, Gary saw he was a well-built man of about thirty-five. The muscle lines under his cardigan told Gary he was a man who cared as much for his own body as those of his patients.

"Can I get you some coffee?" Melanie asked. "Or hot chocolate?"

"Not for me," Derek said. "Thanks."

Alicen declined with a shake of her head. Melanie folded their coats over her arm, thinking how handsome Derek was with his boyish features and dark, wavy hair. Unfortunately, none of his good looks had been passed on to his daughter. Alicen was the sorriest-looking child Melanie had ever seen, with a chubby body and stringy black hair. Melanie noticed she was staring at the mirror backplate of an elaborate wall lamp that hung in the hallway.

"That's called a girandole," she said. "It's an eighteenth century antique. Isn't it lovely?"

Alicen nodded but said nothing. Gary led the group into the living room and indicated seats for everyone. Derek sat on the overstuffed burgundy-colored couch. Alicen kept her distance, choosing a huge slat-back rocking chair near the fireplace.

"You collect antiques, Mrs. VanBuren?" Derek asked.

"Oh, no," Melanie said. "Gary does. He decorated this entire house."

"Some of the furniture came with it," Gary said. "That table there, for instance. It was built around 1795, the same year as this house."

Abruptly Gary changed the subject. "How was your trip?"

"Not bad," Derek said. "It's only two hours from Englewood."

He stood up and went to the fireplace, looking at the portraits that hung over it. There was one of a blond boy and another depicting two little girls looking out a window.

"Dr. Norton said you had three children?" he asked.

"Kyle, Gina, and Nancy," Gary said, pointing to each in turn. "They're in school right now."

"Gina's your age," Melanie said to Alicen.

The little girl mumbled, "I know."

"I guess that's one reason you let me bring Alicen," Derek said. He picked up a pewter vase and fingered its smooth rim. "Most people think she'd be in the way, even before they meet her."

"But you seem like a well-behaved girl, Alicen," Melanie said, smiling at her. Alicen had left her rocking chair and was now sitting on the window seat, watching the rain pummel the azaleas. She said nothing.

"She's a teen-ager, though," Derek said, "and that bothers people. They think she'd bring drugs into their houses or something. It's idiotic. I prefer private work, but it's impossible to get it with a kid in tow. I've been stuck in a clinic for three years."

"We like children," Melanie said, thinking it was very rude of Derek to speak that way in front of his daughter.

"Well, your call was a godsend, Mr. VanBuren," Derek said, ignoring the glare in Melanie's eyes.

"It's Gary," was the reply, "Mr. VanBuren is for clients and children. I'm hoping we'll be friends."

"After a few days of therapy with me," Derek said, laughing, "you may not want to be friends."

Alicen suddenly spoke up, in a clear voice that surprised Melanie.

"Who lives in that house down the road?" she asked, still staring out the window.

"It's empty," Melanie said. "The owner—the owner died last year."

As if to indicate she didn't wish to discuss it, Melanie stood up abruptly. "Well! How about letting me show you your rooms?"

"Sounds good," Derek said.

Gary had rigged a lift along the stairs so that he could get up and down them easily, and was quite adept at sliding himself into it.

Melanie started to push the wheelchair up, as she usually did, but Derek took the handles from her.

"You're too pretty for work like this," he said, putting his suitcases on the seat.

"I've been doing it for months," Melanie said. "I'm not a weakling."

Derek agreed, but still held fast to the chair. They ascended the stairs slowly, so that Gary could keep up with them. As they walked down the hall, Derek stopped to look at the paintings that lined the walls. He saw Melanie's name on a few of them and complimented her. When he saw that the others depicted naval scenes, he asked if they had an interest in that field.

Melanie and Gary exchanged glances, and after a moment's hesitation, Gary said, "The original owner of this house was a captain in the eighteenth-century British navy. Someday I'll tell you about him."

When they came to the last door in the hall, Melanie opened it and led Derek inside. The room was sparsely furnished with only a bed and dresser.

"We can bring other pieces down from the attic," Melanie said. "I thought it would be best to ask what you needed, first."

"This is just fine," Derek answered.

"Now, Alicen," Melanie said, "come across the hall and see your room."

Thinking the original furnishings had been too plain for a young girl, Melanie had added pretty yellow curtains and a white desk. There was a big bouquet of flowers on the window seat. Alicen looked around, then sat down on the bed, which was covered with a yellow and white quilt.

"Well, how do you like it, Alicen?" Melanie asked.

"It's nice," Alicen said in a soft tone.

Derek shook his head in a gesture of eternal patience, then left the room. Out in the hall he turned to Melanie and said, "You'll have to forgive my daughter's lack of enthusiasm. She's been withdrawn like that since my wife died. It's been six years, but . . ."

"Don't make excuses," Melanie said. "I promise, Alicen will get along just fine here. My children are very friendly."

Indeed, Gina lost no time in making Alicen feel at home. After dinner, she showed the girl her collection of records and stuffed animals. They sat on Gina's bed in their robes, Gina's frilly quilted one a sharp contrast to Alicen's flannel robe.

"Do you like Billy Joel?" Gina asked.

"I—I don't know any boys yet," Alicen faltered.

"I mean Billy Joel the singer!" Gina cried. Seeing the confused look on Alicen's face, she said, "Never mind. I'll play some of his records for you later. Don't you listen to the radio?"

"I like to read," Alicen replied. Thinking Gina might ridicule her for being a bookworm, she climbed from the bed and busied herself with a stuffed kangaroo.

"We have lots of books," Gina said, coming up next to her. "Come on downstairs and I'll show you our library."

"You have a library?" Alicen asked incredulously as she followed Gina from the room.

"Uh-huh," Gina answered. "It's got hundreds of books, but we kids have our own special shelf."

Alicen's brown eyes became very round when she and Gina entered the room. Arched bookshelves decorated with carved cherubs' heads lined three of the walls, while a fourth held built-in stands for maps and atlases.

"It's beautiful," Alicen whispered.

"This is our shelf," Gina said. She stood on her tiptoes and pulled a book down. It was so huge that she had to use both hands to carry it to the brown Chesterfield sofa. She laid it down on the long table before her, and Alicen saw the title: *Collected Works of Charles Dickens.*

"Grandpa said the pictures were painted by hand," Gina said. "See the date? 1850!"

"It's just beautiful," Alicen said again.

"My favorite story is *A Christmas Carol*," Gina said. "See this picture of Scrooge? There's this guy named Mr. Percy at school who looks just like him. And he's just as mean."

"Will I get him?" Alicen asked, worried.

"I hope not," Gina said. "You'll probably be in my class. We live together, don't we?"

"Are the kids in your class nice?"

"Real nice," Gina said. "How come you look so worried?"

"I hate school," Alicen said. "All the teachers I've ever had have been mean to me."

"My teacher is nice," Gina said. "So stop worrying."

A knock on the door interrupted their conversation. Melanie poked her head in and said, "Do you know it's almost eleven? Come on up to bed."

"Let me put this book away first," Gina said.

"Well, Alicen," Melanie said, "how do you like our fancy library?"

"Oh, I love it," Alicen said, with more enthusiasm than Melanie had witnessed all day.

"You're welcome to use it any time you like," Melanie said. "If you don't find what you want, I can drive you to the library in town."

"Thanks," Alicen said.

Melanie leaned against the door as the two girls filed out of the room. She hadn't been near the public library since—well, since Gary's accident. Libraries depressed her. They reminded her of a librarian friend she'd had. But that friend had died last year, violently. And though it wasn't her fault that Janice was dead, she still felt guilt twisting at her stomach whenever she thought of her. Why? Why so much guilt?

Stop that, Melanie told herself. *It's the past. It's over!*

With memories of Janice still heavy on her mind, she went to Alicen's room. The girl was surprised to see her and jumped under the covers as if ashamed of the pretty gown that hung over her fat body.

"How do you like it here so far?" Melanie asked.

"It's nice," Alicen said softly.

"I'm glad you like it," Melanie said, wanting to put her arms around the girl. But something in her manner held her back, and she simply said good night.

Alicen settled back against her pillow, all the while thinking how nice everything seemed to be. She hoped Gina would become her friend. Then, exhausted after a long day, she fell asleep immediately. Her dreams, of her mother, were sweet. Alicen was completely unaware of the woman standing over her, considering her as a pawn in a diabolical scheme.

3

Alicen's fears about her first day at Saint Anne's were completely justified. It began when she learned that she had been assigned to the dreaded Mr. Percy, who really did look like the Scrooge in Gina's book. He had white hair and a pointy nose, and he seemed to always be scowling.

He had put her in the seat directly in front of his desk, wanting to keep an eye on his new student. Alicen sensed he was watching her, waiting for her to do something wrong. She looked around the room, lost and afraid among unfamiliar faces. Alicen began to chew her lower lip as she studied the pretty blond girl next to her.

"Eyes front, Miss Miller," Percy snapped. "Let me tell you, I don't tolerate daydreamers in my classroom. Don't let me catch you again, unless you want to spend your first day in the principal's office."

"Yes, sir," Alicen said, feeling tears of humiliation burning in her eyes. She blinked them away.

She tried her best to concentrate that morning, although her mind wandered whenever Percy had his back to her for too long. She knew already that she hated him. Why did she have to be in his class? The principal had said Gina's class was too full, but couldn't they have made room for one more student? And worse than that, Gina's lunch hour was later than hers. So, this first day, she was forced to eat alone.

As she sipped at a container of milk, she noticed a nice-looking boy with red hair approaching her. Not wanting to talk to him, she ducked her eyes and pretended to be busy with her sandwich. When she next looked up, he was sitting across the room.

The afternoon passed more quickly than the morning, since Percy was concentrating on literature. Alicen became caught up in a story, but she was still glad when the bell rang. Like a drill sergeant, Percy barked at them to get on two separate lines. Alicen was surprised to find the red-haired boy from the cafeteria standing next to her.

"Hey!" he hissed. Alicen ignored him, but the boy persisted. "Don't let Percy get you down. No one else listens to him, either."

Alicen managed a smile but didn't say anything. A few minutes later, they were outside, and the two lines broke as children scattered across the schoolyard. The redhead was still with her.

"My name's Jamie Hutchinson," he said. Alicen noticed the braces on his teeth and felt a little less flawed herself.

"I'm Alicen Miller," she said.

"Where do you live?" Jamie asked. "Did you just move to Belle Bay?"

"I came here yesterday," Alicen told him. Then, surprised that she was suddenly talking so much, she added, "I live with Gina Van-Buren. Do you know her?"

"Not really," Jamie admitted. "I've heard of her, though."

Alicen looked around uncomfortably. "There's Gina now!" she cried. She left Jamie without saying goodbye.

"Nice meeting you," Jamie called as he watched her run toward the bus.

Gina grabbed Alicen's arm and took a quick glance at Jamie. "Who was that?" she asked. "He's so cute!"

"His name is Jamie Hutchinson," Alicen reported.

"Gee, you've got a boyfriend already!" Gina squealed.

"He's not my boyfriend," Alicen said, annoyed.

When they arrived home, they found Gary and Derek in one of the upstairs hallways, supervising a group of carpenters at work on Gary's therapy room. The banging of hammers and buzzing of saws was deafening.

In the studio Melanie, in a blue smock, was busy at work on a new painting. A photograph of Belle Bay's town square was pinned to a bulletin board beside her easel.

"Hi, mom!" Gina cried. "What're you painting?"

"A picture of the town square," Melanie said. "I hope to sell it to the mayor or some other local politician. Oh, guess what? I'm going to have another one-woman show. I'll have to paint a lot of pictures of Long Island since it's my home now."

She promised the girls they could go with her to visit Montauk Point and Jones Beach and other local sights. Gina started enthusiastically to plan her summer vacation, talking of nothing else for the rest of the day. But all Alicen could think about was school and how much she dreaded going back.

When she went to bed that night, she whispered out loud, as if her mother were there to hear her, "You'd make it okay, wouldn't you? I wish you'd come back to me, mommy! I need you!"

Tears filled her eyes, and she turned and stared out the window. The moon was bright and full. Alicen gazed at it and tried to remember her mother. The memory of her mother's beautiful, smiling face was still with her; Alicen had made it a point never to forget that face. She had heard adults at the funeral whispering that her mother had been horribly disfigured in the car accident, but she refused to believe they were talking about her. She stamped a picture of her mother in her mind that showed her always smiling, always willing to play with her little daughter. Not like her father.

Alicen's thoughts were suddenly interrupted by a strange, high-pitched laughter. Terrified, she pulled her quilt over her head and held her breath. Was someone in the room, listening to the thumping of her heart? The laughter came again, and she realized it wasn't in her room at all. It had come from the kitchen below, filtering through the grating in the floor.

Alicen was about to get up and tell her father, but she was afraid. This was his first private job in three years, and he'd warned her she had better not do anything to jeopardize it. *Anything.*

"And that means acting like a baby, the way you did at the Laines' house," her father had said.

Alicen had awakened in the middle of the night, crying out for her mother. Her screams had so frightened the Laine children that their parents decided she couldn't stay with them any longer. Derek couldn't afford to send her to a boarding school, so the two packed their bags together. Alicen knew it was her fault that her father had lost his job. So tonight, she pretended she didn't hear the laughter. This time, she swore, she wouldn't have nightmares.

Trembling, she put her fingers in her ears and blocked out the sound. She didn't hear the click of Derek's door across the hall. He had also heard the strange cries and was on his way downstairs to investigate. The long hallway that led to the stairs was pitch black, lit only by dim moonlight filtering through an amber stained-glass window at its end. Obviously the VanBurens were fast asleep, too far at the front of the house to have heard the noise. Derek, deciding he could handle the situation himself, groped his way down the dark staircase.

He stopped short when he heard the laughter again. Then he took a deep breath and burst into the dining room, switching on the overhead light. He scanned the room, taking in the table, chairs, and bay windows. The windows were locked tight. Everything seemed to be in order. Even the fireplace, black and yawning, gave no hint of hiding an intruder. Everything was so silent that Derek could hear a ringing in his ears.

"I must have been dreaming," he said softly, running his fingers through his tousled hair. But then he noticed the kitchen door. Could the prowler be hiding in the kitchen? It suddenly occurred to him that if there was an intruder, he might be armed. Derek wasn't afraid, but he wasn't about to take chances. He needed a weapon.

Looking around, he spotted a pearl-handled pistol on the mantel. It looked like an antique, and Derek prayed the intruder wouldn't know the difference. Refusing to let himself be frightened, he shoved through the kitchen door and switched on the light. The white refrigerator and oven gleamed innocently. He could see his reflection in the backdoor window as he moved carefully around the kitchen. No one was hiding here. He went to the back door and twisted the lock. It was one of those doors where one needed a key to get out as well as in. There had been no time for a prowler to escape—if indeed it was a prowler he had heard.

He sank into a wooden chair. "I'm sure I heard something."

It might have been his imagination. After all, this was an old house, with creaking boards and drafts. He had heard some explainable noises, and nothing more. Laughing at himself, he stood up and headed out of the kitchen.

The door to the basement started to rattle.

Derek turned abruptly, aiming the gun. Why hadn't he thought to check the cellar? Was that just the wind? He heard a scratching noise. The wind didn't scratch. . . .

Derek refused to be afraid. He reached and jerked the door open. His gun was pointed at the black, shiny nose of a puppy.

"I don't believe this," Derek groaned, putting the gun on the counter. He knelt down and stroked the little Weimaraner's ears.

"How'd you get stuck down there?" he asked, wondering if a puppy's high-pitched yapping could sound like laughter. "There's a good boy. Poor doggy, locked in a cellar."

He peered down the stairs into the inklike blackness. "Locked in a dark and cold cellar, too," he said. He stood up and beckoned the dog. Lad followed him from the room. Derek returned the gun to its stand on the mantel, then headed upstairs, Lad at his side. Feeling somewhat embarrassed by the incident, he decided to keep it to himself. Afraid of a little puppy!

He had no idea that Lad hadn't barked once that night.

The therapy room was completed just a few days later.

"It'll be best to get your muscles toned," Derek said as he fastened a cushioned leather cuff to Gary's left ankle. "Once you're used to this equipment, you can move on to bigger and better things."

"Like walking, I hope," Gary said. His leg moved up and down with little difficulty, the cable squeaking from newness.

"Let me add a little more weight to that," Derek said. "It looks too easy." He added a ten-pound weight. This time Gary groaned when he moved his leg.

"Pretty soon," Derek said, "you won't feel it. For a guy who broke both legs, you're in pretty good shape, Gary. Say, nobody ever told me the details of your accident. If you don't mind, I'd be interested."

"They didn't tell you what kind of injury you'd be dealing with?" Gary asked impatiently.

"Of course," Derek said. "But part of therapy is knowing how the accident occurred. I want to know on a professional basis, but if you feel uncomfortable about it, then—"

"No, it's not that," Gary said. "It's just that we don't like to talk about it. Let's just say I came into one of the rooms up here one night and found a prowler. We had a fight, and he pushed me out the window. That's all you need to know, isn't it?"

"Probably," Derek said, wondering why Gary was so reluctant to talk about the accident. He decided it was some family matter and did not pursue it.

Gary asked when he would be able to start using crutches.

"I want to warn you," Derek said, "practicing with crutches is a frustrating and sometimes painful process. You'll probably fall down a lot, and you'll need your muscle strength to get back up again. But don't worry. One of these days, you'll be playing racquet ball with me."

"I don't know how to play," Gary said.

"If you promise to cooperate with me," Derek said, "I promise to teach you the game."

The two men shook on it and continued with the routine. They could hear Melanie down the hall, singing as she worked in her studio.

"Melanie's a beautiful woman," Derek said. "You're lucky to have her."

"I know," Gary said. He studied the sadness in his therapist's eyes for a moment, then asked, "What was your wife's name?"

"Elaine," Derek said. "She was beautiful, too. Her hair was clear down to her hips, and the lightest blond color. She was only thirty-two when she died. Her car was—uh, was struck by a drunk driver doing ninety. The engine exploded."

"I'm sorry," Gary said, feeling uncomfortable. Grasping at straws, he said, "Do you play a lot of racquet ball?"

"Three nights a week and every Saturday, when I lived in Jersey," Derek said, smiling again. "There was a little gymnasium there that didn't charge too much for court time. I miss it."

"I sometimes see ads for a local health club in our town paper," Gary said. "It has a court. Why don't you join?"

On Saturday Derek did drive into town to look up the club. Halfway there, he spotted a young woman hitchhiking. Derek, who never picked up strangers, ignored her. Silver lampposts and patches of sand and sparse, scrubby foliage shot past him. Something about this barren section of Belle Bay made Derek uneasy. Why was that? He was never unsure of anything!

It was the woman, of course. She had looked like a pitiful refugee, her eyes huge and staring. Derek looked in his rear-view mirror, his breath catching in his throat when he saw her eyes. They seemed to be pulling him, making him turn the car around and drive back to her. Without understanding why, he stopped and opened the door for her.

"Where do you want to go?"

The woman said nothing. She stared straight ahead through vacant blue eyes. There was a strange smell about her, a faint mixture of sea wind and rotted meat. Rotted meat? Derek was disgusted at the thought. Close-up, the young woman's appearance disgusted him even more. She was so pale it was painful to look at her, especially since he could see the veins beneath her skin. Her eyes had a filmy quality, and the blond hair that hung around her shoulders looked as if it hadn't been combed in weeks. Even stranger were the clothes she wore—corduroy pants, a flannel shirt, and fur boots. On a warm spring day.

God, have I ever picked up a loser, Derek thought, starting the car again.

"Just tell me where you want to get off," he said as he drove down the road. He was annoyed at himself for giving in to a ridiculous impulse and letting this stranger into his car.

All of a sudden, the woman pressed her hand on top of his. It was as cold as ice. Derek looked down at it, keeping a firm grip on the steering wheel, although he wanted to pull away from the freezing touch of her fingers. Her hand was chapped red. It was as if she had just stepped out of a snowstorm.

"Hey, let go!" Derek cried. "What's wrong with you? Do you need a doctor?"

She made no reply, but took her hand away. Derek turned his eyes from the road for a split second. The woman was making gestures as if she were crying. Derek couldn't see any tears, though her small mouth hung open and her shoulders heaved. She stared down the road.

"Mel . . . Mel . . . Mel . . ." she moaned.

Derek, his eyes on the road once more, patted her arm and told her he would get help. She stiffened. Her sobbing stopped with a huge gasp, and she doubled over as if she were going to be sick. Derek quickly pulled the car off the road, got out, and ran to open the door. But when he tried to help her out, she collapsed to the ground. Her eyes stared glassily, and she made no sound.

"Jesus in Heaven," Derek whispered.

He hesitated, afraid to touch her. All sorts of visions came to his head. Everyone would start asking questions, and they might even accuse him of killing this woman. She had been in his car—how could they think otherwise? Why should he jeopardize his life and career for one crazy addict? He didn't need that kind of trouble.

Derek looked up and down the road, surprised at how calm he was. There was no one around, no one to see him lift her—why was she so stiff, he wondered?—and carry her to a nearby clump of bushes. He put her down there, glad to be rid of her.

"Sorry, lady," he said as he hurried back to his car, "but I don't know you from Adam. I don't need your problems."

He thought at first about forgetting the entire incident, but his sense of decency got the better of him. He parked his car in the center of town and walked to a phone booth.

"Belle Bay police department," a voice said. "Bryan Davis."

"I—I want to report a body," Derek said carefully, keeping his voice low so that passers-by wouldn't hear him.

"A what?"

"A body," Derek repeated. "I saw it behind some bushes on Houston Street, near Walher."

"Hey, wait!" Bryan cried. "Who are you?"

But Derek had already hung up. By the time he reached the health spa and signed the membership papers, he had pushed the incident with the girl from his mind. He was choosing a racket even as Bryan Davis reached the designated intersection.

"Over there," Bryan said to the cop with him. "I think I see something, Jack."

"It's just an old towel," Jack said, kicking it aside to show that the ground beneath was empty. "You suppose this is what our caller saw?"

"I don't know," Bryan said. "He sounded pretty upset. Let's look a little further."

As he poked through the clumps of bushes scattered here and there on the roadside, Bryan took note of the fact that no cars had passed them. Chances were, no one else had seen the body—if indeed there was one. After a few more minutes of searching, Bryan straightened himself and sighed.

"Jack, we're wasting our time," he said. "It was just a wild-goose chase."

"That doesn't surprise me," Jack said. He was looking at some point behind his captain. "Nothing surprises me anymore."

Bryan turned around and followed Jack's gaze. He could see the huge VanBuren mansion at the top of the nearby hill. Bryan wondered how the family was doing, especially Gary.

"I sometimes see his wife driving him through town," Jack said, as if reading Bryan's thoughts. "He's still in a wheelchair, you know."

"It was a hell of a fall he had," Bryan said grimly. He clapped Jack on the shoulder. "Let's get back to the station. We'll just assume the caller was seeing things, okay?"

"If it's all the same to you," Jack said, "I'd like to believe we aren't going to have any more trouble here."

"I couldn't agree with you more," Bryan said as he got into his car.

As soon as breakfast was over, Derek turned to Gary and said, "Why don't we get started now?"

"Right away," Gary said. "I'm having some clients here this afternoon, so I want to get this done early."

Melanie looked over her shoulder. "Honey, I'm going to be taking my new painting into town today. Do you mind if I'm not here?"

"I'm sure I'll be okay," Gary said. Melanie often helped him by answering phones or bringing coffee when he was with his clients.

"I hope you sell that painting," Derek said.

"Thanks," Melanie said. "If I do, I'll probably sell a few more. The mayor's wife is filthy rich."

"Then don't take less than five hundred dollars," Gary said laughing.

Later that morning, Melanie carefully laid the painting in the back of the station wagon. As she walked around to her door, she looked up at the ominous gray clouds in the sky. A faint rumble of thunder told her it would rain within the next hour.

Melanie switched on the radio as she drove down Starbine Court and thought how pretty everything looked that afternoon. The approaching storm gave the air a clean, cool scent. She could see the stretch of beach through the sparse woods; it was empty except for a young couple and their dog. The usually still waters of the bay were churning now, and sea gulls anticipated the storm with high-pitched cries.

Melanie shuddered suddenly. Though it was April, she had felt a wind so cold that goose bumps crept over her skin. Keeping one hand on the wheel as she turned a corner, she tightened the belt on her raincoat. She heard something thump behind her and looked quickly over her shoulder. The painting had shifted a little, but no harm had been done.

"I sure hope I sell that," she said out loud as she drove through the center of town. She pulled into the parking lot next to the town hall, surprised to see how full it was on this gloomy day. She found a spot at last, then switched off the engine. Crossing her fingers for luck, she went around to the back of the car to retrieve the painting. But when she pulled it out, she nearly dropped it. There was an ugly red smudge mark right in the middle of it.

"Oh, no!" Melanie whimpered, propping it against the door. "I don't understand. I worked so hard on it. And I *know* the paint was dry!"

Something told her, though, that this wasn't paint. Carefully she touched the spot. It was thick, but not as thick as oil paint. Melanie brought her finger to her nose. It wasn't paint at all. It was blood.

Quickly she examined her own hands and arms for signs of a cut. That was fresh blood—it wasn't as if one of the kids had touched it earlier on and had been too scared to tell anyone about it. Yet

Melanie's skin was unbroken. It was almost as if someone had done this on purpose. But that was impossible.

Suddenly she heard a voice right behind her. "What happened to your lovely painting?"

An attractive, well-dressed middle-aged woman was at her side. The woman was shaking her head.

"Who'd do such a thing?" she demanded. "It looks as if someone rubbed red paint on it."

"It's—" Melanie stopped. Why should she tell this stranger the red mark was blood? How could she, when she hardly believed it herself?

"Did you paint it?" the woman asked. "It's beautiful, in spite of . . ."

Melanie nodded. "I was going to sell it to the mayor. I don't think I could even give it to him, now."

"It's really not a big smudge," the woman said. "Do you think you could paint over it?"

"I don't know," Melanie said sadly. "I don't know if it would do any good."

"Yes, it would," the woman said, taking Melanie's arm. "Come inside with me, and we'll talk about it. I'm Sarah Kaufman; I'm the mayor's wife."

Melanie and Sarah shared coffee in an empty office, discussing her work as a painter.

At last, to Melanie's delight, Sarah wrote a check for one thousand dollars, explaining that she wanted Melanie to do two paintings for her, one of the duck pond and one of the local church. She asked if Melanie could put pink roses in that one. They were her favorite flowers, she explained. They also agreed that four hundred and fifty dollars would be a fair price for the damaged painting if Melanie could repair it successfully. Sarah Kaufman was a sympathetic woman, and Melanie found herself lingering on after they had completed the transaction, talking about her home and Gary's unfortunate accident.

When Melanie left the town hall, it was starting to rain, so she pulled up the hood of her raincoat and ran down the steps to her car. She was surprised to see a young woman sitting on the back fender. Melanie, feeling elated with the check in her purse, smiled at her. The woman did not return the smile, but watched Melanie as she walked to her door and got in the car.

When Melanie started the car, the woman was still sitting on the fender. Melanie hit the horn, to no avail. Sighing in exasperation, she got out of her car. She tapped the woman's shoulder.

"If you don't mind," she said, "I'd like to move my car."

The young woman said nothing, but stared up at Melanie. There was something in her glassy blue eyes, something cold and vicious, that made Melanie shudder. The woman seemed strangely familiar. Melanie studied her for a moment, then decided she didn't know her after all. "What is it you want?" Melanie asked. "Money? A ride?"

The young woman shook her head and smiled for the first time. It was a thin evil smile.

"I want you to die," she said.

Melanie gasped and turned quickly to run into the hall. She found a security guard and brought him outside. But when they reached the car, the woman was gone. Droplets of rain covered up any indication that she had been sitting there.

"She was right there," Melanie said, pointing.

"She probably ran away when she saw me coming," the guard said. "I wouldn't worry about it. You know kids these days. Probably some smart-ass teen-ager."

"You're right," Melanie said. "I'm sorry I bothered you."

"It's my job, lady," the guard said.

When she arrived home, Melanie gathered the family together and held up the check for everyone to see. She told about her meeting with Sarah Kaufman and how the mayor's wife had commissioned her to paint two pictures.

"That's a lot of money," Kyle said.

"But what about the other picture?" Gary asked.

"I couldn't sell it," Melanie said sighing. "Somehow, part of it wasn't dry yet, and it got smudged." There was no point upsetting everyone with the truth.

"But you finished that several days ago," Gary pointed out.

"I know," Melanie said. "I guess—well, I guess this damp weather we've been having kept it from drying. It's all right, though. Mrs. Kaufman says she'll pay four hundred and fifty dollars for it when I fix it."

Despite her feelings of misgiving, Melanie related the story about the strange young woman. She described the glassy blue eyes and scary smile and related how the girl had disappeared before the security guard could chase her away.

"Probably high on something," Derek said. He thought for a moment about the hitchhiker who had been in his car the other day. Belle Bay was such a nice town. Not the sort of place you'd expect to find a lot of drugged hippies.

"Well, let's forget it," Gary suggested. "This is too happy a day to dwell on something like that. Why don't we all go out to dinner, to celebrate?"

"It sounds great," Melanie said. "Derek and Alicen will come, too, I hope?"

Derek smiled. "Let me get my umbrella."

A short while later everyone headed out to the cars, laughing and talking about the good evening they would have.

The silence of the big house lulled Lad to sleep. His wiry body was stretched out near the front door, ready to waken and jump all over the children when they returned. A twitch of muscle would ripple his smooth gray-brown skin every once in a while, but the dog slept on.

And then something reached his ears, some strange sound that didn't belong in the house. As if he had never been asleep, the dog raised his head and shoulders with a jerk. He looked around, his ears alert from the noise.

Loud wailing was coming from Melanie's studio. With a loud series of barks, Lad jumped to his feet and ran upstairs. A sudden terror overtook him, and he cowered in the studio door and whined, smelling something, but seeing nothing.

Across the room, one of the paintings lifted off its stand as if by itself. It seemed to shake in midair.

She sells paintings, and that's all she cares about. She doesn't care that I was her friend once. She doesn't care about what happened to me.

The painting came crashing down against the easel.

She laughs with her family while I cry for life. But I will have vengeance.

Lad snarled as he saw the painting rise in the air again . . .

Vengeance!

. . . and come crashing down on the easel. But what he heard next was a human voice, disembodied and powerful. He scurried to hide underneath the couch.

"Vengeance! I'll kill them all. I'll make them suffer like I do."

There was a final crash, and then the house was silent once more.

"That was one terrific evening," Melanie said as she and the others walked up the porch steps. She was carrying Nancy, who was asleep, while Derek pushed Gary's wheelchair. "Thanks for everything, guys."

"I wonder why Lad isn't down here to greet us?" Kyle asked.

"Yeah, that's weird," Gina said. "He's always here when we go out."

"Well, he probably got tired of waiting," Melanie said, handing Nancy to Derek as she took off her coat. "We were out very late—so, up to bed!"

Derek offered to carry Nancy to her room. As Melanie followed him down the hall, she noticed she had left her painting there that afternoon and picked it up. Upstairs, she put her sleeping daughter into a pair of pajamas, then tucked her in.

"Sleep good, love," she said, kissing the child's forehead.

She picked up her painting again and carried it down the hall to her studio. Slightly giddy from the wine she had been drinking all night, she was whistling a tune as she opened the door. Her whistling stopped short when she turned on the light.

The room was in complete disarray. Her paintings were scattered everywhere, easels were overturned, and a tube of bright yellow paint had oozed out all over the couch.

"What happened?" Melanie demanded out loud. She could feel her heart start to pound, but she breathed deeply and walked further into the room. She spotted one of her paintings lying on the floor. The frame had been bent completely out of shape, and there were long, ugly gashes running the length of the canvas.

Melanie dropped it as if it were boiling hot and ran out into the hallway. Somehow, common sense got the better of her, and she managed not to scream out in anger. How would she explain this to the children?

Gary was at the bottom of the steps with Derek.

"Gary, could you come to my studio with me?" Melanie forced her voice to remain calm.

"Sure," Gary said. "What's wrong?"

"Oh, nothing," Melanie insisted. "I just want to show you something." She looked at Derek. "Good night."

As she pushed him down the hallway, Gary asked what all the mystery was about. But Melanie refused to speak. Gary's answer came when she opened her studio door.

"My God, this place looks like a cyclone struck it," he said. "What the hell happened?"

"I don't know," Melanie said softly. She walked across the room and lifted the torn painting. "Look at this. This is a painting I did a few years ago of the three children." She brushed back one of the torn edges to reveal a little baby. "That's Nancy, remember?"

"It was one of my favorite pictures," Gary said sadly.

"Mine, too," Melanie answered. "Why, out of all my paintings, was it singled out for destruction?"

"Singled out?" Gary asked. "You say that as if someone did this on purpose. But no one's been home."

Melanie remained silent as she tried to straighten out the mess. She propped her paintings and canvases back on their stands and righted the easels. Tears flowed down her cheeks, and she sniffled.

"Melanie, I'm sure there's some logical explanation," Gary said in a soothing tone.

"There always is," Melanie answered.

A long stretch of silence passed before she spoke again. She had her back to her husband, busily trying to scrape the yellow paint from the couch cover.

"It could be a ghost, Gary," she said.

"Oh, of course not! Some local kids probably broke in and got their kicks by vandalizing your studio," Gary said.

"It isn't impossible that the ghosts are back?" Melanie asked uncertainly.

"No, it isn't," Gary answered. "But it's improbable. Honey, there is no reason to believe all that happened here last year will happen again. You're just tired and upset. Why don't you wait until morning to think this out?"

Melanie burst into tears then and ran to put her head on Gary's shoulder.

"This wasn't supposed to happen to me!" she cried. "I was so happy!"

"It's okay," Gary said, rubbing her back. "Everything's gonna be okay."

He stared across the room. If only he had some proof that all this was the result of mortal hands. And then, as if in answer to his pleas, he saw a small brown paw poke out from under the couch. Then another, and then Lad slowly slithered out. Gary tapped Melanie's shoulder, and she looked up.

"There's your culprit," he said.

Lad slunk toward them, whining in terror.

"He must have been chasing a mouse," Gary said. "And he knocked everything over. The torn painting just caught on an edge of the easel—that's all."

Melanie looked into the dog's big brown eyes and saw fear there. Though she nodded her head in agreement for Gary's sake, she wasn't quite sure the dog was guilty.

An icy touch brought Melanie out of a dream sometime in the very early morning. Without opening her eyes, she tried to brush it away, groaning. But it stayed with her, insistent, pressed against her bare arm. Groggily she rolled over onto her back and squinted up through the darkness.

A woman was leaning over her.

Just a dream, Melanie thought, closing her eyes again. She sighed and opened them a second time to check the clock. The woman was still standing there, moonlight casting a glow over her face and dark hair. She let her hand slide down Melanie's arm and took her hand.

"Come," she said, simply.

Melanie opened her mouth to waken Gary, but no sound came from it. Still half-asleep, she didn't question, but got out of bed and followed the woman into the hallway. In the soft moonlight, colored amber through the stained-glass window at the end of the hall, she could see the woman was a head shorter than she. Could it be Alicen? What did she want? Melanie couldn't open her mouth to ask. She felt as if she were in a dream world, where everything is fuzzy and feet don't make contact with floors.

They went downstairs to the dining room. Now Melanie was beginning to become more fully conscious, and she was aware of the soft rug under her bare feet. But this was a dream, wasn't it?

She knew it wasn't a nightmare, because, somehow, she wasn't afraid.

They entered the kitchen. Someone had left the light on, and in its brilliance Melanie saw the woman's face. It was pretty and childish, framed by long, dark hair. The old-fashioned gown the woman wore was torn to shreds, and she had no shoes.

Encouraged by the gentleness of the woman's face, Melanie spoke at last. Her voice sounded hollow, far away, yet she had the feeling this was all really happening. She wished Gary were down here.

"Who are you?" Melanie asked.

"I have come to warn you," the woman said. "Leave this place!"

"Why?"

"There will be more sorrow," the woman said. "I take great risks coming here—for if she knew of me, she would conjure up the wrath of hell."

"Who would?" Melanie demanded. "Who's she? And who are you?"

Suddenly the woman gave a small cry. "I must go! She walks too near!"

"Wait!" Melanie cried.

The woman turned a panic-stricken face to Melanie and shook her head. Her hair waved slowly from side to side, as if it were floating in water. Then suddenly it started to fall out. The pretty white-and-pink skin began to shrivel and draw away from the skin. Brown eyes disintegrated, and the swan-like neck became a tree branch. Melanie watched in horror as the woman sank to the floor, drawing her arms and legs up in a fetal position. She was nothing but a black, shriveled blob. Then a skeleton. Then, nothing.

"Nnnnooo!"

Melanie screamed and screamed, falling back into a chair. She felt two hands on her arms and tried to pull away, but they held her tightly. And from the other side of her terror, she heard a comfortingly familiar voice.

"Melanie, wake up!"

She dared to open her eyes. Gary was leaning over her in his wheelchair.

"Gary?" she asked weakly. "Where did the woman go? Did you see the woman?"

"What woman?" Gary asked. "Here, calm down. There's no woman here."

Melanie looked around at the empty kitchen.

"Yes," she said, her voice weak but insistent. "Yes, I saw her! She led me down here."

"No one led you down here," Gary said. "I saw you get out of bed and leave the room—by yourself."

"You must have seen the woman, too," Melanie said. "Why didn't you follow us?"

Gary sighed. "Melanie, you were alone. You must have been sleepwalking, although I didn't realize it until I heard you screaming. Luckily, I was awake."

"What about the children? Did they hear me?" Melanie asked, her fears giving way for the moment to motherly concern.

"No one's awake," Gary said. "Now, come back to bed."

Melanie stood up.

"Gary, I saw a woman," she insisted. "She brought me down here. She even spoke to me, warned me to leave this place!" Melanie shuddered. "And then she turned into a skeleton."

"There was no woman," Gary said. "You were sleepwalking, that's all. And it's no wonder, after you found your studio torn apart like that. That was a frightening experience."

"It isn't happening again, is it, Gary?" Melanie asked, her voice almost childish in its pleading.

"Of course not," Gary said. "Come up to bed now, darling."

She did. But she laid awake for hours thinking of the woman. Who was she? What did she want?

No answers came. Melanie considered the possibility that she had been sleepwalking, as Gary said. She only wished she could be sure.

5

---◆---

"Well, today's the day, Gary," Derek announced as the two entered Gary's therapy room the next morning. "I'm going to have you start on crutches."

"It's about time," Gary said eagerly.

"Here, wheel yourself to this mat," Derek said. "That's the way."

"What's it for?" Gary asked, looking down at the heavy vinyl mat.

"Hopefully for nothing," Derek said. "How do you feel this morning?"

"Fine," Gary said. He shrugged his shoulders. "Well, a little tired. Melanie and I were up late last night. She went into her studio and found it ransacked. It upset her pretty badly."

"Did someone break into the house?"

"Oh, no!" Gary said. "I found Lad cowering underneath the sofa. I think he knocked over a few things and got scared. Anyway, it's okay now—so let's get on with this."

Derek positioned a pair of crutches under each of his patient's arms, then lowered the footrest of the wheelchair. After warning Gary to go slowly this first time, he stepped back and said, "It's all yours."

Gary grinned at him, his face a mask of confidence. He had waited so long for this day that he was certain he would just get up and speed right across the room.

Suddenly, as he was leaning forward, the chair shot out from behind him. With a frantic cry, Gary dropped the crutches and grabbed for it, landing sideways in his seat. His hands clutched the back, and he looked up at his therapist with wide eyes.

"What happened?"

"Nothing," Derek said firmly. "Try again."

"I'm not so sure . . ."

"Try again," Derek said, his voice firm.

"Yes, sir!" Gary answered, eyeing him suspiciously. Was he going to let him fall again?

He repositioned the crutches, then took a deep breath. Slowly he started to get up again. And then he sank back down into the chair, frozen.

Memories of his accident came flooding back to him. He saw himself flying through the window, shards of glass flying, sparkling all around him. Down and down and down . . .

His eyes snapped open when his dream-self hit the trash cans below the window. He stared down at his hands, ashamed of his fears. But he still couldn't move.

"I can't do it," he said. "I just don't understand, but I can't do it!"

He was so frustrated that tears began to well in his eyes. Ashamed, he ran his fingers through his hair. This was supposed to be so easy!

Derek was kneeling beside him. "Of course you can do it," he said, with a strange gentleness that Gary had never heard before. "You see, Gary, you associate falling here with the fall that injured you."

Gary blinked and looked at him. "How did you know that?"

"Simple," Derek said, smiling as he stood again. "It's a very common thing with people who were hurt in falls. Why do you think I put that gym mat down?"

"But if you knew that," Gary asked, "why did you let me fall?"

"You didn't really fall," Derek said. "You just got up the wrong way. And I did tell you to be careful. These things take time, Gary."

Gary smiled. "Look at me, will you? An overgrown crybaby. I guess I'd better tackle those damned crutches right now, eh? Before I'm too scared to try them again?"

"That's the boy," Derek said, punching Gary's shoulder.

This time Derek showed Gary how to firmly plant the crutches and to lean forward in such a way that the chair remained stationary. After thirty or more frustrating attempts, Gary was finally able to stand up.

"Now, that's not so hard, is it?" Derek asked.

"What do I do now?" Gary could feel dull pain running up his legs through muscles that hadn't been in this position for months.

"Nothing. You've got a few more days to practice getting up before you try to walk. How do you feel?"

"Achy," Gary said. "But it's a good feeling. You know, like after you've played a hard game of ball?"

Suddenly a delighted yelp and a "Wonderful!" sounded from downstairs. Both Gary and Derek looked at the door, then at each other. Seconds later, Melanie burst into the room. There was a wide grin on her face, but she didn't say anything. She had stopped short to stare at Gary.

"You're standing up!" she cried. "Isn't it wonderful?"

"Isn't what wonderful?" Gary asked as Derek helped him back into the chair. "I'm not walking yet. And what's all the noise about?"

"Oh, Gary," Melanie said, hurrying to put her arms around her husband. "I just got the most wonderful news. My agent booked me into a very prestigious art gallery for the whole month of June—a one-woman show."

"Melanie, I'm so proud of you," Gary said. Melanie leaned down and kissed him. "What do you think of my talented wife, Derek?"

Derek wasn't in the room. He had stepped out, knowing Gary and Melanie might want to be alone at such an important moment. "What do you say we celebrate?" Melanie asked in a soft voice.

Gary smiled. "What've you got in mind?"

"Come into the bedroom and I'll show you," Melanie said.

Though the rough workout that morning made his legs ache from toe to hip, Gary wouldn't let that hinder him. The joyous happenings of that morning made him want Melanie so much that he could ignore the pain. Melanie was the dominant one in their lovemaking now, but today, Gary used his strong arms to embrace her and fondle her more passionately than he had in months. His movements were forced into slowness by his crippled legs, yet Melanie seemed to revel in it.

A while later, when they were leaning against the headboard in a warm embrace, Melanie said, "This is the best of all. Everything is so wonderful."

"What is?"

"Being with you," Melanie said. "More than my art show, more than the fact you're learning to walk again. I have everything I want, right here and now. I've never been happier in my life."

Gary kissed her. "That doesn't sound like the woman who insisted a ghost led her into the kitchen last night."

"I don't know," Melanie said. "I suppose everything that happened today pushed it out of my mind. I don't feel as apprehensive as I did."

"Have you decided it was all a dream?" Gary asked hopefully.

Melanie shrugged. "I suppose so. But even if it was a dream, I wonder who that woman was?"

"Don't even think about it," Gary said. "Everything is just perfect for us now, Melanie. We'll never be afraid again."

His embrace tightened. "I promise you that."

As Derek drove along Houston Street on the way to the racquetball club, he thought of Gary and Melanie and the love they shared. It had been six years since Elaine's death, and in that time he had never let another woman into his heart. Now he felt an emptiness deep within himself. He really needed to love again. A nice, smart, beautiful woman like Elaine.

"No one's like Elaine," Derek whispered.

But he did meet someone that very day. It happened when he was practicing his Z-shot. He was so mesmerized that he didn't pay attention to anyone else around him, and as he dove for the ball, he slammed into a woman, knocking her to the floor.

"I'm sorry!" he cried, turning quickly to look down at her. "I wasn't—"

He stopped talking for just a moment to look at her. She was a vision, a beautiful woman with high cheekbones and almond eyes. She was dressed in a pale green jogging suit, her long legs sprawled out in front of her. Looking at Derek through strands of dark brown hair that had fallen over her face, she held up her hand. Immediately, he broke from his spell and helped her to her feet.

"You have eyes just like Ava Gardner," he heard himself say.

"What?" the woman shrieked with an embarrassed grin.

Derek shook his head. "I'm sorry," he said. "I shouldn't have said that. Are you okay? Did I hurt you?"

"I'm a lot stronger than I look," the woman said, "although I've probably got a nice bruise on my backside."

"I was working on my Z-shot," Derek explained. "I wasn't paying attention. Is my court time over?"

"Well, no. I was watching you, and I guess I became so caught up that I didn't realize I was walking in here. It was my fault."

"I hope you liked what you saw," Derek said, "for the price you paid."

The woman smiled, showing brilliant white teeth. "I've been trying to get that damned Z-shot for weeks, but I can't seem to do it. You make it look so easy."

"Well, I could show you," Derek offered. "Here, stand like this. . . . By the way, what's your name?"

"Liza Crewe."

"I'm Derek Miller. Now, you hold the racket this way, and . . ."

He showed her a perfect shot. Liza tried to copy him, in vain. Laughing, she tried again and again. While she practiced, she and Derek talked. Liza seemed very interested in Derek's work as a therapist. In turn, she told Derek she was a dance student.

Liza missed the shot for the tenth time, and sighing in frustration, she took a step backward.

"See what I mean?" she cried, waving the racket a little. "I just can't get it."

"You're aiming too low," Derek said. "Here, like this."

"Well," Liza said as she tried again, "I may not be the world's best racquet ball player, but I know I can dance. You're looking at the next Fonteyn."

"You'll be better than Fonteyn," Derek said, though he wasn't quite sure who Fonteyn was.

Liza practiced the Z-shot awhile longer, until she did it right a dozen times in a row. She squealed with delight and turned to flash a grin at Derek. She was positively the most gorgeous woman he had ever seen. For a moment he forgot about Elaine.

"Do you live here in town?"

"I have an apartment over a house," Liza said. "I'd like to live in the city, but there're just too many worries there. Belle Bay is so peaceful. It's a nice place to come home to after a long day."

"You don't seem like a worrier," Derek said as they walked off the court.

"Oh, I worry a lot," Liza admitted. "I worry that twenty-eight is too old to take ballet lessons. And stage fright is my pet phobia, believe it or don't."

"I don't," Derek said. "And I think it's great you're studying something you enjoy. Just one question—why did you wait so long?"

Liza sighed. "My father has been sick for many years, and I felt guilty about leaving him down in Florida. That, and the fact I couldn't afford it. But dad's better now, and he even paid half my tuition."

"I'm glad he did," Derek said.

"They went off to their respective locker rooms. Thirty minutes later Liza reappeared wearing a lavender dress that showed off her figure beautifully.

"Will I see you here again, I hope?" Derek asked.

"Sure, when will you be here?"

"Saturday morning?"

Frowning, Liza shook her head. "Sorry, I have rehearsal. How about next Thursday?"

"I'll be here," Derek promised.

He grinned ear to ear all the way home, too caught up in his thoughts of Liza to notice the blond-haired woman watching him from the roadside.

6

Derek wasn't the only one falling in love that day. In the cafeteria of Saint Anne's school, Alicen was sitting with red-haired Jamie Hutchinson, much to her chagrin. Too shy to let the boy be her friend, she had tried to ignore him. But Jamie, who was naturally friendly, had followed her to the lunchroom every day to sit across from her. He tried to win her over with bags of cookies and potato chips, but Alicen always refused. She would stare down at her food, barely glancing up at him every once in a while.

"You're too weird, Alicen," Jamie said one day. He took something out of his lunch bag—a huge chocolate bar—and pushed it across the lineoleum table. "That's for you. And don't tell me you don't like chocolate."

"I love chocolate," Alicen said, gingerly touching the candy. She had never received a present from a boy before and didn't know how to react. Her "thank you" was barely audible.

"Don't mention it," said Jamie. "And listen, don't leave it in your desk. It'll melt."

Alicen nodded. Then suddenly she found her tongue. "Why are you doing this?"

"Doing what?"

"Being so nice to me," Alicen said.

Jamie clicked his tongue. "Because I like you, silly. Can't you take a hint?"

"Why?"

"Why shouldn't I?"

"Because I'm fat and—"

"You're not *that* fat," Jamie said.

Alicen started to protest, but he stopped her.

"You really want to know why I like you?" he asked. " 'Cause I knew from the minute you walked into our classroom that you weren't a phony. You weren't wearing designer jewelry, like all the other girls. I think those things are dumb."

"So do I," Alicen said. She was surprised to find herself smiling.

"Gee, you look pretty when you smile," Jamie said.

He was so charming that Alicen felt herself begin to relax. She learned in their conversation that his father owned a butcher shop in town, and when Jamie asked why she had come to Belle Bay, she told him that her father was a therapist. He became very excited when he learned she was living in the big white house on Starbine Court Road.

"But I already told you that," Alicen said.

"No, you didn't," Jamie said. "You just told me you were living with some girl named Gina."

"Her father's my father's patient," Alicen explained.

"Wow!" Jamie cried. "You live in that spooky old mansion? Did you know it was haunted?"

"That's silly," Alicen said, taking a bite of her sandwich.

"I heard stories," Jamie said. "See, it was built a zillion years ago, and everytime anyone moved into it they either left in a hurry, or" —his eyes became very round, and he spoke slowly, teasing Alicen— "they died."

"You're crazy!" Alicen cried.

"Quiet down there!" the cafeteria monitor yelled.

Jamie was snickering. Alicen frowned at him.

"It is not haunted," she said in a softer voice.

"A bunch of people died there last year," Jamie said. "And if you don't believe me, it was in the papers."

"Liar!" Alicen hissed. "I'm not going to make a jerk out of myself by looking up a story that never happened."

She was glad when the lunch bell rang. She moved quickly away from him, but he caught up with her.

"Hey, I'm really sorry I scared you," Jamie said. "But it is true."

"Well, I'll ask Mrs. VanBuren tonight," Alicen said. "And I still think you're lying."

But somehow, she was unable to ask Melanie. Dinner came, and still she hesitated. She was terrified that they'd make fun of her or that her father would become angry that she'd fall for such a story. Murders? In this beautiful old house?

Still, she wasn't quite so sure. . . .

"Alicen, pass me the bread?" Kyle asked.

Alicen started, jumping out of her thoughts.

"What's up?" Melanie asked. "Daydreaming?"

"No," Alicen said. She handed Kyle the bread basket.

"I'll bet she's thinking about that Jamie Hutchinson," Kyle teased.

Alicen looked at him.

"Kyle—" Gary said in a warning tone.

"Who's Jamie Hutchinson?" Derek asked.

"Just a boy in my class," Alicen said, embarrassed.

"Well, I hope he's just a friend," Derek said. "You're much too young for boys."

"How do you know about him, Kyle?" Melanie asked. "Do you eat lunch at the same time as Alicen?"

"No," Kyle said. "Jamie's brother Mikey is in my class. He told me Jamie talks about Alicen all the time."

Alicen sank lower into her chair.

"That's so neat," Gina said. "I wish a boy would talk about me."

"Somebody will, honey," Gary said. "When that day comes."

Nancy, who had been concentrating on her dinner, held out her empty plate. "Mommy, I want more spaghetti!"

Melanie took the plate from her daughter and went to the kitchen to refill it. She was surprised when she turned and saw Alicen behind her. Alicen shook her head when asked if she wanted more, too.

"Uh, Mrs. VanBuren?"

"What is it, Alicen?"

"I just wanted to know if, uhm—"

She shifted back and forth, staring down at her feet. "Oh, never mind!" she cried, hurrying back into the dining room.

"Now, what was that all about?" Melanie wondered out loud as she watched the door swing shut.

Alicen probably wanted to ask her something about boys but was too embarrassed. Considering she didn't have a mother, she probably didn't know what boys were all about. Derek didn't seem the type to sit down with his daughter and talk about the facts of life.

"The poor kid," Melanie said, picking up Nancy's dish. "It must be tough growing up without a mother."

Later, when Gina and Alicen were helping her with the dishes, she leaned over and whispered, "If you ever want to talk, I'm here. I can keep a secret."

"Okay," Alicen said. She appreciated that, but still couldn't bring herself to ask Melanie if the house was haunted. The more she thought, the more Alicen decided it was just a silly story.

Until that night, when she heard the laughter again. . . .

As before, she was in bed when the laughter started. She turned on her stomach and buried her head under her pillow. The laughter rose to a high pitch, filling her room. Finally, she couldn't stand it any more—she had to convince herself that it was only a draft blowing through the grating in the floor. She climbed out of her bed.

When she switched on her light, the glare blinded her, and she had to grope toward the grating. She was going to put her hands over it, to feel that there was air coming up through it. Then she would know there was nothing to fear.

She dropped to her knees on the carpet and put her hands out. No draft, though she could still hear the laughter. What *was* that? Something made her crawl nearer, and she looked down into the grating.

"EEEYYYAAA!"

She jumped back, screaming. A hideous face had smiled up at her! Even as she stumbled to her bed and sat there crying, she could see it in her mind's eye. The eyes had been blue and filmy, the smile revealing sharp teeth. There was blood caked on the blue-veined forehead.

The door opened just then. Alicen looked up through tears to see her father entering the room, his eyes shadowed with concern.

"What's wrong?" he asked, coming nearer to her bed. "Were you dreaming?"

"I—I saw a face," Alicen choked.

She pointed to the grating in the floor. "I heard funny noises, and when I went over to look, there was this ugly face under there!"

"Alicen, that's just ridiculous," Derek said. "You were dreaming."

Now Melanie was standing in the doorway. "I heard Alicen. What's wrong?"

"Nothing," Derek said. "My daughter was just having a bad dream. I hope it didn't wake the other children."

"They're sleeping soundly," Melanie said. She came up to Alicen's bed. "Honey, what on earth were you dreaming about?"

"It wasn't a dream," Alicen insisted, wishing they would just go away and leave her alone. "I saw a face staring at me under the floor grating."

"It was probably just a trick of the lights," Derek said, standing. He had Alicen firmly by the arm. "Come over here and I'll show you there's nothing there."

"NNNNOOOO!"

"Shut up!" Derek snapped. "You want to wake the other kids, like at the Laines' house?"

"I don't want to go over there!"

Melanie moved forward to intervene, but not quickly enough to stop Derek from dragging his screaming child to the floor grating.

She stood stiffly, with her face turned away, an icy chill crawling over her.

"Look at it, Alicen," Derek ordered. "There is nothing there!"

"No!"

Derek, exasperated, twisted her arm a little. Alicen obeyed him at last and saw the grating was empty.

"Dad, I know I—"

"You were dreaming," Derek insisted.

Melanie felt something in her stomach go sour, something that told her Alicen hadn't been dreaming at all.

"What made you have such an awful dream?" she asked.

"Jamie Hutchinson," Alicen said. "He told me people were murdered in this house. Is that true?"

Melanie gasped a little, then quickly said, "No no, of course it isn't true. Now, you just lie down and go back to sleep. Would you like some tea or hot chocolate to help you relax?"

Alicen was looking into Derek's eyes. The warning in them made her shake her head.

"No, I'll be okay," she said.

Seeing the girl shivering, Melanie went to the bureau and pulled out an extra blanket. To her surprise, Derek took it from her and laid it over his daughter. Then he bent and kissed her forehead.

"You'll be all right," he said.

He walked with Melanie out to the hall, closing Alicen's door very tightly before speaking. "I'm sorry," he said. "I don't know why she behaves so hysterically."

"It's all right," Melanie said, resisting the urge to tell Derek off for being so rough with the child. "I'm sure Alicen will forget all this by morning."

Derek waved his hand. "No. She's had nightmares before this— about Elaine's death. I was certain she was over them. Now she's probably wakened your children."

"I told you they were sleeping," Melanie said. She laughed, trying to ease the tension. "My kids sleep through wars."

"I just don't understand her," Derek said softly.

"It's no wonder she had nightmares," Melanie said. "After those stories Jamie Hutchinson told her about murders. What would possess a boy to do that?"

"Showing off, I guess," Derek said. But something in Melanie's face told him there was more to it than this. Her eyes were just a little too wide, and her smile was just a little too forced.

"Uh, there isn't any truth to that, is there?" he asked. "I know it's a stupid question, but—"

"Derek, nothing bad ever happened in this house," Melanie insisted. "Look, I'm really tired. I'll see you in the morning."

With that, she hurried down the dark hallway. She got into bed, closed her eyes, and pressed herself close to Gary, as if his body could act as a barrier against the darkness. She pulled the covers clear up to her chin, not wanting an inch of her body exposed to the night. Then she buried her face in Gary's chest and breathed deeply. Soon, out of sheer exhaustion, she fell asleep.

Someone touched her arm. Melanie opened her eyes slowly and looking at the clock radio vaguely noted that several hours had passed. She closed her eyes again and snuggled closer to Gary. But when she heard her name, she opened them again and turned around.

The dark-haired woman was standing next to her bed. "Come," she said, taking Melanie's hand.

Without protest, Melanie rose from the bed and followed the woman from the room. She felt sleepy and yet keenly aware of the noises in the house. The wind blew outside, rattling the windows. Nancy was mumbling in her sleep, and Lad gave one yelp from the kitchen.

But Lad was sound asleep when they entered that room. Once again, the light was shining brightly. Able to see her surroundings, Melanie felt stronger; her voice was somewhat harsh when she demanded, "What does all this mean?"

The woman shrank from her words.

"Please," Melanie said, more gently, "I know you're trying to tell me something. What is it?"

"It is not over yet," the woman said sadly.

"What isn't?" Melanie asked, though she felt something gnawing at her stomach. "Please tell me! I can't fight what I don't know!"

"You must leave this place!" the woman cried. She looked over her shoulder, her brown eyes wide with terror. Then she turned back to Melanie.

"I must go!" she cried, wringing her tattered gown. "She comes now. She is evil!"

"Who is she?" Melanie demanded.

But the woman disappeared. Melanie took a step forward, and as she did so, the room light went out. She swung around terrified, expecting to see something hovering behind her in the darkness. But no one was there.

"What do you want?" Melanie whispered. "Who are you?"

No answer. The clock above the sink began to tick loudly. Melanie stared up at it, unmoving. Her eyes began to droop, though she desperately wanted to stay awake. She sank down to the floor.

She forced her eyes open again. But she wasn't looking up at the clock. She was looking at the clock radio next to her bed. It was 7:30 A.M., and the sun was shining.

It was just another dream, she told herself insistently. I just had the horrible incidents of last year on my mind.

In broad daylight it was easier to convince herself not to be afraid.

Much to Alicen's relief, nothing was said about the incident at breakfast. Alicen sat with her head low to her cereal bowl, trying to make herself believe it had been a dream. But it had seemed so real!

Across the table, Derek was also thinking about it. He recalled the series of nightmares Alicen had had after her mother died. Was that happening again? Or was his daughter overly impressed by tall tales of a young boy? Funny, Melanie had seemed a little unnerved about it all, more than she should have been if it was only a dream. He looked over the rim of his coffee cup at her. She was reading an art magazine, nibbling on a piece of toast. Derek recalled the strange way she had behaved the night before. He wondered if she had been hiding a secret—something to do with the murders Alicen had spoken of. But that was just ridiculous, Derek thought. Melanie had flatly denied it, and the VanBurens were hardly the types to be involved in murders. No, it was just a dream. That was all there was to it.

"Mom, you have to sign a permission slip for me," Gina said then, interrupting his thoughts. She pulled a piece of blue paper from between the pages of a book.

"What's it for?" Melanie asked.

"The eighth grade is going on a trip to Vanderbilt Planetarium," Gina explained.

"Are you going?" Derek asked Alicen.

Alicen nodded and produced her own slip of paper. Derek and Melanie read and signed them. Gina smiled at Melanie. Alicen did not smile at her father.

"We'll have to do something special for your graduation," Gary said. "Maybe we could have a family reunion."

"What a good idea!" Melanie said. "Our family hasn't really seen this house yet."

"You never had a housewarming?" Derek asked.

"Well, we were kind of—*busy* the first months," Melanie faltered.

Alicen stirred her cereal. Without raising her head, she looked up at Melanie. What were they busy with? Murders?

"What's the matter?" Gina asked her.

"Nothing," Alicen said, shoving a spoonful of cereal into her mouth.

Later Gary and Derek left for a session of therapy and Gina and Kyle went out to the bus stop but Alicen dawdled, fingering the counter and finding excuses to delay. She bent down to tie a shoe that was already tied. Then she leaned heavily on the counter, finding a place for her elbow amid all the dishes and propping her chin on her hand. She looked up at Melanie.

"Do you think I could have another bedroom?"

"Why?" Melanie asked. "Because of last night?"

Alicen nodded. "I saw a face—I know I did! It had blond hair, and it was *ugly*. I don't want to stay in that room."

Melanie put her hand against Alicen's cheek.

"Honey, it's just a dream," she insisted. "This house is as safe as can be."

"Jamie Hutchinson said—"

"Jamie Hutchinson is a big fibber," Melanie said. "And if I get hold of him I'll—well, never mind. Just realize that boys often make up stories to impress the girls they like."

"They do?"

"They do," Melanie said. "Hey, here comes the bus! You'd better hurry and catch up with the others."

Alicen started to run out the door, but before she did she turned and kissed Melanie on the cheek. Melanie watched her race down the hill, thinking her weight made her look much younger than thirteen. She wasn't happy to hear about that boy teasing her. Wasn't it obvious that Alicen had enough problems? A mother who was dead, a father who had no patience with her?

Melanie went to the sink and tried to concentrate on the breakfast dishes. Somehow, alone in the kitchen with Alicen's "dream" on her mind, she was taken back to the night when Gary had been hurt. She saw a tall, dark-haired intruder fighting with her husband. She heard Gary's scream, then glass shattering.

Somehow, she could believe that Alicen had really seen a face. What had she said? That it was blond-haired and ugly? Now Melanie closed her eyes and saw a face herself. It was of a young, pretty blond woman. She was smiling, but then the smile faded and turned into an evil grimace. Melanie's eyes snapped open.

She felt her lungs constrict, and a weakness in her legs that came when she was feeling guilty about something. But why? She had nothing to do with the woman's death. Why did she always feel such pain to think about her? Last night, when Gary had mentioned the librarian's death, she had wanted to scream. If it wasn't her fault, why did she always feel such guilt about it?

"It isn't guilt," Melanie said. "It's sorrow."

She scrubbed hard at a frying pan. "Oh, Janice," she whispered. "Why did you have to die like that?"

Suddenly the frying pan slipped from her hand. It fell to the floor with a loud clatter and rocked there before settling at Melanie's feet. Sighing, she bent down to retrieve it.

"I've gotten myself so nervous I'm dropping things," Melanie said out loud. "I've got to stop thinking this way!"

She wiped at the pot with furious motions. "Everything is all right," she said.

She was unaware that an unseen hand had knocked the skillet from her, a gesture of anger at her words. Everything was not all right.

You killed me! the being shouted, as if Melanie could hear her. *It's your fault I walk in darkness, and you'll pay for it!*

But not yet, Melanie VanBuren. I won't let you discover me until it's too late.

7

Melanie decided the best way to conquer her fears was to work hard on her painting. She finished the two paintings for Sarah Kaufman sooner than she had expected. One day, she dropped Nancy off at kindergarten and headed toward the mayor's house. It was a mansion on the other side of town, as big as theirs, but much newer.

"Let me see the masterpieces," Sarah said, inviting Melanie to sit down in the living room. "I can't believe you finished them already!"

She tore the brown paper from the two canvases and propped them against the table. Sarah gasped and lifted one of them to study it. Then she carried it to the fireplace, setting it on the mantel in front of a portrait of some distant relative. She stepped back and admired Melanie's painting.

"Look at the detail!" she cried happily. "I love the way the sun's rays hit the church spire. And I can almost count every bud on the rosebushes."

She turned and smiled at Melanie. "They're pink."

"Well, of course," Melanie said. "That's what you asked for."

"Marc is going to be so pleased," Sarah said. "I haven't told him about these, yet. They're a surprise for his birthday."

As Sarah poured coffee into dainty gold demitasse cups, Melanie looked around the elegant living room. "Are these antiques family heirlooms?" she asked.

"Oh, no. I found them in antique shops over the years," Sarah said.

"My husband collects antiques, too," Melanie said. "That's one of the reasons he bought our house. It's the one at the top of Starbine Court."

"Oh, yes," Sarah said. "Marc and I nearly bought it a few years ago."

Melanie's eyebrows went up. She put her coffee cup back in its saucer. "Why didn't you?" she asked, curious.

"Well, I don't really know," Sarah said. She seemed embarrassed and turned to look out the French windows. "I just didn't like the place. There was something about it that made me feel uneasy."

Melanie stiffened. "What was that?"

"Oh, it was silly," Sarah said, waving her hand. The huge diamond she wore on her finger sparkled brightly in the sunlight. "I'd been ill at the time—perhaps I just wasn't receptive to it. Not to say it isn't a beautiful home. But this one is more to my tastes. Your house has a rather masculine air about it, don't you think?"

"I suppose that reflects the man who built it," Melanie said.

"Do you know about him?" Sarah asked, leaning forward eagerly.

"His name was Jacob Armand," Melanie said, not really wanting to talk about it, but there was no way out. "He was a captain in the British navy during the 1790s."

"How interesting," Sarah said.

"Yes, it is," Melanie said, taking a sip of coffee. "But that's all I know about him. Say, these roses are lovely. Do you have a garden?"

"I sure do," Sarah said eagerly. "Would you like to see it?"

They wandered in the garden, then sat outside talking, until Melanie realized her children would be home from school. But before she left Melanie invited Sarah and the mayor for dinner the following week. She liked Sarah, and it wouldn't hurt her career to have the mayor and his wife known as her patrons.

Melanie left the house in a happy mood, whistling as she drove home. All of a sudden, she spotted Alicen Miller trudging down the street. Wondering why she wasn't on the school bus, Melanie honked the horn. Alicen turned and squinted at her. Melanie pulled the car over to the curb and let her in.

"What happened?"

"I missed the bus," Alicen said, wriggling in the seat to get comfortable.

"Wasn't Gina with you?"

"No, she must be home by now," said Alicen. She clicked her tongue and sighed. "Oh! I had to stay after school because I got into trouble today. That's the real reason I missed the bus."

"You?" Melanie asked. "How on earth did you get in trouble?"

"That dumb old Mr. Percy—that's my teacher—sent me to the

principal's office. He said I never pay attention to him. I tried really hard, but I kept thinking about that dream I had."

Melanie took the girl's hand and squeezed it.

"Is that still bothering you?" she asked. "I know it was horrible, but it was just a dream. Keep telling yourself that, and you'll feel better."

"That's what I was doing this afternoon," Alicen said. "And I got into trouble 'cause of it."

"Did you explain the situation to the principal?"

"She didn't want to hear it," Alicen said. She stared down at the books on her lap. "No one wants to listen to me."

"And they call themselves teachers," Melanie grumbled. Louder, she said, "They should at least have driven you home. Your father must be frantic!"

"My father never worries about me," Alicen said. "He probably doesn't know I'm not home yet."

That evening when Derek left for the health club, he packed his jacket and a good shirt in his duffel bag. As he drove to the club, his thoughts were on Liza. He hoped she would accept an invitation to go out for a midnight snack. He was trying to decide where they should go when something made him look in his rear-view mirror. A few hundred yards behind, he saw the blond hitchhiker again. Sighing, he pushed his foot down on the gas pedal. At least he knew she was alive, he thought. But she'd never get in his car again.

He sped down the road a few more miles, putting a distance between himself and the girl before easing the pressure of his foot.

I don't know why I let that girl upset me, he thought as he entered the "safety" of the club.

One look at Liza made him forget the hitchhiker completely. She was sitting in the waiting room, dressed in white terry, racket in hand. She smiled at Derek and stood up.

"Am I late?" he asked.

"Not at all," Liza said. "Go put your things in a locker, and I'll meet you on the court."

Much to Derek's surprise, Liza turned out to be a terrific racquet ball player. She explained that the Z-shot he'd helped her with a week ago was her only problem and that she'd been playing the game for years. She beat him two out of three.

"I probably shouldn't admit this," Derek said as they walked off the court, "but my ego's been shattered."

"It'd be wrong to say I'm sorry," Liza teased. "I played fair and square."

"You play like a man," Derek said. "Just watch out next time, lady."

Liza put her hands on her hips and tossed back her dark hair.

"What do you mean I 'play like a man'?" she asked. "I play to win, and that's all. You're sexist."

"Sorry," Derek said. "It's just that I've never been defeated by a woman."

Shut up, Derek, he told himself. *Before you blow it.*

"It isn't that painful, is it?" Liza asked.

Derek thought for a moment. "No, I guess not. Especially not when you're my partner. Say, would you like to relax in the whirlpool awhile?"

"I was thinking the same thing," Liza said. "Meet you there in ten minutes."

Derek was relieved to find the whirlpool unoccupied. He leaned back, letting the water massage his aching muscles. A day of therapy with Gary, and three games had made him sore all over. He opened his eyes and smiled lazily when Liza sat down beside him.

"That bathing suit is beautiful," Derek said. "Almost as beautiful as the woman in it."

"Okay," Liza said, laughing, "you've earned your Brownie points. I don't think you're sexist any more."

"I mean it," Derek said. "You look as if you're in top physical condition. I—uh—I'm speaking from a therapist's point of view, of course."

"Of course," Liza said, smiling. "Remember I'm a dancer, and I keep myself in shape."

"That's obvious," Derek said.

That's the understatement of the year, he thought. She was downright stunning. Her one-piece suit clung tightly to her, its shiny material showing off her curves. There was just enough fat on her body to make her soft looking, but not an ounce too much. She had rolled her hair up, and now her cheekbones stood out. Derek couldn't help staring at her.

"I've thought about you all week," he said.

"Really?" Liza asked, sounding pleased. "I was afraid you'd forget me."

"Are you kidding?" Derek asked. "I was hoping you'd want to see me again."

Liza moved a little closer to him. A second later, he felt her hand on his thigh. He gaped at her, then grinned. She smiled slightly, teasingly.

"I've only known you for a while," she said, "yet I know you're my kind of man."

"Thanks," Derek said. God, it had been so long since a woman had touched him this way. Unseen beneath the foamy waters, he slid his arm around Liza's waist.

"I think I'm falling in love," he said.

"Me, too," was the answer.

They stared at each other. Without another word, Derek leaned forward and kissed Liza. She moaned a little, pushing herself closer to him. They kissed passionately, so passionately that they suddenly slipped and went under the water. They quickly pulled each other up and sat there laughing hysterically.

"Do all great love affairs start this way?" Liza asked, rubbing her eyes.

"I don't know," Derek said. "But they ought to. I've never been kissed like that before."

He thought for a split second of Elaine, feeling a little guilty. Then he smiled again and took Liza's hand.

"Want to get dressed?" he asked.

"Sure," she said, a little breathlessly. "I've got to get home to practice."

"Practice?" Derek asked. "But I was hoping we could go out somewhere."

"Some other time," Liza said, giving him an apologetic smile. "I have a recital coming up tomorrow."

"You should have told me about it," Derek said. "I would have gone."

"It's private. Only for the dance instructor and class. I'll be advanced according to how I do on this."

"You'll do great," Derek said. "I just wish you could come with me tonight."

"Don't be disappointed, honey," Liza said, kissing him.

"I'll see you soon," Derek said.

"You bet."

They hugged for a few minutes, their wet bodies pressed so close that they could feel each other's heat rising. At last, Derek pulled away.

He didn't wait to see Liza again, but went straight to his Volvo. He unlocked the door, got behind the wheel, and drove out of the parking lot. The car had taken him halfway home when someone suddenly tapped his shoulder and said, "Hello."

Startled out of his thoughts of Liza, Derek turned around and saw the hitchhiker sitting in the back seat. She was grinning.

"What in the hell are you doing here?" Derek demanded angrily.

"I waited for you," the woman said. "I wanted to talk."

"What for?" Derek asked. "Why do you keep following me? We don't even know each other."

"Well, my name is Janice," she said. "And I know you very well."

Suddenly she jumped over the back of the seat. Her hand fell between Derek's legs, grabbing him. He jumped, feeling a pain in his groin as intense as if she had kicked him. The car jumped a curb, and Derek moved quickly to straighten it again.

"Are you crazy?" Derek shouted, pulling over and stopping. "Get the hell out of my car!"

"I want you," the woman said, unbuttoning his slacks.

Derek pushed her hand away. It was like moving cotton. He turned and looked at her, assessing her strength. She'd be easy enough to throw out of the car, but he didn't want to give her a chance to have him arrested for assault.

"Just get out," he said. "I don't want to hurt you. Just leave me alone."

"The way you left me alone?" she demanded as she opened the door. "You'll pay for that, Derek Miller."

She was out of the car before he realized he had never told her his name. He jumped out of the car, calling out: "How'd you know my name?"

But the street was now completely deserted. Filled with curiosity, Derek walked up and down, looking for the strange woman. But she was nowhere to be found. Wondering how she could have slipped into the shadows so quickly, he returned to his car. He had never been a man to fear threats, and so he climbed into the car and tried to put the incident out of his mind.

"What could that crazy little bitch do to me?" he asked himself.

He drove home at a faster speed than usual, unwilling to admit that the thought of the woman knowing his name made his flesh crawl.

8

Derek stared up at the beam of dark wood that ran across his ceiling. He had been awake for an hour, trying to make sense of the evening's strange events. His hands were folded behind his head, and his teeth dug into his lower lip, pressing harder as his thoughts grew more intense. He had already decided how the woman had gotten into his car. It was old, and the lock didn't work very well. But how did she know where to find him? And more than that, how did she know his name?

Derek shook his head roughly, driving away sleep that wanted to claim him. He wanted this mystery solved, *now*.

Thinking the comfortable bed was making his mind wander, he got out of it and pulled on his robe. Walking barefoot out to the hall, he closed the door softly. He stopped when he heard a whimpering noise—Alicen talking in her sleep. Derek ran his fingers through his hair, then reached for the knob of her door. His fingers held it but hesitated.

"Mommy!"

The kid sounded so frantic.

"Mommy, come home."

Derek pulled his hand away from the door. Another dream? When were those going to stop? When was Alicen going to face the fact that her mother wasn't ever going to come home?

But he knew Alicen would never accept the truth. Even though she had seen Elaine's car explode and had stood there watching as the twisted body was pulled from the wreck, she refused to believe it was her mother. That first year had been especially painful. Alicen would look outside every time a car stopped in front of the apartment house, hoping it was her mother.

Derek was struck with the painful memory of Alicen's eighth birthday. Elaine had only been dead a month.

"Mommy told me she'd buy me a new dress," Alicen had said.

Derek could almost feel her small arms around his waist. He closed his eyes.

"I know, darling," he had replied. "But mommy's gone now. And you know how expensive the funeral was. I'm afraid you'll have to wait for your dress."

"Oh, that's all right," the little girl said cheerfully. "I'll have a new dress when mommy comes home."

Derek recalled that he had given her a stuffed animal. Alicen had almost crushed him with her hug. She had once been such an affectionate child. But over the years she had drawn into a shell, until Derek could barely remember their last loving embrace.

He felt a pain for the child that used to be and drove it away.

He shuffled down the hall, then the stairs, and finally entered the kitchen. He always felt as if he were walking into another time zone. Despite the antiques in the rest of the house, the VanBurens had equipped their kitchen with every up-to-date convenience, from the white side-by-side freezer-refrigerator to the gleaming green and yellow tiled floor. The only antique in here was a wooden table with X-shaped legs. He sat down and propped his feet up on one of the X's. At that moment Lad jumped up and barked at him.

"Shh," Derek whispered. He slapped his thigh. "Come here, boy."

Lad rested his chin on Derek's knee. The soulful brown eyes looked up into Derek's, asking for affection. Derek stroked the dog's smooth head and spoke to him as if he were human.

"Can you figure this out?" he asked. "What do you suppose that

woman wants from me?" Lad whined. "I don't know, either," Derek
said, yawning.

He leaned back in the chair and turned to gaze through the back-
door window at the moon. Sighing deeply, he just sat, waiting for an
answer to come to him.

"Wait a minute," he said, turning to the dog again. "I know! Suppose, for some crazy reason she's been spying on me? She must know
I go to the health club a few nights a week. She just followed me
there and hid out in my car."

It made sense, but it didn't answer the most important question:
why? What could she want from him? He had no money to speak
of, and little of value—*nothing* of value, he corrected himself.

Suddenly Lad let out a growl and leaped for the back door. Startled, Derek pushed his chair back and went to investigate. The hitchhiker was staring through the back-door window! She was smiling at
him, her pointy teeth glistening wetly. Her eyes, shining with malevolent delight, had a filmy look to them. She didn't move or make a
sound. She just stood there grinning.

"You bitch!" Derek hissed.

He turned quickly to the cupboard behind him and removed the
back-door key. As he twisted the lock, he glowered at the woman's
hideous face. He wouldn't be afraid. He'd let her in and make her
tell him. . . .

But just as Derek got the door open, she ducked away. He stepped
outside quickly and peered around through the darkness. He could
see the silhouettes of the trees beyond the huge back yard; nothing
seemed to be moving. The moon above cast a silver-gray glow over
everything at such an angle that there were no shadows.

"She must have run into the woods," Derek reasoned, "and there
is no way I'm going to chase her around out there."

Let her go, his mind ordered.

He locked the door behind him. It was all a sick joke, of course.
He shuddered and rubbed his arms to ward off a sudden chill. Lad
nudged him and after receiving a few strokes of reassurance, went
under the table to sleep.

Oh, damn, Derek thought as he headed out of the kitchen.

Never a man to be easily frightened, he decided to forget the
whole thing. How could he let it upset him? It was just some smart-

ass kid in old clothes and Halloween makeup. He'd ignore her. He wouldn't give her the satisfaction of showing fear. Maybe she'd get bored and leave him alone.

He did not know that it wouldn't be that easy.

"God, you look like you've been through the mill," Gary said when he entered the kitchen the next morning to find Derek already up.

"I didn't sleep much last night," Derek answered, yawning into a cup of coffee. He poured another and set it in front of Gary.

"Thanks," Gary said, adjusting himself in his wheelchair. "I thought I heard Lad barking."

"I was here in the kitchen," Derek explained. He took a sip of coffee. "Hey, Gary, are there any other families around here?"

"Not for a mile or so. And we told you the house down the road's been empty for several months. Why?"

"Well, some crazy kid's been bothering me lately. I made the stupid mistake of giving her a lift in my car one day—right down on Houston—and she's been following me around ever since."

"Maybe she's got a crush on you?" Gary asked.

"Oh, no," Derek said, shaking his head. "This isn't infatuation, it's harassment. She is probably out of her mind. You should see her. She has stringy blond hair, blue eyes, and sickly pale skin. I mean, you can almost see her veins through it." He thought a little more, then said, "Oh, yeah, and her hands are always red. Like she has frostbite."

"It's a little late in the spring for frostbite, don't you think?"

"Of course," Derek said. "She's using some kind of makeup on her hands. And on her face, too. She's just too pale—like something out of a horror movie."

Melanie entered the kitchen just then. She greeted them cheerily as Kyle scooted around her to the refrigerator.

"What intense expressions!" she cried. "What's going on?"

"Some girl's been harassing Derek lately," Gary said. He cast a look at Kyle, who seemed to be busy filling his cereal bowl. "Do you know any young women with blond hair and pale skin?"

"Yea," Melanie said, laughing. "Me."

"Paler," Derek said. "Like death warmed over. And her hair was a lighter blond. It's down to her waist and looks like she hasn't combed it in a week or two."

Melanie shook her head. "No, I don't know anyone like that." She went to the refrigerator and took out a container of milk.

"Wait," Derek said. "She told me her name. Do you know anyone named Janice?"

The milk container fell to the floor, the white liquid spilling all over the floor. "Oh, God," Melanie said in a soft voice. She waved her hands. "No, damn it. I don't know anyone named Janice."

She went to the pantry for a mop. Her heart was beating rapidly, and she felt a chill crawling over her. She rubbed hard at the milk, keeping her back to the others. Derek eyed her, wondering why she had reacted so strangely to the mention of Janice's name. Perhaps she did know her?

Later Derek asked Gary about Melanie's reaction. Gary tried to explain it.

"See, Melanie had a good friend once named Janice," he said. "But she died the same night I was hurt. Uhm—I was unconscious at the time, but they told me later that the same—uhm—the same guy who pushed me from the window killed her."

"No wonder Melanie was upset. I probably brought back painful memories," Derek said apologetically.

"Melanie's sensitive about it," Gary said. "She somehow feels responsible for what happened to Janice, but of course that's ridiculous."

"What did happen to her?"

Gary stopped and stared into his eyes. "I don't really know," he said.

"Well, okay," Derek replied. "But I know of course that that Janice isn't the one who was in my car. Not if she's dead. There're no such things as ghosts."

Across the room, an unseen woman laughed silently.

Oh, but there are ghosts, my handsome Derek! she cried, unheard by him. *You'll soon learn how real I am! They'll all learn, and they'll pay for what they did to me.*

*   *   *

Derek decided he would simply ignore the woman the next time she showed up. But a week had gone by with no sign of her. Well, that was fine. Maybe she had seen him with Liza and decided he wasn't single and worth pursuing any more.

Tonight he was dressing in his best clothes for the dinner with Sarah and Marc Kaufman. He had bought Alicen a new dress (much to her surprise). His child shouldn't look like a street urchin around all this wealth.

Down the hallway, Melanie was in Nancy's room, busy tying and retying the blue sash to her daughter's best dress. Kyle bounced on the bed, whining about his seersucker suit. Gina stood at the vanity table with Alicen, combing her friend's hair.

"Kyle, sit still," Melanie said, at last finishing the bow. "You'll mess up your clothes."

"How come I hafta wear these dumb pants?" Kyle asked, settling on the mattress. "They're scratchy!"

"Oh, Kyle," Gina said in a motherly tone, "stop complaining. You look very nice."

Kyle clicked his tongue and jumped from the bed, heading for the door. Just as he reached it, Gary entered the room, on crutches. Kyle stopped short to avoid a collision, his arms spread out at his sides.

"Where are you going so fast?" Gary asked, laughing.

"Downstairs to the kitchen," Kyle said, ducking past him.

"Stay out of the food!" Melanie called. She smiled at Gary. "Say, you look great. It's been a long time since you wore a suit."

"And a long time since I was walking," Gary said. "I hope I do okay tonight."

"You'll do fine," Melanie reassured him. This was the first time Gary would be using his crutches in front of strangers. Melanie went to him and slid her arms around his waist. They kissed warmly.

"We make a beautiful couple," she said.

"You're beautiful," Gary said, running his hands over her peach-colored jersey dress. "And you've really done a great job tonight. I've never seen the kids so immaculate."

He looked over his shoulder at his daughters. Gina was dressed in an eyelet-trimmed denim jumper, while Nancy wore a red-and-white flowered dress. Even Alicen was attired neatly. Her father had bought her a stylish shirtdress with tiny vertical stripes that made her chubby body look a little thinner.

"You'd think it was Easter Sunday," he said.

"It isn't going to kill you," Melanie responded, picking up a comb from Nancy's dresser to brush her hair for the fifth time.

Now Nancy opened her little jewelry box, revealing a tiny dancing ballerina. She lifted out a silver and turquoise bracelet. Gina offered to help her put it on, but Nancy refused, insisting that her father do it. Gary obliged, smiling at his little daughter.

"Why don't you kids go downstairs?" Melanie said after he had finished. "You can make sure everything looks right."

"Yea," Gary said. "Your mother's expecting the queen of England."

"It's just the mayor," Nancy said.

"The way your mother's got you kids dressed up," Gary said, "she might as well be the queen of England."

"Gary!" Melanie cried.

Gary left the room laughing. Melanie had to admit he was right, though.

Sarah arrived wearing a pale pink suit. Four gold chains hung from her neck, and gold earrings dangled from her ears.

"Boy, she looks rich," Kyle whispered.

Melanie aimed a swat behind her to hush her son, then smiled and greeted Sarah and Marc Kaufman. Marc, who had brown hair just turning gray and a thin mustache, offered a stark contrast to his wife in his plain, though expensive, gray suit.

"Sarah and Marc," she said, "I'd like you to meet my husband, Gary."

"Glad to know you," Sarah said.

Marc hesitated to extend his hand, seeing Gary's crutches. But Gary reached out and took his firmly. Marc grinned.

"This is Derek Miller," Gary said, "my therapist."

Derek and Marc shook hands, then Melanie introduced the children. Sarah leaned down to Nancy and chucked her under the chin.

"My, aren't you a pretty little thing?"

Melanie saw Alicen shuffling in the background and quickly said,

"This is Alicen Miller, Derek's daughter. She and her father live with us."

"Hello, dear," Sarah said.

"Hello," Alicen replied, shyly averting her eyes from this stranger.

Sarah and Marc followed everyone down the long hallway. Sarah commented that something smelled luscious, and Melanie told her they were having rib roast for dinner. In the dining room, Sarah complimented Melanie on the centerpiece of azaleas and baby's breath as she settled herself into a massive oak chair. Melanie suddenly remembered Gary's comment about the queen of England and bit her lip to suppress a giggle. She turned into the kitchen to get the food, aided by Kyle and Gina.

Gary's chair had been placed near the sideboard so that he could serve the wine. He turned around and lifted a heavy crystal carafe, filling five matching goblets.

"Excellent wine," Marc said. "What is it?"

Gary laughed. "You're asking me? I hardly know the difference between red and rosé!"

"Well, let's see," Melanie said, leaning toward the sideboard.

She picked up the empty bottle that sat behind the carafe and brought it closer to read it.

There was a sudden crash, and giving a cry, Melanie jumped away from the table. The bottle had exploded in her hand. Shocked, she held out her palm to Gary, showing a trickle of blood that ran from a gash in her skin.

"Kyle, get the first-aid kit," Gary said quickly.

He reached for his crutches, but Derek was already on his feet and leading Melanie into the kitchen. He held a white napkin to her hand to stop the flow of blood. Melanie grimaced in pain.

"I don't know how that happened," she cried as Derek put her hand under a running faucet to wash it.

"You'll be okay," Derek said, examining it. "It's a long cut, but not a very deep one."

Melanie shuddered. "It hurts."

Kyle entered the kitchen with the first-aid kit and put it on the counter. While Derek opened it to take out a bandage, the little boy stood on tiptoe to see his mother's hand. Gary, who was standing in the doorway, called to him.

"Kyle, leave your mother alone," he said.

"Is she gonna be okay?" Kyle asked. "Mom, does it hurt a lot?"

"It just stings," Melanie said, smiling for his benefit.

Derek wrapped the cut with gauze, then closed the first-aid kit. Holding her hand upright, Melanie reentered the dining room while Gary held the door open for her. She looked around at her guests. Sarah and Marc looked worried, Gina and Nancy were whispering, and Alicen kept her eyes on her lap.

"Wait until you see what I do for an encore," Melanie joked, hoping to ease the tension.

Everyone laughed. Melanie was glad, for this night was very important to her. She wouldn't spoil it by letting them know how much her hand hurt.

"What do you suppose happened?" Marc asked.

"Maybe a tremendous pressure built up inside the bottle while it was sitting there for so many months. Melanie just happened to pick it up at the wrong time," Gary theorized.

"That makes sense," Derek agreed.

"Yes, I'm sure that's what it was," Melanie said, a slight inflection in her voice betraying her uneasiness. She just wanted to forget the whole thing. "Come on, eat the food before it gets cold. Gary, will you carve the roast for us?"

"Yeah," Kyle said. "I'm hungry."

Beef, mashed potatoes, and peas made the rounds, and at last everyone settled down to eat. Sarah noticed Melanie was having problems and asked, "Would you like me to cut that meat for you? You really should rest your hand."

"I'd appreciate it," Melanie said. "It is kind of awkward."

"I know how frustrating it is to be helpless," Sarah said. "When I had a heart attack a few years ago, I was unable to do anything for myself for weeks."

"I never knew you had a heart condition," Melanie said. "You seem so healthy."

"I'm better now," Sarah said. "I haven't had a second attack."

"Thank God," Marc said, squeezing his wife's hand.

Sarah turned to smile at her husband, and as she did so she noticed that Alicen was staring intently at the diamond ring she wore. Sarah smiled a little at her, thinking how different she looked from the VanBuren children. While they were listening alertly to the conversation around them, Alicen seemed lost in another world. And while they were beautiful to look at, Alicen was plain and overweight. A feeling of pity ran through Sarah. Poor child, she thought, deciding to talk to her to make her feel comfortable.

"Do you like my ring?"

Alicen nodded, staring as if entranced by the reflection of the chandelier on the facets. Sarah took it off and handed it to her.

"It's beautiful," Alicen said softly. "My mother had one just like it."

Now Derek recalled the engagement ring he had given his wife. It hadn't been as big as this one, but it was as beautiful. He felt his stomach twist as he remembered the last time he had seen the ring on the charred, twisted remains of Elaine's hand.

"You were wearing that the other day, weren't you?" Melanie asked, cutting off Derek's gloomy thoughts.

"I always do," Sarah said. "It's a family heirloom, passed down to me from my great-grandmother. It's a very dear possession."

Alicen, responding to a prod from Gina, turned to show the brilliant gem to her friend. The two girls sighed over it.

"All right," Derek said then, "you'd better give that back." He didn't want the ring to make Alicen start talking about her mother.

"I'm sure Alicen wouldn't hurt it," Sarah said, accepting the ring and placing it on her finger.

After dinner, at Sarah's request, Melanie took her guests on a tour of the house. They ended up in Melanie's studio. Sarah noticed the yellow paint stain on the couch.

"Accident?" she asked, sympathetically, looking at Melanie.

"The dog ran through here one night and knocked over a few things," Melanie said. A glance at Gary produced a smile from him, as if he were telling her he was glad she had accepted that reasoning. It was one less thing for Melanie to worry about, he thought. He had expected her to be upset after hearing Derek mention Janice's name, but she hadn't said a word about it all week. In fact, she looked very sure of herself tonight. Gary wanted to kiss her but restrained himself.

"May I have a glass of water?" Sarah asked, coughing a little.

"Let me get it for you," Derek said.

"I'll manage," Sarah said. "I need to exercise to work off that delicious dinner."

She patted her stomach and went downstairs to the kitchen. Passing through the dining room, she paused to smell the flowers on the table. She was admiring the arrangement when she heard the voice from the kitchen.

"Murderers!"

Sarah tilted her head. The voice had certainly come from the kitchen, and yet it sounded so far away. Was it one of the children, playing tricks on her? Trying to frighten her?

"Murderers!"

"The little monkeys," Sarah said laughing, pushing through the kitchen door.

Her smile vanished in an instant. It wasn't a child at all, but a woman, one whom Sarah recognized. Horrified, she took in the stringy blond hair and pale skin. It couldn't be—this woman had been dead for six months!

"Oh, dear," Sarah moaned, touching her forehead. She felt the cold of her diamond against her skin. Trying to tell herself it was only her imagination, she moved to leave the room. But an arm wrapped around her neck, drawing her back. Sarah grabbed it. Her fingers squished through flesh and blood and bone as if the arm were made of clay. But it wasn't clay. It was much too real, squeezing Sarah's neck tighter and tighter. She couldn't scream.

"You saw me," her assailant hissed.

"No," Sarah managed to whimper.

"You saw me, and you have to die now!"

Sarah's heart began to pound. Pain rushed from the center of her chest to her underarms. Sarah knew the pain—a heart attack. And she somehow knew also that she wouldn't survive this one.

Hail Mary full of grace . . .

"Die!"

. . . the Lord is . . .

Something muddled her thoughts. Sarah saw lights flashing over her head, blinding lights. She couldn't close her eyes.

This can't be happening.

"DIE!"

Oh, please, God, I'm so afraid. I'm so fri—

Sarah Kaufman prayed no more. Her murderer stood back, letting the body sink to the floor, and looked at her handiwork. There were no marks on Sarah's neck.

The ghostly being grinned. She had taken life, and she wanted more. . . .

Marc Kaufman turned around from a painting of Fire Island and said to Melanie, "You don't suppose my wife got lost somewhere in this big house?"

Melanie laughed. "She probably stopped to talk with the children. I'll go rescue her."

She left the room. For some reason a sudden chill rushed over her as she descended the stairs, a cold feeling in her stomach. She had felt like that after hearing Derek mention the name Janice, but she had forced her fears away. After all, it was a very common name. It was only a coincidence that Derek had mentioned it. But why did she feel that same way right now, when nothing had happened?

Sarah wasn't in the playroom. Melanie went to the kitchen and pushed at the door. It wouldn't budge.

"Sarah?" Melanie called, pushing heavily against it with her shoulder. "Sarah, are you all right?"

No answer came, and Melanie stepped back to ram her body against the door with all her strength. Breathing heavily from the effort, she stumbled into the kitchen—half-tripping over Sarah's prone form.

"Oh, my God," Melanie whispered.

Sarah was staring up at the ceiling, her mouth open in a silent scream. Her wide and glassy eyes were fixed on the overhead light.

Melanie sank to the floor, reaching to touch Sarah's face. Still warm. She looked so terrified—what had she just seen, Melanie wondered? She looked around nervously. But the kitchen was empty.

It was Kyle who broke her spell. Melanie jumped to her feet when she heard the door open, blocking her son's way. He looked up at her in confusion and said, "I just wanted a glass of milk. What's the matter?"

"Kyle, honey," Melanie said, pushing him gently from the door so that he wouldn't see Sarah, "run upstairs and get Mr. Kaufman. Tell him his wife had an—an accident."

"What happened to her?" Kyle asked, trying to look around his mother.

"Kyle, please—"

"I'm going," the little boy shouted, running away from her.

Melanie turned back to Sarah. Why couldn't she stop looking at her? What in the hell did she expect to find in that frightened expression?

Marc and Derek entered the kitchen a few moments later.

"Gary's calling a doctor," Marc said. "Kyle said my wife hurt herself?"

"I—I think she had a heart attack," Melanie said.

Marc's reaction upon seeing his wife was barely audible. "Oh, dear Lord, Sarah—"

Without wasting a moment, Derek pushed Marc aside and dropped down next to Sarah's body. At his instruction Melanie left the room to find a blanket. Derek pressed his mouth to Sarah's, vainly trying to get her breathing again. She did not respond.

"I'll try CPR," he said, looking up at Marc.

"Just help her, please!"

Now Derek pressed the palm of one hand against the back of the other, intertwining his fingers. He positioned himself over Sarah and pushed down on her chest. The muscles in his arms trembled with the effort, yet none of that strength would seep through to Sarah's heart.

"I'm sorry," Derek said, standing. "There's nothing more I can do."

"Sarah . . ."

Sirens sounded in the distance just as Melanie returned with a blanket. Derek took it and laid it carefully over the woman. Marc watched all this, stunned and not believing. He hardly noticed the ambulance attendants when they lifted Sarah's body and carried it out of the house.

Marc rode in the back of the ambulance, biting his knuckles. He was so shocked that he did not notice the heirloom diamond missing from his wife's finger.

*　　*　　*

Melanie had another dream that night. She woke up with a start to feel a cold touch on her arm. But then she saw the woman with dark hair and somehow lost her fear. Without protest, she followed her downstairs. The woman turned to her. "It is beginning again."

"What is?"

But there was no answer. Melanie felt her eyes closing, unable to stay awake. When she opened them again, she was back in bed with Gary snoring beside her.

9

◆

Sarah Kaufman was laid to rest in an ancient family plot two days later. On her death certificate, heart attack had been written under cause of death. Marc Kaufman, though deeply grieved, accepted that. It did not occur to him to ask if his wife's death had truly been from natural causes.

Melanie, feeling as great a loss as if Sarah had been a dear friend, walked slowly to her car from the graveside. She was sweating in the hot May sun, her dark brown suit making her uncomfortable. Underneath its bandage, her palm began to itch. Melanie tried to endure the pain, to make it dominate the memory of Sarah's face. But that look of horror hovered in her mind like a dark cloud, menacing her.

"Wait a minute," Melanie said to herself as she took off her jacket and got into the car. "Sarah had a heart attack. That's *all*. It has nothing to do with anything that ever happened in my house."

She turned on the radio to drown out her thoughts. But still her memory was overpowering. Vivid pictures came to her of the night of Gary's accident. She could hear the screams of her children, echoing her own screams. She could see Gary flying out the window, glass sparkling in the moonlight.

And she saw a blond-haired woman sitting in her kitchen, looking up at her with wide blue eyes. . . .

"GO AWAY!" Melanie shouted at her memories.

She gritted her teeth and concentrated on the road ahead, but still there were tears on her cheeks.

"You've been crying," Gary said when she got home. "Funeral upset you?"

"No," Melanie said. "I was thinking about the—well, remembering the look on Sarah's face."

"Why?" Gary asked. "It was sad that she died, and a shock, too. But she did say she had a heart condition."

"She looked *terrified*, Gary," Melanie said. "As if she had seen something."

Gary sighed very deeply and said with patience, "Melanie, she didn't see anything. What would she see in an empty kitchen? She had a heart attack—maybe she'd rushed down the stairs too quickly when she left us."

"I don't know, Gary," Melanie said. "I wish I could believe it was that simple. But I had another one of those 'dreams' last night."

"What dreams?" Gary asked with concern.

"Do you remember the night you found me in the kitchen? When you said I was sleepwalking?"

"Yes?"

"I had two more of those dreams," Melanie said. "Once that night Alicen saw a face under her floor grating, and again when Sarah died."

"Both highly emotional incidents," Gary pointed out.

"Maybe," Melanie said. "And maybe they *were* only dreams. But I heard once that recurring nightmares mean there's something heavy on your mind. What could a girl in old-fashioned, ragged clothes mean? Or the kitchen? It's always in the kitchen."

"Symbolism," Gary said. "Is the girl so hard to figure out? She represents the olden days—Jacob Armand's days. You're thinking too much of him, Melanie. No wonder you have nightmares."

"I don't know." Melanie sighed. "It seems the woman was trying to give us a warning. She even said: 'It's happening again.'"

"You're the one who always insists it's happening again," Gary said. "You just put those words in another woman's mouth. Your dreams simply state what's on your mind."

"Okay," Melanie said. "Then what does the kitchen symbolize?"

Gary waved his hands. "I don't know. Oh, God, Melanie! Don't start talking about evil doings in this house. Your dreams are simply the result of too much emotional stress. They aren't a warning of anything—except, maybe, that you need to get your mind off of all this."

"There's nothing wrong with my mind," Melanie said darkly.

"Melanie, look," Gary said, losing patience, "Sarah Kaufman died of a heart attack, that's all! People die in houses all the time."

"They seem to die more often in this house, don't they?" With that, Melanie turned abruptly and went to her studio.

What was wrong with him? Melanie pondered as she daubed paint on her canvas. Why couldn't he, just for once, give her the benefit of the doubt? Sarah *must* have seen something! It had started this way the last time, so subtly, the old lady next door dying on the hill between their houses.

But this time, Melanie vowed, *I'll be ready for it.*

As she worked on her painting and occasionally stopped to look out of the studio windows, the beautiful sunny day gradually overcame her fears and worries. When she saw the school bus pull up, she was no longer in a dour mood. She watched the children climb the hill, racing each other. Kyle was first to reach the steps, Alicen last. Just a few minutes later, Kyle burst into her room.

"Hi, mom!"

"Hi," Melanie said, laughing. "How'd you get up here so fast?"

"I ran all the way," Kyle panted. His fair skin was flushed red. "I told Gina I could beat her upstairs."

Gina entered the room a moment later, panting, too. Alicen, who had obviously given up, came in after her, breathing normally.

"You win, Kyle," Gina said. She fished in her pocket and produced a quarter for her victorious brother.

"My kid's a gambler?" Melanie asked.

"I didn't think he could do it," Gina admitted.

Now Kyle climbed onto one of the stools in the room, his book bag on his lap. From it he produced a box made from ice cream sticks, painted bright yellow. He held it out to his mother.

"Look what I made," he said proudly. "My teacher said it was the best one in the class."

"Well, good for you, Kyle," Melanie said. "It's very nice."

"I'm going to give it to dad," Kyle said. "To put in his office."

"You should give it to mom," Gina said. "Mother's Day is coming up soon."

She turned to Alicen and without thinking said, "What are you going to give your mother for—"

She cut herself off, her eyes opening wide. Looking at her mother for help, she began to blush. Then she turned back to Alicen and said, "Gosh, I'm sorry! I wasn't thinking, and—"

"It's okay," Alicen said, though she felt a pain deep inside. "It's okay."

Melanie, seeing how uncomfortable both girls were, quickly changed the subject. "Say, when is that class trip of yours?"

"It's tomorrow," Gina said.

"Already? Well, you'll have a great time."

"I can't wait to go," Gina said. "I've never been to a planetarium."

"You know," Melanie said, "I think there might be some books on the planets in our library. Why don't you go see?"

Gina pulled Alicen out of the room. "Let's go look, okay?"

Melanie laughed. With kids like that, how could she ever have sad thoughts?

Alicen had tried to pay attention when Gina read off the statistics of Jupiter and Saturn. She had tried to listen to the conversation at dinner and to laugh at a joke Kyle told. But she was still smarting from the way Gina had carelessly mentioned Mother's Day. She hated that holiday, when people sent cards and flowers to their mothers and stores were filled with sentimental posters. Why did they all have to remind her she didn't have a mother?

She put her forehead down on her desk and cried softly. It just wasn't fair! Some people had mothers and treated them horribly. But she wouldn't, if her mother was alive. She'd be good to her, better than her father had ever been.

"Oh, mommy," she whispered. "Why did Gina have to make me think of you dead?"

She sat up, shuddering. Drying her eyes, she looked over at her clock and noticed it was well past midnight. She'd have to fall asleep now, or she'd never be able to get up for the class trip. Trying to wear herself out, she got up and paced the floor. The rug felt soft and warm beneath her feet. She did not go near the grating.

"Mommy," she whispered. "Mommy, mommy . . ."

Something creaked behind her.

"Aaallliiicceeeennnn!"

The voice sounded hollow and far away. Her heart beating loudly, Alicen hurried to the door to lock it. Who was out there? Was it just Kyle, teasing her? Or was it someone else?

"The door is locked," she whispered aloud. "I'm safe in here. I'm safe."

But suddenly she didn't care who was in the hallway. Her muscles became like jelly, too weak to support her body. Her eyes drooped shut as she sank to the floor. Without warning, she had fallen asleep. But this wasn't a real sleep that took her over.

In a minute she was on her feet again. She unlocked the door and pulled it open. Though the hallway was pitch black, she didn't have to grope her way to the stairs. It was as if some unseen force had her by the hand and was leading the way downstairs.

Alicen heard laughter in the kitchen and pushed through its door. Obeying a silent command, she sank to the floor and waited. She didn't feel the cold of the linoleum.

There was a woman standing above her. Alicen couldn't see the features of her face. But she saw the blond hair and smiled, unafraid. Her mother had had blond hair.

"You've come to me," she whispered.

A hand touched her forehead, and Alicen tilted her head back. She held up her arms to the apparition, her fingers spread wide like a little child's.

"Please hold me tight, mommy," she said.

It was the seven-year-old Alicen asking for affection, the Alicen of all her dreams, where her mother came to love her. But her mother did not embrace her this time. Instead, she pulled her to her feet. Alicen looked at the watery features, wishing she could see them more clearly. She'd waited so long.

"Gina VanBuren made you sad today," the vision said.

"Yes, she made me think of you, mommy."

"That was bad of her," was the reply. "She must be made to pay for it, right?"

"Yes, mommy."

"Then do as I say," the vision ordered. "Tomorrow there is a bus trip."

"Yes."

"Gina must sit directly behind the driver of the bus. Then she will die."

"Die," Alicen breathed.

"And when we are rid of her," the vision said, "I will give you this."

Smoke billowed around the apparition's hand as she raised it to Alicen's face. In the white cloud sat the huge, brilliant diamond that had once been on Sarah Kaufman's hand. Alicen reached for it, mesmerized. She saw it not as Sarah's ring, but as the ring her mother had always worn.

"She must sit up front," the vision said, snatching her hand away.

"She will," Alicen promised. "Oh, mommy, I'll be so happy to wear your beautiful ring!"

The next morning, Alicen woke up in her bed. She went down to the kitchen for breakfast, completely unaware that she had been sitting on its floor just a few hours earlier.

"Look at that bus, Alicen!" Gina cried as they stood together in the school yard. "Isn't it beautiful?"

"Yeah, it sure is," Alicen said, yawning. She was exhausted but didn't know why.

It was an enormous touring bus, one with a completely flat front covered with shining glass. The two girls climbed up inside of it and looked down the narrow aisle at the rows of high, upholstered seats.

"Hey, there's Doreen and Beverly," Gina cried, pointing.

Her friends had taken over the seat under the back window. Gina waved and started to go to them, but Alicen grabbed her arm.

"Can't we sit up front?" she asked.

"Why?" Gina responded. "Everyone else is in the back."

"I'd rather sit up here," Alicen said, indicating the seat behind the driver's.

"What difference does it make?"

Alicen shrugged. "I don't know. Uh—I sort of get sick sitting in the back."

Gina still felt guilty about mentioning Alicen's mother. Maybe she could make up for that by humoring her friend. She nodded.

"Okay," she said, "but I think you're weird. A seat's a seat!"

Alicen slid into the seat. Gina followed, then leaned out in the aisle to talk to Doreen and Beverly, moving back every few seconds to let other children walk past.

Alicen leaned forward and pressed her hands against the glass partition behind the driver's seat. Suddenly she felt sleepy. She yawned, and all at once her yawn became a groan. Gina looked at her.

"What's the matter?"

"Percy's the bus monitor," Alicen said. "And Jamie Hutchinson's coming in right behind him."

"We could have sat in the back," Gina said. "The bus is full now."

"I guess it's okay." Alicen groaned. She turned to look out the window, hoping neither Percy nor Jamie would see her. She was still mad at the boy for telling her stories of murders and making her look like a fool in front of her father and Melanie. But Jamie was too busy reading. Mr. Percy, after a few orders to the children about behavior and staying in groups, sat down and opened up a copy of the *Wall Street Journal*.

The driver came in next, her face hidden behind a curtain of stringy blond hair. Percy scoffed at her, then turned his eyes back down to the paper, wondering why the bus company would hire such an unkempt woman. The driver climbed behind the wheel of the bus without a word to anyone and started the engine.

Just then, Alicen felt a tap on her shoulder. "Hi, Alicen!"

"I'm not talking to you," Alicen said plainly, recognizing Jamie's voice.

"Oh, come on," Jamie said. "Are you still mad at me? Don't you want to look at my book? It tells you all about the planetarium."

"No."

"It's real neat," Jamie said. "Don't you want to see the pictures?"

"No!"

Jamie shook his head at her and sank back down into his seat. Now Gina turned and pinched Alicen's arm.

"Are you crazy?" she asked. "He's trying to be nice to you, and you're acting stuck-up. Why are you mad at him?"

"It's none of your business," Alicen said, not wanting to mention the incident that had so embarrassed her. "He's stupid, and I don't like him any more."

Alicen gazed out at the passing highway. She saw a station wagon with several black dogs in the back, a van driven by a young man with long hair, and a hitchhiking pair of girls. The van stopped to pick them up. This was such a perfect day for a field trip, Alicen thought. The sky was bright blue, and the sun was shining warmly. Why, then, did she feel so uneasy?

She felt a pain in her eyes from the glare of the sun and closed them. Her head dropped against the window, bobbing in rhythm with the vibrations of the engine. She could still hear the children around her talking. Someone started singing, and others joined in. It sounded as if they were singing through a long tunnel. She was far, far at the other end.

"A hundred bottles of beer on the wall, a hundred bottles of beer, if . . ."

Someone was talking inside Alicen's head. She recognized the voice, but couldn't place it. The words made her shudder.

Gina must die, must die, must die.

"Ninety-five bottles of beer, if one of . . ."

Alicen snapped upright and looked through the glass partition at the back of the driver's head. She felt lightheaded, as if she were floating in air and not on board the bus at all. The song the children were singing seemed further and further away. Now the pact she had made in the night came back to her. She knew who the bus driver was. Alicen longed to reach through the glass to touch her mother, but she simply leaned forward and stared. She saw the back of the woman's neck turning from pink to alabaster. Marks of veins began to travel under the skin, like droplets of rain racing on a window-pane. Beyond the woman's shoulder, Alicen could see the soft pink hand twisting as its skin tightened. No one else saw this but her.

She knew the terror had begun.

"Eight-six bottles of beer on the wall, eighty-six . . ."

Suddenly, with a loud growling noise, the bus shot forward.

"Hey!" a boy cried.

"What are you doing?" Percy demanded, leaning forward. "Slow down at once!"

The woman ignored him. The bus picked up speed at such a rate that the trees along the road mashed together in one long, green blur. White lines slipped under its wheels with immeasurable speed.

"Everyone!" Percy shouted, anticipating an accident, "on the floor!"

The children immediately ducked under their seats, too frightened to ask questions. Gina wanted to obey, too; she tried to move but somehow was frozen to her seat. She squeezed her eyes shut, covering them as she screamed.

But no one could hear her cries over the revving of the motor. It spun faster . . .

"Heeelllp!"

. . . and faster . . .

"MOM!"

. . . and faster.

"STOP THIS AT ONCE!" Percy shouted, his old man's voice straining. He grabbed the steel bar in front of his seat, his newspaper flying to the steps below. The old teacher pulled himself to his feet now and stumbled across the rubber-matted floor. His hand shot forward in an effort to grab the driver.

It went right through her.

"What the—?"

Percy backed away in horror, hitting the front window. The driver looked up at him, grinning. Her face was a death mask, grotesquely like blue-veined marble. Percy opened his mouth, but no sound came from it.

Screams jerked him from his dazed state. He looked down the bus at the fifty youngsters crouched on the floor, helpless. He saw a girl with braided brown hair still sitting in the first seat. Her hands were over her face, and she was screaming. Alicen Miller sat next to her, staring at him with hateful eyes.

Percy had the irrelevant thought that she was a disobedient brat. Why wasn't she on the floor?

Alicen smiled slightly and pointed to something beyond Percy's shoulder. He turned and looked out the huge front window of the bus, seeing a sign that read DETOUR and behind it a construction site.

"Oh, dear God," he whispered.

Now a surge of bravery made him lunge again at the driver. But as he touched the steering wheel, ice-cold hands grabbed hard at his wrists. His fingers pulled away in a curling, jerking motion. He whimpered softly as he felt the sickening crunch of his bones under the viselike grip of the phantom driver.

He screamed. The driver roared at him, knocking him back to his seat with breath so foul that Percy felt a wave of nausea. But that pain was cut off by another sharper pain that ripped through his neck like a hot knife. His hand went to his throat, feeling something sharp there. He stumbled toward Gina's seat, blood dripping from his opened mouth.

Screams of the children. The angry motor, honking horns, sirens. These were the last sounds Percy ever heard.

The bus collided at last with the tall wooden fence that surrounded the construction site. It shot over the rim of a pit, rising twelve feet into the air before it dove down into the deep excavation. Small bodies thumped from ceiling to floor as the bus rolled. But somehow, Gina's body didn't move at all. She had not yet opened her eyes, even to see what had knocked her to the floor a second earlier. She could feel Alicen's legs underneath her. Something warm and heavy pinned them on the floor behind the driver's seat.

The bus rolled, bumped, and skidded. It landed nose-first, its entire front crushing, the steering wheel becoming one with the partition. Shards of glass flew like missiles, striking the now-empty upholstered seats.

Though it happened in less than a minute, an eternity passed before the bus finally skidded to a halt and toppled over on its side. Gina at last opened her eyes.

Percy's unseeing eyes stared down at her, inches from her own face. Blood was spurting from a wound that surrounded a shimmering piece of glass in his throat.

"GET HIM OFF OF ME!" she screamed, struggling frantically.

"Gina, you're crushing me!" Alicen cried, the spell broken. She wriggled out from under her friend, grateful that only her legs had been caught. Then she leaned against the top of the bus, now its side, and stared down at Percy's corpse.

"GET HIM OFF! GET HIM OFF!"

Jamie Hutchinson was the first to collect his senses. He pulled himself to his feet, clutching the soft cushion of his seat. Rubbing his temple, where a painful bump was growing larger, he walked ahead to see why Gina was screaming so. In the shock that is the aftermath of a terrible accident, it didn't register in his mind that his teacher was dead. He only thought that Gina was being crushed as he wrapped his fingers around Percy's upper arms. Glass crunched beneath his feet as he pulled hard at the body, to no avail. It was wedged in too tightly, and at thirteen, Jamie wasn't very strong.

"Jamie, please," Gina cried. "I can't breathe."

"I'm trying," Jamie answered, desperate. He turned around. "Hey, somebody help me up here!"

No one responded. They were too caught up in their own terror. Jamie saw one boy holding his arm at an odd angle. A piece of raw bone jutted from a rising bruise at his elbow. A girl with blond braids sat on the floor with the back of her hand to her nose, trying to stop the flow of blood. Another girl was crying about her fingers, and a boy was lying on the floor, his eyes closed, blood trickling from his forehead. Jamie turned his head quickly away.

"Gina, push hard when I tell you," he ordered. He tugged at Percy's arms. "Now!"

Gina pushed with all her strength, and still the body did not move. A pounding noise over her head made her look up. There she saw two policemen sawing away at one of the window frames. One shouted through the small opening.

"Stay still, everyone! We'll have you all out in a minute!"

The first cop sawed with all his might, trying to make an exit. The door itself was useless, lost somewhere in the twisted front of the bus. He could barely make out the steering wheel. He knew the bus driver could not have survived. Yet for some reason, there was no sign of a body.

"Where the hell is the driver?"

"Beats me, Tim," the other cop answered.

Gina had started crying again, fighting the pressure of Mr. Percy's corpse. Tim looked down at her as he sawed the metal window frame. Assuming the body on top of her was the driver's, he continued to work. At last the frame gave way, and he jumped down into the bus. Walking carefully along the row of broken windows pressed flat against the ground, he went to Gina and wrenched the body from her. Without a word, he hoisted it up to the opening, where his partner dragged it out. Moments later, it was covered with tarpaulin.

"Easy now," Tim said, sliding his arm under Gina's back. Behind him, two paramedics climbed down into the bus to attend to the injured children.

As he helped Gina to her feet, Tim noticed the seat and realized something like a miracle had just occurred. Three ugly triangles of glass poked out from the vinyl seat, in exactly the place where Gina might have been sitting if the man's body hadn't knocked her to the floor. He looked at her as he held his hand out to help Alicen.

"Are you hurt?"

"No," Gina said softly, not sure of herself. She turned to Alicen, who stood staring at the twisted frame of the partition. There was no expression on her face.

"How about you, honey?" Tim asked, squeezing her hand.

Alicen shook her head mutely. Now Tim led the two of them to the opening in the ceiling, where they waited their turn to be lifted out of the bus. Once outside, the teen-agers blinked at the flashing red lights and bright sunshine. Gina put her arms around Alicen and stood watching as the others were helped out. She was shocked to see one of her classmates, Tommy Jones, on a stretcher with his eyes closed. Someone had bandaged his head.

Hank Emmons, manager of the construction crew, climbed down into the pit to survey the damage. When he reached the bottom, he ran his fingers through his silver hair and looked around in awe. The last of the group were being helped out of the bus. Several of them were put on stretchers and carried to the ambulance waiting at the top of the pit. As far as he could see, these were the only serious injuries.

"This is the kinda thing that makes you believe there's a God," he said to a policeman.

"How do you figure that?"

"Well, no one was killed," Hank said. "And from the looks of that thing"—he indicated the bus—"no one should have lived. Yeah, God was looking out for these kids."

"Not for the driver, though," the cop said. "He was killed."

Hank frowned. "I can't say I'm sorry. I saw that bus coming down the road. Serves the jerk right, speeding down a busy highway with all those kids."

Within the next half hour, all the students had been brought to the top. As they waited for another bus to take them home, they shared a soda and snacks with the construction crew. The food somehow helped them forget the accident.

Gina had had enough time to realize she was all right and to calm down a little. Some of her classmates had also relaxed and were talking together in excited groups. But for the most part they stood silent, numbed by the experience and wanting nothing but to see their mothers. Alicen was one of the silent ones.

Gina offered her a soda, but Alicen shook her head. "Why aren't you afraid?"

"Because I'm all right," Gina said. "Besides, a lot of worse things have happened to me."

Alicen nodded, knowing Gina was right but unable to share her strength. She felt a terrible fear. Why, since they were all right? But that was just it. Something deep inside Alicen made her feel they weren't supposed to be all right, that something was supposed to have happened and didn't.

"I just want to go home," Gina said.

"Me, too," several of her friends who stood nearby agreed in unison.

"But we'll probably have to go back to school and answer a lot of questions," Jamie said. Seeing a cop approaching, he said, "Starting right now."

"All right," Tim said. "I'd like to ask you some questions about your driver."

All the children started to speak at once.

"One of you, I said," Tim interrupted. He pointed to Jamie, who by his height seemed to dominate the group.

"Tell me, son," he said. "Did you get a good look at the driver? Did he seem to be tired, or drunk, or—"

"I don't know, exactly," Jamie said, pushing a lock of red hair from his eyes. "I was reading, so I just kinda glanced up at her."

"Her?" Tim echoed. "The driver was a woman?"

"Yeah, why?"

"Have you seen her since the accident?"

All the teen-agers shook their heads.

"Percy made us all duck under our seats," Jamie said. "After that, we didn't see a thing."

"I heard a scream," Beverly said. "But I sure wasn't going to look."

There was a silence, and then Gina asked, "What did happen to the driver?"

"I don't know," Tim said. "Can anyone tell me what she looked like?"

"I think she was wearing boots," Doreen said. "But I was at the back of the bus."

"Yeah, she was," Jamie agreed. "I remember because I thought it was kinda weird."

"Boots?" Tim said. "In May?"

Doreen and Jamie nodded. Tim could see sincerity in their faces and wondered if the driver might have worn boots to make her foot heavier on the gas pedal. If that was the case, then it probably meant she had planned the entire thing. Was it meant to be a combined suicide-mass murder? Tim's job now would be to find the body—or, judging from the remains of the bus, what was left of it. He thanked the group for their help, then went to find his partner Rick.

He made his way through the clusters of police, construction workers, and students until he found Rick at the edge of the pit, watching a tow truck haul the bus to the surface. Before he could tell him what the children had said, Rick started talking.

"Look at that thing," he said. "Smashed like a beer can. You know, if the driver hadn't been knocked from his seat like that, those two girls would have been killed? I have it figured that when his body wedged between their seats, he acted as a sort of anchor and kept them down on the floor. If they'd have been in that seat when the partition broke—"

Tim cut him off. "Rick, Dwight Percy wasn't the driver. The kids say it was a woman."

"How can that be?" Rick demanded. "There isn't another adult on that bus."

"We couldn't have missed her?"

"Impossible," Rick said. "Miss a full-grown woman in that little package of metal? No way Percy isn't our driver. The kids are suffering from shock. Or else they're lying."

"I don't think they're lying," Tim said.

"There's no one else on that bus," Rick insisted.

Later, back at the school, the children still swore the driver had been a woman. And out of fifty of them, not one remembered her face. Police Chief Bryan Davis asked each individually. They had to know something. And yet they had no answers.

Bryan was surprised to see Gina VanBuren, remembering her from another incident long ago. He asked about her father.

"He's doing okay," Gina said. "He doesn't have casts on any more, and he's learning how to walk again."

"That's great," Bryan said. "You send him my best, okay?"

"Perhaps we should allow them to leave," an elderly nun suggested. "They need their rest. You may return again tomorrow, when their minds are clear."

"Good idea," Bryan answered. "I'll be back after lunch tomorrow."

The children were relieved to hear they were going home. It had been two hours since the accident, and most were still frightened and upset. Originally Bryan had wanted to send them home right away but then decided it was best to get information while the incident was still fresh on their minds. Obviously that hadn't worked. Now he stood in the doorway, watching the children file outside. Their parents had been called, and a number of cars were waiting. Beverly, Doreen, and Jamie, who had working mothers, joined Gina and Alicen.

"Thank God you're all right," Melanie said, putting her arms around her daughter. "I called several times wondering when I could take you home, but they made me wait here. I've been frantic!"

"The police had to ask some questions," Gina said.

"Couldn't it have waited?" Melanie asked as she started the car. "You should have all been sent home at once."

"It wasn't so bad," Gina insisted.

Melanie turned to Alicen. "How about you?"

"I—I'm fine," Alicen said. She fixed her eyes on the road ahead.

Poor kid, Melanie thought. *She must be taking this worse than any of them.*

"Hey, I have an idea," she said aloud, in an effort to cheer everyone. "Why don't you let me treat you all to lunch?"

"That's a great idea," Jamie said.

"Yeah, neat!" cried Beverly.

"Can we go to Nino's pizza place, mom?" Gina asked.

"Sure."

After they had driven for a few minutes, Alicen felt her head growing heavy. She heard a voice inside it, calling to her, commanding that she come home. She looked around, but no one else heard it.

Suddenly she brought one leg up under her body, clutched her stomach, and started to groan.

"Alicen, what's wrong?" Melanie asked with concern.

"My stomach hurts," Alicen wailed. "I want to go home!"

"Maybe you're just hungry," Doreen suggested.

"I want to go home!" Alicen insisted.

"Okay, honey," Melanie cooed. "We'll drop you off. It's on the way, anyway."

She reached behind Gina and touched Alicen's cheek. It felt cool. "Just lay back," she said.

"I sure hope you're okay, Alicen," Jamie said.

Melanie turned the car around and headed toward the house. On the way, they passed the boarded-up gray mansion that had once belonged to the VanBurens' only neighbor. Jamie leaned over the back of Melanie's seat and asked, "Who lives in that spooky old place?"

"No one now," Melanie said. "But it used to belong to a very old woman named Helen Jennings. She was eighty-four and died of a heart attack."

"Geez," Beverly said. "Eighty-four? That's like a million years."

Melanie laughed, and Jamie asked, "Is anything inside there?"

"No, it's been empty for months," Melanie said.

She sighed, remembering Helen Jennings, who had tried to help her family when they were in trouble, during the months leading to

Gary's accident. Helen had been a little eccentric, watching their house from her bedroom through a pair of binoculars. But Helen had paid a price for helping them. She had died not of a heart attack, but of a broken neck—murdered by the same intruder who had crippled Gary.

But Melanie didn't want to think about that. She drove up to the front door of her house and let Alicen out. The girl left them without saying goodbye or thanks. Melanie watched her climb the porch steps with her head hung low, like a dog anticipating a beating.

"Everything scares her," Gina said.

"Maybe she really is sick," Doreen said.

"She'll be all right," Melanie said.

A little voice inside her added, *I hope.*

10

———◆———

Alicen laid her white purse on a table in the foyer and walked down the long hallway. She passed several doors before finally opening the one that led to the library. For some reason she wanted to look at the picture of Scrooge in Gina's book, the one that looked so much like Mr. Percy. She heaved it down from its shelf and lugged it to the sofa.

Scrooge was shaking his fist at someone. (Mr. Percy was wagging his finger at Alicen.) Scrooge was running scared from a ghost. (Mr. Percy was running scared from a . . .)

A what?

Alicen stared at the ink drawing and wondered what she was doing in here. She hadn't felt right since the accident. It was a feeling of failure, as if she were supposed to have made something happen and hadn't. She sighed and looked up at the carved angels that watched the room from atop the bookshelves.

She shivered. The room had suddenly grown cold, even though the sun was shining warmly through the windows. Alicen placed the book on the library table in front of her and stretched out on the sofa. She pressed a finger to one of the buttons in the upholstery and started to twist it. She could hear the squeak of metal on metal upstairs as Gary worked out in his therapy room. Outside in the yard, Lad barked at something. Birds sang, someone laughed—

Alicen sat up abruptly. It had sounded as if the laughter were right there in the room, and yet she was alone. She looked around. It was the same high-pitched laughter she had heard in her bedroom. Now she found its source. It was one of the angels that was carved in the shelves, its mouth opened wide, emitting short, cackling guffaws. Alicen looked up at it, mesmerized, watching its head loll back and forth as it screamed. She sat up straighter.

The other angels joined in the laughter. Alicen looked from one to the other, seeing angels no longer, but demons. Hideous demons with sharp teeth and bats' wings and blood dripping from the vines that hung around their necks.

"Ohhh," Alicen moaned, trying to stand.

Something pushed her back down on the couch.

"You defied me today," a voice said angrily. "Gina is still alive!"

Something snapped inside Alicen's head, and she was reminded of the pact she had made the night before. She bit her knuckles hard and stared up at the filmy mass before her. Though she could not see them, she could feel cold hands around her wrists.

"I tried, mother," she whispered. "I made Gina sit up front, but—"

"Shut up!" the vision snapped. "The VanBuren brat is still alive. Do you want to see your mother again?"

"Yes!"

"I don't think you do—"

"Yes, I do," Alicen cried, tears streaming down her face. "Oh, mommy. Why don't you show me your face?"

There was a long silence.

"You must make them go away from here," the apparition said at last, ignoring Alicen's plea. "They must all die."

"Mommy, why must they all die?"

But the vision was gone. Alicen looked around the room. The angels were still. Her head felt very heavy, and, unable to stop herself, she let it flop back as she fell asleep.

*   *   *

"I'm telling you, I never saw the driver of that bus," Hank Emmons insisted. It had been just a few hours since the accident, and he was sitting in Bryan Davis's office.

"You must have seen it coming," Bryan said. "You could hardly have missed a huge vehicle like that, heading right for the fence."

"Hey, look," Hank said, waving his hands, "I was busy. The union just ended a strike, and there's lots of work to do, you know? I don't waste my time running to investigate every car that comes speeding down that busy highway. Sure, I heard the thing. I think everyone from here to Montauk heard it. But I didn't see the bus till it came crashing through the fence. Geez! Everything happened so fast after that."

"What about your men?"

"What about them?" Hank asked. "Oh, I get it. No, they didn't see any more than I did. My guys pay attention to their work, you know? They'd better, at least, for what I pay them."

Bryan ran his fingers through his hair and sighed. He was getting nowhere and wished the case had been left entirely to the Suffolk County Police. He shouldn't have volunteered to ask questions. Sure the kids were from his town, and he owed it to them, but where was all this getting him? Nowhere. He had no answers after hours of questioning, and doubted he'd get any more in the days to come.

"Listen," Hank said then, "I want to find this driver as much as you do. I want to know who she is when I sue the bus company for damages. Say, why haven't you called the depot? They'd have her name on a sign-out sheet, wouldn't they?"

"One of my men is seeing to that," Bryan said, a little resentful that this other man should tell him his business. "The office was closed for lunch, but we ought to be hearing from him shortly."

The phone rang.

"That's him," Bryan said, lifting the receiver. "Belle Bay Police. Well, no ma'am, we're working on it." He shook his head at Hank. "I'm sorry about your boy. How is he? Gonna be okay? That's good. Yes, ma'am. It is a shame, ma'am. We'll let you know. . . . Yes, yes. Goodbye now, ma'am."

He hung up. "Damn! That was the mother of the boy who broke his arm. I wish I had answers for her."

"You've been getting a lot of calls," Hank commented.

"People are angry," Bryan answered. "They want to know who this driver is. I've got a lynch mob out there, Mr. Emmons."

The phone rang again. Bryan shifted a little before answering it, bracing himself for another barrage of unanswerable questions. This time, it was the cop at the bus depot.

"What can you tell me, Mike?" Bryan asked. "Who's the driver?"

"Nobody," Mike said, his tone serious.

"What?!"

"I mean it," Mike said. "There isn't any name next to the bus number on the morning register. The supervisor says he saw her writing in the book, but there's nothing on the page. Not even an indentation from an empty pen."

"Damn," Bryan whispered. "Mike, did the supervisor get a good look at her?"

"I asked," Mike said. "He was too busy to notice her. All he remembered was her blond hair. And get this—she was wearing fur boots."

"Must have been on drugs or something," Bryan said, "dressing like that. Okay, Mike, that's all. Why don't you go to lunch now?"

"I'll do that," Mike said, hanging up.

Bryan put down his own phone and looked at Hank Emmons. The man was sitting across the desk with his chin in his hands, studying Bryan's face. Now he sat a little straighter, ran his palms over the front of his shirt, and said, "You haven't got the slightest idea what to do about all this, do you?"

"No," Bryan admitted. He started to bounce a pencil on his desk. "Say, I have to get back to work."

Bryan looked up. "Huh? Oh, sure. Sure. I'm finished with you."

With a wave of his hand, Hank indicated a piece of paper.

"You have my number if you need me again," he said.

"I know," Bryan answered.

He stood up and walked from the room with Hank. The two men parted company out in the hall, Hank heading for the front door and Bryan for the men's room. When he returned to his office, he was surprised to see a girl sitting in a wooden chair near his desk. He looked over her long black hair and chubby face and remembered her from the school. He smiled at her.

"Alicen, right?" he asked.

"Right," the girl said, not smiling.

"My memory's pretty good, isn't it?" Bryan said, sitting behind his desk. "So, what can I do for you?"

"I came to tell you what happened on the bus," Alicen said. "I saw everything."

"Yeah?" Bryan asked, a little skeptical. "Why didn't you tell me before?"

"Everything happened too fast, and I was scared," Alicen cried, her expression becoming frantic for a moment. Then it quickly dissolved again into blankness. "Now I remember things. Just before the bus hit the fence, the driver opened the door and jumped out."

"She did, huh?"

"You have to believe me!"

"Okay, okay," Bryan said, waving a hand. "So what happened after she jumped out?"

"I saw her roll down a slope," Alicen said. "I don't remember anything else."

Bryan picked up a pencil and started to bounce it again, his habit when thinking. This was possible, he thought. Anyone crazy enough to drive a bus at over eighty miles an hour might be crazy enough to jump from it. That would explain why Hank hadn't seen her. But then again, none of the other children had witnessed this feat.

"I think I remember some of the kids saying Mr. Percy made you all lie down on the floor?"

"Yeah."

"Then how could you have seen what the driver was doing?"

"I wasn't on the floor," Alicen said. "My friend Gina was too scared to move, and I was supposed to hold her—I mean, she was holding onto me, and I couldn't move, either."

"But Gina didn't tell me she saw the driver jump," Bryan said.

"She had her hands over her eyes," Alicen said. "She was scared, but I wasn't."

"I'm just glad she wasn't hurt," Bryan said. "I like Gina."

"You know her?"

"Yeah, from some work I did with her family last year," Bryan said. "Nothing that concerns you."

"Were people really murdered in her house?"

Bryan's eyes widened. "Who told you that?"

"People," Alicen said, shrugging.

"Well, it's not true," Bryan insisted, his tone a little uneasy. "Listen, honey. I appreciate you coming here, and I'll call the Suffolk police. They'll take a look along the roadside."

Alicen nodded. To Bryan, her expression looked a little smug. He was suspicious of her, and yet her explanation was the only one he had to go on right now.

Half an hour later, Derek found his daughter sitting on the porch swing, tickling Lad's fur with her bare toes. He sat down next to her, putting an arm along the edge of the seat back.

"I saw your purse in the hallway," he said. "Why didn't you tell me you were home?"

"You were busy," Alicen said. "I didn't want to bother you."

"You wouldn't have bothered me."

"You always tell me to work out my problems for myself," Alicen replied.

"But this is different. This is not one of your nightmares. It was a serious accident, and I'm concerned about you. I heard what happened to Mr. Percy. You must have been terribly frightened."

"I wasn't," Alicen said.

"I don't believe you."

"I'm glad he died," Alicen said, staring at a ladybug that crept along the white railing. "I hate him."

"Alicen," Derek said gently, "you shouldn't ever hate anyone."

Alicen looked up at him, her brown eyes deep. "Don't you hate anyone?"

"No one," Derek said.

"Not even the man who killed my mother?"

Derek sighed deeply and put his arms around his daughter. Unaccustomed to such affection, she stiffened. Derek drew his arms away.

"Alicen, of course I hate what that man did," he said, "and I'll never get over losing your mother. But I can't hate the man himself. He'll have to live with his guilt, and that's enough without my hatred, too."

Alicen closed her eyes. "Sometimes I talk to mommy, and it feels like she's really here."

"Alicen," Derek said patiently, "you know what I told you about those dreams. It's nice to wish your mother was alive again—God knows I do—but you have to accept the fact that she just isn't coming back."

"She's coming back for me," Alicen said, opening her eyes to glare into her father's. "We're going to be together again."

Derek wasn't about to encourage Alicen's fantasies by arguing with her. Ignoring her bizarre words, he stood up and walked to the porch railing. The azaleas were starting to wither now, but their fragrance was still sweet. Derek watched a flock of birds shoot up from the nearby woods and heard the swing creak behind him as Alicen rocked it.

She didn't seem upset by any of this, and that bothered him. Had he scolded her so many times for being overly emotional that she was now afraid to let him know her feelings? He didn't like her having nightmares or pretending to talk with her mother. But he had never meant for her to hide her fears when those fears were justified. He had to make her understand she could trust him.

"Say, Alicen," he said, turning around, "would you like to go out to dinner with me?"

It worked. Alicen's dull expression suddenly brightened, and she nodded eagerly. He hadn't taken her to dinner in years. Derek glanced at his watch; it was still early afternoon.

"Well, it's too early for dinner yet," Derek said. "We can go in a few hours."

The look on his daughter's face was one of such disappointment that Derek tried to think of a quick remedy. He ran his fingers through his dark hair and said, "I know. We'll spend the afternoon in the city. Would you like that?"

"Okay," Alicen said, sounding genuinely eager.

"Then get your shoes and raincoat," Derek said. "And I'll meet you down here in fifteen minutes. I just have to let Gary know we're going out."

After changing his clothes, Derek walked out into the hall. He heard Alicen talking in her room. Knocking at her door, he asked if she was ready. When she didn't answer, he pushed the door open a little. Alicen was sitting on the edge of her bed with one foot propped up and her fingers wrapped around her shoelaces. She was not moving and had a frightened look on her face. She seemed to be staring at something. Derek followed her gaze and saw a milky cloud hovering near the window.

"What the hell is that?" he demanded.

"Dad!"

Alicen jumped, pulling her hands away from her shoe. The cloud disintegrated and became a beam of sunlight. *Just sunlight*, Derek thought. *My eyes must be playing tricks on me.*

"Sorry if I startled you," he said, "but you didn't answer when I knocked at the door. Are you ready yet?"

"Yea," Alicen said, resuming her tying. She got up at last and pulled her raincoat from the closet. Derek noticed her hands trembling a bit but thought it was because he had startled her.

It was hard to believe the day had gone from brilliantly sunny to gloomy gray. But the air was heavy with moisture, and rain would be welcome. The breeze blowing now made the drive to Manhattan more pleasant, and the Volvo rode smoothly along. Derek turned on the radio and hummed with the music. Alicen rested her head on the window ledge and let the breeze blow her hair back.

"Hey, that's it for today for the Charlie Grinn show. I'll be back tomorrow with more hits, old and new."

An interlude of music led to the news.

"Good afternoon. In Washington today, President Carter . . ."

Derek looked across the seat at his daughter. She seemed lost in a dream world, her eyes squinted against the wind. He returned his own eyes to the road and said, "Alicen, do you want to talk about the accident?"

"I've been talking about it all day," Alicen said. "That cop Bryan Davis asked so many questions."

"Talking might make you feel better," Derek said. "You can't face your problems until they're out in the open."

"I don't have any problems!" Alicen snapped.

"Don't use that tone of voice with me," Derek cautioned.

Alicen clicked her tongue. "Oh, dad! Can't we just have a nice time tonight without talking about dumb things like that accident?"

"I don't think it's so dumb, Alicen," Derek said. He glanced at her again. "Stop pouting. We won't talk about the accident if you don't want to."

"I don't," Alicen said.

They sat in silence for a while longer, listening to the news broadcast. There was a report on the bus accident.

"Here on Long Island, police are baffled over a bus accident involving fifty children from Saint Anne's school in Belle Bay. The bus, en route to the Vanderbilt Planetarium in Centerport, collided head-on with the fence surrounding the construction site of the Louis Pasteur Hotel. Speed of the bus was clocked at over eighty miles per hour. The mystery? No driver could be found in the wreckage. Described only as a young woman with long blond hair, she is being sought by police for endangering the lives of minors and for the death of Dwight Percy, the children's teacher. Percy, aged sixty-one, was sitting in the front of the bus at the time of the collision. He had no survivors.

"Miraculously, only four children were seriously injured. A broken arm, nose, and fractured skull were reported. One girl who complained about twisted fingers was treated and released. Police are investigating the incident and request that anyone having information should call . . ."

Derek switched off the radio. "You didn't tell me about the driver," he said.

"You didn't ask," Alicen replied.

"I shouldn't have to," Derek said. "And what do they mean, they couldn't find her?"

Alicen shrugged, not turning her head from the window.

"She sort of disappeared, I guess."

"How does anyone 'sort of disappear' from a speeding bus?" Derek wanted to know. When Alicen didn't reply, Derek tapped her impatiently. "Will you please answer me?"

"I don't know!" Alicen cried. "It happened too fast! Everyone's asking me so many questions." She sniffled, fighting tears.

"I'm sorry," Derek said. "I promised you we wouldn't talk about the accident, didn't I?"

From the corner of his eye he saw Alicen nod.

"Then we'll drop it," he said. "So, what do you want to do today?"

"I want to see the Central Park Zoo," Alicen said, cheering up again.

"That's the girl," Derek encouraged.

As she tried to forget the accident, Alicen told her father all the things she wanted to see in the city. She didn't tell him that she dreaded coming home again.

11

◆

Balancing himself with outstretched arms, the policeman named Tim hurried down the steep slope that led from the roadside. Under orders from their captain, he and his partner Rick were investigating the scene of that morning's bus accident. Rick walked up ahead, holding fast to the leashes of a pair of German shepherds. The animals whined and looked about in bewilderment, not picking up a scent. Tim kept his eyes to the ground, looking for footprints, pieces of clothing, or anything to indicate someone had been there. He was becoming as frustrated as the dogs; they had been walking for a mile and had yet to find a thing.

"I don't know why Davis took the word of some kid," he said, kicking aside a rusted can.

"I'm telling you," Rick answered, "that guy named Percy must have been the driver. I don't know why we're looking for some woman who doesn't even exist."

"Fifty kids can't all be lying," Tim pointed out.

"Well, the kid who talked to Davis was," Rick said. "You can't tell me a woman jumped from a speeding bus and just got up and walked away."

"I'm not telling you that," Tim said quietly.

They moved on in silence, walking further and further from the construction site. The sun was starting to go down now, and the air was growing pleasantly cool. Every once in a while, Tim would look up at the cars passing on the road, squinting against the brilliance of their lights. He laughed a little to see them slow down at the sight of the police car's flashing red light. Then he looked down at the ground again.

"It's six, Tim," Rick said some time later. "Let's call it quits."

"Yeah," Tim said. "We aren't going to find anything here."

Back at the police station, they turned the dogs over to the kennel master, made their report, and went home. Chief Morris contacted Bryan Davis, telling him no body had been found, let alone evidence there had been one at all.

Several miles away, Bryan hung up the receiver and got up from behind his desk. A while ago, he had been looking forward to the end of a long day. But now that his only lead to the driver's whereabouts was gone, he knew he wouldn't be able to rest until he had some answers. That Miller kid had to know something more. She'd looked so spaced-out that afternoon, and she had been overly adamant that he should believe her story. There had to be more to it.

Was it possible, Bryan thought, that she had been told to bring that story to him? An innocent kid doing someone's dirty work? Bryan decided the best way to find out would be to talk to her at home. It was only eight o'clock, not too late to make a call on the Miller house. Pulling the folder on the accident from the file, Bryan looked up Alicen's address in the list of children. His eyebrows went up when he read it.

"Three twenty-eight Starbine Court Road," he said aloud. "What's that kid doing in the VanBuren house?"

He'd find out soon enough, he thought. Thinking the girl might be more relaxed if he was out of uniform, he changed into jeans and a plaid shirt in the locker room. Then he went out to his car. As he drove through town, he recalled the night he had last been at the VanBurens' some six months ago. He remembered comforting Melanie after her husband's accident. Even now, Bryan shuddered to think of it.

"This has nothing to do with what happened last year," he told himself firmly.

But tonight it was too clearly stamped on his mind. He reluctantly recalled the events that had taken place at the house, when a "maniac" had tried to destroy the VanBuren family. It had been so terrifying, so unbelievable, the things that had happened that snowy No-

vember night. And he and the five other cops with him had vowed
never to talk about it again.

The main street of Belle Bay was active right now, filled with teen-
agers hanging out in front of well-lit stores, young couples shopping,
and elderly people out for strolls. Bryan looked up at the trees that
lined the street, seeing rich foliage of late spring silhouetted against
the moonlit sky. As the stores and people faded out, the homes became more numerous, old Colonials mixed in with modern brick and
aluminum-sided houses. Bryan noted the finely trimmed lawns and
painted picket fences. People took care of their homes in Belle Bay.
That was one reason why he loved this town. He didn't need any
trouble here.

Now the houses thinned out, and Bryan found himself on Houston Street. From here, he could see the huge VanBuren mansion,
sitting regally upon a hill. Though only one upstairs light was on, the
entire house seemed to glow. Bryan was surprised to feel himself
shudder.

No cars passed him on the road as he neared Starbine Court. He
swung onto it, driving close to the beach for several hundred yards.
He could just barely make out a couple sharing a blanket at the
water's edge. In a few weeks, he thought, it would be beach season.

Just before he reached the hill that led to the mansion, he passed
another house, huge and gray. It was empty now, ever since its elderly owner's death a year earlier. The house made Bryan think of
hell, as if one could enter the eternal darkness by stepping behind
one of the boarded-up windows.

He shook that ridiculous thought from his mind and drove up the
hill. Parking his car in the driveway, he went to the front of the
house, climbed the wooden stairs, and rang the bell. Seconds later,
the porch was flooded with light. Melanie VanBuren opened the
door, dressed in a robe. Recognizing him, she stepped back and
smiled a little.

"Captain Davis," she said pleasantly, running her hand over her
just-washed hair. "Come on in."

"It looks like I've come at a bad time," Bryan said. He saw Gary
behind his wife, leaning on crutches. "But I had the idea to ask
some questions about the accident."

"Is this official?" Gary asked, leading the police chief into the living room. "You aren't in uniform."

"I thought this was a little less intimidating," Bryan said. He sat down on the couch, sinking comfortably into the overstuffed cushions. "I'd like to talk with Alicen Miller—I understand she lives with you?"

"Yes, she does," Melanie said. "But she's not here right now. She's out with her father."

"I thought you asked questions at the school today," Gary said.

"I did," Bryan answered. "But I got nowhere." He thought for a moment, toeing the ball-and-claw feet of the coffee table, then said, "I thought the children would be more comfortable if I spoke to them in their homes, with their parents there beside them. I'm hoping to get more information this way."

"It's a good idea," Melanie said. "But why did you choose to start with Alicen?"

"She came to see me today," Bryan said.

Gary rocked a bit on his crutches. "Alicen didn't tell anyone she went out," he said.

"Well, she came to the station around twelve-thirty," Bryan reported.

"Oh, that's impossible," Melanie said, leaning forward in her chair. "I dropped her off here at noon. She couldn't have had time to walk back into town!"

"Then she managed to hitch a ride," Bryan suggested. "But she was there, and she had quite a story to tell me. I want to hear it from her again."

"A story?" Melanie echoed. "Alicen hardly seems the type to tell stories. She's a very shy girl."

"Didn't seem that way to me," Bryan answered. He stood up. "Well, if she's not here, I'll see her tomorrow. Sorry if I disturbed you."

Gary called to him before he reached the door. "I thought you wanted to talk to all of the children?"

"Huh?" Bryan answered, turning. "Oh, yeah. I said that, didn't I?"

"Let me get Gina," Melanie said. "She's still up."

She had left the room before Bryan could protest. Sighing, he returned to the couch and sat down again.

"How did she take the accident?" he asked.

"Not too badly," Gary answered. "My kids are pretty tough. They've been through worse, remember."

"I remember," Bryan said quietly. "It just seems wrong that one girl should suffer so much. I mean, after what happened last year. . . ."

"We don't talk about that," Gary said.

Bryan nodded. "Smart thing." He shifted on the couch, making himself more comfortable, then indicated Gary's crutches. "You look like you're doing well, though," he said. "Am I right?"

"I do the best I can," Gary answered. "I've been on crutches for a few weeks now. My next challenge is the stairs."

"You have to go to some clinic for that?"

"No, I've got a private therapist," Gary said. "He—Derek—is Alicen's father."

"That explains why she lives with you," Bryan said.

"You were wondering what a kid is doing in this spooky house, huh?"

"Sort of," Bryan said. "It surprised me to see she had the same address as Gina. Does her mother live here, too?"

"Alicen's mother is dead," he heard Melanie say. He turned and saw her enter the room with Gina, who was dressed in chinos and a T-shirt with a rainbow painted on it. She looked at him with questioning brown eyes, then went to sit on the armchair across from the couch.

"Hello," she said.

"Hey, there," Bryan said, smiling. "How're you?"

"Fine," Gina said. "Do you want to ask me some questions?"

"That's right," Bryan answered. "I was hoping you could remember something new."

Without hesitation, Gina shook her head. "I told you everything this morning."

"Tell me again," Bryan said. "And take your time. I'm not going anywhere."

Gina brought her legs up under her and folded her hands in her lap. She looked around the room, her brow furrowed as she tried to remember the morning's events. At last she fixed her gaze on the bronze fireplace screen and started to speak.

"We were supposed to go to the planetarium," she said. "I wanted to sit in the back, but Alicen said she'd get sick. So we sat right behind the driver."

"Did you see her?"

"Sure," Gina said.

Bryan straightened. "You did? What did she look like?"

"Well, I didn't see her face," Gina admitted. "I just saw the back of her. I was turned around when she got on. I was talking to Doreen—she's my friend. Anyway, all I know is that the driver had blond hair."

"Did she talk to you kids at all?"

"No, she didn't say anything. We told you that this morning, remember?"

Bryan smiled, nodding, then let her go on.

"We were all talking and fooling around," Gina continued. "Then one of the boys yelled something, and all of a sudden the bus started going faster and faster. Mr. Percy yelled at everybody to get on the floor. That's Alicen's teacher."

"You did that?"

"I couldn't!" Gina cried, looking at him with huge eyes. "I was so scared that I couldn't move at all. I just hung on to Alicen and covered my eyes. You know, like you do when you're on a scary roller coaster?"

"Calm down, honey," Gary said.

Bryan said nothing, thinking. It was exactly the same story Alicen had told him, yet . . .

"Gina, did you see the driver fighting with Mr. Percy?"

Gina shook her head. "I didn't see *anything*. I didn't even open my eyes when Mr. Percy—uh, when he knocked me from my seat."

She turned to gaze back at the fireplace. Melanie went to the chair and sat on the arm, taking her daughter's hand.

"Are these questions absolutely necessary?" she asked.

"Yes," Bryan insisted. "But they can wait until tomorrow if—"

"It's okay," Gina said. "What else do you want to know?"

"Did you see anything the driver did before the bus crashed?"

"I said I had my eyes closed."

"You didn't see her jump from the bus?"

"Is that what she did?" Gina asked. "Is that how she disappeared?"

"We don't know," Bryan said, standing. "That's enough for tonight, I think. If you remember anything more, you can tell me at school tomorrow. I'll be there again."

"Sure," Gina said.

Gary walked Bryan to the front door while Melanie sat in the living room with her daughter.

"Are you really going to all the children's homes?" Gary asked.

Bryan shook his head. "No. I really just wanted to talk to Alicen. She told me she saw the driver jump from the bus, but now I'm beginning to think I'm wasting my time following that lead. The Suffolk police couldn't locate a body near the construction site."

"Why would Alicen lie to you?" Gary asked.

"Beats me," Bryan said. "Maybe she's got an overactive imagination."

"Do you want me to have her father contact you?"

"Nah," Bryan said. "I've got enough parents breathing down my neck." He opened the door. "Call me if you learn anything new."

"I'll do that," Gary promised.

He stood unmoving as Bryan left the house, listening until his car started and drove away. Then he locked the front door and returned to the living room. Melanie and Gina were sharing an armchair, Gina's head on her mother's shoulder. Melanie looked up at her husband.

"Gina says he made her think of the night you were hurt," she said. "Don't you think he could have shown a little more tact?"

"He's just doing his job," Gary said gently. "Gina, you know this has nothing to do with that time."

"I know, daddy," Gina said. She climbed out of the chair. "I'm tired. I think I'll go to bed."

"Don't think about it," Melanie said. "Just get a good night's sleep."

But Gina did think about it, lying alone in the darkness of her room. Over and over she heard Bryan Davis asking, "Did you see the driver?" Gina rolled over and clutched at her pillow, trying to relax.

The last thing she saw before falling asleep was Davis, standing over her in his blue uniform.

Minutes ticked by, and Gina sank deeper and deeper into sleep. She was warm and safe in her bed, under a cotton comforter that surrounded her with gentle softness.

And then something made that softness disappear, ripping it from her body. She bolted upright, her bare legs sprawled out in front of her. She couldn't move her arms to cover them.

"Hey, there," she heard Bryan Davis say.

She looked around. The room was empty, and yet someone had to be in there because the light was on. She leaned forward, her eyes darting. Everything seemed okay. But her clock radio was playing music, and she couldn't remember having turned it on.

"Did you see the driver?"

"I'm cold," Gina heard herself say.

"Did you see the driver?"

Next thing, Gina was leaning over the side of her bed, face down into a black pit. Two eyes glared up at her through the darkness, pinpoints of red light. Her stuffed kangaroo suddenly came into view, floating up toward her. No, just its severed head. Gina's hand dropped into the pit, grabbing for it. It turned into a piece of glass.

"Did you see the driver!"

"No!"

The glass dropped, down and down. The pit closed up, but it was not her floor she saw next. It was the sand of the beach, flecked with snow. Everything was icy cold in her room.

Bryan Davis was leaning over her, smiling. He looked so nice, and yet there was an evil glimmer in his eyes when he said, "Hey, there. Did you see the driver?"

"Go away!"

Bryan grinned more broadly and grabbed hold of her wrist. His features began to change, his graying hair turned darker, thicker. The blue uniform swirled and became a cape. The round face became more chiseled. Something flashed in Gina's dream consciousness, making her remember this face against her will. She wanted to get away, and yet she could only lay helplessly as cold fingers wrapped around her neck.

"Did you see the driver?"

"No!"

The fingers tightened.

"You must die, you know," the man said.

"Nnnnnoooo!"

The man smiled.

Gina screamed and bolted upright, alone in her room but unable to realize yet that it had all been a terrible dream. She screamed and screamed, terror churning in her stomach. The door opened; Derek was there with Alicen at his side. They were walking toward her bed, eyeing her strangely.

"Go away!" Gina shouted at them.

"It's only me," Derek said. "Derek. You're dreaming."

Gina simply stared at him, tears falling from her huge eyes. Her mother burst into the room just then and said in a soft voice, "Oh, my God."

She climbed onto the bed and took Gina into her arms. The girl was trembling all over. Melanie could feel her heart beating. She stroked her hair and rocked her.

"It's all right," she whispered. "I'm here, my baby. It's okay."

Gary came into the room, Kyle and Nancy behind him, sleepy-eyed. He glanced briefly at Derek, then hobbled to his daughter's bed.

"Were you having a dream about the accident?" he asked, taking Gina's hand.

Gina shook her head. "That man was here."

"What man?"

"The man with the cape," Gina said hoarsely. She stared down at her blanket with round eyes. "The man from the beach last year, who tried to hurt me. He was here!"

Alicen gasped. Derek quickly hushed her.

"Daddy—" Nancy said.

Gary looked over his shoulder at the two younger children. "Kyle, take your sister back to bed," he ordered.

"I wanna hear about Gina's dream," Kyle whined.

"You want a kick in the pants?" Gary snapped. "Get back into bed!"

Kyle took Nancy by the wrist, not daring to question his father when he acted that angrily. Once he was gone, Gary turned back to

Gina and said, "Honey, you know that man will never come back."

Gina looked at her mother.

"Aren't you worried that he will, maybe?"

Melanie didn't answer at first. She thought of the day she had found the bloodstain on her painting, and then of the ransacked studio. Sarah Kaufman's face tried to creep into her mind, but she forced it away.

"No, of course I'm not," she insisted.

"Gina, why don't you try to go to sleep again?" Gary suggested. "You'll probably feel better."

Gina lay back down and held fast to her mother's hand. The room was silent, and soon she was sleeping again. Carefully, Melanie let go of her and left the room with the others.

"It's that cop's fault," she whispered. "Asking her all those questions!"

"I thought Gina didn't care about the accident," Alicen said.

"Go to bed, Alicen," Derek ordered. "It's late."

"Is Gina okay?"

"She's fine, I'm sure," Gary said, not believing it.

Alicen tapped Melanie on the arm. "Did someone try to kill her last year?"

"Alicen, did you hear me?" Derek said. "I told you to go to bed!"

"I'm going," Alicen said, walking away, pouting.

After she turned the corner Derek looked at Gary and said, "Is there really no chance that the man who hurt you might come back again?"

"None at all," Melanie said. "He was a prowler, and the police took care of him."

"I just want to be sure my daughter is safe here," Derek said.

"She is," Melanie insisted. "There's nothing for you to worry about."

"No, wait a minute," Gary said. "Derek's got a right to know the truth."

"Are you sure you want to tell him?"

"Of course I am," Gary said. "Derek, remember the day you moved in, when I told you the owner of our house had been a captain in the eighteenth-century British navy?"

"What's he got to do with this?"

"Take off your coat and come into my study," Gary said. "It's time you heard about him."

12

Derek had always liked Gary's office. It was a decidedly masculine room, with dark paneling and leather-covered furniture. A huge antique map hung on one wall, and near the window stood a brass stand that had once held a telescope. Now, as promised weeks earlier, Derek was about to learn of the man who had put them in here. He couldn't see the connection with Gina's dream, but curiosity made him anticipate the upcoming story with interest. He hung his raincoat up on a brass coat rack and sat in a chair. Melanie and Gary shared a small couch across from him.

"To begin with," Gary said, "our 'hero's' name was Jacob Armand, a British naval captain who came to America during the early 1790s."

"The colonists, of course, didn't care much for the British at that time," Melanie put in. "Which made life rather difficult for him, added to the fact that he was in the enemy's militia."

"So he built a house far away from the town," said Gary, tightening the belt on his robe. "He hoped they'd leave him alone. It turns out he had to pay a sort of protection fee to keep them from stoning his windows out."

"It didn't hurt him to pay it," Melanie said. "Jacob Armand was a very wealthy man."

"I can see that by this house," Derek answered.

"One day," Gary went on, "Jacob met a beautiful young woman named Lydia Browning. They fell in love, and everything was fine and dandy. But there was a hitch—Lydia was married."

"Her husband detested the British with a passion," Melanie said. "When he found out her lover's nationality, he became enraged. It wasn't enough to have Lydia punished for adultery. He had to throw in a charge of witchcraft, too. And to make matters worse, he forced his two young children to testify against their mother."

Gary pointed out the window. "So Lydia was dragged down to the beach and burned at the stake. Jacob Armand saw all of it but couldn't do a thing. When his beloved Lydia died, he vowed to avenge her death."

"Wait a minute," Derek said. "Why wasn't he executed with her?"

"Don't forget he was putting a lot of money into the town with his protection fee," Gary reminded him. "They were willing to forget his part in the 'crime' just to keep getting the money."

"Jacob himself died just a few months later," Melanie said. "Literally of a broken heart. He carried his vow to avenge Lydia's death to the grave."

"That was the end of him, then," Derek said. "So why the history lesson?"

Gary and Melanie exchanged glances.

"It wasn't the end of him," Gary said in a low voice. "We bought this house last year without knowing his spirit still walked its grounds."

"Whoa!" Derek cried. "Hold on a minute. Spirit? As in haunted? You're trying to tell me this place is haunted?"

He was looking at them as if they were crazy, but Gary was undaunted.

"*Was* haunted," he corrected. "We drove Jacob Armand out last November. He had become attached to my wife and tried to kill the rest of us to have her."

Melanie took Gary's hand and looked at him with sad eyes. Remembering the events that led to this story, she spoke in a soft, choked voice.

"He saw me as his Lydia," Melanie said. "And Gary and the children as the husband and children who led her to her death. In order to save me—Lydia—he first had to get rid of them. And he almost succeeded."

She shuddered and turned to put her head on Gary's shoulder. Gary put his arms around her and kneaded the hair at the back of her neck.

"On the night it ended," he said, "he pushed me from a window upstairs." He motioned toward his legs. "That's why I'm like this."

"You said it was a prowler," Derek said quietly, a little over-whelmed.

"Would you have believed the truth?" Gary asked. "We hardly believe it ourselves. In fact, we promised each other not to talk about it ever again. But, considering Gina's dream, we might have made a mistake. It was wrong to expect the children to forget that night."

"The bus accident made Gina remember what had happened," Melanie put in. "And she was tormented as horribly as any of us that night. I don't think I'll ever forget—" She began to cry now. "Oh, God, Gary!"

"Jacob Armand tried to murder my daughter on the beach," Gary said. "In the same spot where Lydia had been executed. Fortunately, Melanie got to him in time to prevent him from taking another life."

There was silence for a while. Derek considered all this, wanting not to believe it, and yet unable to think of a reason why they would be telling him such a fantastic yarn. Were they hiding something behind the fantasy? A thought came into his head.

"Those murders Alicen mentioned," he said quietly. "They really happened, didn't they? Is that what you meant by his taking another life?"

"Yes," Gary said. "In his pursuit of Melanie, he murdered three people. The first was an old woman named Helen Jennings, who used to own that house down the road. Then there was a young cop, Tony DiMagi. And last of all, Melanie's best—"

"Gary, please," Melanie begged. "Don't talk about her."

"It's okay," Derek said. "I know about your friend Janice. Gary told me the day you got so upset when I mentioned that name."

Melanie looked at him through tears. "He told you what happened to her?"

"Not that Jacob Armand murdered her," Derek said.

"Well, he did," Melanie answered. "He hit her across the head and killed her."

She said that in the tormented way of someone who wants the truth to be known. It was as if she were afraid he wouldn't believe her. In truth, he wasn't quite sure what to believe. His loyalty to Gary made him want to buy the story, and yet his own common sense told him it couldn't be true. Ghosts! But Melanie looked so upset and Gary so solemn that he figured it was best to humor them right now.

"So Gina was reliving that night?" he asked. "Just because of the bus accident? I know it was a horrible experience, but Gina seemed so calm at dinner tonight."

"Well, it was more than the accident," Melanie said, sniffling back the last of her tears. "Bryan Davis—the police chief—came to talk to her tonight. He'd been here the night of Gary's accident."

"Why did he come here at night?" Derek asked. "Didn't he spend enough time questioning the kids at school? At least that's the impression I got from talking to Alicen."

"Actually, your daughter was his reason for coming," Gary said. "He said she'd been down at the station telling him she'd seen the driver jump from the bus."

"I don't see how it was possible," Melanie put in. "He said she was in his office at twelve-thirty, but I only left her here at noon. It takes longer than half an hour to get into town. So Bryan thinks she might have hitchhiked."

"Oh, brother," Derek said, recalling the woman who had hidden in his car. What if Alicen had met with that evil woman named Janice? He shook the thought from his mind.

"I find the fact that Alicen went at all even more unbelievable," he said. "Funny she didn't tell me about the driver. She didn't seem to know anything at all."

"Maybe Bryan mistook her for another child," Melanie said.

"There isn't anyone like Alicen," Derek answered. He clapped his hands together. "Well, if she did go, I'm glad. It just means she's starting to come out of that shell of hers. It's about time she started taking things into her own hands."

"Thirteen seems a little early to start taking things into your own hands," Melanie said softly.

"What did you say?"

"Nothing, Derek," Melanie said in a clearer voice. "I didn't say a thing. Gary, finish the story for him."

"Just tell me how you finally got rid of your ghost," Derek said, running a finger under his lip.

"We weren't the ones who did it," Gary said. "It seems he'd been tormenting other families who had lived in this house. All their spirits came to fight him, and they sent him to hell. In the process Lydia herself showed up. Now that Jacob had her again, his spirit was put to rest."

"Where was Lydia before this?"

"Waiting for him to come to her," Melanie said. "Remember, in her day women would wait for months, even years, for their men to return from the sea. I—uh—suppose that in the afterlife, two hundred years is like six months."

"It sounds interesting," Derek said.

Gary eyed him. "But you don't believe it."

"How can I!" Derek asked. "I hardly believe there's a God, and I'm not quite sure there's an afterlife. I never believed in supernatural powers, and I'm not about to start."

"Then you must think we're a pair of fools," Melanie said bitterly.

"Not at all," Derek said. "I'm sure you have your reasons for telling me this story. Hey, look, what do I know, right? Just because I don't believe it doesn't make it untrue."

He stood up. "I'm very tired. Sorry to run out on you, but I'd like to hit the sack."

"We didn't lie to you," Melanie said darkly.

Derek didn't answer her. He opened the door, then turned and said, "My daughter's a hysterical type. Make sure she doesn't hear about this, okay? Her nightmares are frequent enough."

With that, he was gone. Melanie stared at the closed door for a long time without speaking. And then she said, in a quiet voice, "You didn't have to tell him about Janice."

"Honey, he was bound to find out," Gary said. "Why let it bother you so much?"

"My best friend is dead," Melanie snapped, "and I'm not supposed to let it bother me?"

Gary waved his hand at her. "Of course you are. But why do you single Janice's death out in particular? Why didn't you stop me from mentioning Helen Jennings and Tony DiMagi?"

"That's different," Melanie said.

She stood up and headed for the door, not waiting for her husband. The hallway was dark, in spite of the light pouring into it from the study. Melanie's nerves were on edge, as if anticipating that cold fingers would reach out through the blackness to grab her. But whose fingers?

At the end of the hallway, the small stained-glass window burst open, crashing against the wall.

"What?" Melanie cried out, turning around. She saw Gary in the doorway of his office.

"Just the wind, Melanie," he said, hobbling to the window to shut it. When he looked out, he noticed the trees were perfectly still.

"Wait for me," he said as he latched the window. "I'll walk back to our room with you."

He thought he heard someone laughing in the distance. But he blocked the sound from his ears and went to his wife. He wasn't about to join her in thinking every little noise was the herald of something evil.

The next day Gary called his family together. After what had happened that night, he knew it was very important to talk to his children. He and Melanie shared a loveseat, while the children sat on the couch. Nancy bounced up and down playfully, until Gina stopped her. Gary noticed the dark circles under his oldest daughter's eyes.

"I have to ask you kids something," Gary said. "Kyle, Gina, Nancy —do any of you ever have dreams like Gina had?"

Kyle looked at the fireplace, as if in deep thought. Nancy brought her thumbs to her mouth. Melanie frowned as she noted Nancy's gesture. It had been two months since Nancy had sucked her thumbs, and all it took was this suggestion of Gary's to start her again. Maybe the children had the incident with Jacob Armand more deeply rooted in their minds than she thought?

"I had a lot of dreams right after the accident," Kyle said. "But you knew about them, 'cause I came into your room a couple of times, remember?"

"I remember," Gary said. "And that was to be expected so soon after what happened. But I'm asking if you've been having dreams lately?"

"No, dad," Kyle said. "You told us not to think about those things."

"How about you, Nancy?"

The little girl shrugged.

Melanie looked out the window and saw the bus coming. "Hey, you'd better get going," she said.

Gary hoisted himself up from the chair and said, "Now, listen. If you ever want to discuss what happened that night, you just come to your mother or me, okay? Don't bottle your feelings inside."

"We won't, dad," Kyle said, heading out into the hall.

"They'll be okay," he said, putting his arm around Melanie. "I just wanted to let them know we won't make fun of them if they're still afraid. Now listen," he said, abruptly changing the subject, "I've got news for you that'll take your mind off of all this."

"What's that?"

"Guess where I'm going tomorrow?"

Melanie shrugged.

"To the medical center for tests. Melanie, if I do okay, I may be able to go back to work."

Melanie's smile broadened and became genuine. "Gary, that's wonderful! It'll be just like it was when we first moved here! The way it was supposed to be—with you going to work and me doing my painting."

She threw her arms around him. She wanted so much to be happy, to believe that nothing but good could happen to her family from now on.

13

"Hey, Alicen, wait up!"

Alicen recognized Jamie Hutchinson's voice and quickened her pace toward home. She had been made to stay after school that day. The accident had been heavy on her mind, and she had been caught daydreaming—*again*. This new teacher was worse than Mr. Percy had ever been. She had yelled at Alicen, humiliating her in front of the whole class. Oh, God, the girl thought, isn't this day bad enough? All I need now is Jamie Hutchinson teasing me.

"Alicen, I know you can hear me," Jamie said, his voice right behind her. "Why don't you stop?"

"Why don't you go away?" Alicen replied.

"You want a ride home?" Jamie asked, ignoring her remark. He came up alongside her on a bicycle.

"No," Alicen said plainly.

"It's a long walk," Jamie coaxed. "Come on, will you? I rode all the way back to school just 'cause I thought you'd want a ride home."

Alicen stopped, considering this. "Really?" she asked. "You really came back for me?"

"Sure," Jamie said. "Now, hop on, will you?"

He stopped the bicycle and patted the fender behind him. Alicen studied it doubtfully.

"I think I'm too heavy for that," she said.

"It's stronger than it looks," Jamie said. "And besides, I already told you, you aren't that fat. Get on."

Alicen sighed with defeat and climbed behind him. She hoped none of her classmates would see them riding together.

They rode on in silence, until they reached the bottom of the hill that led to the VanBuren property. Alicen jumped off the bike, knowing it wouldn't make it up the hill under their combined weight. She adjusted her skirt and books.

"Thanks, Jamie," she said. "I'm sorry I acted so stuck-up before."

But Jamie wasn't listening. Straddling his bike, his sneakers toeing the asphalt, he was staring at the big gray house. It fascinated him, with its boarded-up windows and brown, overgrown grass. He turned back to Alicen.

"I want to look inside there," he said.

"You can't," Alicen replied. "It's private property. And besides, how would you get in?"

"I'll find a way," Jamie said.

He jumped off his bike and walked it toward the house, dried weeds and crab grass crunching beneath his feet. Alicen ran after him.

"Jamie, you can't go in there!" she cried. "You'll get in trouble."

Jamie stopped and turned to her. "If no one tells on me," he said, a warning tone in his voice, "I won't get in trouble. Besides, I'm just looking."

He found a place to hide his bicycle in the bushes that surrounded the house. To his dismay all the windows and doors were tightly boarded over. Alicen hoped it would discourage him.

"Ah-ha!" Jamie cried. He had discovered an entrance to the basement. An empty, rusted milk can rested against the slanted doors.

"Help me tear some of this up," he said, pulling at the weeds. Alicen joined him, somewhat reluctantly. "See? They forgot to secure this lock."

Jamie removed it and set it on top of the milk can. With a heave, he jerked one big door open. The basement below was a black pit, silent and frightening. But this only sharpened Jamie's curiosity. He hurried down the stone steps. Alicen hesitated but decided she didn't want to be alone out here and ran after him.

"Brr!" she mumbled. "It's so cold!"

"Shh," Jamie said, as if the house had ears. "Help me find the stairs."

They groped through the darkness, Alicen holding fast to Jamie's belt. She was struck by a mixture of smells. Cats, rusting metal, old wood. Her hands felt the stucco of a wall, then pulled back when cobwebs brushed her fingers.

"I don't like this," she said.

"Here're the stairs," Jamie said. "Follow me up."

Unused for months, the wooden stairs creaked in protest under this new weight. Alicen felt the banister wobbling and tightened her grip on Jamie's belt. At last he opened the door. They were in the kitchen. A beam of light shining through a crack in the window illuminated the empty floor. Jamie and Alicen stepped further inside.

"I'll bet she's watching us," Jamie said.

"Who?"

"The old lady," Jamie said. "Helen Jennings. You know she died out on that hill last year?"

"Mrs. VanBuren said she had a heart attack."

"Uh-uh," Jamie said. In the half-light, Alicen saw his head shake back and forth. "I'll bet she was one of the murder victims I told you about."

"That was a lie!" Alicen cried.

Jamie didn't reply. He opened a door and walked out of the kitchen. His sneakers made squeaking noises as he moved across the bare wooden floors, investigating each empty room. Their barrenness made them very cold, and Alicen wished she hadn't come in here after all. Jamie poked around a fireplace in the living room, hoping to discover some treasure the movers had left behind. Alicen looked around the big room but didn't move from Jamie's side.

Suddenly something moved in the entranceway to the dining room. Alicen took a step toward it but quickly found herself unable to move. A woman was staring at her. She pointed at Alicen, her long arm glowingly white.

"Leave this place!" she cried. "There is danger, child!"

Alicen was frozen to the floor. The vision continued to point at her, a frothy light in the darkness of the dining room. Alicen wondered what was hidden in that darkness.

"Alicen, let's look up—"

Jamie turned to see Alicen staring across the room. He snapped his fingers in front of her eyes.

"Alicen!" he cried. "What's the matter?"

His cries broke her spell, and giving a gasp, Alicen turned to face him. She pointed to the entranceway. "There's someone standing there!" she hissed.

Jamie squinted his eyes and looked through the darkness. He saw a shimmer of white where Alicen pointed. Someone was standing there, all right, blocking their only exit! For the first time since entering the house, Jamie was scared. Slowly he unbuckled his belt and pulled it through the loops of his jeans. Winding an end around his hand, leaving the buckle free, he walked carefully toward the white light. It did not move.

He raised it in the air, ready to swing it forward with all his might.

"Go away!" Alicen cried. "Leave us alone!"

Jamie gave a cry then and let the buckle of his belt swirl though the air at the unmoving form. It made a loud sound as it struck wood. The sound reverberated through the house like mocking laughter. There was no one there at all.

"Alicen, it's only a curtain," Jamie cried. "I just made a fool of myself over a dumb curtain."

"I know I saw someone there," Alicen insisted. "She pointed right at me and said, 'Leave this place. There is danger, child!'"

"I think your brain is in danger," Jamie scoffed. "I didn't hear a thing."

"It's true," Alicen said.

"Oh, you're seeing things," Jamie said. "If you're so scared to be in this house, I'll leave."

He took her by the hand and walked through the darkness to the kitchen. Alicen didn't protest, only too happy to be getting out of there. But she had seen something. It had spoken to her.

They cut across the dark basement, heading toward the light of the doorway. Once outside, Jamie closed the doors. Then he turned to Alicen, and squinting in the bright sunlight, he said, "If you tell anyone what happened in there, I'll kill you. I feel like such a jerk—hitting a curtain with a belt!"

"I won't tell a soul," Alicen promised. She pulled her hand from his and ran across the lawn, wanting to get as far away from the house as possible. Jamie went to fetch his bicycle, pondering over Alicen's overactive imagination.

"She's nuts," he said, then sighed. Climbing onto his bike, he rode back to the road and headed home.

He didn't know he was being watched.

I try so hard to warn them, the dark-haired woman thought. *I have spoken to Melanie many times, but she ignores me. They all ignore me.*

I don't know that I can save them.

After shepherding Gary through a number of tests and X-rays, Doctor Norton announced that he could go back to work on a three-day-a-week schedule. Derek readily agreed to drive Gary into the city, provided he promise that the remaining days be dedicated to therapy.

"After the bus accident, I knew something good had to happen to this family," Melanie said when she heard the news. Thoughts of the mysterious dark-haired woman flashed in her mind, but she shook them away. This was a happy occasion, and nothing would mar it.

"You've waited so long for this," she went on, "and now it's here."

*   *   *

The next morning, all the children gave Gary kisses of encouragement before they left for school. Around ten, Derek helped Gary put his things in order, then carried the briefcase and crutches downstairs while Gary rode the lift. Derek made a mental note to begin stairs therapy that week.

Gary took the crutches from him at the bottom, then hobbled into the kitchen to say goodbye to Melanie. There were tears in her blue eyes. He laughed and ran a thumb under one of them.

"Hey, this is a happy occasion," he said.

"Why do you think I'm crying?" Melanie blubbered.

"Well, I'll see you later tonight," Gary said, kissing her. "Stop crying and wish me luck."

"Good luck, Gary," Melanie said, smiling.

The sun was shining brightly as the two men got into Derek's car. There was a low hum in the air, the buzz of insects heralding summer. Gary opened his window and breathed in the aroma of flowers on the warm, soft breeze.

"Summer's so close you can smell it," he said.

"I love this time of the year," Derek replied, turning his key. "I met Elaine on a day just like this."

He looked up at the blue, cloudless sky and pressed his foot on the gas pedal. "Funny how a certain kind of day can make you remember things," he said.

"For sure," Gary agreed, wondering if Derek wanted to talk about his wife.

"I don't think I could ever forget the way Elaine looked that day," Derek said wistfully. "She was so beautiful." But he forced his voice into a more cheerful tone. "I'm happy that I met Liza Crewe. She's giving me something to look forward to in life. I'm hoping to marry her."

"Hey, that's great," Gary said. "Any idea when?"

"I haven't asked her yet," Derek said. "I don't think the time is right, since we've only known each other a few weeks. I don't want to scare her off."

"It's usually smart to take it easy," Gary said. "Although Melanie and I only knew each other for a few months before we tied the knot."

"Those kind of marriages usually don't work," Derek said.

"Which is why I hesitate to ask Liza this early on. You and Melanie were lucky."

"We've had our problems," Gary said.

"So I gathered from what you told me the other night," Derek said. "Hey, listen. I wanted to apologize for laughing at you."

"Don't worry about it," Gary said. "It is an unbelievable story."

"Are you taking it back?"

"No," Gary said. "It's true. I just hope nothing ever happens again to prove it."

Derek put on his signal as he headed for the exit ramp. He thought about the things Gary and Melanie had told him and wondered if there wasn't a germ of truth in them. Not ghosts, of course. Derek firmly believed those things didn't exist. But he knew some crazy people practiced the occult. Could the prowler who murdered those three people have been one of those?

Whatever, it didn't concern him. He looked up into his rear-view mirror to be sure no one was tailgating him. Then he returned his eyes to the road. Seconds later, he did a double take.

"Damn!" he cried. "She's back again."

"Who?" Gary asked, trying to look out the back window.

"The hitchhiker I told you about," Derek said, looking in his mirror at her. She was waving slowly. "I was hoping that bitch had decided to leave me alone."

Gary hadn't seen anything on the road but thought perhaps that the woman had moved out of his line of vision. He noticed that Derek's forehead had broken out in a sweat and that his usually calm therapist was chewing at his lips.

"Hey, she's really gotten to you, hasn't she?"

"Huh?" Derek jumped a little. "Oh, Jesus in Heaven. I guess so. I had forgotten about her, but it looks as if she's moving in on me again."

"Somebody ought to call the police about her," Gary suggested.

Derek reached the parkway exit, and he sped onto it, glad to be getting away from the woman. He didn't understand why she frightened him so much. But he had seen something in her eyes a moment ago—the look one sometimes sees in the faces of killers pictured in the newspapers. If Jacob Armand—or whoever the prowler was—had belonged to some occult group, could she have also been a member? Was that why she was hanging around the VanBuren house?

WELCOME BACK, GARY!

The sign was stretched across the waiting room, from a translucent glass door that read Warren Lee to one that read Gary VanBuren. Gary rocked on his crutches, grinning up at it. The secretary, who had been hired during his absence, asked politely if he needed help.

"I work here," he said, grinning at the sound of those words. "I'm Gary VanBuren."

"Oh!" the young woman said, standing. She rounded the desk, a petite redhead with a broad smile. She held out a hand, and Gary shook it. "I'm Judy Palance. Mr. Lee's told me so much about you! Can I help you sit down? Then I'll go get—"

Gary assured her that he was fine. The door to Warren Lee's office opened then, and a handsome young Oriental stepped out. Seeing Gary, he smiled and went to put his arms around his partner. Then he stepped back and looked him over.

"It's been a long time," he said. He gave him a slight punch. "You look terrific. Are those muscles I see under that suit?"

Gary looked from one arm to the other. "I guess that's from lifting weights. The way my therapist pushes me, you'd think I was training for the fight of the century."

"At least he's got you walking again," Warren said. He turned to Judy. "Get the champagne out, okay? We're going to have a party."

"You bought champagne?" Gary asked. Warren nodded, smiling. "And what about my appointments?"

"I set the first one up for one o'clock, so we'd have time to talk. And you're only getting one today. You don't need to overburden yourself."

"Yes, doctor," said Gary.

Gary, Warren, and Judy shared champagne, joking together so joyfully that they barely heard the phone ringing over their laughter. Judy leaned over her desk to grab the phone. "Mr. VanBuren? Yes, he's in. Hold on."

Gary looked at Warren. "I didn't think anyone knew I was coming back today."

Warren shrugged his shoulders in response. Gary turned and went into his office. For a moment he stopped to admire it. It looked exactly as it had when he had left it last November. Even the calendar hadn't been changed. He flipped through it to the right date and settled down in his leather chair. God, that felt good! It was wonderful to be back on familiar territory. Propping his crutches against the window behind him, he paused for a moment to look out at the city. Then he finally answered the phone.

"Mr. VanBuren?" a voice asked. It was vaguely familiar.

"Yes?"

"It's Marc Kaufman," the man said.

Gary leaned back in his chair. "Oh, yes. How are you, mayor?"

"Under the circumstances—" Marc began. Gary could hear him sigh. "Well, I should get right to the point. It's about Sarah's diamond ring. I don't want to seem as if I'm making accusations, but it was missing from her hand when . . ."

"The heirloom she was wearing that night?"

"Yes," said Marc. "Mr. VanBuren, I was wondering if you might have seen it? Perhaps she dropped it in your house."

"Did you call my wife?" Gary asked.

"I tried," said Marc. "No one answered the phone."

"Then she's probably out shopping," Gary said. "How about the people at the hospital? Or in the ambulance?"

"I've talked to them," Marc said. "And to the police. Please don't think I'm saying anyone at your house took it. But it was the last place Sarah wore the ring."

Gary thought a moment, then said, "When I get home tonight, I promise I'll have the whole family look for it. Come to think of it, we gave you two a tour of the house that day. It could be anywhere."

"I'd really appreciate it if you'd look," Marc said.

As soon as he hung up, Gary's door opened. Into the room walked his partner, carrying a pile of folders. He dumped them on Gary's desk and told him they were backlogged files that needed to be gone through.

"Hey," Gary said. "I thought you weren't going to overburden me today?"

"Admit it," Warren said. "You love every minute of this."

Gary smiled crookedly and opened the top folder. At last he was back at work again.

While Gary readjusted himself to the working world, Derek Miller waited outside Madame Martin's Dance Studio for Liza to finish her class. He sat on a cushion-covered bench in the waiting room, looking at the pictures of a magazine written in French. He heard a French voice from behind a door.

"Un et deux, un et deux," it repeated over and over to the beat of the piano music. "Et c'est assez, mesdames. À demain!"

Seconds later, the door opened, and a thin woman with hair pulled back in a bun came out. Derek looked past her at the small group of students and signaled to Liza. She waved and indicated the locker room. Derek went back to his seat and waited.

Liza came out at last and in front of several other dance students, threw her arms around him and kissed him.

"That's the kind of greeting I like," Derek said.

"Have you been waiting long?"

"Not really," Derek answered. "But I'm ready for lunch if you are."

"I'm famished!" Liza cried, patting her flat stomach. "And I know a terrific Chinese restaurant."

It was only three blocks away, but Derek insisted upon carrying Liza's case. It wasn't heavy at all, and Liza was a little embarrassed when a few classmates saw her handing it to him. But Derek wasn't worried about their opinion.

"Women shouldn't have to burden themselves," he said.

"You're such a chauvinist," Liza teased, "but I guess I love you, anyway." At the restaurant Liza opened the door before Derek could get to it.

The restaurant was crowded, but recognizing Liza, the maitre d' led them quickly to a table. In silence Derek and Liza ran over the menu, then placed their orders. When the waiter left, Liza folded her hands together and leaned forward.

"How's your daughter?" she asked. "You told me about the accident over the phone but no details. Did it upset her very much?"

"I wouldn't know," Derek admitted. "I took her out to dinner that day, but she didn't want to talk about it. Alicen has a habit of clamming up like that."

"I can't blame her," Liza said. "I saw the picture in the paper. What a horrible mess!"

"Thank God none of the children were seriously hurt," Derek said. "But that poor teacher . . ."

Alicen's words came back to him: *I'm glad he died. I hate him!*

Derek shook his head roughly.

"What's wrong?"

"Nothing," Derek said. "Dwight Percy was Alicen's teacher. I understand, though, that they weren't too fond of each other. Alicen has a tendency to daydream, and Percy was a no-nonsense type."

Liza laughed, a bell-like sound that relaxed Derek at once.

"Oh, I used to daydream all the time," she said. "I used to pretend I was a prima ballerina when I was supposed to be doing equations. I think all girls go through a time like that. How old did you say Alicen was?"

"Thirteen," Derek said. "And I don't think this is a passing phase. She's been having these dreams for six years." He lifted his fork and dropped it. "Ever since Elaine died."

"Oh . . ."

Looking up at Liza, Derek realized his mistake.

"Oh, hey, I'm sorry," he said, reaching across the table to take her hand. "I shouldn't have said that."

"You're just upset because of the accident," Liza said. "I understand."

"I don't want to spoil our lunch," Derek replied. "Let me think of something better to talk about. Do you like ghost stories?"

"Sure," Liza said.

"Then listen to this one," Derek answered. "You'll love it."

He proceeded to relate the story of the VanBuren hauntings. Liza listened intently, her almond eyes as bright as a child's. When Derek finished, she stabbed a shrimp on her plate with a fork and said, "That's interesting, but a little unbelievable, don't you think? I mean, haunted houses?"

"I don't believe it," Derek said, "and yet I don't disbelieve that something went on in that house last year. I think the VanBurens made up that story to push the truth from their minds. But one thing that is true is the fact that three people died at the house. One of them was a young woman named Janice. She was Melanie's best friend, and needless to say, my patient's wife gets rather upset at the mention of her name."

"The poor thing," Liza said. "It must have been a horrible experience for her."

"Melanie tends to get emotional about it," Derek said. "But who can blame her?"

Liza ate a few bites of food, then said, "I'd sure like to see that house. I'll bet it's eerie."

"You wouldn't be disappointed," Derek answered. "But the Van-Burens do keep the cobwebs swept."

Liza laughed. "Do you suppose I could come there one night?" she asked. "I mean, after giving Alicen time to adjust after the accident? I think meeting her father's new girlfriend would be too much for her right now."

"You missed your calling," Derek said. "You should have been a child psychologist."

"I worked with one for eight years," Liza said. "That's how I saved money to come to New York."

Derek lifted her hand and kissed it. "You're a very kind woman," he said.

"I was just thinking about Alicen."

"Shh," Derek said. "Enough about Alicen. You'll meet her soon, I promise."

Making his nightly rounds of the bay area, Harold Kent, a security guard for one of Belle Bay's prestigious private communities, drove his dune buggy along the water line. His headlights danced off the little ripples made by the wind, competing with the golden reflections of the moon. The bay was so peaceful at this hour, just before dawn. Harold began to whistle.

But something caught his eye, an interruption in the golden ripples of the bay that made him stop whistling. He stopped his truck and went to investigate.

It was a woman's body. Harold bent closer to it, waving his flashlight over the wet, sand-covered flesh. In the moonlight the bloated face seemed to be grinning with evil pleasure. Blond hair was braided with seaweed. Some of it had wrapped around the woman's throat.

Harold rushed back to his truck and drove up to the guard house. There, he phoned his discovery in to the Belle Bay Police. Within two hours the body, named Jane Doe for lack of identification, was taken to the Belle Bay funeral home for storage. There it would wait until someone came to identify it.

14

◆

"As soon as you kids are through with your homework," Gary said at dinner that night, "come downstairs. I have a chore for you."

"What is it, dad?" Kyle asked.

"Well, Mayor Kaufman gave me a call today," Gary explained. "It seems Sarah lost that big diamond ring of hers, and he wondered if it might be in this house somewhere. So we're going to look for it."

"Gary, I've cleaned this house since then," Melanie said, serving beets to a grimacing Nancy. "I didn't see it."

"Well, it wouldn't hurt to look," Gary said.

"Alicen and I will help you," Derek said.

Alicen, picking listlessly at her food, didn't hear her father say that. She was thinking of the old house down the road. Jamie hadn't mentioned a word of what had happened in school the next day. And true to her promise, Alicen had kept her own mouth shut. She wasn't quite sure what she'd say, anyway. That she had seen a ghost that turned out to be a curtain? Having had time to decide the whole scene just had to be her imagination, she felt as silly now as Jamie had. Still, she wished her mother were there. Her mother would make her feel better about all the crazy things that had been happening.

Her head felt funny tonight, the way it had just before the bus accident. She stabbed a beet and saw red juice flow over her plate like blood.

"Nancy!" Gina cried then. "Stop feeding beets to Lad!"

"Yeah, little girl," Gary said. "You eat those. They're good."

"Alicen isn't eating hers," Nancy said, pouting.

Melanie looked across the table at her young house guest. She frowned to see Alicen staring dully at her plate, pushing her food around. The fork looked ready to drop from her fingers.

"Are you all right, Alicen?"

No answer.

"Alicen!" Derek shouted.

She jumped. "Huh?"

"Mrs. VanBuren asked if you're all right," Derek said, studying her face.

"I'm just real tired," Alicen said. "Can I go to my room?"

"Eat first," Derek insisted. "It'll make you feel better."

"Please?"

"Alicen, just eat dinner," Derek snapped.

Alicen obeyed him. She ate as quickly as possible without making herself obvious, wanting only to get upstairs. She had heard a voice in her head, a voice calling her to her room. When at last her plate was empty, she excused herself and all but ran from the dining room.

"I'll never understand that kid," Derek said, looking over his shoulder.

"You don't try very hard," Melanie mumbled.

Derek ignored the remark.

Upstairs, Alicen sat down at her desk and waited. Her head was light as a cloud now, her ears deaf to the noises around her. Only her mind listened, waiting for the voice that would mean her mother had come once more to talk with her. The conscious Alicen was suppressed now, and she waited in a trance.

"Alicen," she heard.

"I'm here, mommy. Why did you wait so long to talk to me, mommy?"

"Selfish brat!" the apparition hissed. "Do you think I have nothing better to do than talk with you?"

"Mommy, please don't be mad," Alicen begged. She squinted at the cloud of smoke, shaped like a human body one moment, then unidentifiable the next, and tried to see her mother's features.

"Tell me of the man Davis," she heard.

"He came back to school a couple of times," Alicen reported. "I told him about the driver jumping from the bus, like you wanted. But he didn't believe me 'cause none of the other kids said they saw it." Alicen looked down at her hands. "They didn't find a body."

"If they want a body," the vision said, "I will give them one. Then they'll be satisfied. But you must help me. You'll know what to do."

There was a deep silence for a few moments. Alicen felt something cold press against her forehead, but she didn't move away from its stinging touch. Then the vision spoke again.

"You will know what to do. Succeed, and I will give you this."

Alicen saw the diamond ring floating before her. She reached for it, taking it in her hands. It glowed in an almost unnatural way, as if possessed by the very soul of the apparition. Alicen gazed into it.

Someone knocked at the door. "Alicen?"

The girl turned around at the sound of her father's voice, the spell that held her breaking. She became her own person in a split second, in the same time that the cloud of smoke disappeared and left her holding the ring. Momentarily confused, Alicen didn't think to hide it when her father opened her door.

"Are you okay?" Derek asked. "I want you to come downstairs and help look for the—"

Alicen realized that her father had seen the ring. Not knowing how she'd come to have it and afraid her father would think she'd stolen it, she dropped the ring in the pocket of the cardigan that hung over the back of the desk chair. Derek waited for his daughter to tell him about the ring, but she said nothing.

"I was just putting on a sweater," she said quietly, standing. "It's cold in this house."

"I was rather warm myself," Derek said. He debated whether or not to take the ring forcefully but decided against it. Why create a scene in front of the VanBurens?

"Get busy looking for that ring," he said. "It's very important that we find it."

He left the room and went to the staircase, pretending to look for it. As he poked around the carpeting, knowing there was nothing to be found, Derek tried to understand what he had just seen. *Jesus*, he thought, *my daughter's a klepto! How'd she get the ring? And what the hell am I going to tell the VanBurens?*

"Nothing," he said out loud. With three kids of their own, they wouldn't want a little thief around. They would call her a bad influence and kick her out—and him with her.

He sank down on the step and punched one of the balusters. "Damn you, Alicen," he whispered. "I've waited too long for a job like this to have you ruin it for me."

He'd have to get the ring from her and plant it somewhere in the house where Sarah could have dropped it.

Hearing soft steps on the carpeting behind him, he turned to see Alicen coming down the stairs. She barely glanced at him when she said, "I'm going to look in the dining room."

Derek said nothing. He clutched hard at the baluster, resisting an urge to grab and shake her. When she disappeared into the dining room, he got up and hurried back to her room.

It looked so innocent, with its yellow curtains and white furniture. Derek went first to the desk, pulling open all the drawers. He found stationery, pencils, and a roll of tape, but no ring. Next he went to the bed and pulled back the yellow coverlet. The ring wasn't under the pillow, nor was it between the mattress and box spring. And it wasn't anywhere else in the room.

"She's still got it in her pocket," he guessed. He left the room and walked down the hall, meeting Melanie.

"Is Alicen still in the dining room?"

"I sent her to help Gina look in the living room," Melanie replied. "Honestly, I don't think any of us will find that ring. One of those hospital people probably took it."

"It—uh—doesn't hurt to check," Derek said, moving down the stairs.

He stood in the doorway of the living room for a few minutes, wondering how he could get the ring from his daughter. He couldn't tell her to give it to him—not with Gina standing right there. He watched Alicen make a big production of the search, masking her guilt. She poked around the fireplace, looking like such a little girl in front of the huge structure that Derek momentarily forgot his anger. Could he have made a mistake? Maybe he hadn't seen the ring at all but had imagined it. Alicen had never stolen anything in her life!

Still, he had to be certain. He walked into the room and reached to touch the pocket of her sweater, in a gesture that would appear to be an embrace. Alicen jumped away from him.

"Dad!" she cried. "You startled me!"

"Me, too," Gina said. "I didn't hear you come into the room."

"I walk softly," Derek said.

His smile was a false one—he had felt the ring. Nervously, his daughter had resumed her search, moving to the window seat. She would not look her father in the eye. Derek saw that her hands were trembling. That was good. Let her suffer a little. He'd get the ring tonight.

By midnight, Derek decided it was safe to enter Alicen's room. To be certain, he listened carefully at her door until he heard her even breathing. Then he pushed it open and groped his way inside. His hands touched the sweater, hanging on the desk chair again, but found that the pockets were empty. Holding his breath, he carefully searched the desk. When it came to nothing, he turned and crept to the bed.

Derek stood over his daughter for a long time, wondering why she had done this thing. She looked so innocent, lying there breathing softly. Her hair was spread out on her pillow, her lower lip jutted out in a slight pout. She looked more than innocent. She was like a little child, the way Derek remembered her being before Elaine's death. My God, she had been a pretty little girl. What the hell had happened these past six years? Was Alicen's crime the result of their struggles to get by on catch-as-catch-can jobs, living in motels or basement apartments? Or was it the fact that Derek had been just a little ignorant of a growing girl's needs?

He had never admitted that possibility to himself. But now, seeing the trouble his daughter was in, he wondered if he should have been a little more understanding. After all, she was a child, and—

No, Derek told himself firmly, *I did the right thing when I tried to make her independent. You have to control your emotions to get by in this world.*

And right now, I have to get that ring.

Derek snaked his hand under her pillow. His daughter turned in her sleep, mumbling something. Thinking he had awakened her, he stepped back into the shadows. Alicen moved again, and in the thin shaft of moonlight, Derek saw the glistening facets of the diamond in her opened palm. Carefully he took it.

He could barely make out the banister and wheelchair lift as he reached the stairs, and he touched them both as he walked down. The dining room was dimly lit by moonlight shining through the bay windows. By contrast, the kitchen was almost blinding. Someone had left the light on, and he squeezed his eyes shut until they could adjust. At last, removing the ring from his bathrobe pocket, he walked to the oven. If he hid the ring there, it would look as if Sarah had dropped it when she fell.

Derek bent toward the floor but stopped when he heard a noise behind him, a dull thud, like a heavy footstep. He looked over his shoulder. There was no one behind him, and when he turned back to the oven, he saw only his reflection in its glass door. He laughed at his fears, then proceeded with his task.

All at once there was another thud, and he felt a flash of pain. This noise had sounded from his own back, something knocking against it and sending him flying forward. His face came down hard on the oven door handle, a pain shot up through his forehead. He dropped to the floor in a flurry of gray mists and twinkling lights.

He was too stunned to react when he heard laughter. Then, as if through water, he saw a young woman standing over him, her smile a familiar one. He wanted to scream, but he couldn't. He couldn't even open his mouth.

She bent closer to him, smiling all the while, and ran her fingernails over his stomach as if to rip it open. From far away, Derek heard the sound of cloth tearing, and he thought it was his flesh. *No, no, no!* His mind echoed the plea over and over.

"I wanted you," he heard her say, in an eerily seductive way. "I've wanted you for so long, Derek Miller."

"No," Derek said aloud, barely hearing his voice.

She was on top of him, her small frame somehow crushing his muscular body. He closed his eyes tightly, something deep inside his will making him do so. He would open them again, and she wouldn't be there. She didn't exist. She was his imagination.

She was still there.

"My Derek, my handsome lover Derek," she breathed.

Her face came closer and closer to his. He could see the repulsive veins, the thin blue lips, the filmy eyes. He couldn't turn from her, for when he did, he felt something rip at the sides of his head. She had him by two handfuls of hair.

"Give me what you would give a woman," she whispered, pressing her lips to his.

It was cold. My God, it was so cold! Something like a fish was pushing into Derek's mouth. He realized with horror that it was the woman's tongue. Her hands left his hair and slid down his chest, kneading the matted black hair. Mercifully, her lips left his.

Why can't I move? I'm stronger than her! I'm str—

She bit him hard on the stomach, then kissed him over and over as if to make up for the wound. It was impossible, crazy. Derek didn't want this. Not from her repulsive lips, her cold hands. He tried to push her away, but it was like moving lead.

But for a moment her touch shattered him so that he had no thoughts. His arms dropped weakly to his sides. He felt himself floating, higher and higher. Only when he was still again did he dare to open his eyes. She was sitting up, straddling him, her smile red. He wanted to kill her for using him this way, and yet something told him that that was impossible.

Something told him she was already dead.

"No," he whispered, falling at last into blackness.

The woman stood up, holding the ring in her hand. This was good, but it didn't satisfy her lustful needs. She wanted him through his own free will, not forcefully as tonight. And she would have him, soon. She smiled to think of owning that handsome man, of having him as her lover. And her anticipations made her desire to destroy the VanBuren family all the stronger.

She found Alicen waiting for her in the upstairs hallway. She handed the child the ring, then stepped back into the shadows. There was no need for words. Alicen knew exactly what to do. She entered her father's room, barely seeing the bed and dresser there. Walking to the floor grating, she knelt down and pushed her fingers between the woven strips of iron. It creaked softly. She felt pain where the iron pinched the soft underside of her hands, but she did not stop.

At last, the grating gave way, and she lifted it out. Alicen reached deep inside the cavity and dropped the ring. It made a soft tap against the floor. Then she replaced the grating, pushing it down hard so that it would not come loose again. Less than five minutes later, she was in her own bed. The smile on her face as she fell asleep was a triumphant one.

The night watchman at the Belle Bay Funeral Parlor sat up a little straighter in his chair when he felt a cold breeze brush past him. He looked behind him, saw that the back entrance was tightly closed, and shrugged. It was an old building, and drafts like that weren't uncommon. He checked his watch: 5 A.M. Two more hours and his shift would be over.

He was flipping through the pages of a girlie magazine when he heard a dull thud from one of the other rooms. He stood up, fingering the nightstick in his belt, and walked carefully toward the noise.

"Who's in there?" he asked.

Across the icy, refrigerated room, he could see the sheet-wrapped body of the latest Jane Doe to enter the morgue. A young blonde who had been found rotting on the nearby beach. The autopsy said it was a drug overdose but that the actual cause of death was probably drowning.

"Too many low-lifes in this town," the guard said with a quick glimpse at the shrouded corpse. The bump made by its nose under the sheets cast a long, grotesque shadow in the lamplight. The guard saw now that an ashtray, left here by the coroner, had fallen to the floor. He put it back up on a table and left the room. The night was silent once more.

Bored, he decided to put his head down and rest—for just a few minutes. He didn't feel the touch on his arm that turned that rest into a deep, deep sleep. Nor did he see the back door opening. He was snoring when the body of Jane Doe was dragged feet-first through the door into a back alley, pulled by unseen hands.

15

◆

Melanie entered the kitchen the next morning to find Derek slumped in a chair, an icepack to his swollen mouth. A thin bruise covered the bridge of his nose and spread out under each closed eye.

"Derek?"

He opened his eyes. "Good morning," he said groggily.

"It certainly doesn't look like it's been a good morning for you," Melanie said. "What on earth happened?"

Conscious for about an hour, Derek had prepared himself for the questions he knew would come. He shifted in his seat and adjusted the icepack to speak more easily.

"I was up in the night to get a cup of tea," he said. "I slipped on the floor and hit the oven handle."

Melanie shook her head in sympathy, then went to the cupboard to find a bottle of aspirin. She shook two of the tablets into her palm and handed them to Derek with a glass of water.

The cold glass felt strange against his teeth, and Derek grimaced when he put it down on the table. Melanie gasped.

"Derek, you've broken your teeth!" she cried.

Not for the first time that morning, Derek ran his tongue around his mouth. It scraped over the remains of one front tooth and the thread of the tooth beside it. He tasted blood. Then he pointed to the oven door handle in explanation.

Melanie took the sponge from the sink and tried to scrub the stains from the chrome. She looked over her shoulder at him. For the first time, Melanie felt sorry for Derek. He looked so vulnerable, obviously hiding a good deal of pain. But sorrow turned to shock when she noticed a circle of red dots on his stomach, where his robe had fallen open.

Teeth marks?

She turned from the sight. It was just a love bite, of course. Derek did have a girlfriend, after all. It had nothing to do with his accident and was none of her business.

"Melanie?"

"Hmm?"

"Would you do me a big favor?" Derek asked. "Would you drive Gary into work today? I couldn't make it, and I don't want him to miss a day because of me."

"Sure," Melanie said. She rinsed out the sponge, then thought better of using it again and dropped it in the trash can.

"Derek," she said, "you should really see a dentist today. Why don't you let me call ours after breakfast? Then I could drop you off on the way to the city."

"I can call a taxi," Derek said.

"Never mind," Melanie answered. "It isn't out of the way. And don't worry, you'll feel better soon."

He didn't feel better. Not now, several hours into the morning with a numb upper lip. He rested on the couch in the library, two temporary teeth in his mouth. It was more than the physical hurting that fatigued him. It was the mental anguish, the trying to remember. Derek needed to recall what had happened the night before so much that all thoughts of Alicen and the ring were obliterated. Maybe he had gone to get tea and had fallen, just like he told Melanie. But bits and pieces of a nightmare kept coming back to him, making him think there was much more to it than that.

It must have been an erotic dream. Derek figured that much out by the dull ache he had felt in his groin when he had picked himself up off the floor early that morning. In his patchy memory, he saw a blond woman straddling him, laughing at him. She looked like that woman Janice, that crazy hitchhiker. Yet Derek knew she couldn't have been in the house. The door had been locked all night.

How, then, could he explain the teeth marks?

He looked down at his stomach and pulled his shirt out of his jeans. He ran his finger over the red bumps, as he had done many times that morning, trying to tell himself they weren't what they seemed. He knew they looked like a human bite, but he wanted another, saner explanation, something to tell him the terror he remembered so vaguely was nothing more than a dream.

Suddenly the phone rang. Derek considered ignoring it, then

thought that it might be Gary, or even Liza. He crawled off the couch and stumbled out into the hall, the phone's high-pitched ringing hurting his ears. He lifted the receiver and mumbled a greeting. There was no reply.

"Hello?" he repeated, his voice sounding slurred because of the Novocain. He started to hang up but heard his name. "Yes, this is Derek," he said, putting the phone to his ear again. "Who's this?"

"The woman who craves you," a voice said, teasingly passionate. Derek laughed. "Liza, you're pretty fun—"

A loud, ear-shattering screech made him drop the receiver. It wasn't Liza on the phone at all, but some crank. Wisely, Derek hung up. When the phone rang again a moment later, however, he picked it up against his better judgment.

"Hello?"

"Don't hang up."

"I won't," Derek promised. "Is this the woman from the roadside? Janice?"

"Yes."

Derek sighed. "I thought I had made it clear that you weren't to bother me any more. What is it you want?"

"You, Derek Miller," she said. "I want you."

Derek swung the cord of the phone over the banister, then went to sit on the stairs. Leaning against the double-twisted rungs, he answered, "I'm flattered. But you see, kid, you're wasting your time. Why don't you find another fellow, someone your own age? I already have a girlfriend."

"EEEEEYYYYYAAAA!"

"Don't do that!" Derek ordered. "Stop screaming."

"I want you!" the woman shouted. "And I'll make you want me!"

"Just leave me alone," Derek said in an angry tone.

"I'll never leave you alone," Janice hissed. There was a silence, and then suddenly her voice took on the pleading quality of a little girl's. "Please, Derek! We can have so much fun together. Once I get rid of those people in that house."

"Wait a minute," Derek interrupted. " 'Those people'?"

"The VanBurens," Janice said with a click of her tongue, as if Derek should have known. "I want them out of there. I want them *dead!*"

Derek resisted an urge to hang up and asked with forced calm, "Why? What did they do to you?"

"I'll tell you," the woman said. "One night, I came to this house to visit Melanie. But first I met the spirit of the house's original owner. He sought my aid in his getting revenge against the VanBurens. But not Melanie! He *loved* Melanie. He'd been following her for nearly two hundred years, and that night I was going to help him have her, at last."

Derek recalled the story of Jacob Armand and Lydia Browning. Was this some lunatic who had also heard that tale? Someone making fun of the VanBurens' troubles?

"But those evil children tried to stand in my way," Janice said. "When I tried to rid myself of Kyle, Melanie came to his defense. She defended a devil-child by striking me across the head with a pistol! And now"—she paused—"I will walk in this limbo until I have vengeance!"

Struck in the head? Derek thought. She must be brain damaged! That would explain it. And Derek would bet all his money that Melanie had nothing at all to do with it. This woman was just plain nuts!

"I don't think this is very amusing," Derek said soberly.

"I'm serious," the woman said. "I'll get rid of them, one by one. Melanie goes today."

"What?" Derek cried. "What does that mean?"

But she had hung up on him. For a long time Derek sat holding the receiver on his lap, not believing what he had just heard. This woman was deranged, no doubt. What reason could she possibly have for hating the VanBurens?

He got up and returned the phone to its stand. Whatever that lunatic tried to do, she wouldn't frighten him into giving in to her!

Bryan Davis stopped working on his report and reached across his desk to answer the telephone. "Belle Bay Police," he said. "Bryan Davis speaking."

"Captain Davis?" a woman asked. "It's Joan Mead, from the funeral parlor. I'm afraid we have a problem."

"What can I do for you, Mrs. Mead?" Bryan asked.

"It seems someone stole one of our residents," Joan said. "Do you remember the Jane Doe brought in a few nights ago?"

"Yes," Bryan said. "The one found on the beach. Are you certain she's missing?"

"Definitely," Joan said. "As a matter of good business policy, I always have my employees check each room before we officially open. People so need to be catered to at times like these."

"Of course," Bryan said.

"But when we entered the morgue," Joan continued, "Jane Doe was gone."

There was a pause, and Bryan heard the old woman sigh. "To think I found the security guard sleeping," she said. "Of course, I fired him. But he's still waiting here if you need to question him."

"Thanks," Bryan said. "I will. I'll send someone down there right away."

He hung up the phone. Wasn't it bad enough that he hadn't yet found the bus driver? Now there was another mystery to solve.

"Oh, God," Bryan sighed. "Who'd guess what a peaceful town this was, just a year ago?"

Derek waited all morning for the phone to ring again. At lunchtime, while he sat on the steps with a sandwich, his daughter was making a call of her own. She had told the cafeteria monitor that her father had been sick that morning and that she wanted to have flowers delivered to him.

"That's sweet of you," the monitor had said.

"I'll have to use my whole allowance," Alicen said. "But I don't care. I love my father."

Now she stood up in the little hallway just outside the cafeteria, thumbing the phone book for a number she never intended to call. With the pages opened to "Florists," she instead dialed the police.

"Belle Bay Police," a voice said. "Bryan Davis."

"Yeah, hi," Alicen mumbled, turning her back to the cafeteria doors. She covered the receiver with a napkin. "Listen, I read in the papers that you guys are looking for a body? Some bus driver?"

"What about it?"

He sounded eager. That was good.

"I sorta saw one," Alicen replied. "At that construction place, you know? I was driving by, and I saw this big dude dump this thing in a green trash container. Looked like a body, but I can't be sure, you know? I just figured I should call."

"We appreciate it," Bryan said. "Would you tell me your name?"

"Never mind," Alicen said. "Just go—"

Alicen heard a tap at the door and nearly dropped the receiver. Hanging up, she stuffed the napkin into her pocket. Then she opened the door and smiled at the monitor.

"I had to call three florists," she said.

"Had a hard time of it, huh?"

"Everything's just fine now," Alicen said, smiling.

Tim and Rick were certain they were being sent on another wild goose chase, but they couldn't question their captain's orders. So now they stood banging on the newly repaired fence of the construction site, their shirts sticking to them under the merciless sun. The crane above them drowned out the sound of their knocking, and Rick was inclined to give up until the machine stopped. He removed his cap and wiped his forehead.

"Damned hot, ain't it?" someone said. A broad-shouldered, shirtless man had opened the gate. Hank Emmons tilted his helmet back. "Are you guys back again?"

"We received a call this morning pertaining to the case," Rick said. He stepped inside the fence, followed by his partner. Over the din of the crane, he said, "Do you have any trash bins around here?"

"Of course we do," Hank said. "What do you think? But you can't come in without a helmet. Wait a second."

He left and returned a moment later with two hard hats. Rick and Tim donned them, then followed Hank past work crews and machinery. Along the back fence of the site, they found two five-yard containers.

Rick went close to one and asked, "How long has it been since you opened these?"

"That one was emptied yesterday," Hank said. "But this one here hasn't been opened in a few days. Since the accident, I guess. We use it for dry rubbish—wood scraps, you know? Stuff that keeps for a while."

Rick turned to his partner. "You brought the body bag, didn't you?"

"Right here," Tim replied, holding it up.

Hank looked around at his work crew and saw they were still busy. Then he said in a low voice, "What in the hell is the body bag for?"

"What do you think?" Rick asked, almost sarcastically.

Now Hank laughed at him. "Oh, hell! There ain't nothing in there but trash. Just get out of my way and I'll prove it."

Before Rick could stop him, the foreman climbed up the side of the container and threw it open. The smell that shot up from it was so horrendous that tears welled in his eyes. He backed away, choking.

"Shit! That's like rotten meat!"

"She's in there, then," Tim said.

"Damn right she is," Hank growled. "And you'd better get her out."

Tim and Rick had brought special masks with them, and they tied them around their mouths and noses. Rick was first to climb to the top of the bin, and what he saw made his heart skip a beat. The young woman's twisted body had been thrown on top of the trash, a broken two-by-four pushed into her stomach. One arm reached for the side of the container, the fingers at its end clawing as if the woman had tried to climb out. Tiny worms made a feast of her flesh, or what was left of it.

"She looks like she's been dead for six months," he said.

Tim was looking at her now, too, a grimace on his face. At last, wearing canvas gloves, he jumped down into the container. He had to fight a wave of nausea as he knelt down on the floor, feeling the wet, bloated flesh through his gloves. He pulled the heavy-weight bag over her head-first, glad her face was down. When he reached her feet, he stopped to study them for a moment.

"Want me to come in?" Rick shouted.

"I can do this," Tim said, resuming his work. "Just be ready to lift her out."

Something about her feet bothered him. They had been white and bloated, cut by the thin straps of her sandals. It was horrible, horrible. But why did he single out that one feature?

At last he tied the end of the bag, stood up, and lifted the gruesome parcel to Rick. He climbed from the container as his partner laid the body on the ground. The work crew stood at a distance, curiosity taking precedence over their duties. Suddenly Tim understood what bothered him about the victim's sandals. Determining that Hank had kept the crew far enough away so as not to hear him, he turned to Rick and asked, "Didn't the kids say their driver was wearing boots?"

"I think I remember that."

"This one's in sandals," Tim said quietly.

Rick shook his head at his partner.

"Do you want to spend the rest of your life looking for a body?" he asked. "Who the hell else would she be?"

"But the kids said—"

"The kids were lying," Rick interrupted.

"You said that before," Tim reminded him.

Rick didn't answer. He stooped down and grabbed an end of the bag. Tim picked up the other, and in silence they carried the body to the car. Rick made it clear that he didn't want to discuss this any further. He had his body, and he didn't care what she was wearing.

Bryan Davis's emotions were mixed when he heard the news. He was sad that a woman had died but happy that he at last had something to say to the irate parents who called all day long. Horrifying as all this had been, it was at last over. Bryan could return to keeping the peace in Belle Bay while the county worried about finding the woman's next of kin.

Melanie glanced at her watch and saw it was time to meet Gary. She walked toward the exit of the art gallery she had been visiting. The street outside was filled with people and cars that seemed to glow in the hot sunlight. Melanie could see ripples of heat rising from the cracked sidewalk as she opened the door to her car and climbed behind the wheel.

The engine turned over easily, as it had done every day since she had had it overhauled. Looking behind her, she turned the front of the car just slightly into the street. A taxi came speeding down it, forcing her to stop. Another followed, then a bus and a few cars. It was five minutes before Melanie was able to pull out.

"Nice way to waste gasoline," she mumbled, zooming into the road while she had the chance. Following traffic, she crossed Sixth, then Fifth Avenue. Except for the stops and starts expected of New York City traffic, the going was smooth. And then, just as Melanie turned onto Madison, the car began to choke. It slowed down to a complete stop.

Angered, Melanie pumped the gas pedal and tried to start it again. How could this be happening now? She was embarrassed to hear a dozen horns honking behind her. Angry drivers cursed loudly. Melanie was about to answer them in kind when a loud thud cut off her words. Someone had hit the car, sending it spinning. Melanie heard herself cry out and felt her body stiffening in reaction to the impact.

The car skidded across the road and sideswiped a lamppost. Melanie never saw it coming.

A moment of stunned silence followed, and then suddenly a dozen people were swarming about the wreck.

"Did you see that guy? Hit and run!"

"She's bleeding!"

"Of course she's bleeding, you idiot! Someone call an ambulance!"

The proprietor of a nearby men's store had already taken care of that, and even now the group could hear sirens wailing. More curious than helpful, they didn't move when the ambulance turned the corner. A police car followed, and two policemen jumped out to push the crowd back as the paramedics tended to Melanie. They carefully pulled her from the wreck and laid her on a stretcher. Twenty minutes later, she was wheeled into the emergency room of nearby Saint Joan's Hospital.

In the meantime, Gary was waiting patiently in his office for Melanie's arrival. It didn't surprise him that she was late, since traffic was always heavy at this hour.

The secretary announced that Derek Miller was on the line. Wondering what he wanted, Gary picked up the phone.

"Saint Joan's Hospital just called," Derek said. "Gary, your wife was in an accident just a short while ago."

"What?!" Gary cried. "When did this happen? Where is she?"

"At Saint Joan's," Derek repeated. "They found this number in her handbag and called here. But they wouldn't tell me anything."

"I'll go there at once," Gary said, reaching behind him for his crutches.

"Don't go by yourself, okay?" Derek said.

"My partner will take me," Gary assured him.

It only took twenty minutes to get to the hospital, but to Gary it might have been two hours. Warren opened the glass door for him, and the two men walked up to the reception desk.

"Can you tell me where my wife is?" Gary asked.

"Melanie VanBuren," Warren explained.

The nurse flipped through a file. "She was admitted just a short while ago," she said. "Would you please wait over there while I call the doctor?"

She indicated a small gathering of orange vinyl couches in a corner of the lobby. An elderly woman frowned at Gary over the top of *Reader's Digest*.

"What about my wife?" Gary asked, turning back to the nurse. "Is she all right?"

"The doctor will tell you everything, sir," the nurse said politely. "Please sit down."

"But is she—"

"Gary, come on and sit," Warren said. "The doctor will be out in a minute."

Half an hour, then an hour passed with no word, and Gary found himself knocking his crutches together in frustration. At last, though, the doctor appeared.

"Your wife had a bad blow to the head," he said quietly. "She's suffering from a concussion."

Gary closed his eyes and steeled himself. "What else is wrong?"

"Nothing," the doctor said. "She has a nasty cut on her forehead, of course. But there's no internal bleeding. She'll be able to go home after a few days of rest."

"How did the accident happen?" Warren asked.

"It seems Mrs. VanBuren's car had stalled," the doctor said, "and was struck by a speeding car. She hit a lamppost, but luckily there wasn't much damage done to her."

"Not much!" Gary cried. "You just said she had a concussion, and—"

"Relax," the doctor said. "Would you like to see her?"

Gary nodded. The doctor led him down a long hallway and opened a door at its end. Gary felt his stomach twist to see his wife lying in that bed, her face swollen beneath a gauze bandage. Her hair was in disarray, some of it plastered to her cheeks. Gary leaned awkwardly on his crutches and brushed it gently away.

"God," he whispered, "can we ever live in peace?"

16

———◆———

Kyle was at first delighted to find pizza on the table for dinner, until he realized his mother wasn't there to serve it. When he and his sisters had come home from school to find her studio empty, they had assumed she was still in the city with their father. But why wasn't she home yet? Why was Derek taking care of dinner?

"I'm afraid your mother isn't coming home tonight," Derek said, tearing the top off of one of the boxes. "There was an accident today."

"Oh, no!" Kyle cried.

"Hey, it wasn't that bad," Derek said, realizing he had spoken too bluntly. "Another car hit hers. All she has is a little concussion, and she'll be home in a few days. Nothing serious."

"What's a ca-cussion?" Nancy asked.

"Concussion," Derek corrected. "It—uh—it just means her head hurts a little bit. But everything else is okay."

"Are you sure my mom's okay?" Gina asked, concerned.

"That's what your father said. He'll be spending the night with her. Hey, start eating this food before it gets cold."

"I'm not hungry," Kyle said.

"I sure am," Alicen said.

Derek put out the pizza. "Please eat at least one slice," he said. "What would your father do to me if he came home and found you starved? I promise you, your mother's okay."

"Then why does she have to stay in the hospital a few days?" Gina asked. "Why can't she come home now?"

"Because the doctors want to keep her under surveillance," Derek said, not quite sure how to handle this. "It's just routine. Now, eat!"

He said that in such an authoritative way that the children obeyed, though they didn't taste their food. The room became silent, each person busy with his or her own thoughts. Derek's mind was filled with the sound of that voice over the telephone that morning, the one telling him "Melanie goes today." What did it mean? That it was no accident that Melanie was in a hospital right now? Derek had thought of phoning the police about the call—especially now that the threat had come true. But having no idea where to find the woman who'd called him, he changed his mind. It had to be coincidence, of course. Melanie was miles and miles away at the time of the call. The woman named Janice didn't know she was going to be in the city today.

Besides, the VanBurens had enough worries without him bringing up a new one. That was why he decided to keep the call a secret. And it was also why he hadn't yet brought up Sarah's ring. Even though he knew Alicen must have taken it when he passed out last night (he tried not to think of it in any more detail than that), he didn't want to confront her in front of the children. But later . . .

Just then, his thoughts were interrupted by small, squeaking noises. He looked up from his plate and saw Nancy's shoulders quivering. He reached across the table and patted her hair.

"Nancy, everything's all right," he said. "Your mommy'll be home before the weekend."

"I want my mommy now!" the little girl wailed. The word accident had frightened her terribly, making her remember the accident that had hurt her father. Would her mother be a cripple, too?

"Nancy, it's just a *little* accident," Gina said firmly, as if trying to convince herself. "Derek said mom was fine—didn't you, Derek?"

"I sure did," Derek said, grateful that she was backing him. "And I wouldn't lie to you."

He thought for a moment, trying to change the subject. "Hey, guess what?" he said at last.

"What?" Nancy asked, looking at him through tearful blue eyes.

"We're having company tonight," Derek said. "I called a friend of mine to come over and help me out. Her name is Liza, and she loves kids. I think you'll like her."

Alicen's eyes became wide. She put her glass of milk down and raised her head to glare at her father. Liza? He had a girlfriend? But how could he do such a thing, when he was supposed to love her mother?

Derek returned the glare with eyes that told Alicen she'd better not ask any questions. Okay, so he had meant to introduce Liza to her at a better time than this. But he needed last-minute help tonight, not knowing how to handle a houseful of children. And it was his life; he wasn't about to let a thirteen-year-old run it.

"When's Liza coming?" Kyle asked.

"Around seven," Derek said. "She's at school right now."

"She goes to school?" Gina asked.

"Dance school," Derek replied, still looking at his daughter. "She'll tell you about it when she gets here."

Alicen finally dropped her gaze to her plate and finished her dinner. When the meal was over, Derek sent the VanBuren children from the kitchen with the announcement that he and Alicen would take care of cleaning up. He wanted to be alone with his daughter.

He didn't waste any time. "Did you take Sarah Kaufman's ring?"

"Of course not!" Alicen cried. "Why?"

"I found it in your room last night," Derek said. "So don't deny having had it. I was going to put it down here in the kitchen—to make it look as if Sarah had dropped it here when she fell. I was trying to protect you, Alicen. And what do you do? You steal the damned thing again!"

Alicen tore angrily at the empty pizza box and stuffed the pieces into the trash can.

"I didn't take any old ring," she insisted, remembering nothing.

"Alicen," Derek said, forcing himself to be patient, "do you have any idea what would happen to my job if the VanBurens learned you stole that ring?"

"I didn't!" Alicen cried, tears welling in her eyes. "And I don't care about your dumb old job!"

Derek slammed a dish he was washing against the sink, breaking it. "You damned well better care!" he shouted. "This job was a godsend for me, and you know it. Do you want to go back to living in a roach-infested apartment again?"

Alicen was crying openly now, staring down at her feet. She was confused, not understanding why her father was accusing her of this crime. She hadn't done a thing.

"Look, all I ask is that you give it back," Derek said. "I'll mail it to Mayor Kaufman, and no one will ever know where it came from."

"I don't have it," Alicen blubbered.

"Liar!" Derek cried. His head was starting to hurt him, and he rubbed at the bruises under his eyes. "This is a terrible thing you did, Alicen. Give me back that ring, or so help me, I'll—"

"Don't you hit me!"

Derek drew his hand back. He had been so close to slapping her, hating her for all her lies. But no, this wasn't the way to handle her. And the other children didn't need to hear an argument. What was the matter with him? Was he upset because of the mysterious fall he'd taken the night before? Or was it because that crank caller had predicted Melanie's accident? So damned much had happened in the last two days.

"Alicen, you're grounded until that ring shows up again," Derek said. "God knows I'd like to beat the hell out of you, but I can't prove you're guilty. I just hope your conscience takes care of that. Now, get out of here. Go do your homework."

Alicen threw her dish towel on the counter and stormed from the kitchen. How could her father say such terrible things about her? She had never touched Sarah's ring! She heard Gina calling her from the playroom but ignored her and ran upstairs. In her room she threw herself on the bed and started pounding the mattress.

"I hate him!" she seethed. "I hate him!"

The room was growing chilly, and she pulled the bed's coverlet around her like a cocoon. "I wish he was dead."

Something was pressing against her back. Alicen rolled around and looked up. She heard her name called, and she answered very softly. A moment later, a cloud, shaped like a woman, appeared. Alicen's trembling stopped immediately, and the room became very quiet. Slowly she reached up. But no one took her hand.

"Why do you want your father to die?"

"I hate him," Alicen said plainly. Under a spell, there was no emotion in her voice. "He called me a liar."

"It isn't his time to die, you little fool!" the vision cried.

Alicen jerked away as if stunned by her mother's angry words.

"I'm not ready yet for him," the apparition said. "There are things that must be done first. Melanie is still alive—but not for long. They'll all go, one by one. They'll all die!"

"Mommy, why do they have to die?" Alicen asked. "I don't under—"

The loud ringing of the doorbell downstairs shattered the spell like a sledgehammer through glass. Alicen was alone again. She sat up, feeling as if she had just wakened from a deep sleep. She rubbed her eyes and went to her door, opening it. Voices from the downstairs hallway were carried up to her room.

"Hi, Liza," her father was saying. "Come on in."

Alicen heard kissing noises, and her stomach turned.

"How're you, darling?" Liza asked. "Where are the children?"

Alicen closed her door and missed the rest of the conversation. She prayed her father wouldn't make her come downstairs. But a moment later she heard his voice calling her. Alicen thought of ignoring him but remembered his anger and left her room. She walked slowly.

"What's wrong with you?" Derek asked. "Get a move on!"

"Derek, let her be," Liza said quietly.

Alicen stopped at the bottom step and rested a hand on the post. She stared at Liza without speaking. In the soft light, she could see that this woman wasn't at all like her mother. Unlike Elaine, she had dark hair and eyes. And she was much taller than Alicen remembered her mother being. How could her father like a woman who was so different?

"Hi, Alicen," Liza said then.

"Hi," Alicen said perfunctorily.

"Looks like a lot has happened in this house," Liza said, making conversation. "Poor Mrs. VanBuren had an accident, and your daddy fell. Would you like to tell me about that?"

"No," Alicen said plainly, staring at her.

Liza shrugged. "Okay. Then how about taking me around this house? It sure is pretty from the outside, with those towers and the big porch in front. And look at all those doors! What's behind them?"

"I don't know," Alicen said. She turned her eyes to her father. "I have homework to do."

Derek sighed and put his arm around Liza's shoulder. Alicen's eyes narrowed. Her father was doing this to spite her. Without waiting for permission, she turned and ran up the stairs. Derek let her go, leading Liza into the kitchen.

"Derek, I hate to say this," Liza commented, "but if looks could kill . . ."

"Alicen was very rude to you," Derek said. "She'll hear about that."

"Oh, Derek, let it go," Liza said. "I expected her to act that way. Any normal child would! She probably thinks I'm trying to take her mother's place."

"That doesn't give her an excuse to be impolite," Derek answered, filling the teapot. He set it on the stove, then turned around to Liza. "It isn't just that, anyway. Alicen's being punished for stealing, and she's angry about it."

"What did she steal?"

"A ring," Derek said. He proceeded to explain everything to her, glad he had someone he could trust with his terrible secret.

"Oh, Derek," Lisa said when he was finished. She reached across the table and took his hand. "Maybe Alicen really doesn't remember taking the ring. Maybe she's upset about something. Have you considered that?"

"There's nothing wrong with her," Derek insisted.

Something in his eyes told Liza he didn't wish to discuss Alicen any further. So, to get his mind off his troubles, she went to him and sat on his lap. Running her fingers through his thick hair, she bent and kissed him passionately.

"I love you, Derek," she said.

"And I love you, Liza," Derek answered.

The phone began to ring.

"Ignore it," Liza said.

"I can't," Derek replied. "It might be Gary." He stood up. "I'll be right back."

He walked through the dining room and out into the hallway, where the phone sat on its little stand. "Hello?"

"Get rid of her!" someone shouted, the voice high-pitched. "I know you have that woman with you!"

Derek pulled the phone away from his ear, grimacing.

"Get rid of her, or she'll be next."

"Look, I'm getting damned sick of your threats," Derek said angrily. "What are you doing now, following my guests around? How'd you know she was going to be here?"

"I know everything you do, Derek Miller. Just get her out of there!"

"You go to hell," Derek said quietly, hanging up the phone.

He shook his head in exasperation and headed back into the kitchen. Liza had already poured the tea and was setting the cups down on the table. She sat and looked up at him quizzically. Derek realized there was still a look of anger on his face, and he tried to erase it. But Liza's concerned expression didn't fade.

"Is something wrong?"

"No, Liza," Derek said. "Wrong number. I—uh—hate wrong numbers."

Liza could tell that he was lying, but she knew that he'd tell her what had happened if he wanted to do so. She poured a little milk in her tea and began to stir it. Derek, usually strong and self-assured, looked so pitiful right now with his swollen eyes and cut lip that Liza wanted to throw her arms around him. But something made her keep still.

The room was silent, except for the clanking of teaspoons against china cups. Then suddenly Derek blurted out, "Everything's wrong!"

"Derek?" There was encouragement in Liza's voice.

"It isn't just the fact that Alicen stole that ring," Derek said. "Liza, something else happened today. I—I don't think Melanie is in that hospital by accident!"

"What do you mean?"

"I got a phone call this morning. From some crazed woman who apparently hates the VanBurens. She told me Melanie would be in an accident today."

"Derek!"

"Well, not exactly that," Derek corrected himself, "but she made indirect threats toward the family and said, 'Melanie goes first.' Next thing I know, Saint Joan's Hospital in Manhattan was calling me."

"And then you called the police?"

"No. I was going to," Derek said, "then I thought that there was no way I could prove that the woman ever called. I don't know where to find her, or if she even meant what she said about Melanie. Maybe she's just trying to get me upset."

"Why?" Liza asked. "And who is she, anyway?"

"She told me her name is Janice," Derek said. "And that's another reason I don't want to mention this to the VanBurens. Melanie had a best friend named Janice who died violently last year. The similarity in names—"

"I remember you mentioning her at lunch the other day," Liza interrupted. "But surely they wouldn't connect the two! There are a lot of Janices in the world."

"After that story they told me about ghosts the other night," Derek said, "I'm inclined to believe the VanBurens will think anything. This woman is just plain nuts. I met her a few weeks ago, just after I had moved in. She was hitchhiking on Houston Street, and she looked lost and lonely. Like an idiot, I gave her a lift. She's been bothering me ever since."

He searched Liza's almond eyes and found sympathy and deep interest there.

"I should have driven by her," he went on. "But I didn't, and now I'm stuck with her. One night she even hid in my car. It seems she has some sort of crush on me. But, by God, she's the most hideous woman I've ever seen!"

Liza took a sip of tea, then set the cup down again. Her thick lashes seemed to fan out as her eyes widened. *She's so beautiful*, Derek thought as he reached across the table to take her hand and kiss it.

"What does she look like?"

"I might sound like I'm exaggerating," Derek warned. "Her skin looked like a coroner's mistake, it was so pale. You could see her veins right through it. And her eyes—there was no life in them, not even when she was angry. Not to mention hair that probably never saw a comb and the fact that she always wears the same winter clothes."

"She sounds insane," Liza said. "Who would let themselves look like that?"

"Who would threaten to kill off an entire family?"

"Derek, I really think you should go to the police."

"No," Derek insisted. "No police. The VanBurens have enough to worry about."

"But shouldn't they be warned?"

"I don't think this woman was serious," Derek said. "You know crank callers—all talk. The accident today was pure coincidence."

"I find that hard to swallow," Liza said quietly, her mouth turning down a little. She sighed. "But you do what you think is right. And remember I'm here if you need someone to talk to."

"I know that," Derek said. "And I love you for it."

He stood up and walked around the table to put his arms over Liza's shoulders. Her lips felt warm and full against his, and he wanted to take her upstairs with him. But with four children in the house, he knew that was impossible.

"I wish we were alone," he whispered.

"So do I," Liza said. "But there will be other times."

Other times. Across the room, an unseen woman resisted the urge to throw something at Liza. Other times? There would be no other times! The next time Derek made love to a woman, it would be with her, not with this Liza!

She would get rid of that beautiful bitch, she vowed, when Derek was least expecting trouble. . . .

17

"Melanie?" Gary kissed his wife's hand. "Honey, come on. Open your eyes. It's morning."

Melanie stirred a little bit, her lashes fluttering. "Gary, where am

I?" she asked weakly. The sheets on her bed felt cool beneath her fingers.

"In the hospital," Gary said. "You had a little accident, but you're going to be okay. How do you feel?"

"My head hurts." She breathed deeply as if to fall asleep again. Then she opened her eyes and blinked at the glow of the track lights overhead. She turned to look at Gary.

"What do I look like?" she asked, her voice only slightly clearer.

"You always look beautiful to me," Gary answered.

"You're evading my question," Melanie said, raising a hand to touch the bandage on her forehead. It was a small one, yet she couldn't be sure there was nothing more wrong with her. Or else, why would she be in this room with an i.v. in her arm and all sorts of unfamiliar machinery near her bed?

"Trust me," Gary said. "It's just a small cut. The worst thing is that you've had a concussion. Your head is going to ache quite a bit for a few days."

"Right now," Melanie said, "it feels as if someone's using it for target practice. How long am I going to be in here, anyway?"

"Just a few days," Gary said. "You need to rest, and they want to run some more tests."

He lifted her hand again and kissed it. "I wish someone had seen the accident. Two dozen people, and not one of them could tell the police anything about the car that hit you."

"You called the police?"

"Warren did," Gary said. "But I doubt it did any good."

Melanie thought for a moment, trying to remember something that had been in her mind before the car was hit. But it evaded her, and Gary was talking again.

"You'll be home before you know it," he said.

Melanie nodded slightly. She stared up into the light, squeezing Gary's hand. What was it she was trying to remember?

"Oh, my God, Gary!"

It had come to her, and now she looked up at her husband with panic widening her eyes.

"Gary, the car stalled," she said frantically. "The car stalled, and I didn't even have the brakes on. And we just had that engine overhauled last month."

"It's an old car," Gary reminded her. "I told you I wanted to buy you a new one, and that's just what I'm going to do when we go home."

"N-no," Melanie stammered. "No, it isn't as simple as that. Gary, that car shouldn't have stalled. There was no reason. Someone must have tampered with it. Somebody wanted to kill me!"

"Nobody wanted to kill you," Gary said. "Why would you think such a thing?"

Melanie was crying loudly now. "Those dreams. That woman trying to warn me. She tried to tell me to get out of the house, but I didn't listen to her. Oh, Gary, something's wrong at the house again. I know it. It's Sarah's death and the bottle that broke in my hand, and now this! And the bus accident and—"

"Melanie, please calm down," Gary ordered. "Nothing is going on in Belle Bay. It's just coincidences."

"Coincidences?" Melanie said. "Oh, Gary! After what happened last year? How can you stand there, crippled by something no one would believe in, and not see that it's starting all over again?"

"Melanie, for God's sake," Gary said. "Jacob Armand is *gone*. He got his Lydia, didn't he? What the hell would he want to come back for? Now, please quiet down."

"I can't quiet down!" Melanie screamed.

Just then, a nurse came into the room, alerted by Melanie's cries. Seeing that Melanie was hysterical, she called in a doctor to administer a shot. Gary was then asked to leave the room. Having had no food since the previous morning, he decided he'd better have breakfast to keep his strength up.

As he ate the bland eggs and toast, he felt sorry for Melanie. It was no wonder she was having such fears, considering all that had occurred in the last weeks. But like he said, they weren't connected at all. Didn't every other family on earth have its share of problems?

"She's just sensitive to this sort of thing," he reasoned. "She'll be okay as soon as she gets home."

Derek came in from walking the dog later that afternoon to find Alicen on the phone. Didn't being grounded include use of the telephone? And then Liza's name caught his attention. As he unhooked Lad's leash, he pretended not to be listening.

"Sure, Liza, you can come for dinner," Alicen was saying. "You can help my dad out like you did last night."

A pause.

"I guess about six?"

Alicen looked down the hall at her father. Derek nodded without emotion. "Six is fine, Liza. See you then!"

She hung up and smiled down the hall at her father. Derek approached her, eyeing her warily. Why this sudden friendliness toward Liza? Especially now, when she and Derek were having differences? It didn't make sense that she should invite his girlfriend for dinner. Unless—

"This isn't going to change anything, Alicen," he said. "You're still grounded."

"I know that," Alicen said, smiling. "Can't I invite a guest for dinner?"

"I didn't think you liked her."

"I never said that," Alicen replied. "I only just met her." She shifted a little. "Dad, I have homework to do—"

"Go ahead," Derek said, wondering what Alicen's game was. No matter. He liked the idea that Liza was coming for dinner.

As promised, she arrived at six on the dot, bearing four giant cookies, one for each child. Alicen was all smiles and thank-yous, which sharpened Derek's suspicions. She ran to her room to put the cookie away for safekeeping.

"Is that the girl who shot daggers at me last night?" Liza asked with disbelief.

"She's up to something, I'm sure," Derek said. "I wonder why she called you? I can't believe she wants to be friends."

"Give the kid a chance, Derek," Liza said as they entered the kitchen. "Maybe she really does want to make amends. Did she tell you anything about the ring?"

"Of course not," Derek said.

At dinner that night Alicen surprised everyone by talking to Liza as if they were good friends. Derek knew he should be happy about that, but there was something in the glistening of Alicen's eyes that made him uneasy. Her words were polite enough, but there was an underlying sharpness to them that set him on edge. Not quite sure what to make of it all, Derek ate in silence and listened.

"Do you like the beach?" Alicen asked.

"Sure, I love it," Liza answered.

"Well, why don't you ask my father to take you down there after dinner?" Alicen suggested. "It sure is pretty when the sun goes down."

"Alicen, it looks like rain out there," Derek said. Why would his daughter want him out of the house?

"It's a beautiful night," Alicen insisted.

"Oh, let's go down!" Liza cried eagerly. "It probably won't rain for a few hours."

"There are umbrellas in the hall closet if it does," Gina said. "Want me to get two for you, Derek?"

"That's okay," Derek said. He smiled at Liza. "If Liza really wants to go, I don't think we'll mind getting wet."

"You'll like the beach at night," Alicen drawled. "It's so pretty."

An hour later Liza and Derek were headed toward the bay. They walked hand in hand, forgetting the events of the past few days. Impulsively, Derek swung Liza around and kissed her.

"You know I love you?"

"Yes," Liza said. "And I love you, Derek."

He kissed her again.

"I was going to wait," he said, "but I can't. All this nature is turning me into some kind of romantic. Liza, will you marry me?"

A beautiful smile spread across Liza's face. Leave it to Derek to be this abrupt! She nodded enthusiastically, letting him pull her close. "Of course I'll marry you," she said.

They held each other tightly, then Liza said, "Derek, let's spend a long time on the beach. I don't care if it is raining."

"Well, let me run back to the house for an umbrella," Derek said. "I don't want you to catch cold."

"Hurry back," Liza said.

She settled down on a log and watched him run back to the house. The rain increased in intensity, and she was grateful for the thick evergreen above her. Breathing in the damp, pine-scented air, she bent forward to pick one of the tiny white flowers. Something crackled behind her.

She turned abruptly, startled. There in the thick undergrowth stood a young woman, a patch of blood matting the blond tendrils at her forehead. The woman's face was corpse-like, her smile blue and thin. Liza found herself standing up, staring at her. She knew this was the woman Derek had spoken of, and yet she was too stunned to scream for help. That moment of hesitation was the last mistake she would ever make.

The woman jerked her to the ground, pulling Liza's face close to her own. Frantically Liza tried to turn away from the horrible, putre-factive flesh. But this woman was too strong. She had a gleam in her eyes that burned into her victim's, draining the fight in her. Some-thing twisted Liza's hand, and a cold line of metals slipped over her wrist as the bracelet she was wearing broke off and fell to the ground. Her sanity slowly drained by the piercing, evil eyes above her, Liza stopped thinking she was going to die and saw only blackness.

Her spirit had given up her body to the malevolence that longed to possess it.

A few minutes later, the body that was once Liza Crewe's heard the sound of Derek's whistling. He appeared in the clearing with an umbrella, a smile on his face. She smiled back at him, giving no clue to the evil that had just taken place here.

"Ready?" Derek said.

"Quite ready, Derek," 'Liza' said.

She smiled slyly at him and hooked her hand around his elbow. She liked the hardness of his biceps. They didn't speak until they reached the bay, where they kicked off their shoes and walked bare-foot in the sand. The light rain had stopped, the sky was growing pink, and the salty wind was cool. Derek took Liza's hand and squeezed it hard.

"Melanie's going to be all right, isn't she?" Liza asked.

"That's a funny thing to bring up now," Derek answered. "Well, yes. She's going to be fine."

Liza nodded. "That's too bad."

"You sound as if you *wanted* her to be hurt," Derek said.

They caught each other's eyes, and Derek noticed there was no light in Liza's eyes. Her voice sounded dull when she said, "I meant it was too bad about the accident."

"I know," Derek said, toeing the water that rippled along the beach. "I was only kidding."

He had brought a blanket with him, and when they found a huge pile of rocks, they sat down together and wrapped themselves in it. Derek kissed Liza gently.

"You're trembling," he said. "Do you want more of the blanket?"

"I only want you, Derek Miller," Liza said.

She began to pull him down, pressing her lips to his as they sank into the pit of sand in the center of the rocks. It was their own private shelter, where no one else could see them. As Derek kissed Liza, his desires grew. So did hers, and she was suddenly sitting up and unbuttoning her blouse.

He watched her, tucking his hands behind his head, until she was kneeling over him wearing nothing but a necklace. This Derek fingered gently and then let his hand travel down the length of her body. She undressed him, and he stared into her eyes, his head filling with the mixed scents of her perfume and the wet, briny air.

"Funny," he said.

"What?"

"In the twilight," he said, "your eyes look blue."

"Yes, Derek," she said, leaning toward him.

She felt so warm to his touch. He covered her with kisses, not missing an inch of her dark, soft skin. Liza pressed herself hard against him. Derek was in ecstasy, never remembering a time when their lovemaking had been this intensely pleasurable.

When it was over, he opened his eyes and looked again into hers. Their blue had become lighter, but Derek was too filled with passion to really notice. Liza smiled up at him, digging her nails into the taut muscles of his arms.

"I knew I could have you, Derek Miller," she said. Her smile revealed pointed teeth.

Liza had always had perfect teeth.

"What?"

Stunned, Derek rolled off of her. He gazed down at the nude woman lying on the sand, studying her face. It was Liza's face, and yet the eyes and smile . . .

"Liza, what's wrong with you?" he whispered.

She threw back her head and let out an ear-shattering screech. All at once, Derek felt himself being flipped over, his back crashing down against the flat rocks. Before he could right himself, the woman knelt over him, pinning his arms to the ground with superhuman strength. Her face twisted and stretched and became the hitch-hiker's. She grinned at him, knowing he was now in her power and that she could do anything to him that she desired. But there was still a flicker of defiance in Derek's eyes, and he dared to lean his head back and spit at her.

"AAAAAUUUUGGGH!"

The cry was deep and guttural, not a woman's cry at all. Angered, Janice-Liza willed her face to change once more. What Derek witnessed now tore away the last shreds of his resistance. For looming above him were the horrid remains of his wife Elaine's face, just as she had looked after her terrible accident. Derek screamed, reliving that long-ago afternoon. Elaine's car had gone up in flames, her body melting in an inferno. Her face, once beautiful, had become so twisted and ugly that Derek had passed out after identifying her at the morgue.

And now she was back again. . . .

"NNNOOOO!"

He tried desperately to turn away from the sickening vision. He screamed and kicked and pleaded, and yet the hideous face still hovered over him.

"Please, oh, dear God," Derek cried. "I'll do anything! Just get her away. Please!"

The face drained away and became the hitchhiker's, smiling at him. He had said exactly what she wanted to hear.

"You'll remember that face from now on, won't you?" she said.

Derek nodded.

"And you don't ever want to see it again, do you?"

Derek shook his head.

"Then remember this," she hissed, "if you don't want to suffer again, you'll do everything I say." Her voice took on a sing-song sweetness. "Won't you?"

"Yes," Derek whispered.

"Good," the woman said. "Go back to the house now. You'll go straight to bed, and when you wake in the morning, you'll remember nothing but a pleasant evening with Liza."

"Y-yes," Derek choked.

He did not move when she climbed up the rocks and left him, carrying Liza's clothes in her hands. She padded, naked, across the beach, her feet leaving no marks in the sand. A few moments later, she was behind the wheel of Liza's car. This she started without a key and drove down the hill. When she reached the strip that followed the edge of the beach, she didn't turn onto Houston, but instead found a sand-covered boardwalk, just wide enough to support the vehicle.

She drove on it, without lights, straight for the bay. The car splashed into the water, sending out a series of soft ripples. At first it floated, rocking gently. And then it was drawn down into the murky depths, moving slowly and lazily. When it hit the bottom, Liza's body slumped forward against the steering wheel. The soft sand offered little resistance, and within moments the car had wedged itself in permanently.

On the beach Derek finally stood up and dressed himself. Then he hurried to the house, where, obeying a command, he went straight to bed.

18

◆

"Are you okay?" Gary asked Melanie as they sat in the back of a yellow cab on the way home from the hospital.

"Why wouldn't I be?" Melanie asked, smiling at him. Then she nodded. "I get it. You think I'm nervous to be in a car again."

"It would be understandable."

But Melanie looked calm today. After her outburst about someone tampering with her car, Gary had been afraid for her. Fortunately, she hadn't mentioned it again. Realizing she might have been delirious from the blow to her head, Gary was quick to pass that incident off as hysteria.

Melanie took his hand. "I'm fine. Trust me."

They were home within an hour. Gary paid the driver, then hobbled on his crutches to the front door. He expected Derek to be waiting inside. Instead, it was Lad who gave them a warm welcome-home.

"Hey, puppy," Gary said, rubbing the dog's head. "Where's Derek?"

Lad barked. Gary looked at Melanie. "He's probably right behind us," he said. "Must have gone out for something. He wouldn't let the kids come home to an empty house."

"I should think not," Melanie said, feeling a little angry at Derek.

She and Gary walked down the hall to the stairs, then Melanie carried her overnight bag up to her room. By the time she finished unpacking it, she heard the sounds of her children downstairs. Happy to see them again, she hurried down.

"Mom!" Kyle cried, running to her when she reached the bottom landing.

Hugs and kisses were exchanged, and even Alicen managed an embrace for Melanie. She noticed a change in the child. Alicen seemed to be *glowing* today; her smile made her very pretty, as a matter of fact. Melanie wondered what had happened to cause the change.

"You don't look bad at all, mom," Gina said. "It's just a little bandage, like Derek said."

"Derek bought pizza for dinner two nights!" Nancy cried.

"Mom, are you gonna cook for us now?" Kyle wanted to know.

"Of course," Melanie said. "By the way, where is Derek?"

"Maybe he had to go to the dentist again," Alicen suggested.

Well, that's another switch, Melanie thought. *Alicen making excuses for her father?*

"He should have been here when you kids came home," Melanie said. "He didn't know daddy and I were coming today."

Alicen shrugged. "We can take care of ourselves."

"I know that," Melanie said. "But I still don't like the idea of you being alone. Anything could happen here."

Gina's eyes darkened. "Mom, don't talk like that," she said softly.

Melanie smiled at her, realizing she might have frightened her. The dining room door opened now. As if in answer to Melanie's question, Derek stepped into the hallway. There was a shadow of a beard on his face, and underneath his eyes were dark circles. He blinked twice at the group near the front door.

"I thought you were out," Melanie said. "Aren't you feeling well, Derek?"

"I'm fine," Derek said without emotion.

"You look terrible."

Derek yawned and forced a smile that came out like a grimace. "I guess I fell asleep at lunch. I was up late last night."

Melanie looked at him for a few minutes, disturbed to see that he, too, had changed. It was as if he had switched personalities with his daughter. Where she was now cheerful, he was gloomy. And Melanie could tell by his eyes that he was hiding something.

But Nancy was pulling at her arm, and it was more important to enjoy the children than to have worries.

"Where's my daddy?"

"Upstairs in his office," Melanie said. "He had to make a phone call. Why don't you go up and say hi?"

"Come with us, mom," Kyle said, taking her hand.

Melanie had wanted to talk to Derek, but Kyle was insistent. So now Derek leaned against the doorjamb and watched them go up the stairs. He sighed. The slight heaving of his shoulders made his back ache terribly. He felt as if he'd been severely beaten over every inch of his body.

He had been sitting in the kitchen for hours, staring out the back door. Something had happened the night before, Derek knew. He couldn't remember having said goodbye to Liza. He knew they had had a pleasant evening—that much was clear in his head. But when had it ended?

A month, a week ago, Derek would have racked his brains to find a logical explanation for his loss of memory. He was a therapist, after all. He was supposed to always be in perfect physical and mental health. But now his physical being felt like a rat dragged out of a river, and his mental self was frayed to bits.

And for some reason, he didn't give a damn.

He stopped rubbing his arms long enough to go upstairs to the bathroom. He could hear Gary's voice, and he had the vague idea that they should get back to the therapy sessions as soon as possible. Then he reached into the tub and turned on the shower.

The water was like ice, invigorating. Shivering under it, Derek felt the fatigue draining from his body. The pain in his bones lessened a bit, and by the time he dried himself off, he was feeling a little better. Not much—the tiredness was still there. But enough to hide his uneasy feelings from the VanBurens. He wrapped a big towel around himself and hurried down the hall to his bedroom to change. He caught sight of himself in the floor-length mirror. To his shock he saw that his back had a bruise on it from his shoulder blade to the bottom of his ribs.

"Where the hell did that come from?" he asked himself aloud. He couldn't remember falling last night. And his eyes—they weren't like his eyes at all. There were dark circles under them, like a man who hadn't slept in weeks.

What the hell went on here last night?

There was one way to find out: call Liza. Derek wasn't sure if she would be home from school yet, but he'd take a chance. He dialed her number on the downstairs phone and let it ring twenty times before hanging up.

"She must be in school yet," he said sadly.

He tried to call her again after dinner, to no avail. The fact that she wasn't home when he needed her angered him so much that he slammed the phone down with a curse.

"Derek, what's the matter?"

He turned to see Melanie behind him. Her eyes widened, and he knew it was at the sight of his angry face. He closed his eyes and breathed deeply to calm himself, then said, "Sorry. I've been trying to get Liza all day, but she isn't home."

"Well, I'm sure she'll call you when she is," Melanie said, reassuring him. She moved past him and went up the stairs, looking at him over her shoulder. It was as if she couldn't wait to get away from him.

She found Gary in his office upstairs. "Gary, did you notice something funny about Derek today?"

"He looks a little tired," Gary said.

"It's more than that," Melanie said. "Derek usually has energy to spare."

"What are you doing?" Gary asked. "Giving yourself something else to worry about? He's just fatigued after taking care of four kids for two days. He isn't used to that kind of work."

"It looks like more than fatigue, Gary," Melanie said. "The man looks ready to drop."

"Maybe he's coming down with something," Gary suggested. "We've had some damp weather here lately. Even therapists catch cold, you know."

Melanie considered this. "You know, you're probably right," she said. "I'll find some cold capsules and give them to him to take tonight."

That night Derek took the pills, thanked Melanie, then dropped them into his wastebasket as soon as she left his bedroom. She had said they would make him fall asleep, and though he wanted that, a firm voice in his head told him he must stay awake. He sat up reading until midnight, then finally turned off his light and settled back against his pillows.

Suddenly, in the total darkness, he felt himself trembling. His knees turned to jelly, his stomach flipped, his heart pounded. In seconds his pillow was wet with perspiration. All the doubts he'd had earlier drained away, and in their place came a feeling of raw terror. He remembered everything of the previous night now. Liza's face loomed over him, then the hitchhiker's, and then, oh, my God, Elaine's. Derek started to scream, but lips pressed hard against his to stifle it. A tongue pressed between his lips and sought his. Derek gave in weakly and wrapped his arms around the ghostly body above him. It felt strangely warm, not what he had expected. When she pulled away from him, he saw Liza's face.

"I want you, Derek Miller."

It was Janice's voice.

"Yes," Derek said.

He knew he would have to give in to her. He knew she would show him Elaine's face again, if he protested. So tonight, he didn't try to get away from her. He didn't dare.

She stood up now, pulling him onto his feet. When they passed through the beam of moonlight, he saw to his surprise that she was completely nude. It was Liza's body, beautiful and firm. Derek reached out to touch it and heard Janice's laugh. His hand shot through her.

"Please," he whispered. "I want you, Liza."

"Janice," he heard.

They left the room, Derek following Liza-Janice like a little boy. He could feel his heart beating with anticipation, and did not try to fight it. He wanted her! He wasn't afraid! He craved her more than he had ever craved anyone or anything in his life. And so he let her lead him down to the kitchen, to where Lad slept soundly under the table. As if they weren't there at all, the dog didn't stir.

Derek sank down to the floor, pulling Liza-Janice with him. His organ was stiff, his veins throbbing all through his body.

"I want you now," he breathed. "*Now.*"

Janice fell on top of him, kissing him passionately. Then she sat up and smiled down at him. This was *perfect.* He was completely under her spell. This was exactly what she wanted.

"Make me feel like a woman," she ordered.

Derek tightened his arms around her, crushing her. This time, there was substance there, warm flesh like a living mortal's. And under Janice's spell, he saw her only as Liza. She was good, pure, beautiful. She was not a thing of evil.

If Derek had been listening, he would have heard the sound of Melanie's door opening. She had wakened up in the middle of the night with a splitting headache and was shuffling down the hallway to the bathroom. The bright light made her head ache all the more, and she clutched at the sink as she opened the medicine cabinet. To her anger, she remembered that she had left her painkillers in the kitchen.

She couldn't stand the pain enough to go back to bed, so she decided to brave the dark house and go get her medicine.

Liza-Janice suddenly looked up with a start. She and Derek were embracing on the kitchen floor, completely naked. Derek's underwear and robe were scattered on the floor near where the dog still slept, undisturbed.

"She's coming," Janice hissed. "That bitch Melanie is coming."

"Keep her out of here," Derek said.

"I'll kill her."

There was a coldness in Janice's voice that made Derek shudder. He grabbed her wrist.

"Don't go away," he begged.

Janice looked at him. His eyes were so beautiful in the moonlight that she felt her evil passions growing again. She smiled crookedly. "I'll get rid of her," she said.

Melanie was halfway into the dining room when a loud noise behind her made her turn around with a yelp. It was the sound of a motor revving. Melanie listened, not knowing which way to turn. Something was drawing her away from the kitchen door.

Come out to the stairs, Melanie. Come out to the stairs.

She ran into the hallway. To her shock she saw that the lift had somehow started up by itself. Its pulleys and gears whirred wildly, but it wasn't moving. Melanie switched on the hall light and stared up at it in confusion. A moment later, Gina appeared on the top landing. Kyle came up behind her, rubbing his eyes.

"Mommy?" he whimpered. The yellow hall light made his mother's face look all distorted, and he moved closer to Gina.

"Mom, turn that off," Gina ordered. "It woke us up."

"I don't want to touch it!" Melanie screamed. "Just go back to bed."

"I don't want to," Kyle said. "I'm afraid."

Gary was here now. "Kyle, listen to your mother. I'll fix it."

Reluctantly, the children obeyed him. Gary glanced at Melanie, then grabbed the banister to try to get to the lift. It had stopped halfway down the stairs. Melanie, realizing Gary didn't know how to walk on steps, suddenly shot up the stairs after him.

"Let me get Derek—please," she begged.

"Derek isn't in his room," Gary said. "I want that thing off before it wakes Nancy."

"Gary, *please*," Melanie said. She was terrified that he might fall and hurt himself again. She began to cry.

Gary frowned at her, then turned his gaze to something over his shoulder. He watched a shadow move across the floor as the dining room door opened wider. Melanie turned and saw Derek.

"What are you doing down there?" she demanded. "Why—"

Gary interrupted her. "Could you please turn that thing off for us?"

Nodding, Derek walked up the stairs. Pulling a wire, he at last silenced the machine. Then he took something soft and warm into his hand and held it up. It was a dead rat.

Melanie groaned.

"He must have gotten caught in the gears," Derek said calmly.

"Oh, get it out of here!" Melanie ordered, unable to take her eyes off the tangled mass of fur and blood. The rodent's teeth glistened viciously in the light. Derek turned back down the stairs to dispose of it.

"See that?" Gary said. "It was only a mouse."

"Rat," Melanie corrected.

"A mouse," Gary insisted. "Like you always find in big old houses."

Melanie stared down the stairs in silence.

"It really is happening again, Gary," she said quietly.

"No," Gary said.

"Someone's coming for us," she said.

"Oh, damn it, Melanie!" Gary cried. "You're supposed to be the strong one in this family, remember? Stop being ridiculous."

Melanie glared at him. Suddenly she wanted to get away from him. She hated him for mocking her fears.

"I think I hear one of the kids up," she said, hurrying past him.

"Oh, Melanie," Gary whispered. "Don't you see it can't be happening again? It just can't be."

He didn't hear strange, feminine laughter. He didn't hear a voice saying:

It is happening again, you fool. And nothing is going to stop it.

Derek returned to his room after dumping the rat in the trash. Now he lay in his bed on his stomach, his face buried in his arms, trying to breathe deeply and fall asleep.

But sleep wouldn't come to him. He felt too dirty, too shamed to allow himself the peace of sleep. Too scared. How could he have let himself fall into her trap? He should have seen this coming when Janice called him by name that day in his car. He should have known there was something different about her by the insane look in her eyes and the crazy way she talked.

Shame was a painful thing for him. It twisted at his muscles and made his stomach burn. He claimed to love Liza Crewe, had even asked her to marry him. Yet he had been unfaithful to her, with the woman he hated most. Janice had lured him from Liza's arms into her own evil embrace.

But he was a man, after all. A man deprived of sexual love for many years. Janice's lustful embraces had awakened some sort of animal feelings in him, and he had been unable to control himself.

He was making excuses. Wasn't he always the one who claimed to be strong? Why couldn't he fight this woman?

"What is it you're ashamed of, Derek?" he asked himself out loud. "That you cheated on Liza or that you fell under that bitch Janice's powers?"

But what kind of powers were they? How could she change her face to Elaine's—God, don't let me think of that, he prayed—to Liza's, to any face she knew would control him? How could she have such a hold on him, so much so that he couldn't get up right now, pack his bags, and leave?

What was she?

He felt panic-stricken. How could he explain this to anyone? How could he explain it to himself? It was crazy. If he ever told anyone, they'd think he was crazy.

He was trembling and wished Liza were there by his side. She would hold him in her arms, tell him everything was all right, protect him. She would understand.

Derek had never thought he would need to be protected by a woman. But where was Liza now? He'd been unable to get in touch with her since the night he asked her to marry him. Had something happened to her? He had the sick feeling Janice had something to do with that. And the only way to find out would be to stay here and give in to her. If it meant finding Liza again, Derek would do anything.

But he knew he would hate himself for his weakness. . . .

19

At breakfast the next morning, Melanie explained to Kyle and Gina how the lift had started. Not wanting to frighten them, she changed the rat into a little field mouse. She related the events less to ease their fears than to make herself believe her own had been unjustified. In the darkness she had been terrified. But somehow, the daylight made her strong again. She was willing to believe it had been "just one of those things."

"Poor mouse," Gina said. "How do you suppose it got in here?"

"Probably crawled through a hole under the house," Derek suggested, shifting a little to ease the aching in his muscles. He knew exactly where the animal had come from. Janice had lured it into the house and had planted it in the gears of the machine.

"I'll have to have that checked out," Gary said. "And God knows what else we'll have to have fixed this summer. We'll have to have the roof repaired, too, before we have floods."

"That's to be expected of an old house," Melanie said.

Gary looked at her.

"So are a lot of other things, darling," he said.

Melanie smiled at him and got up. She wasn't completely convinced that he was right. But what good would it do to mope around, waiting for something to happen? Wouldn't it be better to fight her terrors? The best way to do that, she knew, would be to throw herself completely into her work.

She went up to her studio, and Gary and Derek headed up to the therapy room. Derek wasn't really in the mood for a workout, but what excuse could he give? So he motioned toward the mock stairs and said, "We're going to start on them today."

Gary studied the four steps. "It doesn't look difficult."

"That's what you said about getting out of the wheelchair," Derek reminded him.

Gary looked over his shoulder. "Thanks for the vote of confidence," he said.

Without answering, Derek proceeded to show Gary the right way to use crutches on stairs. Then, yawning, he told him to practice. He was supposed to stand and watch Gary, to support him if he fell. But instead, he went to look out the window. He thought he saw Janice walking through the woods—but then there was no one there.

"How long do you think it'll take me to get used to this?" Gary asked.

Derek ran his fingers through his dark hair, but didn't say anything. The previous night still weighed too heavily on his mind, and the shame and sickness he felt were competing too strongly with his work.

"Derek, come see if I'm doing this right," Gary requested, loudly. Still, his therapist was silent. "Hey, what's the matter with you?"

"I—I'm sorry," Derek said, turning. "Hey, look. You're almost at the top. One step to go."

Gary frowned at him and continued up the stairs. His legs ached only a little from the effort, since months of lifting weights had made them strong. Still, he hesitated a little as he turned and looked down the stairs. One slip of the crutch . . .

Cut it out, he said to himself. *You aren't going to fall.*

Five minutes later, he reached the bottom step. Five minutes! Gary sighed with frustration.

"Tired?" Derek asked.

"A little," Gary admitted. "But I suppose you want me to try again."

"I don't care—" Derek cut himself off. "Sure, sure go ahead."

Once more, Gary ascended the stairs. He was nervous about coming down. He moved slowly and held fast to the railing.

"I hope this gets easier," he said. Derek didn't answer. "I mean, I don't know what to put down first sometimes."

Derek cleared his throat and realized he had let his mind wander. "You'll get the hang of it," he said, catching the last of Gary's sentence. "By the time your wife comes back home, you'll be an old pro."

With all his strength, Derek tried to drive away the memory of the previous night. It was daylight, and he wasn't alone. Why should he be afraid now?

He knew, though, that he dreaded the fall of darkness. And worse than that, he knew he couldn't run away from it.

"Do you feel any better today?" Gary asked his wife as they sat together on the living room couch after dinner.

"A lot," Melanie said. "Getting into a new painting was a smart move."

"You're not afraid any more?"

"No," Melanie said slowly.

"Nothing should scare you," Gary said, kissing her. "We're safe here, I promise."

Across the room an unseen being sat in the huge rocking chair, watching them. So they thought everything was all right? The idiots! They had escaped her wrath up to now, but no more. She wouldn't rest until they were punished for what they had done to her. Tonight, she would move in first on the easiest victim.

Later in the night, when all the house was sleeping, she went to Alicen. The little girl had been dreaming of her mother. Elaine looked so beautiful, not mysterious or cloudy at all. Alicen reached up for her.

"Hold me, mommy," she cried.

Something cold took her hands, and her dream mother faded away. Alicen's eyes fluttered open, and she sat up slowly.

"Mommy?"

"I have something for you to do, Alicen," her vision said, pressing a small, hard object into the girl's palm. Alicen looked down at a tiny black vial, then back up at the vision.

"I want you to put that in the dog's dish."

"Why?"

"Don't question me," the apparition said firmly. "Do as you're told."

"Okay, mommy," Alicen said quietly.

Wanting to make her mother happy, she walked silently, hardly seeing the long stretch of doors or the darkened rooms downstairs, and went into the kitchen. She found Lad's dish in a corner and emptied the bottle into it.

Lad, disturbed by the sound of her footsteps, sat up with his ears perked. He got on his feet and went to his dog dish, where he sniffed the strange new scent. . . .

At the same time Gary was learning to walk on stairs that Saturday morning, a plane touched down on the runway at LaGuardia Airport, just in from Fort Lauderdale, Florida. It taxied to its final destination, where a collapsible tunnel was fixed to its door. Bearing garment bags and overnight suitcases, the passengers filed out. Children wearing Mickey Mouse hats held fast to their parents' tanned hands, while old couples discussed moving to Florida for good. A blond, tan young man burdened with an overnight bag filled with books exited, pleased to be in New York. He was here on business, with the hopes of seeing his sister Liza during his visit.

Owen Crewe shifted his bag from one muscular shoulder to the other and brushed a strand of mustache from his lip. Liza would be surprised to see it; he hoped she'd like it.

Walking through the tunnel, Owen headed first for the phone booth. To his disappointment Liza didn't answer his call. She hadn't answered the night before, either. But then she had no idea that he was coming to visit. He had had no idea until yesterday that he'd be assigned to a psychiatrist's forum here in Manhattan. It had been a last-minute decision by his superiors to let him sub for one of their sick colleagues.

Owen had ordered a car for himself and was pleased to find it was air-conditioned. He climbed behind the wheel and took out a map of Long Island. He located Belle Bay on the Nassau-Suffolk border, then switched on the ignition.

Traffic was heavy this Saturday morning, and it took him nearly an hour. Owen was almost convinced he had passed the town when he saw a sign showing Belle Bay at the next exit. Guiding his car onto the ramp, he found himself on Houston Street, a long, barren stretch of road that skirted the edge of the town.

With Liza's address memorized, he drove up to the first person he saw and asked for directions to her street. Liza's apartment, he found, was on the top floor of a comfortable-looking house. He went up to the door and rang the bell.

"Can I help you?" a middle-aged Italian woman asked, opening her window.

"I'm Owen Crewe," he replied. "Liza's brother. Is my sister home?"

"Wait a minute," the woman said. She shut the window and came out to the steps. "Liza didn't tell me you were coming. Besides, I haven't seen her today. She didn't come home last night."

"No?"

"You don't see her car, do you?"

Owen looked past the newly mowed lawn.

"I wouldn't know it, anyway," he said. "Look, could I wait in her apartment until she arrives?"

The woman eyed him suspiciously. "How do I know you're really her brother? She's a young woman alone, you know."

"I'm glad you're so protective," Owen said, smiling. "Here's my driver's license—it has my name on it, see? And here's a family picture of us."

The woman nodded, convinced. She unlocked the upstairs door for him and held it open while he carried his suitcases upstairs. After setting them in the living room, Owen went to the kitchen. He'd have a beer and watch TV until his sister came home.

20

Nancy, her blond curls catching the early morning sunlight, tugged on her mother's sleeve as she walked with her family to the bay. It was Sunday, and they were going to have a picnic.

"I forgot my yellow rabbit, mommy," she said. "I want to bring him with me."

"Can't you live without that dumb rabbit?" Kyle asked.

"I want it!" Nancy wailed.

"Yeah, well I wish Lad was coming with us," Kyle said. He was in a bad mood because the dog had disappeared in the night.

"Don't worry about Lad," Gary said. "He'll probably show up on the beach in a while."

"Mommy, my rabbit!" Nancy cried.

"Okay, okay," Melanie said, handing Gina the basket she was carrying. "I'll go up and get it. Wait here for me."

"He's on my bed," Nancy told her.

Melanie unlocked the door, smiling at the idea her daughter needed her toy so badly. *Oh, to be a child again,* she thought. *If only a simple toy could make me feel secure!*

Well, that was what this picnic was all about. It had been Gary's idea—something to prove they were nothing but an average American family. Mother, father, and kids. All they needed was the dog, but no one had seen Lad that morning. He wasn't at the breakfast table looking for handouts.

"He's probably digging up the garden," Melanie had reassured the children.

Melanie pushed open the door to Nancy's room. She hardly took a step inside before she started choking. A horrible stench filled the air, permeating her nostrils even when she tried to hold her breath. Holding her hand over her mouth and nose, Melanie walked carefully into the room. What the hell was that?

She found it in Nancy's doll carriage.

Don't scream, she thought. *Don't get the kids up here.*

It was Lad's body, stuffed somehow into the little carriage. One paw was pushed up against the cover, making a dent. Lad's head was bent into his chest.

"Not again," Melanie whispered, unable to take her eyes from the hideous sight.

Pictures flashed in her mind: Sarah's face, a crashing bus, her own car spinning in circles. And through these, she saw Lad's body. Was she justified in her fears that evil had descended once more upon their home?

"Oh, dear God," she prayed. "Don't let that be happening again."

She ran from the room and down the stairs, her heart pounding. In the kitchen she stopped and leaned heavily against the refrigerator. She had fought tears until now, and though her head ached, she didn't want the children to see her crying. They were so happy today—nothing would spoil that. She heard Kyle's laughter, high and sweet. *Hold onto that,* she told herself. *There are good things in this house, too.*

She took a very deep breath, then let it out slowly before opening the back door. Her calm voice belied the pounding of her heart as she called, "Derek, could you come in here?"

"Is anything wrong, honey?" Gary wanted to know.

"Nothing," Melanie insisted. "I—I just want Derek to help me with something."

Derek hurried up to the house. He couldn't help staring at Melanie, wondering why her face was so pale. Silently she motioned him toward Nancy's room. The color drained from Derek's face when he saw Lad's corpse. He looked up into her blue eyes, his own very wide. Melanie returned the gaze, wondering how he could ignore the terrible stench. She didn't know it was meant for her alone and that Derek was unaware of it.

"How did this happen?" he asked, returning his gaze to Lad.

"I don't know," Melanie said. She blinked away tears. "I called you in because there isn't anything Gary can do about it. Please, Derek, can you get ri—put him somewhere? If the children saw him . . ."

"Of course," Derek said gently. "Can you get me a sheet?"

Melanie nodded and went to the linen closet. It was all she could do not to burst into tears.

"You'll have to tell them," Derek said, taking the sheet from her.

"Tell them what?" Melanie asked. "That their pet was murdered?"

"Somebody killed him," Derek said, feeling a twist in his stomach. He recalled the pleasure he'd had with Janice and was sickened. *She* was responsible for this.

"I know that," Melanie said. "And I'm frightened, Derek. But I don't want to spoil this day for the kids. They don't need to know he's dead. I—I'll tell them tomorrow that he ran away.

"Thank you," Melanie said. "For taking care of Lad."

Derek walked downstairs, carrying the wrapped body. Melanie waited a few moments at the top of the stairs, until she heard the front door open and close. Then, forcing a smile on her face, she hurried down and went out the back door. By the time she crossed the vast lawn to her waiting family, she had relaxed, if only a little.

"Is everything okay?" Gary asked.

"Sure," Melanie said, handing Nancy her rabbit.

"Where's Derek?"

"He'll be out in a minute," Melanie said. She looked up to where the children were racing ahead.

"Lad's dead, Gary."

Gary's head snapped around. "What?"

"Someone killed him," Melanie went on, still fighting tears. "I—I asked Derek to hide the body from the kids."

"Melanie, what do you mean?" Gary asked. "Who killed Lad?"

"I don't know," Melanie answered. "I found him in Nancy's room, in her doll carriage." The horror of it finally struck her, and tears began to fall. "Oh, my God, Gary! If Nancy had found him!"

"She didn't," Gary said soothingly, his own grief taking second place to shock. "It's okay."

"It's not okay," Melanie cried. "Nothing's been okay for the past month! It's starting again, Gary. I know it is!"

Gary looked past the trees to the house. Huge and white, it looked beautiful to him. How could it harbor so much evil? How could it be responsible for so much sorrow? Lad dead? But he was just a puppy —bought for the children when Gary came home from the hospital a few months earlier. He was barely eight months old.

"Gary, we have to do something," Melanie said.

"No," Gary said. "We'll tell the children he ran away, and leave it at that."

"I already figured that out," Melanie said. "I mean, I don't know what to do about the house."

"Melanie," Gary said stiffly, "there is nothing going on there. Not again. We've discussed this before, and my beliefs are unchanged."

"Damn, you're stubborn!" Melanie hissed. "After all that's happened—"

Gary cut her off. "You know what I think? I think the culprit behind all this is mortal. Someone so filled with hatred that she'll do anything to hurt others."

"Who are you talking about?" Melanie asked quietly.

"Alicen," Gary said simply.

"Oh!" Melanie cried. "Gary, that's just ridiculous! She's a little girl. I won't have you accusing—"

"Listen to me," Gary interrupted. "You can't deny Alicen isn't like normal children. She keeps to herself for hours, and her mind always seems to be off somewhere when anyone tries to talk to her. Haven't you ever noticed that?"

"Why does it make her a murderer?"

"She's trying to get back at her father," Gary said. "Derek ignores her too much, and she's rebelling."

"I can't say I blame her," Melanie said. "But I refuse to believe she'd do all these things. Sabotage my car? Murder a dog? Damn it, Gary, she's thirteen years old!"

"That doesn't matter," Gary said. "And in spite of your doubts, I think our problems will be over once we get rid of her."

"Gary, we're not sending that child away," Melanie said. How could he be so stubborn? Couldn't he see what was happening? He of all people, who stood there a cripple because of supernatural evil?

Before Gary could answer her, the sound of running feet silenced him. Kyle came up to them and tugged Melanie's arm.

"Aren't you coming?" he asked.

When Melanie turned, Kyle backed away at the sight of her bloodshot eyes.

"What's the matter, mommy?" he asked.

Melanie forced a smile. "I got something in my eye, and we had to stop a minute. But I'm all right now."

"Oh?" Kyle sounded unconvinced. But his excitement about the picnic soon overcame his doubts, and he cried, "Come on!"

He took his mother's hand and pulled her forward. Hating to leave things unfinished, Melanie looked over her shoulder and shook her head a little at Gary. Then she saw Derek coming up behind him. Seeing him made her think of Lad, and she had to turn away to keep from crying again.

"Melanie told you?" Derek asked Gary.

"Yeah," Gary said.

"I wish I had some explanation," Derek answered.

I'll bet you do, Gary thought.

Derek did have one, but he kept silent, even though the urge to tell Gary was strong. Poor Lad. Derek had found a pit in the grounds of the gray mansion that might have once been a duck pond. Thick with ivy and weeds, it was a perfect place to hide the dog. Infuriated that such a thing could happen, and at the same time moved with sorrow, he had dumped the body and marked the grave with Lad's chain.

Melanie had been wise to keep the truth from them, Derek realized as he sat on a rock and watched the children playing in the water. Even Alicen looked happy today. Derek was surprised to find himself admiring her. She had grown prettier. Her hair was neatly combed, and even in her bathing suit, she was no longer fat. But at such a cost . . .

"Aren't they wonderful?" he heard Melanie say. "They make you think everything's going to be all right."

"They're having a great time," Gary agreed. "Look, even Alicen's laughing."

Melanie shot him a glare, embarrassed. But Derek said, "Yeah, isn't that something?"

He stood up, curling his toes in the sand. "I'd like to take a walk with her. How long until lunch?"

"At least half an hour," Gary said. "Although I'm not very hungry."

Derek nodded, then went to his daughter. Gary, keeping his eyes on the therapist, said, "He knows something."

"Gary, please."

To make her happy, Gary said nothing more. He kissed her lightly on the cheek and went back to the barbecue.

Derek tapped Alicen on the shoulder. She turned and smiled at him.

"Want to go for a walk?" he asked.

"Sure!" Alicen cried. She took his hand. "Just me and you?"

"If the other kids don't mind," Derek said.

Gina shook her wet head. "Go on."

"I'll see you at lunch," Alicen said.

When they were a few dozen yards away, Derek spoke to his daughter. "Alicen, do you know anything about the VanBuren's dog?"

"No," Alicen said. "I told Mrs. VanBuren that at breakfast. Why?"

"He's dead, Alicen," Derek said softly.

He heard the choking sound of her breath stopping.

"What do you know about that?" Derek asked.

Alicen was wide-eyed. "Nothing!"

"Don't start crying, please," Derek said. "The other kids don't know about it, and we're going to tell them he ran away."

"I didn't kill him," Alicen said.

"I know."

She looked up at him, surprised. "You do?"

"Yes," Derek said. "Alicen, did you hear anyone talking about hurting Lad? I mean, not one of the VanBurens—but someone no one else knows but you?"

Alicen gazed into his eyes for a long time, not speaking. They had stopped at a jetty, the dividing line between the VanBurens' private beach and the public one. Alicen climbed up on the rocks and sat down. She brought her knees up under her chin and gazed at a boat passing on the bay.

"Mommy told me to kill him," she said finally, distantly.

Derek stiffened. "Mommy told you?"

"She told me to put this funny-smelling stuff in his dish," Alicen said. There was no trace of remorse in her voice. She was simply reporting an order obeyed. "She said she wouldn't come see me any more if I didn't do it." Alicen looked up at her father, all innocence. "Mommy went away once. I don't want her to go away again."

Derek nodded slowly. He understood now why he had heard Alicen talking in her sleep so many times in the past weeks. She hadn't been dreaming at all; she, too, was under the spell of the woman who controlled him. Innocent little Alicen, who sought in her dead mother the love she lacked from her father.

A pang of guilt made Derek's throat tighten. Would it have been so hard to be kind to the child? It might be too late, but—

Suddenly he turned and pulled Alicen very close to him. Alicen returned the embrace, resting her head against her father's warm chest.

"Isn't it wonderful, daddy?" she asked. "Mommy's back, and we can be a real family again."

"Yeah, it's wonderful," Derek said quietly. He couldn't tell her this woman wasn't her mother.

"Daddy," Alicen said, rubbing her bare feet up and down the moss-covered rock. "You'd rather have mommy than old Liza, wouldn't you?"

What did Alicen know of Liza? Could she tell him why Liza never answered his calls? But something in Alicen's expression told Derek she would never answer his questions, so he ignored hers and stood up. Alicen followed him down the rocks and took his hand as they headed back to the picnic.

"Listen," Derek said, "this conversation is our secret, okay?"

"Sure," Alicen said.

"No one has to know about Lad," he said. "Or your mother."

"Mommy told me that already," Alicen said.

"If you ever need to talk," Derek said, squeezing her hand, "come to me, okay?"

"Okay."

Alicen ran to catch up to the VanBuren children. Derek walked slowly, planning. He'd give Gary his notice tomorrow and would hopefully be out of the house within a week's time. Gary had made great progress and would get along fine with another therapist.

Derek looked at his patient. He didn't really want to leave him. Gary was more a friend than a patient now. But that gave Derek all the more reason to believe he should get away from the house before it was too late.

He knew he should warn them. He should tell them about her, about the things she'd done. It was no accident that Melanie's car was now in a junk yard. Her studio had not been torn apart by a mischievous puppy. And there was so much more. Lad's death was only the beginning.

But for the first time in his life, Derek was afraid. All he wanted to do was run away from his problems. God knew he couldn't face them much longer. Not when she drained his resistance each time he saw her. Or she saw him—was she watching him right now?

Derek wished to God he could forget.

But that wasn't going to happen. Late that Sunday night, he was lying with his face buried in his arms when he felt a cold touch on his back. He didn't move, but breathed more evenly as if in sleep. The touch stayed on him, moving up and down. It should have made him feel good, but instead a chill rushed through him.

"Look at me, Derek Miller," he heard.

Derek refused to move. He didn't want to see who shared his bed. But the pain of her nails in his flesh was so great that he was forced to roll over. He glared up at her. Even in the dim light of the moon, she was hideous. Derek fought to keep his eyes on hers, afraid to turn away.

"Good," she said. "You should know by now that you can't defy me, Derek. I own you."

"No one owns me," Derek said.

"I'll make you happy," Janice said. She leaned down and kissed his lips.

"What are you?" Derek asked. "How can you do these things?"

She didn't answer.

"Why are you doing this?" Derek persisted. "Why are you trying to hurt the VanBurens?"

"I was murdered," the vision said. "And I was only twenty-eight."

"Murdered?" Derek asked, confused.

"Silence!"

Before Derek could protest, she pressed her mouth to his and pried his lips open with her tongue. Derek had learned to give in to her. She became violent when he showed his repugnance. But God, how he hated this! How he wished he could throw her away from him, smash her hideous face, drive her away forever. But that was impossible.

At last, satisfied for the time, she rolled away from him. Derek knew what would happen now. He would fall asleep and remember this only vaguely in the morning. But he needed questions answered. "Why did you say you were murdered? You can't be dead. You're here right now."

She screamed, a scream heard only by him. Throwing her body on top of his, she pulled hard at his hair, making him want to cry out. He foolishly tried to grab her wrists. It was like grabbing water.

"Stop it, please," he said. "I won't ask any more questions."

"You must learn to be submissive," Janice hissed. "You must be taught to obey. Look at me."

Derek resisted.

"*Look at me!*"

To Derek's horror, she faded away from him and returned as Elaine. He jerked his head away from the sight, feeling nausea rise in his gut. He had prayed never to see that twisted face again.

"Please," he said quietly. "Please go away."

"Remember this face," Janice said.

Derek nodded, his face buried in his pillow. Several moments passed before he dared to turn around. He was alone once more.

21

———◆———

Because his first meeting was at nine o'clock, Owen Crewe was up very early Monday morning. He sat on the couch in Liza's living room, his blankets tangled up in a knot behind him. Rubbing his eyes, he yawned widely, then looked around. The door to his sister's room was still open, her bed not slept in.

Owen had been certain she'd be home by now, if she was only on a weekend trip. And she couldn't have left for school already—not when the kitchen clock read six o'clock. Owen frowned at it and filled the teakettle. He then walked to the table, where he found the note he had written for her the previous morning. He had explained his presence there and had told her he would be home as soon as orientation was over. But he had returned in the late afternoon to find an empty apartment.

"Easy, Owen," he told himself. "She's a big girl."

Still, anyone seeing him crumble the note and throw it hard across the room to the wastebasket would have known he was more worried than he'd admit. Liza had never been the type to disappear like this. Of course, she hadn't known he was coming. But they had kept a correspondence going over the years, and Liza always told him when she was planning a vacation.

Hearing the kettle whistling, Owen went back to the stove and fixed his coffee. He carried the mug into the living room and sipped it slowly, looking out the window.

Pretty town, he thought, taking in the row of Colonial houses across the street. It was no wonder she had picked this neighborhood to live in. What could possibly happen to her in a town like this?

He finished the last of the coffee, gathered his papers together, then hastily wrote a new note for Liza, propping it up against a vase of dying flowers. Owen checked his pockets for his keys, then left. Surely Liza would be there when he returned.

Gary had spent all the previous night thinking of an excuse to dismiss his therapist. He couldn't accuse Alicen of killing Lad, because Melanie would deny it. But he knew he was right. Alicen was a disturbed child, and he wanted her away from his kids. So now he hobbled up the fake stairs in the therapy room, trying to get up the courage to tell Derek he had to leave. But Derek beat him to the punch.

"I'm afraid I'll have to be giving you my notice," Derek said.

Gary stopped halfway up the stairs and looked over his shoulder. "Did I hear you right?"

Derek nodded. "I'm leaving. Alicen and I will be moving as soon as I find new work."

Though he was grateful it was out of his hands, Gary had questions. "Why?"

"Don't stop in the middle of your workout," Derek said, waving at the stairs.

Gary continued to the top, then turned and started down again. "You didn't answer my question," he said when he reached the bottom. Would Derek admit the truth?

"I feel it's time Alicen and I were moving on," Derek said. "We're becoming too dependent on you—especially Alicen."

He did know the truth about Alicen—that was why he wanted to leave.

"Then send Alicen to boarding school," Gary suggested. He didn't want to lose his therapist. That would mean going back to the clinic.

"You know I can't do that," Derek said.

"And you can't leave me alone!" Gary snapped. "What happened to the guy who was going to teach me racquet ball?"

What was wrong with him? Why did he argue with Derek, when only moments ago he was looking for reasons to get rid of him?

Gary sighed deeply. "It's your life. You do what you want."

"I'm sorry," Derek said. His voice took on a louder, more authoritative tone when he said, "Let's try the stairs a few more times."

Gary obeyed, not knowing what to think. Well, maybe it would be better to just concentrate on his routine. Their troubles would soon be over, once Alicen was gone. Gary hated that child, not just for tormenting his family, but for taking his best friend away from him.

Melanie had gone to visit some art galleries that morning, needing to do something to forget her fears. On the way home, she glanced at her watch. It was about time now for Nancy to be getting out of kindergarten. Melanie, wishing she could have all her children with her now, decided to drive her youngest home. She pulled the car up alongside the play yard and waited. Minutes later, the lunch bell rang, and hordes of children ran from the brick building. She was surprised to see Alicen coming from the building with Jamie Hutchinson.

"Well, that's a surprise," she thought aloud. Puppy love had claimed Alicen Miller at last. And Gary thought she was abnormal.

Melanie spotted Nancy, walking in a line of children. She got out of the car and called to her. The little girl waved, spoke to her teacher, then ran on chubby legs to her mother. Melanie caught her in her arms and kissed her.

"Mommy, stop!" Nancy giggled. "Everybody's looking!"

"How's my girl?" Melanie asked, opening the door for her.

"Fine," Nancy said. "How come you're here today?"

"I was on my way home," Melanie explained. "And I thought you might like a ride."

"Are you coming back for the other kids?"

Melanie thought for a moment: *it wouldn't be such a bad idea.* Then she told herself to stop being ridiculous.

"No," she said. "They'll come home on the bus."

She started the car. Nancy bounced up and down on the seat a few times, then moved closer to her mother.

"Why do you have such dark circles under your eyes?" she asked.

"I didn't sleep very well last night," Melanie admitted.

"Why?"

"I don't know."

Nancy was silent for a moment. Then: "Mommy, that mean man isn't coming back, is he?"

"Mean man?"

"The man who hurt daddy last year," Nancy cried. "Gina had a dream about him—is he back?"

Melanie was glad she had reached a red light so that she could take the child in her arms. "What makes you say that?"

"Because you're so sad all the time," Nancy said. "And you wanted to know if Kyle and Gina and me wanted to talk about daddy's accident."

"That was just in case you were thinking of it, honey," Melanie said, feeling uneasy.

"He isn't back, is he?"

"No, honey," Melanie insisted, her voice carrying more conviction than her thoughts. "I'm just tired. That's why my eyes have dark circles. You know how busy mommy is with all her work."

"It's okay?"

"Sure it is," Melanie said, kissing her. She drove down the road. She could tell the child was frightened.

"How about painting with me today? You could sit at the little table in my studio."

"Sure!" Nancy cried, delighted to share something with her mother.

Melanie was glad Nancy had agreed so readily. She wanted to keep the child in her sight as much as possible. That way, no one could get to her. Nancy would be safe.

After lunch Melanie and Nancy painted and talked until they heard the other children approaching the house. Melanie felt apprehensive; she knew she would have to tell them about Lad without further delay. So she gathered them together in the kitchen, fixing lemonade for everyone.

"There's something I have to tell you," she said as she filled a glass.

"It's about Lad, isn't it?" Kyle asked. "I bet he didn't come home."

"No, he didn't," Melanie said.

"Did you look for him?" Gina asked.

"Yes," Melanie said. It hurt her to lie like this, but what else could she do? "We searched the woodlands, and even Mrs. Jennings' property down the road. I think he wandered off somewhere."

"Maybe you'll never find him," Alicen said darkly.

"Shut up!" Kyle cried angrily. He was more hurt by Lad's disappearance than the others. "Don't talk that way!"

"I'm sure we'll find him," Melanie said, returning Alicen's gaze. When she stared like that, it was almost easy to see why Gary accused her.

Kyle went across the kitchen and opened one of the drawers. He pulled out a colored marker, then fished around a little more.

"What're you doing?" Nancy asked.

"Looking for paper," Kyle replied. "I'm going to make posters and put them all around. Someone will find Lad."

"I'll help," Gina said.

"Me, too!" Nancy cried.

Only Alicen declined. While Melanie was marveling at her optimistic children, Alicen was wondering how they could be so foolish as to think their dog was still alive.

Melanie bent over her sleeping son and gently put his arm under his covers. Kyle had been so excited just a few hours earlier, making the signs for Lad. It seemed impossible that he was so quiet right now. Melanie smiled at his curled-up figure, hidden under a light coverlet. Then she frowned. How could anyone dare to hurt such a beautiful child? Gina and Kyle and Nancy were so precious to her. She had already stopped in the girls' rooms. She didn't want to tell herself it was because she wanted to be certain they were safe. Earlier, she had been tempted to let them sleep in her room, but she knew that was a ridiculous idea. Gary would never allow it, and besides, it would needlessly frighten the children.

But she had to do something to stop her fears. She was terrified of the night. Though the entire day had been peaceful, Melanie recalled tactics used the last time her house was stalked by an unseen predator. Jacob would let a few days go by, then he'd attack when least expected. Melanie knew her family was being tormented that way again. But if this was Jacob Armand's doing, why hadn't he made contact with her?

Melanie yawned and realized exhaustion was muddling her thoughts. She left Kyle's room, closing the door quietly behind her. When she turned into the dark hallway, she bumped into something.

"What—?"

"Shh," a voice said. "It's Gary. What're you doing up?"

Melanie took a deep breath. "You scared the hell out of me."

"Sorry," Gary said. They walked to their room together. "You don't have to watch them every minute, you know."

"I think I do," Melanie protested.

"It's too late in the night for an argument," Gary said. "So if it makes you feel better, it's all right."

"Of course it's all right," Melanie grumbled. "I don't need your permission to safeguard my children."

"You're really serious, aren't you?"

"You go ahead and make fun of me," Melanie said, "but I'll be the one laughing when you find out I'm right."

"You're wrong," Gary said. "And I have something to prove it. Melanie, Derek gave me his notice today."

"You didn't tell me that before," Melanie said.

"I didn't want to say anything in front of the children. But Derek told me today he and Alicen would be moving as soon as he finds other work."

"That's strange."

"No, it isn't," Gary said. "Not when you consider that he might be running away from something. Melanie, Derek is a top-notch therapist. He just isn't the type to leave so abruptly. Unless he knows something we don't. He knows about Alicen. He knows she's responsible for Lad's death."

"Gary—"

"Melanie, your mother instinct is blinding you," Gary said. "Look at the facts, will you? Why would he be running away if he wasn't afraid we'd learn the truth about Alicen?"

"The truth about Alicen?" Melanie echoed. "It sounds like a cheap porno flick!"

"Derek told me once he had to leave a job because of his daughter," Gary said. "So why not now? Melanie, why would he be leaving so suddenly unless he wants to do so before I fire him?"

Melanie couldn't help but see the logic in Gary's argument. It all fit together, didn't it? Alicen was a strange child. But a murderess? That Melanie found hard to swallow. Still, it was late, and she was tired. It was so much easier to believe in a disturbed little girl than a ghost.

"Maybe you're right," she said. "But I prefer to keep an eye on my children."

Bryan Davis hung up his telephone and started to bounce his pencil nervously. He had just received a call from the county coroner. They had identified the driver; the body was that of one Nora Browne, an eighteen-year-old girl who had run away from home. Her parents had positively identified her and had admitted she was heavily into drugs.

"That's what I thought," Byran said, "considering how she drove that bus. But eighteen? I can't believe an eighteen-year-old passed for a bus driver!"

The coroner said, "Captain Davis, there's just one problem. According to my autopsy, this can't possibly be your driver."

"What do you mean?" Bryan asked, closing his eyes. He wanted to be through with this.

"We checked her body for traces of drugs," the coroner said, "before we spoke to her parents, that is. We wanted to have something to report in reference to her behavior at the time of the accident. Granted, it was difficult, considering the condition of the deceased. But we found something we weren't looking for—sand and seaweed. It was in her teeth, her throat, and a small piece was found in her hair."

"So?"

"So this woman didn't die of a fall from a bus," the coroner said. "She drowned—probably accidentally."

Bryan thought a moment.

"Maybe she had been swimming before the accident," he said. "It's a long shot, but I'm willing to go for it. Why don't you tell me what she was wearing? Then I'll know for certain if it's our driver."

"Jeans, a white shirt," the coroner said. "And sandals. That's about all. Oh, yes—there was a tortoise-shell comb in her hair."

"What color hair?"

"Blond," the coroner said. "I understand your bus driver had blond hair."

Bryan nodded, as if the coroner could see him. When he hung up a moment later, his mind started to fill with questions. He bounced his pencil more quickly and tried to fit the pieces together. The coroner had just described the Jane Doe missing from the funeral parlor. Was it possible someone had stolen the body, driven it all the way to the site of the accident, and dumped it there? It was obviously done to get the police off a trail. But by whom? It was impossible to think the bus driver was still alive.

Bryan got up and went to the file cabinet near his windows. He found the folder on the bus accident and scrawled across it: CASE REOPENED.

22

———◆———

Monday night Owen Crewe returned to an empty apartment. His note was still propped up against the vase on the kitchen table. Owen removed its dead flowers and threw the murky water into the sink. He remembered how much his sister loved plants. It was unusual for her to leave them neglected like this. He filled a pitcher and watered the plants around the apartment.

Water spilled over one of the plantholders in the living room and dripped onto a chrome-and-glass end table. Owen mopped it up, then straightened a pile of mail Liza had left there. On the bottom was a greeting card. A giraffe dressed in a tutu was on the front, and in the blank inside, someone had written: *For my favorite racquetball-playing ballerina.*

It was signed "Derek." Owen wondered why his sister had never mentioned anyone by that name in her letters. The date on the card made it two weeks old. Owen wished there was an envelope with it. Maybe this Derek would know where to find his sister. Of course, he shouldn't worry so about her. She was twenty-eight, for heaven's sake. She didn't have to answer to him for everything she did. But Owen was one of those eternal big brothers, and he wouldn't rest until he was sure his sister was all right.

The next day he resolved to try her dance school. It was housed in an ancient brownstone. Owen entered a small, dimly lit hallway. There were no elevators, so he had to walk up three flights. Madame Martin's Dance Studio was written in gold across a black door. Hearing piano music, Owen entered without knocking.

"May I help you, sir?" a young woman asked from behind a desk.

"Yes," Owen said. "I'm looking for my sister. Her name is Liza Crewe—she's a student here."

"Yes, I know Liza," the woman said. "Please sit down until class is over. Madame Martin will speak with you."

"Thank you," Owen said, finding a seat across the room.

He heard French being spoken in the other room, in a lilting rhythm with the music. Finally the music stopped, and there was a shuffle of feet as women headed for the locker room. Madame Martin came out into the lobby for her mail, wiping her neck with a towel. When the receptionist told her of Owen, she turned to him.

"Mr. Crewe? You've come to ask about your sister?"

Owen smiled to hear that she didn't have the slightest accent. Her manner of speech was pure New Yorker.

"Yes," he said, extending his hand. "I came up from Florida for a convention, with the hopes of also seeing my sister. But I've been here since Saturday and haven't heard a word from her."

"I'm afraid I haven't, either," Madame Martin said. "Liza has missed three classes in a row—and it's so unlike her. She may be one of my older students, but she has always been as bright-eyed and dedicated as a young girl."

"You don't have any idea where she might have gone, do you?"

"None whatsoever. I have been expecting her to call me."

"But she hasn't."

"No," said Madame Martin. "I'm sorry, Mr. Crewe. Perhaps you'd like to speak with my other students? Liza had friends in this class."

Owen said he would appreciate that. But as it turned out, none of the other women had any answers, either. After a half hour or so of questioning them, Owen said his thanks and left the building. Now he was determined to find his sister—something was very wrong. When he arrived home, he made a long-distance call to his hospital in Fort Lauderdale. His boss wasn't very happy about his taking a leave of absence so abruptly. But at the moment, Owen didn't care what his boss thought. There was only one more day of the convention, and if Liza didn't show, it wasn't enough time to find her. Still, Owen went to bed that night hoping he would wake to find her home.

Somehow, he wasn't surprised when morning came and Liza wasn't there. This time he didn't bother to write her a note. He dressed and ate breakfast, then left for the Manhattan hotel. Dedicated to his profession, he was able to take notes, look at slides, and listen to speeches without thinking too often of Liza. But as soon as he could, Owen hurried home. Even as he sped along the highway, he knew he'd find nothing there.

He entered the apartment, tossed his briefcase on the couch, and left again. In the foyer downstairs, he knocked on a red door. He could hear an Italian opera playing and someone speaking the language over the music. Moments later, the door was opened by a thin, doe-eyed little girl.

"Is your mother home?"

The child, who couldn't have been more than five, nodded.

"Carmella, who is it?" a woman called.

"Owen from upstairs," he said.

"Owen from upstairs, momma!"

The landlady appeared with a wooden spoon in her hand. She smiled at Owen.

"Hi," he said. "I was wondering if I could talk to you."

"Of course," the woman said. "Has your sister come home yet? I don't see her car."

"No, I'm afraid she hasn't. That's what I want to talk about."

He was led into the apartment and further into the kitchen. Sitting on a barstool, he breathed in the smell of sauce.

"I'll bet you cook all day," he said.

"Company tonight," was the reply.

"By the way, I didn't get your name," Owen said now.

"Mrs. Verdini," the woman said. "What can I do for you?"

"I was hoping you could help me find my sister," Owen said, tugging at his mustache.

"Is there trouble?"

"I don't know," Owen answered. "But she hasn't been home since Saturday, and I'm worried. If I knew where she was, I could go home. But I can't leave without being certain she's safe."

"You're a good brother," Mrs. Verdini said. "You have a large family?"

"There are only four of us," Owen said.

"I have three children," Mrs. Verdini said. "Such angels. But we were talking about Liza. Let me think."

She lifted the lid from a pot, stirred her sauce a little, tasted it, and added more spices before speaking again.

"I know she has a new boyfriend," she said. "He was here a few times. I didn't see him very well, but he looked nice and neat. He drives a Volvo."

"I think his name is Derek."

"That's it," Mrs. Verdini said. "They played tennis together. I know because I saw them carrying bags with rackets."

Owen recalled the card he had found the day before, and corrected her.

"Racquet ball," he said. "Do you happen to know where they play?"

"Not really," Mrs. Verdini said. "I don't go in much for sports. But I do know there's a local health club in town. The Hercules Inn. If you want, you can ask my husband how to get there. He gets home at six."

"No, thanks," Owen said, jumping from his stool. "I can look it up in the phone book. I appreciate this, Mrs. Verdini."

"Anytime," she said. "Liza's a lovely woman. I just hope she's all right."

She walked with Owen to the door. "Listen, if she doesn't come home tonight, don't you eat alone. One more person won't make a difference at my table tonight."

Owen grinned. The smell of sauce was making him famished. "Thanks. Maybe I'll see you later."

The club was easy to find. It was in the heart of town, just around the corner from the main road.

"I was wondering if you could help me," he said to the girl behind the horseshoe-shaped desk.

"Sure," she answered. She studied his tanned face and sun-bleached hair and smiled. "Sure, what do you want?"

"I'm looking for two people," Owen said. "One is named Liza Crewe, the other is Derek. I don't know his last name."

"Why do you want to know?" the girl asked, tilting her head. "You aren't a cop, are you? I'm not sure you're allowed to ask questions like this."

"Liza's my sister," Owen said. "I've been looking all over town for her. Has she been here in the last few days?"

"I don't know any couple named Liza and Derek."

"Liza has dark hair," Owen said. "And eyes like Ava Gardner."

The girl cut him off. "Who's Ava Gardner?"

"An actress," Owen said patiently. "My sister's a dancer. She plays racquet ball here."

"Oh, I know who you mean!" the girl cried. "I remembered Liza when you said she was a dancer—she has those muscular calves, you know."

"Has she been here recently?"

"I haven't seen her," the girl said. "Or her boyfriend."

"You don't happen to know where he lives, do you?"

The girl shook her head, smiling. "Sorry. Even if I did, I couldn't tell you."

Owen sighed so sadly that she was moved to say, "I'll relay a message to them for you if they come in."

"I'd appreciate that," Owen said. "You have something I can write on?"

The girl pulled a short, eraserless pencil from a red cup and handed it to Owen with a pad. After scribbling his message, he pushed it across the counter and thanked her. He left, feeling no better than he had earlier. He'd found a lead, and it had brought him nowhere.

Well, he thought, he could always come back to the club. Liza had to show up soon.

All that optimism didn't take away the burning in his stomach, a sign Dr. Owen Crewe, psychiatrist, interpreted as fear.

23

That Tuesday Gary had gone back to work. Derek, only too glad to have a chance to get away from the house, drove him to the city. So Melanie spent the entire day alone, keeping very busy with her painting so as not to think about what was happening. Nancy was now sitting at her little table in Melanie's studio, coloring. At last the other children came home from school. Melanie, seeing thick gray clouds in the sky, was glad to see them. She knew now that they were safe.

She thought it was possible that Gary's theory about Alicen might be correct, but she couldn't be absolutely certain. Until there was definite evidence against the child—and Melanie doubted there ever would be—she had to keep herself ready for the worst. No matter how much Gary objected.

The studio door opened wide just then.

"Hi, mom!" Gina cried.

"Hi, honey," Melanie said, taking her in her arms and giving the child a tight hug. For a moment she didn't want to let go.

"Mom, you're squashing me," Gina protested. She pulled away and smoothed her hair.

"I'm just glad to see you, Gina," Melanie said. She noticed her son now. "Hello, Kyle."

"Hi, mom," Kyle said. He kept his distance, having witnessed the bear hug Gina got. He was at an age where gushy affection made him shy.

"What's Nancy doing in here?" Gina asked.

"Well, I just figured she shouldn't be alone in this big house," Melanie said.

"Since when?" Kyle wanted to know.

I'm too protective, Melanie thought. *Even the kids see it.*

"Hey, I don't have to explain myself to you," she said in a warning tone. "Nancy's fine here. By the way, where's Alicen?"

"She went to her room," Gina said.

"She's not ill, is she?"

Gina shrugged. "Who knows? She didn't talk to me at all today. Sometimes she's just weird."

"I told you to be nice to her," Melanie reminded her.

"I am!" Gina cried. "But how can I be nice to her when she doesn't talk to me?"

"I know you do your best, Gina," Melanie said. "But everyone gets into moods. Just let Alicen's pass, and she'll be nice as ever before you know it. Now, why don't you kids go out to play? But stay in the yard where I can see you. It's going to rain soon, and I don't want you caught in a downpour."

The children left the room. In the hall Kyle turned to his sister and said quietly, "Mom sure is acting funny lately."

"Yeah," Gina said. "Just like last year, when daddy was hurt. I hope nothing is going on."

"Oh, it's probably okay," Kyle, the eternal optimist, said. "Say, I know something we can do. We can look for Lad in the woods."

"Good idea," Gina said, forgetting her mother's orders to stay within her sight.

They ran from the house, hand in hand. Melanie watched them cut across the lawn and smiled. They were such nice, normal kids. If only Alicen could be that way, too. Then Gary wouldn't have any cause to be suspicious of her.

But Alicen wasn't normal at all. Normal children didn't become liars, thieves, or murderers just out of obedience to a disembodied voice. And they didn't sit in their rooms, staring at walls, waiting for that voice to come again. That was exactly what Alicen was doing at this moment. All during the bus ride home from school, she had heard her "mother" calling her.

The room grew cold, but Alicen didn't mind. She looked around and saw a cloud hovering near the door. She smiled.

"I wish you'd let me see you just once, mommy," she said.

"No," the vision snapped. "Not yet. There is something I want you to do today. The boy Kyle—he's next."

"Am I going to kill him, too?" Alicen asked, with innocence that would have alarmed a sane person.

"Not today," the vision said. "I want him to suffer first. I want them all to suffer, the way I do."

"What do you want me to do, then?"

"Get him up to the attic."

"The attic?"

"Yes," was the reply. "When you get there, you'll know what do do."

Melanie looked out her window and noticed her two oldest children were nowhere in sight. Thunder sounded in the distance, and a breeze blew up through the trees. Very firmly, she told herself not to panic. But she tore off her smock and threw it across the room. Nancy looked up, startled.

"What's the matter, mommy?"

"Nothing, dear," Melanie said. "You go on coloring. I've got something to do."

"I'm making a picture for daddy," Nancy said.

"That's nice," Melanie said, leaping the room. She saw Alicen coming down the hallway but ignored her. A few moments later she was yelling out the back door: "Kyle! Gina!"

She breathed a sigh of relief to hear their faint reply.

"Come where I can see you!"

Gina and Kyle appeared at the edge of the woods, then ran up to the house. They exchanged confused glances to see the angry look on their mother's face.

"Did we do something wrong?" Gina asked.

"Yes, you did," Melanie said. "Didn't I tell you to stay where I can keep an eye on you?"

"I guess so," Kyle answered, fidgeting. "We forgot. Can't you see in the woods from upstairs?"

"I'm not blessed with X-ray vision," Melanie snapped. She brought her hand to her still-bandaged forehead and rubbed away an oncoming headache. "I can't see through a half acre of fir trees."

"We're sorry," Gina said. "But we were looking for the dog."

"Yeah, don't be mad," Kyle begged.

I must sound like an idiot, Melanie thought. *They're big kids.*

"Sure," she said, smiling weakly. "I'm sorry I yelled. But Lad will come home in his own good time, don't you think?"

"I hope so," Gina said. She turned to her brother. "Kyle, I've got some homework to do."

"See you later," Kyle said.

Alicen was standing in the kitchen. Gina was tempted to ignore her, but since her mother was at her side, she said hello. Alicen mumbled a greeting as they passed her. She stared at Kyle for a few minutes before speaking.

"Your mother treats you like a baby," she teased.

"She does not!"

"Then how come she has to watch you?"

"What do you care?"

Alicen shrugged. "I don't know. Except that nine is kind of old to be listening to everything your mother says, isn't it?"

"No," Kyle said. "She's my mother."

Alicen turned on him. "I'll bet you can't even cross the street by yourself!"

"I can, too!" Kyle cried.

"Then prove it," Alicen said, her eyes thinning. "Take a dare."

Kyle hesitated. But how could a little boy resist a dare?

"What?"

"Come up to the attic with me," Alicen said.

"Oh, no," Kyle said. "I'm not allowed up there. Some bad things happened there last year. I'm not gonna get myself grounded just when summer starts."

"No one'll know," Alicen said. "Unless, of course, you're afraid."

It was an old trick, but Kyle hadn't been on earth long enough to be wary of it.

"Okay," he sighed. "But let's get it over with. And you gotta promise to stop teasing me if I do."

"Sure," Alicen said.

The two children walked upstairs together. Melanie's studio was not in the same hallway as the linen closet, which led up to the attic, so no one saw Alicen climb its steps. Kyle was close behind her, his heart beating. If his mother caught him . . .

Alicen pushed aside the cover and hoisted herself up over the ledge. She had never been in the attic before, and she looked around in awe at its contents. There were chests and toys and old furniture, all covered with a thick layer of dust. Mesmerized, she moved into the room to inspect a full-length mirror. A vision in its glass, of a blond-haired, faceless woman, reminded her of her task.

"Okay, I'm up," Kyle said. "I'm going down again."

"Wait a minute," Alicen replied. "Don't you want to see the neat stuff that's up here?"

"It's just a bunch of furniture," Kyle said, stepping down to the top step. He didn't want to leave Alicen up there, so he stopped for a moment to watch her.

She moved through the room, brushing cobwebs out of her path. She walked as if she had been up there dozens of times. At its other end she found what she was looking for.

"Hey, come here and look," she said. "There's a trapdoor in the ceiling."

Of course there was. Her mother had told her so.

"So?"

"So I'll bet you can see for a million miles if you go on the roof," Alicen said.

"I'm not going on the roof!"

Alicen looked over her shoulder at him. "If you don't, I'll tell your mother you did, anyway. And then you'll get into big trouble."

Kyle considered the threat.

"Maybe she'll ground you for the whole summer."

That was threat enough. Sighing, he walked across the room to Alicen and helped her open the trapdoor. Alicen boosted him through it, then climbed out herself.

The loose tiles made a precarious foothold for them. Alicen sat down, putting herself between Kyle and the door. The little boy clicked his tongue, having hoped to get right back inside before his mother came looking for him. But how could he, with Alicen in the way?

"It's going to rain," he said. "I felt a drop."

"Just look at the bay," Alicen said, ignoring him. "Isn't it neat the way the wind makes it so choppy?"

"Yeah," Kyle said, studying her.

"You're not looking!" Alicen cried.

Kyle turned his head and pretended to be interested in the faroff water. Moments of silence went by, and then suddenly he heard a thud and a click. He turned and saw that the trapdoor had been slammed shut. Alicen had tricked him.

"Hey, open up!" he shouted.

Kyle pounded at the door, unable to pull it open. No reply came.

"Alicen, this is stupid!" he cried. "Let me in!"

No answer.

"ALICEN!"

A clap of thunder made Kyle jump. Crying, he grabbed for the door frame to keep himself from slipping. He held his breath and waited for the downpour. It began to drizzle.

"ALICEN YOU STUPID SHIT-HEAD! OPEN THIS FREAKIN' DOOR!"

He was so frightened that he didn't know what he was saying.

"I'LL KILL YOU, ALICEN! LET ME IN! LET ME IN!"

He pounded on the door, his soft young hands scraping over the shingles. A loose nail caught the side of his fist, opening the skin. Kyle's hand flew to his mouth. Praying someone would find him, he sucked on the wound while rain pelted heavier and heavier against him.

"HELP! HELP!"

His words were so muffled by the downpour that no one heard him. Fighting tears, Kyle lay down and drew himself into a ball. One hand held fast to the door frame while the other remained in his mouth. He could only wait.

"Look at that rain," Melanie said to Nancy as she put the finishing touches on her work. "I hope daddy and Derek get home okay."

"Are they coming soon?"

Melanie looked at her watch.

"In about an hour," she said. "Except this rain may delay them a bit."

She took off her smock and laid it across a stool.

"It sure is loud," Nancy said.

"I can't even hear myself think," Melanie answered.

"What are you thinking about, mommy?"

"Nothing," Melanie said, laughing. And that was true. She had been so ashamed of yelling at Kyle and Gina for no good reason that she had forced herself to stop worrying and concentrate on her painting. For the time, it had worked.

"Well, I've got to start dinner," she said. "You be sure to wash your hands and clean up nice for me."

"Okay."

Melanie went downstairs to the kitchen. She opened the refrigerator and pulled out chopped meat for hamburgers, and a package of fries. Seeing a bag of unshucked corn on the counter, she decided to have that, too. That would show her children she wasn't mad at them.

She could hear all the windows of the house rattling from the terrible storm as she walked out into the hallway and called upstairs for Kyle. Her son didn't answer her. But then, the storm was so loud that he might not have heard. She called again and this time heard a door open upstairs. But it was Gina who appeared on the top landing.

"Find your brother and tell him I need some corn shucked," Melanie said.

"Sure," Gina answered.

Melanie went back to the kitchen. She sat at the wooden table, took some meat, and began molding it into patties. The rain pounded the roof above her, and the wind blew furiously as she worked on dinner. A chill went through her—Melanie hated dark, rainy days.

After she had finished making the hamburgers, Melanie suddenly realized Kyle hadn't yet come downstairs. Melanie felt her heart jump to her throat but controlled herself as she went upstairs. She met Gina in a hallway.

"I can't find him anywhere," she said. "I looked in every room."

"Oh, God," Melanie whispered. "Did you ask Alicen and Nancy?"

"They don't know where he is, either," Gina said.

"He must be downstairs, then."

"I already looked."

"Look again," Melanie ordered. "Then come and get me if you find him."

If you find him . . .

Gina hurried downstairs. Melanie walked down the hallway to Kyle's room. She checked his closet and even under his bed, to no avail. He had to be in here somewhere, though. He couldn't have gone out in that storm.

"Kyle?"

The rain had subsided, so there was no reason he couldn't hear her —unless he was in some kind of trouble.

He has to be okay, Melanie told herself as she rounded a hallway. She passed the linen closet and noticed the door was open. She wouldn't have given it a second thought if she hadn't felt an icy wind rush out of it. Melanie stepped inside and looked up. The trapdoor had been left open.

What's he doing up there? she asked herself. But she didn't stop to think of an answer.

She hurried up the stairs, calling her son's name. The attic was hot, which made Melanie wonder why she had felt such a freezing blast a moment ago. Again, she didn't give herself time for an answer. She moved through the half-light offered by the clouded sun, looking behind the chests and pieces of furniture. She hated this place, with all its cobwebs and dark shadows. Had Kyle come up here on his own, or had someone made him do it?

Every time she looked behind something, only to find he wasn't there, she couldn't help breathing a sigh of relief. Her heart was pounding in anticipation of what she'd find. But at last, after a very thorough search, she realized he wasn't up here. The trapdoor had been left open by accident, of course. She'd find out about that later.

She was on the first step when she heard a small noise. It was a squeaking sound, like a mouse. Melanie remembered the rat that had gotten caught in the wheelchair lift and started to hurry away. But then there was a faint tapping noise from the roof.

"Kyle?"

The child had fainted under the chill of the driving rain, and only now had come to. Shivering, he managed to knock a few times on the trapdoor.

"Oh, my God," Melanie whispered. "Kyle, I'm coming!"

She hurried around the clutter of the attic and unhooked the little door. To her shock, she saw Kyle's pale face and plastered hair. There was blood on his lips from sucking his wounded hand.

"Alicen made me do it," he said weakly.

"Shh," Melanie cooed, hoisting herself up onto the roof to take him in her arms. "Come inside."

Kyle held her very tightly, and Melanie felt the trembling of his body. He coughed a little as she moved back toward the door. Then, suddenly, a loud clap of thunder made him jump. His scream mixed with his mother's as his body was torn from her. He slipped down the roof.

"MMOOMMMMYY!"

"Kyle, no!"

She couldn't reach out quickly enough to grab him. He fell over the roof, screaming all the while. Melanie crawled out after him and to her relief saw that he had caught hold of the rain gutters.

"Take my hand, Kyle!" she shouted, reaching down. Because of the decorative trim around the roof, the gutters were a foot below her. Kyle was too frightened, however, to reach up.

"I—I can't!" he protested.

"Kyle, it's okay," Melanie insisted. "I'm right here. I'll hold onto you."

"I can't!"

"Kyle, *please*," Melanie begged.

The child began to cry hysterically. Seeing he would never let go of the gutters, Melanie crawled further out, until half her body was hanging over the ledge. She didn't dare think that someone might be behind her, waiting to push her off the wet, steep roof. She didn't think at all, but worked mindlessly in her efforts to save her child. Those gutters were so old they were rotted, and if they should break . . .

"I've got you!" Melanie shouted, feeling Kyle's wrist in her hand. "Let go!"

"No!"

It began to rain again. Without arguing, Melanie gave a heave and tried to pull her son over the ledge. But he was too heavy for her one arm. Blinking in the rain, she reached her other arm down and grabbed his other wrist. At the very moment she managed to at last pull him on the roof, a piece of the gutter gave way and crashed to the gravel driveway below.

Without a word, Melanie held fast to her son and scurried back into the attic. She closed the door above her and locked it, all the time thanking God that Kyle was safe in her arms. He was coughing violently, his wet body shivering against her. She carried him down into the hall.

Gina and Nancy, who had heard all the shouting, were waiting there. Seeing Kyle's wet clothes and hair, Gina reached into the closet for a blanket to wrap around him.

"What happened?" Nancy asked, frightened.

"Kyle was locked up on the roof," Melanie said, hurrying down the hall to his room.

"Alicen did it," Kyle said weakly.

Melanie laid him on his bed and began to remove his soaked clothes, while Gina looked through his drawers for a pair of warm pajamas and handed them to her mother. Melanie dressed her son more violently than she realized, throwing his wet clothes across the room with such force that they made slapping sounds against the furniture. She was furious that such a thing could happen to a nine-year-old.

At last she tucked him under his covers. "You lay still, darling," she said. "I'll call a doctor."

Kyle closed his eyes. Gina and Nancy stood by the bed, watching him with concern. A hand went into Kyle's, and he opened his eyes to smile at Gina. But his smile never happened. He saw Alicen standing beside his sisters.

"GO AWAY! GO AWAY!" He screamed on, stopping only when he doubled over in a coughing fit. Just then, the door opened, and Melanie hurried to his side.

"Get out of here," she said to the girls, who obeyed immediately.

Melanie sat Kyle up to pat his back. "Easy, honey! Mommy's here!"

Kyle quieted at last and fell against her.

"Okay, now?"

His eyelids began to droop, his voice became a whisper. "Alicen. Alicen. Alicen."

Melanie bit her lip and laid her son back down again. He was delirious, the poor child. She kissed his burning forehead and went out into the hall. The three girls were standing there, wide-eyed.

"Alicen," Melanie said, "did you tell Kyle to go up onto the roof?"

Alicen's brown eyes rounded. "No! Why would I do a thing like that?"

"Kyle said you locked him on the roof," Melanie reported.

"He's a liar," Alicen growled.

"Don't you call my brother a liar!" Nancy said angrily.

"Alicen," Melanie said, her tone grim, "I'll get the truth when Kyle is better. But right now I have to call a doctor. Stay out of his room."

Gina turned to study her friend's face as her mother walked away. There were tears in Alicen's eyes, tears of a child who couldn't understand why she was being blamed for something she didn't do. Gina said nothing to her. She heard the sound of the front door opening and ran downstairs, Nancy at her heels. Passing her mother at the telephone stand, she raced to throw her arms around her father as he entered the house.

"Well, hello!" Gary said cheerfully. "That's just the kind of greeting I need on a day like this."

"Daddy, Kyle's sick," Nancy said.

Gary's smile faded. "What's wrong with him?"

"He got caught up on the roof," Gina said. Confused, Gary walked down the hall with her, his raincoat dripping on the carpet.

"Please, he's feverish and delirious," Melanie was saying over the phone. "He was caught out in the storm for God knows how long. Couldn't you come here?"

A pause.

"Oh, thank you," Melanie said. "You're very kind. I'll see you in a few minutes."

She hung up and looked at Gary. But before she could speak, Derek interrupted her.

"How did Kyle get caught up on the roof?" he asked, thinking the worst.

"I'm not sure," Melanie said. "It seems he climbed out through a trapdoor, and it slammed shut behind him. I didn't hear him calling, because the storm was so loud."

She bowed her head and cried a little. "I didn't hear my child calling me!"

"Melanie, don't blame yourself," Gary said gently. "Let's go upstairs and have a look at him."

"I hope he's all right," Derek said, an uneasy feeling creeping over him.

In Kyle's room Gary bent over his son and brushed back a strand of hair that was plastered to his forehead. Kyle slept fitfully, pulling away at his father's touch and whining a little. Gary straightened up.

"What on earth possessed him to do such a foolish thing?" he asked.

Melanie looked over her shoulder and saw they were alone. But she still kept her voice down. "Gary, he said Alicen made him do it. She must have dared him."

"I believe it," Gary said angrily. "The little—"

"Shh," Melanie said.

"Tell me something," Gary asked. "With Derek leaving us so abruptly and Kyle blaming Alicen for this, do you still think this house is haunted again?"

"I don't know what to think right now," Melanie said.

She put her arms around her husband, her wet hair dampening his shirt. Kyle's room was darkened by the storm outside, and silent but for the wheezing of a little boy in a huge four-poster bed. A short while later, they heard a knock at the door. Melanie let the doctor in, and the young woman came close to the bed. She looked Kyle over carefully and at last stood up.

"It's possibly pneumonia," she said. "I'll take this blood sample in for tests, in case something else is wrong."

"Something else?" Melanie asked.

"Just routine," the doctor said. "All he needs is plenty of rest and fluids. And give him one of these every four hours. I'll leave you a prescription for more."

"Is he going to be all right?" Gary asked.

"He'll be fine," the doctor said. "Call me if his fever doesn't break by morning."

"I'll do that," Melanie said.

That night, she sat by Kyle's bed and didn't close her eyes until exhaustion claimed her sometime in the morning.

24

———◆———

Gary came in sometime the next morning to insist that Melanie come downstairs for breakfast. After all, she hadn't eaten anything for dinner the night before. He had taken care of the children that morning, and now that they were off at school, he had decided it was a good time to get the entire story from his wife.

"Come on, honey," he said, pulling her gently from the chair beside Kyle's bed. "If you don't get food in you, you'll collapse."

Melanie followed him from the room without protest.

Gary poured his wife a cup of hot coffee in the kitchen. She drank it slowly, not tasting it. Gary waited for her to wake up a little more, then said, "While we have the chance, tell me exactly what happened yesterday."

"I'm not quite sure," Melanie said, yawning. "I'll tell you what I think happened. Alicen dared Kyle to go up on the roof—for whatever reason. He knew better, but he couldn't resist a dare."

"Kyle's like that," Gary said. "She probably shamed him into it."

"But Kyle wouldn't have locked himself on the roof," Melanie went on. "And he certainly would have called Alicen right away when he saw it shut. She must have heard him yelling and ignored him. Apparently, she locked him out there on purpose. But when I asked her about it, she denied everything."

"Of course," Gary said.

"I was inclined to believe her," Melanie said, "because she's never been a vicious child. Then I saw the way Kyle reacted when she came to his bedside. Gary, he became completely hysterical!"

"The poor kid," Gary said. "I believe what he said about Alicen. The question is, do you?"

"I still have to force myself," Melanie said, "but I do. I'm not sure she killed Lad—I still can't bring myself to think that. But considering the fact that she did hurt Kyle, I wouldn't put Lad's death past her."

She sipped again at the coffee. "My God," she said. "A thirteen-year-old murderess."

"It's no less believable than a two-hundred-year-old ghost," Gary said. "Melanie, now that you've seen what Alicen did, are you willing to believe our troubles will be over once we get rid of her?"

"I want to," Melanie said. "I don't want to be afraid, Gary."

"We can handle a child," Gary said. "Derek will be gone from here in a week or so, and then everything will be back to normal."

He sighed. "I hate to see him go, though. Derek's a fine therapist. The rest of his life and career are going to be ruined by a disturbed child."

"Alicen should get counseling," Melanie said. "I wish Derek would send her away right now, even if he doesn't leave himself."

"You know he won't do that," Gary said. "In spite of everything, he still feels a sense of responsibility toward her. But don't worry. We'll keep an eye on Alicen. Now that we know who to watch out for, we're perfectly safe."

Across the room an unseen figure began to laugh as she listened to that statement. Perfectly safe! It struck her as so funny that she screamed with delight, a scream heard only by those who dwelt in her own dark world.

Later in the morning, Melanie went to check Kyle's temperature. To her relief it had gone down two degrees. She kissed him and left the room again. With the children at school and Gary busy doing paperwork in his office, she decided to treat herself to a long, warm bath. She had been through such a mental ordeal that even her physical body was taxed.

She and Gary hadn't discussed Alicen with Derek yet. Not because they didn't want to, but because neither of them had had the chance. He had barely said good morning before he hurried from the house, racquet ball equipment in hand. He had tried to call Liza, needing her, but there had been no answer.

I never really liked you, Derek, Melanie thought to herself, *but I never wished this kind of heartache on you.*

She slipped out of her robe and tested the water with her toe. "But I've been hurt, too," she mused, sinking down into the water.

She closed her eyes and leaned back. The water was so hot that steam rose from it, relaxing every bone and aching muscle in Melanie's body. She heard a squaking noise but didn't open her eyes to investigate it.

She began to hum lazily. The squeaking continued.

Probably water in the pipes, she thought.

Her arm flung over the side of the tub, then pulled back with a jerk. Something wet had brushed against it. Melanie sat up with a startled cry, staring wide-eyed at a huge brown rat.

It bared its teeth at her, yellow, vicious teeth. Melanie remained perfectly still, too shocked to move. It was one of the beach rats, the filthy animals that lived among the jetty rocks. What the hell was it doing in here?

It wasn't alone. Melanie heard a whimper and slowly turned to see another one running circles around the base of the sink. At that moment Gary pushed the door open.

"Melanie? I heard you cry—" He let out a groan when he saw the rats.

"Gary, get them out of here!"

The rats moved closer together and hissed defiantly. Gary leaned heavily against the doorjamb for support. One crutch raised high in the air and came crashing down full force on one tiny head. Blood squirted across the room. While Melanie clung to the bathtub faucet, Gary made an attempt at the other one. Instead, the rodent made a blood-curdling hissing noise and flew at Gary, it's long teeth sinking into his side.

"AAAAUUUGGG!"

Melanie, forgetting her own fears for the moment, stood up and stepped out of the tub, nearly slipping on the bloody floor. She whipped a towel at the hideous creature that clung so viciously to Gary's side. Gary screamed in pain, his crutches falling from under his arms as he furiously pried at the animal. Unsupported, his legs flew out from under him, and he fell to the floor.

"Gary!"

Grimacing, he at last tore the animal away. His face was red with fury as he smashed the hideous creature against the tile floor, again and again. Melanie watched him, crying loudly, until at last she could stand no more. She pulled the dead rat from his grip and threw it across the room.

"Stop it, please!"

She moved closer to him. Gary clutched at his side, grimacing in pain. "Where d-did they come from?"

"I don't know!" Melanie cried. "Gary, I've got to get you to a doctor."

"I'm okay," Gary insisted, foolishly trying to get on his feet again. Uttering a terrible cry, he fell to the floor. "Damn it!"

Melanie, still naked, stood up now and walked to the medicine cabinet, her body dripping water that mixed with the blood on the floor, making it dangerously slippery. She found a bottle of hydrogen peroxide and a package of gauze. Carrying these in either hand, she walked carefully across the floor and knelt down beside her husband. She sniffled as she helped him get his shirt off. There was a tiny gash in his side, but it was deep, and so much blood gushed out of it that Melanie was forced to use the entire package of gauze to stop it. Although she shook as she worked, she managed to do a good job. At last she stood up and put on her robe.

"That'll hold until the ambulance comes," she said. "Please don't try to move, Gary."

"I'm okay," Gary said weakly.

"That thing could have had rabies," Melanie said firmly.

She hurried downstairs to the phone. Gary protested when the ambulance arrived, but Melanie refused to listen to him. She followed the paramedics from the house as they carried her husband on a stretcher. To her relief, they had placed the rats in a bag for inspection at the hospital.

"Please take care of him," she said.

"You're not coming?"

"I—I can't," Melanie said. "I have a sick child upstairs. Gary, call me when you can?"

"I will," Gary said. "And don't worry."

Don't worry! How many times had he spoken those words? Now,

feeling tears rise again, Melanie tightened her robe and watched the ambulance drive away.

"MOMMY?"

Kyle's frantic cry broke her spell. She ran as fast as she could. Upstairs, to her disgust, she found him staring at the bloodstained bathroom floor. She hurried to him and lifted him away.

"What are you doing out of bed?"

"I had to go," Kyle said.

Gary's cries had wakened him, and now he stood in his bare feet, trembling. Melanie took him in her arms and suddenly felt the seat of his pants becoming wet. He looked at her, embarrassed. But Melanie kissed him and said, "It's okay. You're frightened and sick. Come on back to your room and I'll get you dry pajamas."

She helped the little boy undress. Weakened by his fever, Kyle didn't protest. Melanie then tucked him under his covers and bent to kiss his perspiring forehead. He was sweating—that meant his fever was going down, thank God.

"Go to sleep, honey," she said. "You'll be all right."

She wished she could feel that way herself.

Derek had come to the spa to work off his frustrations, only to become more frustrated because he had to wait for a court. At this early hour, it was a marvel to see how many people were playing racquet ball. For a while he sat on a blue vinyl couch, staring at a bad oil painting. Then he stood up and fished a dime out of his pocket. For the tenth time that morning, he would try to get Liza on the phone. She couldn't stay away forever, could she?

Derek tried not to think that something might have happened to her. He was glad when someone answered the phone but disheartened to hear a male voice. Idiot? He'd dialed the wrong number. And now they were calling him onto the court.

It was satisfying to take out his anger on those four walls. The loud, repetitive bouncing marked his fury. BANG! That one was for Alicen. BANG! That was for that bitch Janice and how she controlled his life. BANG! That was for this job. He had once called it a godsend, but for all he cared now, God could send it to hell. BANG!

BANG! BANG! He wanted out. Away from Janice, away from Alicen, maybe even away from Liza. Where the hell was she now?

BANG! Liza's name was written on that one.

The ball sped around the court, moving so fast that its echoes were deafening. Derek dove and leaped for it, breathing heavily, sweat marking his T-shirt. It hit a high point above him and bounced to the back wall. But Derek didn't hear it hit.

He turned and saw Janice standing behind him. She was smiling, holding the ball in her hand. Dripping with sweat and panting, Derek frowned at her and held out his hand.

"Give me the ball," he said.

"No," Janice said.

Derek's arm dropped to his side. He closed his eyes and sighed. Then he opened them again.

"What do you want now?" he asked. "Isn't it enough that you forced my daughter to almost kill a little boy?"

Janice smiled. "You shouldn't talk to me like that."

"Why are you here?"

"To ask why you told that slime you aren't going to be his therapist any more."

"Don't call him slime," Derek cautioned.

"He is slime!" Janice hissed. "That whole family is slime, trash, garbage! They murdered me!"

"'They?'" Derek echoed. "Does that include Kyle and his dog? How about Gina? I suppose you engineered that bus accident—with my daughter's help."

"Alicen is a dreamer," Janice said. "I control her, and I control you. I'll keep you from leaving, Derek. I want you!"

Derek stared defiantly into her blue eyes. Why couldn't he run away from her? Why did he stay here and take this? He had a little money. He could survive until he got a job. Mary Norton would take care of him and Alicen.

What was this power Janice had over him?

"You'd better leave," he said. "My half-hour's up, and someone's bound to come onto the court."

"They won't see me," Janice said. "Only you can see me."

She moved closer to him, putting her arms around him. Derek was surprised to find she smelled like flowers. No, like the beach. And

then like the perfume Elaine had always worn. He closed his eyes
and gave in to her.

"Court time is over, sir," a voice said.

Derek's eyes snapped open. He was standing alone, his racket
hanging at his side.

"I'm sorry," he said, embarrassed. "I played too hard."

"Why don't you relax in the whirlpool?" the man said.

Derek smiled. He went into the locker room, looking around, expecting her to show up. She was making him paranoid. Even the
whirlpool didn't help. Derek got out when the memory of Liza came
to him—the day they had slipped beneath the water together. Where
was Liza now?

What had Janice done to her?

Derek cut off that thought, like he had cut off so many others, and
went to the locker room to shower and dress. He was surprised to see
it was nearly two o'clock before he left the building. He passed a
tanned, blond-haired man on his way out, but didn't even notice
him.

Melanie moved slowly back and forth in the antique rocking chair
as she stared out the bay windows at the sky. She had been unable to
work, nervously waiting for Gary's call. Why was it taking so long?

She thought of Alicen and felt a mixture of pity, anger, and of relief. It was easy to handle a thirteen-year-old mortal, wasn't it?

She felt a hand on her shoulder. Gina, who had come home from
school just a half hour earlier, wondered why her mother looked so
sad. It had something to do with daddy, of course. She knew her father would never go out with Kyle so sick.

"Where's daddy?" she asked.

Melanie turned her gaze from the window and leaned sideways
against the chair's slats. Gina was looking at her with worried eyes,
eyes that told Melanie she wanted to know the truth. Yet Melanie
couldn't give in to them. How could she tell this beautiful young girl
about the rats and rabies?

"He went to the hospital for tests," she said at last.

"He had tests done just a short while ago," Gina said warily.

"I know," Melanie said, building the lie, "but this bad weather made his bones hurt so much that he figured he'd better have them checked out. He'll be staying overnight, but I'm sure he'll be back tomorrow."

"Oh, mom," Gina sighed, putting her arms around Melanie's neck. "Everything is so bad lately, just when we were going to start a nice summer." She pulled away. "How's Kyle?"

"Sleeping," Melanie said. "His fever is broken, but his temperature isn't normal yet. I'll call the doctor if things don't change more drastically by tomorrow."

"Poor Kyle," Gina said. "And damned old Alicen!"

"Gina!"

Gina frowned. "I'm sorry. But she is. She wouldn't talk to me again today. Even when I tried to make her think I'd believe her story about Kyle. I mean, we haven't heard her side yet. It's only fair."

"Alicen won't talk to me, either," Melanie said.

"She's weird," Gina replied. "She didn't talk to anyone today. Not even Jamie Hutchinson, and she's in love with him."

"Jamie Hutchinson?" Melanie repeated. "Is he the red-haired boy I met the day of the bus accident?"

"Yeah."

And the one who got Alicen started on all this, with his stories of murder, Melanie thought.

But she didn't tell Gina this. Instead, she used the opportunity to change the subject. She asked about Jamie, and soon Gina was babbling on about the boys in her school. The mood lightened, and both mother and daughter began to relax. Until the phone rang. It was Gary, at last.

"No rabies," he said.

"Thank God," Melanie whispered. She fought tears of relief and managed to laugh at herself for spending the entire afternoon in that damned rocking chair, expecting the worst and accomplishing nothing.

"When are you coming home?" she asked.

"That's the clincher," Gary said. "The fall I took messed me up a little. I'll be here for the weekend."

"Oh, God!"

"Melanie, Derek is there if you need help," Gary said.

"I know that," Melanie answered. "And I can take care of things myself. I'm worried about you. What's wrong with you?"

"Just a bad sprain in my ankle," Gary said. "It isn't too serious."

"But Gary," Melanie protested, "your legs weren't strong to begin with. Are you sure it isn't serious, or are you just trying to make me feel better?"

"I could put Dr. Norton on the line," Gary suggested.

Melanie sighed. "I believe you."

There was a long silence, in which Melanie heard the distant sound of the hospital P.A. system. Then she said, "What am I going to tell the children?"

"Haven't they asked yet?"

"Gina did," said Melanie. "Nancy's at a birthday party, and of course Kyle is sleeping. I told Gina you were just going in for more tests."

"That's good enough."

"But I told her you'd be coming home tomorrow," Melanie said.

"You can think of some excuse," Gary said. "Our kids know how slow hospitals are."

Melanie nodded, as if Gary could see her. "I love you," she said.

"I love you," Gary answered. "Don't worry. I'll be home before you know it."

At dinner Melanie told Gina and Nancy about slow hospitals. They listened sympathetically, Nancy sad that her daddy was sick again, Gina not believing a word of her mother's story. But she knew better than to push things. It was bad enough that just the three of them were sharing dinner. Kyle, of course, was unable to join them, Alicen refused to eat, and Derek hadn't yet come home.

In the loneliness of the house that night, Melanie was unable to sleep. She decided to go downstairs and read for a little while. She curled herself up on the sofa in the library, her head on a bolster, and flipped lazily through a book.

A few pages blew over in a cold wind that swept through the room. Melanie sat up, looking around. It seemed her heart had stopped beating.

She heard a familiar voice. "Melanie," it said.

"You've come back again," Melanie said when the dark-haired, ragged woman appeared. She didn't shrink away, knowing this woman was her friend.

"I've come to warn you for the last time," the woman said. "You must leave this place, before it is too late."

"I can't leave," Melanie said. "I have a sick child, who can't be moved. But—you said this is your last time? Why?"

"I took great risks coming here," the woman said. "If I return again, she will surely learn of me."

"Who is she?" Melanie asked. "At least tell me that!"

"I dare not speak her name," the woman said.

"Then tell me why you've come to help me. I don't know who you are."

"You know me," the woman said. "It is because of me that evil fell upon this house. His love for me has condemned my lover to eternal suffering in hell. But I am a good Christian woman, and perhaps, by the mercy of God, I can lessen his suffering. I came here to temper the evil of this house with kindness. But no one listens to me, and she is still strong!"

Melanie reached out a hand to put it on the woman's shoulder. But the woman shrank away from her.

"I must leave now," she said. "My Jacob awaits my return."

She was gone. Melanie stared at the now empty space where the woman had just stood, unmoving. *My Jacob?*

Melanie shot to her feet and cried out: "*Lydia?*"

There was no answer. But Melanie knew now who the woman was. It was Lydia Browning—Jacob Armand's lover! The woman who had been burned at the stake for witchcraft while Jacob stood witness. It was the pursuit of her that had brought Jacob's wrath down on Melanie's family the year before.

But why had Lydia come? Did this mean Jacob Armand had nothing to do with all this? Lydia kept talking of a woman. Who? What woman had reason to hate the VanBurens so?

There were too many questions. And Melanie feared the answers would come all too soon.

———◆———

25

Alicen could barely make out Kyle's silhouette in the darkness of his room. She stood near his bed, a pillow clutched in her hands, listening to the uneven sounds of his breathing. The doctor had said he had caught pneumonia up on the roof, and they were blaming her for it. As the other Alicen, she had believed in her innocence, but now she remembered the incident on the roof. She smiled. Her mother had been pleased with her.

Now it was time to finish the job . . . .

With her fingers tightening around the pillow, Alicen leaned closer to the sleeping figure. Closer—

Kyle stirred in his sleep, mumbling something. Alicen backed away, her heart pounding. Had she wakened him?

"Do it," a voice commanded.

Alicen nodded. "Okay, mommy."

And the pillow was pressed to Kyle's freckled, angelic face.

Alicen pushed with all her might, hearing her mother's voice. "Kill him, Alicen! Kill the brat!"

Emotionless, Alicen stared down at the little figure. Mommy said kill. Mommy loved her. Mommy made her do the right things—

"AAAUUUGGGHH!"

It was Alicen's own cry. Something had struck her under the chin —a small, bare foot. She regained herself and threw her body on top of Kyle's. Somehow, she had pressed the pillow at the wrong angle, leaving a channel in the folds for Kyle to breathe through. He was fully awake, kicking and screaming.

"*Mommy!*"

"Shhhh!" Alicen hissed.

"*Stop it! Stop!*" Kyle yelled hoarsely, his screams torturing his sore throat.

He was like a tiger under Alicen's body, clawing and kicking and biting. Alicen couldn't handle him much longer. Why wasn't her mother helping her?

At that moment Melanie burst into the room to find Alicen straddling Kyle, her fingers around his small neck. Kyle's face was crimson with rage and fear, and his arms and legs seemed to be everywhere. Without a moment's hesitation, Melanie ran to the bed, grabbed Alicen by the hair, and threw her across the room. The girl cried out in pain and ran out. Ignoring her, Melanie climbed onto the bed and took Kyle in her arms.

"Oh, God," she whispered. "Oh, my God."

Over Kyle's blond curls, growing wet with her tears, she saw a blue-and-white-striped pillow. A pillow that didn't belong in Kyle's room.

"Alicen tried to hurt me," Kyle whimpered.

"Shh," Melanie said. "Mommy's here. It's okay."

"Make her go away!" Kyle cried.

"I'll do that," Melanie promised. "Alicen won't hurt anyone again."

She was furious. How could anyone hurt a little boy? Kyle had suffered so much. Alicen had been cruel to lure him onto the roof through that trapdoor. And now the pillow—

Her thoughts skipped backward. Through the trapdoor? But how did Alicen know about it? Melanie herself had only discovered it a few months earlier.

Was she the someone, that mysterious "she" that Lydia had warned about?

She wished Gary was there. Or even Derek. Where the hell was he? He'd been gone all day long, leaving this mess to her. God damn him, Melanie thought. She's his daughter.

"Mom, what's going on?"

Gina was at the door, holding hands with her sister. Both girls were in pink nightgowns, barefoot. Nancy had her thumb in her mouth. Her blue eyes seemed to fill her face.

"Did you see Alicen?" Melanie asked.

"She ran by me," Gina said. "She was crying. What's wrong?"

"She tried to kill your brother," Melanie said, before she could stop herself. She was too angered to smooth things for her children's sake.

Gina cried out, and Nancy's face contorted as if she would start crying.

"I hate Alicen!" Gina cried. "She's mean and bad! I *hate* her!"

"Make her go away, mommy," Nancy said.

"I will," Melanie said. She opened her arms, and her daughters ran to her.

"Why is Alicen so mean?" Nancy asked, her round face pressed against Melanie's stomach.

"Alicen's sick," Melanie said. "She's a sick little girl."

Gina's frown deepened, but she didn't say anything. Melanie could almost feel the child's emotions. She crushed her children to her and said, "No one will hurt you. Never again."

She knew she should leave the house at once. If Lydia had been telling the truth, then their unseen enemy could strike at any moment. But how could she leave? How could she move the children, when one was so very sick? More important, where would she go at this hour of the night?

So, Melanie did the next best thing. That night she took the room next to Alicen's, leaving the door open. There was no way she could get past Melanie's room without her knowing. Melanie's eyes didn't close once that night, and her eyes were turned for any unusual noise. The house was deadly silent, except for an occasional mumble from Alicen's room. What was she saying, over and over? *Mommy?*

She thought about the trapdoor, meaning to ask Derek about it when she saw him tomorrow. She prayed he would say he had told Alicen it was up there.

At four in the morning, Melanie heard the front door open. Derek had returned home at last.

Melanie had gotten her daughters off to school the next morning and had gone upstairs to paint. But how could she concentrate? An hour's work had produced a hideous piece of garbage. It was the work of an amateur, not the professional she was supposed to be. The colors were all wrong, the buildings out of proportion. Angrily, Melanie picked it up and threw it across the room.

"Hey!"

It had struck Derek. Well fine, Melanie thought. He deserves it.

"It's about time you're up," she snapped.

Derek bent to pick up the painting without answering her. He propped it on the sofa.

"I was in late last night," he said.

"I know," Melanie said. "Where the hell were you?"

Derek backed away a little. He couldn't tell her where he had been. After leaving Janice, he had driven for miles and miles, clear out to Montauk. He'd driven until he was ready to drop from exhaustion, and then had fallen asleep at a rest stop. He hadn't wanted to come home to that woman or to Alicen. And now Melanie was giving him this.

"I don't think that's any of your business," he said quietly.

Melanie lifted a small can of turpentine and slammed it down on a table.

"It damn well is my business!" she screamed. "That brat of yours tried to murder my son last night!"

Derek fell down to the couch as if Melanie had punched him. His mouth hung open, and he stared up at Melanie in disbelief. Alicen had tried to kill Kyle?

But why was he so surprised? He had known this was coming.

"Oh, don't sit there like an idiot," Melanie growled. "Don't you have anything to say?"

Derek breathed deeply. "Tell me what happened," he said with forced calm.

"I heard Kyle screaming and ran to his room," Melanie said. "I found Alicen in his bed, with her hands around his neck. And there was a pillow on the floor that didn't belong in his room. She had tried to smother him, Derek."

Derek rubbed at his eyes. "Dear God."

He looked up at Melanie. "Where is my daughter?"

"She locked herself in her room," Melanie said. "Derek, I want her out of this house. No later than Monday, even if she has to go without you."

"I'll do what I can," Derek said, knowing he would never be able to get away from the house. "Let me talk to my daughter."

A few moments later, he knocked at Alicen's locked door, but there was no answer.

"What should I do, mommy?" Alicen whispered.

"Let him in."

"Alicen!" Derek called.

Alicen walked across the room and opened the door. Derek entered the room, saw a filmy cloud by the window, and frowned. He knew what that cloud was, even if Alicen didn't. And it was about time Alicen *did* know.

"That isn't your mother," he said abruptly.

In the silence that followed, Derek waited for the consequences. But Alicen merely gave her head a shake, and disembodied laughter filled the room.

"Derek, she's as much in my power as you are," a voice said. "She thinks I'm her mother, the little fool!"

"You bitch!" Derek roared, pushing Alicen aside to lunge at the filmy mass hovering over the floor. His hand slammed hard against the window. The laughter continued.

"Derek!"

Melanie had entered the room just as he fell against the window. She looked at him, then at Alicen. Derek straightened himself, rubbing his wrists.

"Please leave this to me, Melanie," he said, approaching Alicen. "She's my daughter."

"I heard someone yell, and—"

She turned back to Alicen when she heard her speaking. The girl was rocking back and forth on the bed, glaring at Melanie.

"I want you to die," she sneered. "I want *all* of you to die."

It wasn't Alicen's voice at all. Melanie stared wide-eyed at her, terror filling her. Why did she recognize that voice? Where had she heard it before?

"Go away!" Derek yelled, not at Melanie, but at the spirit in Alicen's body.

"Derek, what's wrong with her?" Melanie demanded.

"Die!" Alicen screeched. "Die! Die! Die!"

Suddenly Derek burst into tears. His macho, self-assured image was shattered, and he felt no shame when he ran to Melanie's arms.

"Please help me," he sobbed.

"Derek, she'll be okay," Melanie soothed, as much to reassure herself as him. She felt terror creeping inside her. Alicen's voice stayed in her mind, taunting her. She knew that voice. But how? From where?

"Derek, come out of the room," she said. "There's so much to discuss. Alicen will be okay for a while."

And then, as she had done so many times when comforting her children, she kissed him gently.

There was a scream, and suddenly Alicen was on her father's back, pummeling him. "You're mine! You're mine!"

Derek fought her, gathering his strength back together. He knew it wasn't his daughter who reacted so jealously to that simple kiss. And it wasn't his daughter he struck so violently. As Melanie watched in horror, he threw her on the bed and slapped her again and again. Melanie grabbed his arms and tried to pull him away.

"She's out, Derek! Stop it!"

He ignored her, seeing Janice's face.

"Derek, let it go!"

At last she managed to jerk him away from the child before he killed her. Derek stared down at Alicen, his mouth open in shock. What had he done? She was innocent Alicen again, her round face covered with ugly red marks. A bruise grew under one eye.

Ashamed of himself, that he had let himself give in to his emotions, Derek let out a wail. He turned and ran from the room, wanting to get as far away as possible.

"Derek, come back!" Melanie cried, chasing after him.

She caught him just as he reached the front door and raced around him to block his path. Breathing heavily, she pointed to the living room and said, "Please come inside and talk to me. There's something going on here, and I want to know what it is."

"My daughter—"

"I think it's more than your daughter, Derek," Melanie said. "I don't know why, but I do. Please sit down and talk to me!"

Derek nodded slowly, not knowing what he'd say to her. The two entered the living room together and sat on the burgundy sofa. Melanie brushed her hair out of her face and said, "Derek, some things have happened lately that make me wonder if your daughter is simply disturbed, or if she's somehow—say, possessed."

"There's no such thing as possession," Derek said, though no one believed in it more strongly than he.

"Derek, you don't really know the history of this house," Melanie said. "What we told you of Jacob Armand was only the beginning. But there's much more. This is an evil house, Derek. And a young girl like Alicen could easily fall victim to it."

And a full-grown man like me, Derek thought bitterly.

"What—uh—what makes you say this?" he asked.

"Two things," Melanie said, "although I'm sure I could think of a few more. Firstly, the fact that Alicen knew there was a trapdoor to the roof. I never told her that, and as far as I know, neither did Gary. Why would he? And secondly, that voice I heard. I know that voice, Derek! I can't place it, but I've heard it before."

Derek said nothing. He turned and stared into the cold fireplace, trying to come up with an answer. Then he heard a voice in his head, telling him exactly what to say. He turned back to Melanie, his expression serene.

"There are simple answers to those things," he said, repeating the words in his mind. "Gary told me of the trapdoor, and I mentioned it to Alicen, not realizing she'd be foolish enough to investigate it."

"That makes sense," Melanie said. "But the voice?"

"Liza's voice," Derek said very quickly. "Alicen is tremendously jealous of my relationship with Liza. She was tormenting me, using that voice. That's what you recognized."

"Derek, I never met Liza," Melanie said.

"But you did speak to her on the phone once or twice," Derek said. "Which would explain why you didn't recognize the voice right away."

Melanie thought a moment. It made so much sense, and she desperately wanted to believe in Derek's explanations. Why then, did she still feel so uneasy?

"Derek, that child should be put in a hospital," she said. "Not only for her sake, but for my children's safety."

Derek, who on the outside appeared very calm, was being torn apart by guilt and shame. The mention of a hospital for Alicen made him want to scream with rage. He'd beaten his daughter. He'd beaten a little girl.

"No!" he cried. "No, she stays until I leave. Monday—I promise you."

"Derek, she needs a doctor *now*," Melanie insisted.

"No!" Derek jumped to his feet and ran from the room. Before Melanie could stop him, he was out to his car and climbing behind the wheel. He ignored Melanie's calls and sped down the hill.

As he drove along the beachside, he saw mothers with their children. Their fresh faces and smiles made him think all the more of his hateful deed. He was grateful when he was at last able to turn onto Houston Street. Its steel and asphalt simplicity were soothing to him.

When he reached the intersection of the main street into town, he stopped and caught his breath. He could keep going straight, of course. Houston Street led to an exit ramp for the parkway, and the parkway would take him far, far away. He could forget Alicen, Liza, the VanBurens—

Suddenly he felt a touch on his shoulder. It was Janice.

"Can't you leave me alone for a moment?"

"Not when you try to get away from me," Janice said. Anger flashed in her blue eyes.

"How did you know what I was thinking?"

"I know everything in your mind," she said.

Derek began to drive again. "You made me hurt my daughter."

"You hated her anyway."

"I never hated her!"

Janice ignored the outburst. Keeping his eyes on the road, Derek turned the car into town. He tried to pretend she wasn't there, so hideously close to him.

"Where are you going?" He didn't answer. "Where are you going?" Janice asked again. "You're going to that bitch Liza's house, aren't you? Well, you won't find her! You'll never see her again. She'd dead, Derek Miller."

"Leave me alone!" Derek shouted.

He heard her laughter and wanted to strike her with all his might. But when he turned, she was gone. He sped to Liza's house, all the time praying Janice was only taunting him. He wanted to stop and catch his breath but somehow found himself running up the stairs and pounding on Liza's door.

"Hold your horses!" someone yelled from inside—a man's voice. The door jerked open, and Derek found himself looking at a blond-haired man. The two studied each other for a moment before Owen spoke.

"What do you want?" he asked. "You could've broken the door down!"

"I—I'm looking for L-Liza Crewe," Derek said, panting heavily. The run up the stairs had exhausted him—he wasn't in the shape he used to be.

"You're Derek, right?"

"Yea," Derek said. "Who're you?"

Liza's found someone new.

"Owen Crewe," was the reply. "I'm Liza's brother."

Derek simply nodded. He had almost hoped it was a new lover that kept Liza away from him. That would at least prove she was still alive.

"Come in," Owen said. "I've been looking for you."

Derek sat on a couch he had shared with Liza several weeks earlier, while Owen sat in a leather and chrome chair across the room. He studied his face for so long that Derek felt himself becoming nervous. There again, that was Janice's doing. He'd never been paranoid in his life.

"You seemed in a rush to get in here," Owen said at last. "What's the matter?"

What was the matter? How could Derek answer that? There was no voice in his head to tell him what to say now. So he thought carefully before answering.

"I was driving through town," he said finally, "and I was thinking about Liza. I've been trying to get in contact with her for a week. I thought she was mad at me, but she would have come around with an explanation by now, wouldn't she?"

Owen nodded.

"Anyway," Derek continued, "I decided to come up here and confro—make her listen to me once and for all. If I did something to offend her, I'd like to know what it was. But I know I didn't do anything wrong. I keep wondering, then, why the hell she disappeared."

"That makes two of us," Owen said. "I came up from Florida for a convention last week. I have to say I found it a little unnerving to come here and find my sister missing. Liza's not one to go wandering off somewhere without letting anyone know."

"No, she isn't," Derek said.

"Why don't we go over that last time you were together?" Owen suggested. Seeing a defensive look in Derek's eyes, he added, "I think it would help, don't you? There may be a clue."

"I've been over it a thousand times," Derek said. "She came to visit me at my home. We went for a walk on the beach, and I asked her to marry me—we've been dating awhile. She said yes and seemed ecstatic. So, after a while, we said goodbye and made plans to see each other again."

That was a lie, since Derek had made no such plans. Or maybe he just didn't remember them, he thought defensively.

"There was no argument, then," Owen said.

"None whatsoever," Derek answered.

He stood up and walked to the window at the back of the room. Staring out at the town, all green and bright with summer, he felt something rise from his stomach. He held his breath for a moment, then said quietly, "I think something happened to her."

Owen stood up now. "I've been trying to keep that thought from my mind," he said. "What makes you say so?"

"I don't know," Derek lied. "There are just too many unanswered questions."

"We could look for her together," Owen said.

Derek's reply was too swift. "No!"

He slowed himself down. "I mean," he said, "it would probably be best to let the police handle this."

He wouldn't admit he was terrified of what he'd find if he looked too hard. Owen was staring at him again, the suspicious bastard. Did he think Derek was responsible for Liza's disappearance?

He made an excuse to leave. "Listen, my daughter is home sick," he said, hating the truth in those words. "I should be with her. What if I come back tomorrow?"

"Please," Owen said, feeling uneasy about Derek's swift goodbye.

Without saying anything more, Derek left the house. He was too busy with his own thoughts to look up in his rear-view mirror a few minutes later to see that Owen was following him.

26

---◆---

Smiling, Melanie stepped away from Kyle's bed. His fever had gone down considerably and was now only a degree above normal. He'd be his old, energetic self in just a few days. She wished she could say the same about Alicen. Applying lotion to the cuts on her face had brought out the mother instinct in Melanie. Seeing that little girl, all battered and so frail, she couldn't help feeling sorry for her. She was sick and in need of help and understanding. She wasn't responsible for her actions.

But, then, who was?

The voice she had used in her threats stuck in Melanie's mind. She wanted to believe that it was Liza's voice, but something made her think otherwise. She had an uneasy feeling that she had heard that voice before, and not when talking on the phone with Derek's girlfriend. Still, it made sense. Alicen might have mimicked the voice to make her father angry. Melanie knew that Derek had been unable to get in touch with his girlfriend. And, for God's sake, who else would the voice belong to?

Gary would have fits if he heard you now, she told herself. *Stop it! It was Liza's voice you heard.*

She went downstairs to the kitchen. The children would be home soon, and she wanted to fix them a nice dinner. She would do it more to prove to herself than to them that nothing supernatural was going on. A good, ordinary meal on the table would show Gina and Nancy that, in spite of the bad things that had happened in the last few days, everything was going to be all right. Or so Melanie hoped.

But to her frustration, she opened the refrigerator to find it practically empty. In all the confusion of the past week, she had forgotten to stock up on groceries. And the weekend was coming.

Melanie hated to leave Kyle alone with Derek, remembering his angered outburst that morning. But what was she supposed to tell the girls when they came home? That she was too frightened to go out of the house? But she wanted them to see that life would go on as usual, and that meant having dinner with their mother. So Melanie reasoned that Derek had been angered only momentarily at Alicen, and wouldn't harm Kyle. Besides, if she left soon, she would be home before the girls. And Kyle would probably sleep all afternoon.

Just then, she heard the front door open. She left the kitchen and went out in the hallway to meet Derek. He looked tired, his eyes rimmed with red. Melanie went to him.

"I suppose you called a doctor for Alicen," he said.

"I thought I should let you do that," Melanie said.

"Thank you," Derek said, grateful no one else would have to know of his terrible crime.

"Now I have a favor to ask of you," Melanie said. "Would you stay with Kyle for just a little while so I can go to the store? The refrigerator is empty, and I don't want my kids starving on top of everything else."

"I guess it would be all right." Derek sighed.

"Don't worry," Melanie said. "I'll be back before the girls are home."

She left the house.

It was so silent. Derek hated that. He wanted the house to creak and moan, just to let him know it was like any other old house. But it wasn't, was it? Any moment, that heavy silence could fall down on him. She'd be back, for certain, knowing how vulnerable he was right now.

But the house remained silent. Derek opened the door to his room and looked around, expecting to see her. No sign of her. He stretched himself on the bed, putting his hands behind his neck and staring at the ceiling.

He waited.

Hearing the sound of an engine, Owen Crewe ducked behind a tree. He watched the car drive by him on the gravel road, seeing a blond woman behind the wheel. When she passed, he came out of his hiding place and continued up the road. Not wanting Derek to see him, he had parked his car at the public beach and had walked the mile to these woodlands. He could see the huge white house at the top of the hill. How could anyone afford a place like that, he wondered? He thought of Liza's reaction upon seeing the place, with those towers and that porch.

But he was more interested in the woodlands that surrounded it. They were so thick that anything could have happened to Liza in them—and no one would have seen. They led to the beach, no doubt, the last place Derek said he had been with Liza. Owen had a feeling that Derek had been lying when he said he knew nothing of Liza's disappearance.

At last he found a path that cut through the woods. Looking around to be sure no one was watching, he turned onto it.

"I don't see mom's car," Gina said as she and Nancy climbed up the hill, leaving the school bus behind them.

"Maybe she went out to a gallery or something?" Nancy suggested.

"Yeah, but she wouldn't have left Kyle alone," Gina said. "Not with crazy Alicen."

She broke into a run, her long legs covering the ground in strides. Nancy protested, unable to keep up with her, and finally let her sister go on alone. She climbed the porch steps and entered through the door Gina had left open.

"Gina!" she cried.

"I'm up in Kyle's room," Gina called back.

Nancy found her sister sitting on Kyle's bed. The little boy was fully awake, propped against his pillow. Nancy, too, jumped on the bed. The three children began to talk.

"Do you think all this stuff is scarier than last year?"

"I don't know, Kyle," Gina said. "Everybody got hurt, like last year. But this time we know why. It wasn't a ghost."

"I don't wanna talk about ghosts," Nancy pouted.

"Okay," Gina said. "But if you ask me, Alicen's scarier. How could she do all this?"

"I hate her," Kyle stated.

"Where is she, anyway?" Gina asked.

"How should I know?" Kyle said. "As long as she stays there."

"And where's mommy?" Nancy asked. "We didn't see her car. Did she go away?"

"No, she had to go to the grocery," Kyle said. "I started yelling for her, and Derek came in and told me." He brought a hand to his throat. "Boy, that hurt when I yelled."

"Mom left you alone with crazy Alicen?" Gina said.

"Derek said there was no food in the house," Kyle reported. "Gina, can't we stop this? Talking about Alicen gives me the creeps."

"Sure," Gina obliged. She looked around the room for something to do, and underneath Kyle's dresser, she spotted a Monopoly game. She pulled it out and set it up on Kyle's lap.

"Mommy'll be home soon, I bet," she said as she shook the dice.

They tried to concentrate on the game, pushing aside their fears. But Melanie didn't come home soon, and after a while it became too much to wait for her. Nancy started to whine, and Kyle became listless. Trying to cheer them, and herself, Gina put the tiny metal dog inside the little car and pretended it was driving around the board. The trick worked, and soon all the children were laughing. It was nervous laughter, uncontrollable and silly. To the unseen woman who saw it, it was also hateful. Janice went to the bed and knocked the board from it.

"Kyle, you kicked it!" Gina said.

"I guess so," Kyle answered, still laughing. "Isn't it funny?"

Funny! Janice echoed. *When I'm through today, you won't be laughing.*

She willed herself to Derek's room. Gathering herself into her most solid form, she climbed onto the bed. Derek's eyes opened wide when she planted an icy kiss on his lips.

"It's time," she said.

"Time?"

"You know what I mean," Janice replied. "They're alone, aren't they?"

She kissed him again, running her cold fingers through his thick hair. Then she sat back on his hips. The bed did not sag beneath her, but Derek felt pressure. He frowned.

"They're just kids," he said. "What the hell could they have done to you?"

"Don't ask questions," Janice said, rising. "Stand up and come with me."

Derek sat up, pressing his fists into the mattress. But he didn't move. Somehow, the visit with Owen Crewe had strengthened him. He wouldn't listen to anyone who hurt his beloved Liza.

"No," he said.

Janice turned, her eyes surprised.

"What did you say?"

"I said no," Derek repeated. His strong voice belied the weakness in his stomach. But he wouldn't stop now. "If you want to hurt them, I know I can't stop you. But I won't help you."

"You bastard!" Janice screeched. "You'll do as I say!"

She lunged at him, her fingers curled like talons. They sought the flesh of his cheeks and ripped down them. Derek cried out and pulled away.

"You're my slave!" Janice hissed, striking him.

"No!"

He stared into her eyes, and saw them change. The face blurred, widened, became Elaine's face. But this time, Derek was able to look at it. He knew it wasn't his wife's face at all, but a cruel apparition. Janice screamed with rage and struck him again.

"You're my slave!" she cried. "My slave and my lover! You'll obey me!"

How could he dare defy her? She would show him. He would learn what terrible things she could do to him, in spite of the fact that she craved his affections almost above vengeance against the VanBurens.

She threw herself at him, pressing her fingers to his throat. He gagged and tried to grab for her wrists. Stupid thing to do, they passed through them as if nothing were there.

"Go away!" Derek cried. "You don't exist!"

Janice laughed and bent to kiss him. He was so handsome. Her tongue pried his lips open, found his tongue, and sucked hard at it, as if to drain his courage. Derek sank down away from her, wishing he could fall through the bed, through the floor. Anything to get away from her passionate kisses!

"Let me alone," he demanded hoarsely.

"Never," Janice said.

She tossed her head back, the lackluster hair falling over her thin, lifeless shoulders. She began to stare at him. The filminess in her eyes began to drain away, and the irises became as sharp and clear as they had ever been when Janice was alive. In those eyes there was a devilish power, a power Derek could not resist. It weakened him more than the sight of Elaine's twisted face, more than the thought that he might never see Liza again. Why? Why did those eyes have such power over him?

After all his resistance, it took only a pair of eyes to turn him inside out. He sat up and put his head against her, not realizing what he was doing. The room began to spin, and her voice sounded as if she were speaking through a long tunnel.

"Take them where their mother won't find them," she said, stroking his thick hair as if he were a child. "I will be there in time to punish them. But first they must suffer in darkness."

"Suffer," Derek said.

Janice kissed him. And then she was gone.

Derek sat up on the bed, his head dropped down to his chest. His heart thudded so loudly that he thought everyone could hear. He tried to quiet it. Otherwise, how could he sneak up on them?

Rubbing his eyes, he stood up and walked from the room. Alicen was waiting in the hallway, dressed in a loose white nightgown.

"Daddy?"

Derek moved past her without answering. Alicen watched his retreating figure, feeling tears rise. She had been lying in bed, knowing he was across the hall, waiting for him to come apologize for beating her that morning. Why did he have to hurt her so, now that mommy was back again? Why couldn't they be a happy family again?

She'd get even with him, that's what she'd do. She'd go into his room and tear it apart and mess up his clothes and use a crayon all over the furniture and . . .

The three VanBuren children, having grown bored with the Monopoly game, were now coloring—even Gina, who was too old for such things. But it made Kyle happy when she shared things with him. They colored the pictures, leaving the game board and all its pieces on the floor. Cleaning up could wait until later.

"Nancy, the sun is yellow," Kyle said. "Why are you making it purple?"

"I like purple."

"Well, I think it's dumb," Kyle said. "Everyone knows—"

His words were cut off when the door swung open. Derek entered the room and stopped to look at them. The three children didn't speak, mesmerized by the coldness in his eyes. He looked so mean.

Gina moved closer to Kyle and pulled Nancy to her. The three children huddled together, watching Derek move to Kyle's closet. He removed a flannel robe and held it out to the boy. At last Gina spoke up.

"What's going on?" she demanded.

"Put this on, Kyle," Derek ordered. "We're going out."

"Out?" Gina echoed. "Are you nuts or something? Kyle can't go out!"

"Don't talk back," Derek said in a warning tone.

"But why do you want us to go out?" Kyle asked. "Mommy'll be home soon, and she'll be so mad."

"If you don't put on the robe and come with me," Derek cautioned, "I'll get my belt and—"

He moved closer to the bed, away from the door. Seeing a chance, Gina jumped from the bed and ran as fast as she could. Derek tried to grab her flying hair, but she was too fast for him. She disappeared around the corner of the hallway, Derek running after her.

I have to get to the stairs! Gina thought.

But someone was standing there. A blond woman. Gina stopped in her tracks. Her mouth dropped open, and she gaped wide-eyed at the woman who blocked her way down. She couldn't be there, she was dead! Crazy Derek was making her so scared she was seeing things.

"You aren't real," Gina said, her voice trembling. "You're dead!"

But the woman didn't go away. Frozen, Gina stood her ground, not thinking that Derek was coming to find her. She could hear him yelling down one of the hallways. But she was too mesmerized by the vision. The woman smiled wickedly at her. Once Gina had loved her smile. She had been so sweet then. Mommy had met her when they were having all that trouble with Jacob Armand, and she always made them feel better. But Jacob had killed her, mommy said. She was dead.

"Gina, you God-damned brat!"

Derek's shouting broke the spell, and just as he lunged for her, she found her feet. Hardly feeling the floor, she sped down the hallway, reaching its end only to find there was no place to go. She turned, bursting into a bedroom with Derek only a few feet away.

"No!" Gina screamed even as she threw the door shut and locked it. Derek's body fell against it, pounding. The girl could feel vibrations all through her body as she leaned heavily against the door, crying. But after a few terrifying moments, the pounding stopped.

"I'll be back, Gina," Derek said.

Gina listened to the soft thudding of his shoes on the carpet as he retreated. Then, trembling, she turned around. Her breath caught in her throat—the room was in a complete shambles. Someone had torn the covers from the bed, and now they were tossed here and there. So were Derek's clothes, ripped from the room's single dresser and hanging from the bedposts and curtain rods as if they had been thrown around by a madman. Worse than this, the lovely antique bed and dresser were covered with crayon marks.

Gina looked around at all this in a stupor, not believing it. Her eyes fell on a message scrawled across the mirror on the closet door.

MOMMY AND DADDY LOVE ALICEN.

Now she heard a whimpering noise and turned to it. A moment later, Alicen stood up. She had been hiding behind the bed, and now she threw herself on it, oblivious of Gina. The other child felt herself crying again. No! She couldn't be locked here in this room, alone with crazy Alicen!

"I'm sorry, daddy," Alicen whimpered into the bare mattress. "I'm sorry."

Hearing her babbling made Gina all the more nervous, and she burst out sobbing. Alicen sat up, glaring at Gina. What was she doing in here? But then her eyes softened. Gina was her friend. She had made her happy that first day she'd come here. And she needed someone to talk to so much.

If she couldn't have a mother and father right now, a friend would do nicely. Just for now.

"Hi, Gina," she said, as if nothing were wrong.

"H-hi, Alicen," Gina replied, not knowing what else to say. How do you talk to a crazy person?

"I'm sorry I messed up this nice room," Alicen said. "I was mad at my father, 'cause he hurt me."

Gina took in the girl's bruised and bloodied face. For a moment, seeing that Alicen was just as vulnerable as any other girl, Gina forgot her fears. She went to the bed and sat down.

"Your father tried to hurt me, too," she said. "And he's got Kyle and Nancy. What'll he do with them?"

She was afraid of the answer, but didn't get one anyway. Alicen simply nodded.

"My father has a terrible temper," she said. "He's going to beat me for doing this, but I don't care."

"Your father shouldn't beat you," Gina said. "It's wrong."

What was he doing now, with Kyle and Nancy? She should run from the room to rescue them, but she was so afraid. Why didn't her mother come home?

"My mother won't let him hurt me, though," Alicen was saying now.

"Your mother?" Gina replied. "But she's dead."

"She is not!" Alicen cried. "She's right here in this house!"

Gina backed away, suddenly understanding. Janice had made Alicen believe she was her mother.

"Alicen, that isn't your mother at all," she said. "It's a woman named Janice Lors. She was murdered here seven months ago."

"No!"

"You don't have a mother!"

"Yes, I do, yes, I do! Dead people don't give beautiful presents!"

She jumped to the floor, pounding it with her fists and screaming. She grabbed at the heavy floor grating and ripped it up with no effort and threw it across the floor. Her hand thrust into the dark crevice, and when she drew it back, she was holding Sarah's ring. Gina gasped.

"Mommy gave this to me!" she shouted triumphantly.

"Alicen, that's Sarah's ring! Your mother is—"

The door burst open. Derek was standing there, holding a gun.

"You're going to come with me quietly," he said, "or I'll blow your brains out."

Slowly, keeping her eyes on the round hole of the barrel, Gina stood up and went to him.

27

Melanie removed the purchases from her shopping cart and quickly filled the conveyor belt. She was angered at herself for having left the shopping until today, when everyone else was shopping for the weekend. A half-hour trip had turned into more than an hour. And there were still six people ahead of her on line.

She knew the children had been home about an hour now. If only she had sent Derek out to do this. The kids were probably worried about her. But at last she reached the cashier. Two prices had to be checked, slowing her down all the more. She almost ran out to her car when she was finished.

She would be home in a few minutes, she reassured herself.

But that wasn't to be. She turned a corner and found her way blocked by a truck pulling out of a factory driveway. There were four cars in back of her, and no way out.

"Well," she said, sighing, "they've done without me for an hour. They can survive a few minutes longer."

The cellar was cold. It gave no hint of the intense summer heat outside. Kyle coughed violently, the icy air constricting his lungs. Angered at the noise, Derek pressed the gun to the boy's head. Kyle forced himself to stop coughing.

Worse than being cold, the cellar was dark. Nancy began crying loudly. "I want my mommy!"

"Shut up!"

Derek waved the gun. Kyle stared up at him, wondering if the gun was loaded. In the next thought, he prayed his mother would come home soon. What was taking her so long?

Derek pushed them ahead of him. They walked slowly in the darkness, brushing away cobwebs, their shoes making soft noises on the concrete floor. At last, Derek stopped at a door on the back wall. He flung it open and motioned them inside.

"I don't wanna go in there," Nancy protested. "I want my mommy!"

Derek picked her up and threw her into the dark cave. Her little body landed on the sand floor of the storage room like a sack of flour. Before she could right herself, Gina and Kyle were pushed in beside her. Derek stooped down to let himself under the low door and placed a big flashlight on the floor. He turned it on, shining it at the three cowering children, then crawled over to them.

"My mommy'll be home real soon," Kyle said, his voice hoarse. He started coughing again.

"Shut up," Derek said. So much in Janice's power, he didn't know what he was saying. He worked without thinking, tying their small wrists and ankles with pieces of clothesline, and gagging their mouths. Then he went to the door and, lifting the flashlight from the floor, said, "It'll be over soon. Once she's punished you, it'll all be over."

Only Gina knew who "she" was. But why did Janice want to hurt them. Jacob Armand was the one who killed her, not them.

Derek shut the wooden door, sealing the room in total darkness. Nancy started to whimper behind her gag, and Gina moved through the darkness to lie beside her. Soon she felt Kyle's head on her shoulder. All they could do was pray their mother would come home soon.

Owen kicked a stone out of his path and continued on his walk. But he had been searching the woods for over an hour, and his feet ached. Spotting a log, he sat down to rest. No sooner had he stretched his legs out than his eyes were attracted by something glittering in the dirt. He leaned forward and lifted a silver and turquoise bracelet from a pile of wet leaves.

"This is Liza's," he said, recalling that he had given it to her a few Christmases back.

"It's *my* bracelet," he heard someone say.

Owen turned around to see a frail blond woman standing behind him. She looked insane, like the patients at the Fort Lauderdale mental hospital. He backed away from her.

"No," he said calmly. "This is my sister's bracelet. Do you know where she is? Her name is Liza."

"It's my bracelet," the blonde screamed. "*Mine*. I knew you were out here. I knew you'd try to steal it."

Suddenly, to Owen's disbelief, she bent down and wrapped her thin arms around the log. She lifted it high in the air, as if it were made of paper.

He didn't wait to see if she could swing it at him. His feet were taking him off at top speed, running for dear life. He ran and ran until he reached the beach, not looking back when he heard her call his name.

"You're next, Owen Crewe!"

How did she know his name? As his feet pounded the sand and his lungs took in the hot, salty air, Owen told himself over and over not to be afraid. He had handled people like her before. It was his profession.

Yet something made him keep running, even when his shoes became heavy with water. He didn't stop until he reached the flat rocks of a jetty, where he threw himself down and panted loudly. He looked over his shoulder, expecting to see her behind him. But the beach was empty.

"You ass," he said to himself, turning on his back. "Some psychiatrist you are!"

He needed a place to rest and collect his thoughts. Then he would go back to the big white house, knock on the door, and confront Derek Miller face to face, as he should have done earlier. Then he might learn who that strange woman was. He climbed over the rocks to the public beach. Once he crossed them, he removed his sweat-soaked shirt and wet shoes and walked toward the crowds. God, how far away this all seemed from the loneliness of those woods.

He found an empty spot and sat down, bringing his knees up to his chin. Radios blasted all around him, children squealed, people talked loudly. Liza, who loved people, would love a place like this.

A sudden commotion in the water made him avert his eyes from the jetty he'd just left. Two young boys in scuba gear were running to the shore, shouting something. The lifeguard stood up and blew his whistle at them. Curious, Owen got to his feet and shuffled to the small group that was gathering around the teen-agers.

"There's a car under the water!" one shouted, pointing. "We saw a body in it!"

"Sure, there is," the lifeguard drawled. "You think I'm crazy?"

"It's true," the boys insisted in unison. "It's true!"

"I think you'd better call the police," Owen said, staring at the innocent-looking blue water of Belle Bay.

He believed the boys. And, his stomach turning, he knew what the police would find when they came.

"Home at last," Melanie sighed to herself as she propped a grocery bag on one hip and unlocked the back door. Inside the kitchen she put two parcels down on the wooden table. Then she turned to go back outside, where two more bags were waiting in the trunk. But she decided she'd better go upstairs first to let them know she was home. She had been stuck in that traffic jam for twenty minutes.

Her voice, calling her children, rang through the house. But she heard no response. Melanie went upstairs to Kyle's room.

It was empty.

"What is this?" she demanded out loud.

She saw the Monopoly board on the floor, resting against the unmade bed, its pieces scattered everywhere. Kyle wasn't a messy child, but he was mischievous; he had probably used the golden opportunity of her absence to leave his bed. Melanie noticed his robe was missing from the closet and prayed he had taken it out himself.

She went out into the hall.

"Kyle?"

No answer. God, the house was quiet. Why didn't she hear the children talking or laughing? She went to Gina's room and when that proved empty, tried Nancy's. Then her studio and Gary's office. Why didn't her children answer her calls?

They couldn't have gone outside, she thought, her panic building.

Derek would know where they were. He'd tell her they were off playing somewhere. As angry as Melanie would be with Derek, she hoped to God that was the case. But Derek didn't answer when she knocked at the door. Thinking he might be taking a nap, Melanie carefully opened the door. She stepped into his room and cried out.

Like Gina, Melanie was at first too stunned to move when she saw the junkpile Derek's room had become. Sheets and blankets were torn from the bed, clothes strewn everywhere, swirls of crayon marked the headboard of the bed. Melanie almost screamed when she read the lipstick scrawling on the mirror.

MOMMY AND DADDY LOVE ALICEN

And below:

MOMMY AND DADDY KILL BAD CHILDREN

"Kill bad children," Melanie repeated, her voice choked.

Alicen's reflection appeared in the mirror. "They're all going to die," she sneered, in that horrible voice.

And suddenly Melanie recognized it.

"No!" she screamed. She went to Alicen and grabbed her roughly. "What have you done with my children? Where are they? Where are they?!"

"Mommy's going to kill them," Alicen said, in her own voice. "They're *bad* children."

"Oh, no," Melanie said, shaking her head. "No, they're good children. Why does she want to hurt them?"

Alicen shrugged. "I don't question my mother."

"Alicen, please," Melanie begged. "Tell me where she's taken my children."

Alicen shook her head and refused to answer. With a disgusted, frightened cry, Melanie pushed by her. She raced down the hall, crying loudly, "*Derek?*"

If he was there, he didn't answer. Neither did the children when she screamed their names. Derek must have kidnapped them.

It had to be. She couldn't possibly have heard that sneering voice a moment ago. It belonged to a dead woman.

(MOMMY AND DADDY KILL BAD CHILDREN)

"No," Melanie said. "No, this isn't happening."

She reached for the phone—it was dead. Trying to calm herself, she reached for her car keys and headed into the kitchen. She would drive to the police for help. She knew she couldn't handle this herself.

But the back door was closed tight, and locked.

"I *know* I left that open," Melanie cried. Quickly she opened the cupboard behind her to find the key. She was shaking so badly that she could hardly slide it into the lock. It clicked and turned, but the door wouldn't budge. It was as if someone had nailed it shut.

Without a moment's hesitation, Melanie ran to the front doors. She tried one, then the other. But they were sealed just as tightly, and she wasn't strong enough to break through them. She panicked for a moment, then realized the windows in the living room were big enough to crawl through. She hurried inside and saw to her shock that someone had snapped off their brass handles.

She grabbed the old slat-back rocker and lifted it high above her head. Using a strength unknown to her, she swung it forward, flying with it.

"Oh, God," she said, looking at the results. She had broken only a few panes, not enough to get out. Her shoulders felt as if she had torn them out, but she ignored the pain. She had to get to her children.

With a cry, she lifted the rocker again and tried to swing it forward. But she couldn't. Someone was holding it fast, behind her back. Melanie closed her eyes, afraid to turn around.

"Look at me, Melanie VanBuren," a voice said.

Melanie turned slowly, dropped the chair, and screamed.

"Are you so surprised to see me?" Janice asked. "You knew I was coming back, you murderess."

"No!" Melanie cried. "I'm not!"

"You are," Janice hissed. "You murdered me. You hit me across the head with a gun."

Suddenly Melanie remembered everything. She recalled the night of Gary's accident, when Janice had fallen under Jacob Armand's evil spell. She had tried to hurt Kyle, and Melanie had defended her son by hitting her with that pistol. But she had only stunned her. Jacob Armand was her murderer.

"No, it was *you*," Janice sneered, reading Melanie's thoughts. "*You*."

"Go away."

"Oh, no," Janice drawled. "Not until you pay for what you did to me."

Melanie found her legs and ran for dear life back to the—where? Where could she escape?

There was no chance. Derek was waiting in the dining room for her. As she lunged for the kitchen door, he tackled her and threw her to the floor.

"Let me go!"

She wrestled with him, feeling the sweat on his body, hearing him growling at her. Her fingers found his eye sockets and dug in, yet somehow only scratched his eyelids. Giving a roar, Derek slapped at her hands.

"HELP! HELP, SOMEBODY!"

Down in the cellar, three terrified children cried softly as they heard their mother's screams. And in the dining room the smiling ghost of Janice Lors watched the two fighting. She wanted to see Melanie beaten, made to suffer for what she had done.

"Hurt her, Derek," she ordered, her voice filled with passion.

Melanie saw Derek's fist rise in the air. She screamed as it came down. There was a flash of pain, and then darkness.

Owen felt the muscles in the back of his legs tighten, and he started to breathe more deeply to calm himself. But no matter how hard he tried, he couldn't let himself believe the car being dragged out of the water wasn't his sister's. He was standing in the crowd, behind wooden police barricades. One look at the bumper sticker on the rusted, soaked automobile made him cry out and run forward, knocking down the barrier. It read:

FLORIDA: EVERY DAY IS SUN DAY

"Liza!" He screamed, running toward the car.

"Hey!" a cop shouted, lunging at him. He caught Owen by the arm.

"Let me go, damn you!" Owen shouted. "That's my sister!"

Still holding him fast, the cop turned and said, "Captain Davis? This guy says that girl's his sister."

Bryan Davis hurried to them and took Owen by both his shoulders. Owen's face was red with fury, his eyes flashing.

"Calm down, fellow," Bryan said gently. "Calm down and tell me what's going on."

"M-my sister has been missing for a week," Owen stammered. "I-I went up to the—"

His words were cut off when he heard the car door crash open, giving way to a crowbar. Jerking away from the policeman who held him, he walked in a daze to the car. Two other cops were pulling a corpse from the wreck, laying it carefully on the sand.

But, no, that couldn't be Owen's sister. That bloated, green, hideous thing wasn't beautiful Liza. Not when the face looked so round, the skin so tight it seemed ready to burst. And Liza had always smelled like roses. . . .

And she was nude. Someone had murdered her. And someone would pay.

Owen turned away from the horrid sight and started to cry. Bryan patted his arm gently, as pictures of the body were taken for evidence and notes were scribbled in reporters' pads.

When Owen calmed down a bit, Bryan at last said, "You were saying you went up somewhere?"

Owen nodded. "To that big house on the hill. My—my sister's lover lives there."

Bryan felt his heart jump. The VanBuren house?

"Come on," he said. "We're going up there."

"I want him to get the chair for this," Owen seethed.

"Yeah," Bryan said, not certain if Liza's boyfriend was the killer. But he didn't want to think of that right now. He gave orders to his men and had two cars follow him up the hill. Once at the house, he ordered them to stay put until called. If Derek Miller had murdered Liza Crewe, he might become violent upon seeing the police. So only Bryan and Owen walked up the stairs to the double doors. Bryan pounded loudly and rang the bell at the same time. No one answered.

"Open this door!" Owen shouted.

"Shh," Bryan said. "If he's here, he might be hiding. And there are other people in this house—innocent people. We don't want to scare them."

"What other people?" Owen demanded. "I don't care about other people."

He turned and continued to pound on the door. Inside the house, Melanie's ears perked to hear it. She turned, as if she could see the source of the noise through the walls of the kitchen. She tried in vain to cry out, but her mouth was gagged, and ropes held her fast to a chair—the same chair where Janice had sat seven months ago, when Melanie had killed her.

It had all come back to her, everything she had blocked from her mind since the night of Gary's accident. Jacob Armand hadn't killed Janice, *she* had. Janice had tried to hurt Kyle, and Melanie had stopped her. She had only meant to stun her friend but instead had killed her with that gun. Melanie understood now why she felt so guilty about Janice's death all these months. But it wasn't her fault. It was self-defense.

Now Janice and Derek were standing in front of her, their arms around each other. Derek's face was expressionless, but Janice's wore a smile, tasting the sweetness of revenge. She was making Melanie wait—death for a murderess couldn't be swift and painless. Melanie's tears made her all the more angry.

"Go ahead and cry," she sneered. "I haven't even begun with you."

The pounding on the front door stopped. *Oh, please*, Melanie thought. *Please come to the back door.*

Downstairs, the children had also heard the pounding. Had somebody come to rescue them? Was that why the knocking was so loud?

Little Kyle became so excited that he suddenly began to cough. Phlegm filled his throat, gagging him. He couldn't spit because of the gag.

He made strangling noises, falling forward. His coughing became so violent that Gina rolled toward him and tried to lift her hands from behind her and slap his back. But she couldn't. Someone had to find them before he choked.

Crying with fear and praying this would work, Gina lifted her bound feet and kicked the wall. They made a loud, satisfying thud.

Again and again she kicked at the walls, and soon Nancy was joining her.

"What's that?" Derek asked, looking around.

"Those brats!" Janice cried.

She disappeared. Seconds later, Owen and Bryan were at the back door. Alerted by the pounding, Bryan had ordered his men to surround the house. Derek saw them through the window and ran from the room. There was a loud crash, and suddenly the door was hanging by one hinge.

"Oh, Lord," Owen said.

Quickly Bryan tore off Melanie's gag as another cop cut her ropes.

"She's got my children somewhere!" she cried, her voice hoarse.

"She?" Bryan echoed.

"You mean Derek Miller," Owen said.

"No," Melanie said firmly. "*She*." She looked into Bryan's eyes, "Janice Lors."

Bryan backed away. Janice Lors? But she had been dead seven months.

And Jacob Armand had been dead nearly two hundred years on that November night when . . .

"Spread out over the house," he said over his walkie-talkie to his men. "We're looking for four kids, and a man."

No use telling them to look for someone they couldn't see.

"Where did the pounding come from, Mrs. VanBuren?" he asked.

Melanie shook her head. Where? It had come from everywhere, carried through every wooden beam of the house.

"Just find my babies, please," she cried, standing.

She hurried from the kitchen, Owen and Bryan at her heels. They broke off in separate directions, Melanie hurrying upstairs in spite of Bryan's protests. She knew where to find Derek. And she'd make him tell her where her children were.

He was in Alicen's room, holding the girl on his lap. Melanie stopped in her tracks. Why was her face so pale, her head hanging back like that?

Derek stared at her through tears.

"She's dead," he said softly. "Janice appeared to her, and when she saw it wasn't her mother, she collapsed."

"Oh, God," Melanie whispered, moving closer to them.

She reached out and touched Alicen's body. It was still warm. And then she drew back and screamed:

"*Derek, where are my children?*"

"I don't know," Derek whined.

"You have to know," Melanie cried. "She's got them somewhere, and she's going to kill them, too. Please, Derek!"

"I don't know where they are."

"Derek, this house is filled with police," Melanie said, her voice filled with rage. "They'll arrest you for murder if you don't tell me where Janice has my children!"

Just then, Owen and Bryan burst into the room. They took in Melanie, standing there with her fists clenched, Derek, crying softly, and the little girl flopped in his arms. When Bryan tried to pry the child loose, Derek spat at him and tightened his arms.

"I never wanted this to happen," he sobbed. "Jesus, she's just a kid. I never wanted her to die."

But Bryan had seen a soft rising in the girl's chest. He forced Derek's arm away and listened to the child's pulse. "This child is alive," he said, standing. "She needs an ambulance."

"Oh, Derek!" Melanie cried. "Can't you see what she's done? Janice almost killed your little girl. She'd made both of you her slaves. Don't give in to her, Derek. Please tell me where she has my children."

Derek rocked his daughter back and forth. Alive? She was alive?

"The—the cellar," he stammered. "She's got them in the storage room."

Without hesitation, Owen and Bryan ran from the room. Even as they hurried downstairs, Janice was standing over three cowering children, her eyes blazing.

"You wicked children," she said. "You tried to call for help, didn't you? And now Derek's sent help down here—but he'll pay for defying me."

She took a step forward. "But first—"

Gina screamed as best she could and kicked at the massless body. Janice laughed at her.

"Don't try to stop me," she said. "You deserve to die, all of you." She grabbed Nancy's curls and lifted her off the floor. The child struggled like a fish, with no arms or legs to flay. Janice shook her roughly and threw her to the ground. "You're all going to die."

But just then, the door crashed open. In the same instant Janice was gone, leaving Bryan Davis alone to gape in wonder at the children. Quickly, he untied them. Melanie appeared in the doorway now, and Kyle and Gina ran to her.

"Oh, my babies!" Melanie whispered. "It's all right."

"Nancy's hurt!" Gina cried.

Melanie looked up at Bryan, who had taken the child in his arms. He passed by her and carried her upstairs. Moments later, all three children were in the back of an ambulance. But Melanie wasn't with them.

"Where's my mother?" Kyle shouted.

"I don't know," Bryan said, hurrying back to the house. Owen was at his side, and Bryan turned and snapped, "Stay out here. This doesn't concern you."

"He killed my sister!" Owen yelled.

"Derek Miller didn't kill your sister," Bryan insisted.

He ran into the kitchen. Melanie was standing there, holding hands with Derek, speaking in firm tones.

And Janice was standing across from her.

"You can fight her, Derek," Melanie was saying. "You're a strong man. Don't let her control you."

"You fool," Janice hissed. "I *do* control him. Derek, I want her to die. *Now.*"

Derek shook his head slowly. "No."

"What did you say?" Janice demanded.

Bryan took a step forward but stopped when Melanie spoke again.

"He isn't going to listen to you any more," she said. "Not since you tried to kill his daughter."

"Derek, you're my lover." Janice screamed. *"Kill her!"*

"Melanie, get out of this house," Derek said.

"Where am I going to go?" Melanie demanded. "I want to see this ended now, or I'll never escape her."

She began to cry again. Suddenly, infuriated by her tears, Janice pounced forward to grab her—but somehow Bryan managed to beat her to it. Without looking back, he dragged Melanie out to the ambulance.

"Get them to the hospital," he said to the drivers.

He turned back as the ambulance drove away, carrying a mother hugging her three children for dear life. Suddenly, Bryan realized Owen Crewe was now nowhere in sight. He raced to the house. Owen was in the kitchen, staring at something with wide eyes. Bryan turned to where his eyes were fixed.

Janice was on top of Derek.

"My God," he whispered. "She's tearing him apart."

He knew that he and Owen would be next if they didn't run *now*.

"Owen, get out of here!" he shouted, pulling at the other man.

He had seen so much in his years as a cop—so much gore and horror. But nothing would be imprinted in his mind more clearly than the picture of Janice Lors digging her hands into Derek's flesh, ripping at it. Clutching at his stomach, Bryan slid into his car and started the engine.

"I don't understand any of this," Owen said softly, watching the house. "I don't understand why Liza had to die. Why did Derek kill her? Who was that woman in there?"

"That house," Bryan answered vaguely. "It was that house. It ought to be burned to the ground."

Angrily he slammed his foot down on the gas pedal and sped into town—into the peaceful town of Belle Bay.

28

◆

"Gary, I'm not going back to that house," Melanie said.

She sat with her husband on a couch in a hotel room, her head on his shoulder. They had been here two days, ever since the hospital checked them over and released them. Gary had been released at the same time and had found a place to hide from reporters just a few miles out of town. It was a small room, with only one king-sized bed, where Kyle and Nancy now slept away their fears. Gina was sitting in a chair, listlessly flipping through a magazine.

"Of course we won't," Gary answered, kissing his wife.

She looked at him in disbelief.

"You aren't going to argue with me?"

"No," Gary said. "We should have left that house seven months ago. We should have known this would happen again."

He squeezed her tightly. "I'm sorry I doubted you, Melanie," he said quietly.

"Lydia Browning tried to warn us," Melanie said. "Perhaps it was to make up for all the wrongs Jacob committed out of love for her."

She waved her hand. "But we're safe now—that's the important thing."

Gina stood up now and walked to them, putting her arms around Gary's shoulders.

"Daddy?" she asked. "Where are we going to go?"

"I was thinking of staying with your grandparents a few months," Gary said. "Would you like that?"

Gina nodded.

"That's a wonderful idea, Gary," Melanie said. "My parents have plenty of room."

"Are we going to leave the furniture?" Gina asked. "And all our nice things?"

"No, honey," Gary said.

"We can't go back to get them!" Melanie cried.

"I'll call a moving van once we're at your parents' place," Gary said. "We never have to set foot on that property again."

"Thank God," Melanie said. She looked at Gina. "Honey, it's late. Why don't you try to get some sleep?"

"I can't sleep," she said, shuffling her feet on the rug.

Melanie stood up and put her arms around the child. As she stroked her hair, she asked, "You aren't thinking of what happened at the house, are you? You shouldn't. None of it was our fault."

"Janice said you killed her," Gina said softly.

"Gina—" Gary cautioned.

"No, Gary," Melanie said. "She's old enough to hear the truth. Gina, I did kill Janice. But it was blocked from my mind until a few days ago. I believed Jacob Armand had done it."

"That's why she came back to haunt us?" Gina asked. "It was your fault?"

"Gina, please," Melanie said. "Janice had tried to hurt Kyle, and she had led you into Jacob's trap. I had to defend you—so I hit her across the back of her head with a gun. I didn't mean to kill her. I only wanted to save my children."

She had begun to cry. Now Gina was crying, pressing her head into Melanie's heaving breast. Her mother held her tightly. Gary, feeling helpless, reached for his crutches and got to his feet. Melanie and Gina moved closer to him.

"Go ahead and cry," he said. "It'll make you feel better. But don't worry. We're going to get as far away from that house as possible."

He looked at the two children sleeping in the bed.

"No one will ever hurt you again," he vowed.

"Wh-what about Alicen?" Gina blubbered.

"Alicen?"

"She must be so lonely in that old hospital," Gina said. "It wasn't her fault this happened. Janice made her do those awful things. And now she doesn't have a father or a mother."

"She's right, Gary," Melanie said. "We can't just leave that child."

Gary nodded. "I'm a lawyer. I know who to ask about taking care of her."

He kissed each of them.

"Alicen can come with us," he said. "And then, I swear to you, we'll never be afraid again."

Owen tugged at his mustache and stared at the carved double doors of the big white mansion. God, he thought, how could any place so beautiful hold so much evil? From talking to Bryan Davis, he knew now that his sister had been murdered by a ghost and that the ghost had also murdered Derek Miller.

But who would believe it? How could he tell his parents, who lived so peacefully in their Florida condominium, that their precious daughter had been murdered by a ghost?

"You don't have to tell them anything like that," Bryan had said as they sat together in the police station that morning. "We have a likely suspect. The man you first accused—Derek Miller."

"But he's innocent," Owen said.

"And dead," Bryan answered. "He can't defend himself. And who's going to defend him? A thirteen-year-old kid? Alicen's going to be in a hospital for a long time, and by the time she gets well, she won't remember any of this."

"Poor kid," Owen said. "But tell me about her father."

"Derek Miller had no family except for his daughter," Bryan said. "And only one close friend—a doctor named Mary Norton. I've already told her Derek was going slowly mad over the death of his wife Elaine, and she accepted that theory."

He lifted a pencil and bounced it a few times.

"Besides, I like the VanBurens," he said. "If we accuse Janice, they'll have all sorts of nuts bothering them the rest of their lives. But if we don't accuse someone, the blame will lie on them. And I don't want to see that happen."

God only knew the VanBurens had suffered enough. Bryan should have seen it coming when Gina was involved in that bus accident. The driver had been Janice Lors. She had taken little Alicen Miller into her power and had sent her to the police station with a story about the driver jumping from the bus. That mystery was now solved, too. Bryan would worry about what he'd say in his report later.

"Neither do I," Owen said, standing. "You go ahead and tell the papers it was Derek who killed my sister. But I won't rest until the real murderer gets what's coming to her."

"Stay away from that house," Bryan cautioned. "If I find you there, I'll have you arrested. That place is deadly."

Owen stared at him, considering the threat.

"All right," he said at last. "There's nothing I can do to a ghost anyway, is there?"

Yet now he was walking around the house to the back door, barricaded only by a rope since the door had yet to be fixed. A paper sign hanging on it said: POLICE AREA DO NOT CROSS. Owen climbed over it.

Pending an investigation into Liza and Derek's deaths, the house had been left exactly the way it was two days ago. Chairs were overturned, paintings knocked from the walls, the glass windows in the living room were shattered. Absently, Owen bent down and righted the rocking chair, setting it near the fireplace. He looked around in awe at the beauty of the room, with its plush sofa and antique furniture. And then he felt a touch on his arm.

"I knew you'd be back," a voice said. Owen turned and saw the woman named Janice smiling at him. "I noticed you alone among all those other people here the day I killed Derek. I knew I wanted you."

Stunned, Owen said nothing. Her eyes were powerful, holding him fast.

"I thought I wanted Derek," Janice said, moving closer to him. "But he betrayed me. He let those murderers escape."

She turned to stare through filmy eyes at the fireplace. "But I will have my revenge one day."

Owen found his tongue and was surprised to hear himself speaking to her as if she were simply one of his patients.

"Why do you want revenge so badly?" he asked. "So far as I know, Melanie was only defending her child. Jacob Armand had turned you into a madwoman. What was she supposed to do?"

"She had no right to kill me!" Janice snapped. "I was only twenty-eight. I was beautiful."

She leaned forward to kiss Owen, but he backed away.

"Don't do that," he said, feeling weak. What was it about her eyes?

"I want you, Owen Crewe," Janice whispered.

Calling himself a fool for coming here, Owen tried to turn and run away. But he couldn't feel his legs.

Janice pulled him down to the floor. "Make love to me, Owen," she whispered passionately.

"Let me go," Owen said, feeling powerless as a baby. This was happening too fast.

"I waited for Derek," Janice said, "because I needed him for something. That was a mistake—I lost him. But I won't lose you, my handsome Owen. I want you."

Her lips pressed his, her tongue pried them open. Suddenly Owen found his strength and tried to knock her away. She sat up and slapped him, hard, again and again. Her face changed then, bloated and turned green, and became Liza's face. Blood dripped onto Owen.

"No!"

"I want you with me, brother," Janice teased, in Liza's voice. "I'm so alone without you. Oh, so alone! Die, big brother!"

Owen closed his eyes and felt his heart jump. When he opened them again, there was nothing above him but stars and blackness.

Epilogue

◆

When the moving company came Monday morning, they found Owen's body on the living room sofa. His arms were folded across his chest, his hair neatly in place. The effect was like a wake, but Bryan Davis insisted the death certificate should read heart attack. The coroner accepted a sum of money and obliged. Who was Owen Crewe to him?

Though she didn't know him, Melanie cried when she read the obituary. She was sitting on the porch of her parents' house, with Gary at her side and the children sitting nearby. They kept close to her these days. Nancy stood up from the game she was playing with Kyle and came to put her head on Melanie's lap.

"Mommy, why do we all cry so much?"

"Because many sad things have happened to us," Melanie said, gently rubbing the child's back. It was a hot day, and Nancy's sunsuit was soaked with perspiration.

"I don't want to be sad any more," Nancy said. "Daddy promised we wouldn't be sad—didn't you, daddy?"

"I did," Gary said. "Melanie, what are you reading there?" Melanie showed him the paper. "Don't think about it," Gary said. "You didn't even know the guy."

She leaned across the wicker sofa and kissed him. In spite of all that had happened, she still had her career, didn't she? And her beautiful family. Nothing bad could happen to them again. Not if they stayed away from that hateful, evil house.

Still, the next day, she couldn't help driving back to it for one last look. She didn't cry to see the high white towers and bay windows, nor the porch and bay windows. She felt a loss, of course, but also a joy that the terror was at last over. She would have sat there, near the car, looking at it for hours, remembering the good times they had had—and there had been many in spite of everything—if a sight in the upstairs window hadn't broken her spell. She saw two blond people. Melanie could barely make out the mustache on one. Was that Owen?

"My God," she said. "The papers were wrong. He didn't die of a heart attack—she killed him!"

She saw Janice pointing at her. Before those eyes could take her into their evil power, Melanie turned and ran to her car. It carried her at top speed to the highway, to safety. By the time she reached the main street of Belle Bay, she had forced herself to calm down. She had escaped. And it was over.

Her only worry now would be her career, and nothing else.

There didn't need to be any other worries, for Janice no longer wanted revenge. She had found something in Owen Crewe that satisfied her. He had become her total slave, easily forced into submission by the sight of his sister's face.

No one ever came back to the house after that, except for a crew to block the door and put up a condemned sign. Gary had wanted the place torn down but was told it would be too expensive. So now the house sat regally upon the hill, rotting and lonely. Winters passed and tore at the shuttered windows, summers made the white paint crack and peel. And as the house grew uglier, legends by the townspeople grew around it.

They called it the Ghost House. And sometimes, if the wind was blowing just right and imaginations were tense, people would swear they could hear the laughter of two people sounding from behind its ancient, dilapidated façade.

ABOUT THE AUTHOR

CLARE MCNALLY attended the Fashion Institute of Technology in New York City where she studied advertising and communications. She has worked on a children's wear magazine, freelanced as an advertising copywriter and edited a technical magazine. She lives on Long Island.